T0246207

AN ANGEL CALLED PETERBILT

THE RING OF FIRE SERIES

**To purchase any of these titles in e-book form,
please go to www.baen.com.**

AN ANGEL CALLED PETERBILT

ERIC FLINT
GORG HUFF
PAULA GOODLETT

AN ANGEL CALLED PETERBILT

This is a work of fiction. All the characters and events portrayed in this book are fictional, and any resemblance to real people or incidents is purely coincidental.

Copyright © 2024 by Eric Flint, Gorg Huff, and Paula Goodlett

All rights reserved, including the right to reproduce this book or portions thereof in any form.

A Baen Books Original

Baen Publishing Enterprises
P.O. Box 1403
Riverdale, NY 10471
www.baen.com

ISBN: 978-1-9821-9319-5

Cover art by Tom Kidd

First printing, February 2024

Distributed by Simon & Schuster
1230 Avenue of the Americas
New York, NY 10020

Library of Congress Cataloging-in-Publication Data

Names: Flint, Eric, author. | Huff, Gorg, author. | Goodlett, Paula, author.
Title: An angel called Peterbilt / Eric Flint, Gorg Huff, Paula Goodlett.
Description: Riverdale, NY : Baen Publishing Enterprises, 2024. | Series: Assiti shards ; 5
Identifiers: LCCN 2023043262 (print) | LCCN 2023043263 (ebook) | ISBN 9781982193195 (hardcover) | ISBN 9781625799487 (ebook)
Subjects: LCGFT: Time-travel fiction. | Novels.
Classification: LCC PS3556.L548 A83 2024 (print) | LCC PS3556.L548 (ebook) | DDC 813/.54—dc23/eng/20231006
LC record available at https://lccn.loc.gov/2023043262
LC ebook record available at https://lccn.loc.gov/2023043263

Printed in the United States of America

10 9 8 7 6 5 4 3 2 1

This book is dedicated to Eric Flint.

It was his project.

It wouldn't have been written if he hadn't come up with it. Neither of us would have been involved with it if he hadn't pulled us in.

CONTENTS

PART I

PART I

CHAPTER 1

THE PETERBILT

As Michael and Melanie Anderle were leaving the diner in the Love's Travel Stop outside of Ina, Illinois, followed by their twelve-year-old daughter Shane holding their bag of leftovers, two men approached them. Both were well dressed and middle aged.

"Excuse me, folks," said one of them, "could you give us a moment of your time?"

Michael didn't judge them to be any sort of threat, so he readily came to a stop. People rarely threatened him anyway—not when he stood six feet four inches tall and weighed almost three hundred pounds. Besides, the man had a definite English accent—of the upper-crust variety, not Cockney or Scouse—and Michael shared the usual American reaction to it: *Must be a polite fellow.* And never mind that, as a British friend whom he'd met in his first tour of duty in Afghanistan who was from Liverpool and *did* speak with a Scouse accent had pointed out to him, the British reputation for brawling was far worse than that of Americans.

"Sure," he said.

"I'm Doctor Malcolm O'Connell—the doctorate is in mathematics, not medicine—and my companion here is Colonel Sam Peffers, recently retired from the United States Army. We're with a private company that's researching some aspects of four-dimensional space-time. To that end, we've developed some instruments that allow us to probe the fourth dimension while shifting constantly through the other three. Ah...to put it another way—"

"You're studying time while moving through space," said

Melanie. She gave the Englishman a sweet smile at the startled look that came to his face. Michael didn't give a damn himself, but his wife could get irked at people who assumed that a truck driver was a semiskilled Neanderthal. Neither of them had completed college, but they'd both spent time at community colleges. Perhaps more to the point, they both liked to read science fiction. Listen to it, mostly; audiobooks were a blessing to people in their line of work. Melanie's reaction might have had something to do with the fact that she was blonde and buxom, and a lot of males tended to assume an inverse relationship between breast size and IQ.

The colonel grinned. "Right on the money, ma'am."

Melanie made a face. "I figure I'm still at least two decades short of needing that term. I'm Melanie Anderle. The oversized fellow next to me is my husband Michael. And this is our daughter, Shane. So what do you want from us?"

"We've found that having over-the-road truckers carry one of our instruments is the best way, at a reasonable cost, to get the data we need."

"Define 'reasonable cost,'" said Melanie. She was the one who always did the dickering when money came up.

"We'll pay you three hundred dollars a month, transferred directly to whatever bank account you choose."

"How big is this instrument?" asked Michael. Michael considered what the colonel was saying. He knew about the event in West Virginia. By now the blogs were all over the fact that when Grantville disappeared, it was replaced with a chunk of seventeenth-century Germany. There were even reports of the government hiding Germans from that time in Area 51. The same was true of the prison that apparently went all the way back to the Jurassic. And the cruise ship. They'd found a bit of Formentera Island in the Bahamas after that one. It was clear that these guys were studying those events and possibly others like them. But Michael would confirm that before he agreed to anything.

Peffers gestured with his hand, indicating something the size of a small valise. "We have lots of ways to attach it, too."

"I'd like to see it first, if you don't mind." Michael and Melanie were in the business of hauling stuff, so hauling a small case was natural enough. But before he agreed to anything, he'd know that he wasn't hauling a bomb. His time in Afghanistan had left him very careful about what exactly he took on board.

Peffers headed off, toward a car parked not too far away. He lifted something out of the trunk and came back holding it. From the way he was carrying it, the gadget didn't seem especially heavy.

"Open it up, please." Seeing the skeptical look on the retired colonel's face, Michael shook his head. "I don't expect to understand any of the widgetry. I just want to make sure it's actually a scientific widget."

"He's a little paranoid," said Melanie.

Michael shrugged. "A couple of tours of duty in Afghanistan in a combat unit makes you twitchy about anything that might be an IED." He nodded toward the case. "I want to see what's in there."

Peffers fiddled with a couple of latches and opened the top lid. Anderle leaned over and studied the innards. After a minute or so, he straightened up. "Okay. That doesn't look like anything that could go 'boom.' So I'm betting you're investigating the events that seem to be moving stuff through space and time." He waited for Peffers' nod, then said, "I want to know what's been happening too. You got a deal." *And*, thought Michael, *the extra three hundred bucks a month will pay for some diesel.*

While his wife and O'Connell worked out the financial details, Michael and Peffers went over to his vehicle, which turned out to be a Peterbilt tractor hauling a tanker trailer. The tractor was flamboyantly painted to resemble a dragon breathing fire. On the door of the cab was a logo reading:

Anderle Trucking
Evansville, Indiana

"What's in the tanker?" Peffers asked.

"Mostly diesel. Some gasoline in a separate compartment."

They attached the case to the back of the tractor's cab, in a spot where it wouldn't interfere with anything. There was plenty of space and the glue that Peffers used was impressive. It'd be easy to remove when the time came, too, since all that actually touched the cab were four little legs.

Not long thereafter, the Anderles climbed into their truck. The engine fired up, and off they went.

"Follow them?" Peffers asked, pointing to the Peterbilt containing the large blond man and his family.

O'Connell nodded. "For ten miles or so. That'll be enough time to make sure the instrumentation's working properly."

Six miles from the truck center, the monitor in O'Connell's laptop suddenly came to life—and very dramatically. From Peffers' angle at the steering wheel, it seemed as if every light was flashing and every dial was going berserk.

"Dear God!" exclaimed Malcolm. "I think...Sam, I think we're about to intersect a temporal bolide." That was the term they used for what they postulated were objects/forces/whatever that were striking the Earth and producing the time transpositions. "I'm getting readings from the detector in the Peterbilt and the detector in our car."

Peffers, on the other hand, had a clear line of vision in both the rearview mirror and the side mirror. Nothing was showing any indication in the three visible dimensions.

Malcolm shouted, "STOP!"

Peffers slammed on the brakes and the car swerved off the road onto a grassy shoulder. He looked at Malcolm. "What the fuck!"

O'Connell, pulling up a camera, pointed ahead where the Peterbilt was making a slight curve following the road. Directly in front of them, but no longer directly in front of the Peterbilt, was a country store.

There was a flash of light. It looked like ball lightning, but it was huge, the length of a football field. No. More! Then it was gone. So was the Peterbilt and about half of the store.

None of the occupants of the Peterbilt saw anything at all until the flash of light. Shane was curled up on the lower bunk of the sleeper portion of the cab and was playing a game on her tablet. She couldn't have seen anything from there anyway.

For their part, Michael and Melanie were debating which audiobook they should listen to and neither of them was looking in a side-view mirror. People driving vehicles that weigh close to forty tons tend not to worry overmuch about what might be coming up on their rear. It wouldn't have mattered. There was no indication until the flash of light.

One moment they were in the twenty-first century. There was a flash of light, and they weren't.

There was a double bump as the Peterbilt's left, then right, front tires climbed a six-inch step to get from the road to the prairie. The rear wheels of the Peterbilt made the transition from blacktop to prairie more easily. The front tires had converted the step into something approaching a ramp the trailer's wheels barely noticed. But by then Melanie was already braking.

"Oh, shit," Peffers said. The whole thing had taken a fraction of a second and as he looked ahead he realized that if they hadn't stopped they would have been caught in the Ring of Fire.

The Peterbilt, the road, about half the store and more than half its parking lot, were just gone. There was nothing in the distance beyond a stretch of prairie where a road had been, and the land behind the store which ended not more than fifty yards past the store.

Peffers lowered his cell phone and turned off the video. Malcolm did the same with his much fancier video camera.

"Jesus wept," said the mathematician.

"We'd better get over there and help any survivors," said Peffers. *If there are any,* but he left that unspoken. He and Malcolm climbed back into their car and headed carefully across the prairie toward what was left of the store.

As they drew near, Peffers abruptly put on the brakes. "Malcolm..." He pointed out the window. "Please tell me that isn't what I think it is."

The mathematician got out and approached the object lying on the ground a few yards away. He didn't get any closer than a couple of yards. After studying it for a few seconds, he came back. "Green around the gills" was a pretty apt depiction of his face.

He got back in. "It's the top part of a human body—male—that's been cut in half just above the pelvis. The cut's at a steep angle, from the middle of the rib cage through most of the hip on the other side. The cut looks as if it were made by a razor blade. A giant razor blade." He stopped and took a deep shuddering breath.

"The pickup truck's gone," mused Peffers. "It was inside the diameter of the ring. The guy on the ground was probably its owner, coming back from putting something in the dumpster over there."

Malcolm nodded, took another deep breath and jerked his chin toward the store, which was now about ten yards away. "Let's keep going."

When they reached the gutted store, Peffers called out: "Anyone here?"

A voice to their right responded "yeah," in what sounded more like a croak than a word. Looking over, they saw the counter with the cash register that would be where people paid for whatever they'd picked up. But no one was in sight.

Malcolm stepped from the prairie onto the floor of the country store and walked over to the cash register. Sam moved around to the right, where he could get behind the counter it was on. As soon as he did so, he saw the source of the croaking voice: a young man—he might be just a teenager—sitting on the floor and clutching his knees to his chest. If Malcolm had been green around the gills, this poor fellow's figurative gills looked gangrenous.

"Is it over?" the youngster asked.

"Yes," Peffers said firmly. That seemed a better answer than *we think so, but who knows?*

Malcolm had leaned over the counter to bring the fellow into view. "You can come out now. Is there anyone else in the store?" By then, he was pretty sure there wasn't, but that question was less likely to trigger off the boy's terror than *any corpses you know about?*

The cashier rose to his feet and looked around. Then, pointed to his left. "There was a black lady over there. Next to the baked goods..." He looked in the direction of the baked goods and swallowed. "Where the baked goods were. They're gone. But she was there. Her and two little kids."

Holding his breath, Sam went over to the area indicated and looked around. Thankfully, what he had feared seeing wasn't there—neither corpses nor any body parts. The woman and the children, presumably her own, must have been caught fully in the ring's passage. They would be wherever the truck was.

Probably. It wasn't as if they really had much of an understanding of these temporal bolides and what they could or would do.

"Nobody here," he called over to Malcolm. He turned to the kid at the cash register. "What other customers did you have before the... event happened?"

"Mr. Dawes had just left. He must be..."

Peffers shook his head. "I'm afraid he didn't get out in time. Anyone else?"

The cashier looked at the open space where half the store had been and shook his head.

"Just hang tight," Peffers said in as reassuring a tone as he could manage. "The authorities will be here soon and everything will get straightened out."

That was probably the most ridiculous statement Sam had ever made in his life. He looked over at Malcolm, who used his head to nod toward the door. Where the door had most likely been, anyway.

When they got outside, he asked the mathematician, "*Did you notify the authorities?*"

"Not yet. We need to spend a few minutes getting all our ducks in a row." He'd taken out his cell phone and was tapping in a number. "I'm calling the company offices first. We finally have what we need to break through the government bureaucracy's *see no evil-speak no evil-hear no evil* bullshit and get them to stop prattling about terrorists and take these bolides seriously. Dammit, something—or someone—is bombarding the Earth."

"Malcolm," Peffers asked, "did we cause this? Did the sensor pack we stuck in that Peterbilt call the temporal bolide?"

"We've done at least a dozen of these installations," Malcolm said. "And we've followed every one of them for a few miles to make sure everything was working. Nothing like this has happened before."

Peffers looked at the scientist's face and saw a man trying hard to convince himself. It was a good point. On the other hand, the odds that a bolide would hit a specific place and time were astronomically low, which suggested that even if it hadn't happened to the other trucks they'd put instruments on, it might have caused this one. He prayed that it hadn't, and even more, he prayed for the Anderle family in the Peterbilt.

General Store
April 11, 1005 CE

Melanie was at the steering wheel when the flash of light blinded her, then came the bumps as the Peterbilt climbed from blacktop to prairie. She hit the brakes and the wheels tore up the soil. She hadn't been going very fast, since they were on a secondary state road, not an interstate. Even so, a truck with a fully loaded tanker attached to the tractor weighs more than thirty-five tons. It takes a while to stop.

When the truck halted and the dust cleared away, both she and her husband stared at the road ahead of them. To be precise, the *nonexistent* road ahead of them. They were looking at a prairie field; an untouched one, to all appearances. In most places they could see, the prairie grasses were several feet tall.

"What the fuck?" demanded Melanie.

Michael opened the door on his side of the cab and looked out; then, down. He was looking at the same prairie.

"Wait here," he said, as he climbed out of the cab and onto the ground. Once there, he walked to the back of the tanker. From that vantage point, he could see the last stretch of road, which ended fifty or so yards behind them.

He walked back to the cab and climbed back in.

"What is it?" asked Melanie.

He shrugged. "Damfino. The road comes to a stop about fifty yards back. From there, we were driving on prairie land."

"Could you see the store we were passing? It was on our right."

"Part of it's still there," said Michael. "Part of where it was is prairie now. And, yeah, I saw what was left of it."

They looked at each other for a moment. During the pause, Shane stuck her head between the front seats and demanded, "What's going on?"

"We don't know, honey," said her mother. "I figure we should turn around and go back to the store, Michael."

"Yeah, so do I. But do it carefully. The prairie looks flat and pretty solid, but who knows what might be hidden under all that grass and stuff. That grass comes up to my shoulders in some places."

CHAPTER 2

THE COUNTRY STORE

The Country Store
April 11, 1005 CE

The first thing that grabbed their attention as they drew near to the store were three people huddled together by a bisected small car. A woman and two young children. All were African-American.

Their heads turned to look at the truck as it came near. A look of relief came to the woman's face and she started waving her arms vigorously.

After Melanie got the truck on what was left of the state road and brought it to a stop, she and Michael climbed down from the cab, followed by Shane, and went over to the woman and—presumably—her children.

"Are you okay?" asked Michael.

The woman ran fingers through her thick, black hair, and issued a little bark of a laugh. "I have no idea how to answer that. Physically, yeah, we're fine. Not a scratch on any of us—and how the hell we managed that when that lightning strike blew half of the store away is a mystery to me."

She looked down at the collapsed automobile. "And my trusty old Honda Civic sleeps with the fishes. Dammit. I've had it since my first year in grad school." The Honda Civic was parked in the country store's parking lot and one side's tires were right there, where they were supposed to be. The other side was missing and the blue car looked like it had been sliced by a razor blade. About half the passenger side seat was missing, and the body of the car was angled over where it had fallen to the prairie, where there wasn't a parking lot anymore.

Melanie looked at the two kids. They were staring at the car and looking terrified. She wanted to hug them and tell them everything was going to be all right. There were two problems with that. She wasn't at all sure everything was going to be all right, and they weren't her kids. About all she could think of to do was act normal and avoid turning the terror into panic.

Looking for a distraction, Melanie asked, "Did you get a degree? And if you did, what was it in?"

The woman had followed Melanie's eyes and apparently followed her thoughts. She took a deep breath. "I have a Ph.D. in chemistry. For the last few years I've been an assistant professor at Southern Illinois University in Carbondale."

"That's impressive. You don't look to be any older than your early thirties."

The woman nodded. "Just turned thirty-two. My parents were fairly well-off and supportive. So is my husband. He's a manufacturer's rep in the chemical industry. I met him at a professional conference and we hit it off. Three months later we were married, and it wasn't much more than a year later that we had Miriam."

Both of her children were clinging to her tightly. She brought up her hand and placed it on the girl's head. "Miriam's almost six and Norman"—the other hand came up and rested on the boy's head—"is four and a half. Oh. I haven't introduced myself, have I? I'm Alyssa Jefferson."

"I'm Melanie Anderle"—her hand came out for a shake—"and this is my husband Michael."

He extended his hand also.

Alyssa shook his hand, nodded, then hesitated for a moment. "I know this is a lot to ask, but can we hook up with you folks? We"—her voice choked—"don't have a car anymore—even if I had any idea where to drive it. We've just got two suitcases and my laptop. Wherever we've found ourselves, I don't think me and a couple of small children have much of a chance on our own."

Melanie frowned at her. "Do you really think we'd leave you stranded out here?"

Alyssa didn't flinch from the hard gaze. "With our skin color, there are plenty of people who would, Mrs. Anderle."

Melanie's mouth opened; and... nothing came out.

"She's right, hon, and you know it," said Michael. "Mrs. Jefferson, my wife and I have our faults, but one thing we're not are racist assholes."

He gestured toward the Peterbilt. "If I remember my Spanish correctly, *nuestra casa es su casa.* Okay, it's a truck, not a house, but it's one hell of a truck, if I say so myself. There's plenty of room in there for all of us."

"We've got an upper bunk, too," said Shane. "Except 'bunk' doesn't do it justice. It's not as wide as the lower bed but it's plenty big enough to fit you and your kids." It was apparent that Shane had been looking at the kids too and was working pretty hard to be a calm, rational grown-up.

"We opted for a second bunk rather than the usual storage shelf," said Melanie, thinking *just keep talking like everything is ordinary. Get through this. I can panic later.* She took a breath and continued. "Once we decided we'd sell our house and I'd become Michael's driving partner, we needed to rearrange our lives. I'd had it with never seeing him for weeks at a time. Once it was almost three months."

She smiled down at her daughter and placed a hand on her shoulder. "That left the problem of Shane. But she was okay with living with Michael's parents during the school part of the year and living with us in the Peterbilt during the summer and school breaks."

"It wasn't any big sacrifice," said Shane cheerily, but it was false cheer. Melanie could tell. Shane was trying to distract herself just like the rest of them. "I knew my mom and dad were unhappy hardly ever seeing each other and this way I got to spend one third of the year driving all over the country. I like that a lot." Her eyes flicked to the two smaller children. "Besides, grandparents are a lot easier to wheedle than parents are."

"Sure are," said Alyssa, smiling. "And fathers are softer touches than mothers. Our kids each figured that out by the time they were two. They'd always hit on Jerry before they came to me." The chuckle that followed had a sobbing undertone. Alyssa's terror for what could happen to her children—herself, too—had kept thoughts of her husband at bay, at least partly. Now that she could start relaxing...

She was desperately afraid that she'd never see him again. This was so weird that she couldn't figure out a way to get back. She wanted to climb back in her car, turn around, and go back the way she'd come in hopes of undoing whatever had happened. She looked again at what was left of her car. That wasn't an option. It looked like her only option was to hook up with this trio of Nordic blonds. She looked at them. The man was huge and a little frightening with his short blond hair under a baseball cap that said "Peterbilt" across the front. The woman was shorter, only a little taller than Alyssa's five-foot-six height. And the daughter, Alyssa thought her name was Shane, was shorter and thin, five two or three.

"So what do we do now?" asked Melanie, turning to Michael. Michael had been in Afghanistan. He knew about survival in a way that Melanie didn't.

"Our first and top priority," said Michael, "is finding a source of clean water—which means either running water or a big lake. Best would be a large creek with a rapid flow of water. We want water for sanitation purposes too, not just drinking and cooking, but also cleaning."

He turned and pointed at the surviving portions of the general store. "There's probably some bottled water in there, maybe even a lot of it. But however much there is, it'll run out sooner or later. Before it does, we have to find another source.

"Our second priority is stocking up on food." He nodded toward the remnants of the store. "We need to strip whatever store shelves are left of any food on them. Yeah, I know that means we'll be mostly subsisting on junk food, but it'll keep us alive until we can find other sources."

"What about calling someone?" Alyssa asked. She didn't know where they were, but in her experience there were always people that could be called. She pulled out her phone. There was no signal, not even any GPS signal, and there should be. Anywhere on Earth, there should be GPS and her phone had the chip to receive those signals and provide her a location. That worked everywhere except underground, so it should work here.

It didn't. No phone signal, so no cell towers in range and no GPS so...So what? They weren't on Earth? No. The plants, the sky, the sun...this was Earth. It had to be. "We should be getting GPS signals, even if we don't have cell service. At least, we should be if we're anywhere on Earth."

"We're not getting any signals either," Michael confirmed. "I think for now at least we have to assume we're on our own. Which means we need food."

"Hunting?" said his wife. "We've got the guns for it—but only so much ammunition for them." She looked around warily. "And we have no idea what sort of animals we'll encounter out here. Some of them might be more than our guns will handle."

"Are your guns deer hunting rifles?" asked Alyssa.

"Yeah. Michael's got a 30-06 Remington 300 firing 180-grain bullets. My rifle's a Winchester Model 70 .308. I prefer a lighter 150-grain round."

Alyssa nodded. "Either one of them will take down any game in North America, although it might be a little dicey using a .308 150 grain on a polar bear."

Michael and Melanie both stared at her. Alyssa smiled. "Chemists have a wide range of knowledge. Plus, my father and husband are both avid deer hunters. The funny thing is that I haven't fired a gun all that often and I'm not a hunter myself. I just know a lot about them."

"Okay. Before we do anything," said Michael, "we need to check out that pickup over there." It was a Ram 1500 with a regular cab.

He headed toward it, but as soon as he came around the back he came to an abrupt stop.

"Melanie. Alyssa. Keep the kids away from here."

Naturally, that stimulated the interest of the three children, especially Shane, who started toward her father. But Melanie caught her by the shoulder and pulled her back. For her part, Alyssa gathered both of her children to her side.

"What is it, Michael?" asked Melanie.

"A corpse," he said tersely. "Part of one, rather."

He moved forward a few more steps and was now looking almost straight down at something at his feet. He took a deep breath and muttered, "Jesus. Talk about a land of nightmares."

Then, after hesitating, he bent over, seemed to grab something—no one else could see exactly what he was doing because he was on the other side of the pickup—and began dragging it away toward a nearby patch of tall prairie grass. He stooped over again for a few seconds with his head out of sight. Then, arising, seemed to brace himself. With a heave, he pitched whatever it was into the grass, which shook back and forth for a few seconds.

When he came back around the pickup he was holding a wallet in his hand and looking through it. He found a driver's license and studied it for a moment.

"The guy's name was George Dawes. White, seventy-seven years old." He looked back up at his wife and Alyssa. "Keep the kids here. I can search the pickup on my own." He glanced at the bed of the pickup, which was empty except for the kind of aluminum truck toolbox that spanned the entire width of the bed and was about eighteen inches wide and high.

"On second thought, see what's in that big toolbox. Just keep the kids away from this side of the vehicle and the interior."

"Come on, Shane," said her mother, unlatching the back gate to the truck bed and climbing up into it. "Let's see what we've got."

While they started investigating the contents of the big toolbox, Michael opened the driver's door of the pickup. Not more than a second elapsed before he half-shouted, "*Hallelujah!* He's got a rifle on a rack in here. Looks like a Ruger Mini-14. Let's hope…"

He started searching behind the driver's seat. This time, not more than two seconds elapsed before he issued another *Hallelujah* and extracted a large ammunition storage box. He set it on the ground and opened it up. "Well, our hunting capacity just went way up. I was worried about how soon we'd run out of ammunition for our rifles."

Melanie looked over the edge of the pickup bed. "This toolbox is loaded, too. There are two smaller boxes in here holding a lot of different tools—screwdrivers, wrenches, a couple of hammers, that sort of thing—several ropes, two tie-down ratchet straps, an ax, a hatchet and a spade."

"Good deal," said Michael. He leaned over to reach the glove compartment from the driver's seat. His arms were long enough to manage it.

As soon as he opened the glove compartment his eyes were drawn to the prominent object within it.

"What the hell?" He drew out a very large pistol. "Why in the world is a man in his late seventies carrying around a Desert Eagle?"

"Retired special ops soldier?" suggested Melanie.

Alyssa shook her head. "That pistol's almost never used by military forces. It's too heavy and the ammunition it fires isn't standard. I think it's the only pistol in the world that'll fire a .50 caliber round. My uncle Jethro, who *is* retired from Special Forces, says it's a weapon without a purpose. He's pretty derisive about it. Says it's just a gun for civilian enthusiasts who want to have bragging rights on the firing range."

"He's probably right," said Michael. "We'll take it, though."

He put the Desert Eagle back in the glove compartment, closed the door, and headed toward the store's remains. The first thing that drew his attention when he entered were a pair of ice cream freezers against what was left of one of the store's walls. Walking over, he saw that they were about two-thirds full of various ice cream products.

Melanie and Alyssa came over, with Alyssa's children in tow. Shane was off inspecting a different part of the store.

"Well, at least we get a treat for everyone," said Melanie. "Do your kids like ice cream, Alyssa?"

"Be serious. Miriam, Norman—come pick something out from the ice cream coolers." The two children eagerly complied.

Alyssa looked on, her mouth quirking into a wry smile. "Too bad we can't make these a steady diet."

"Are you kidding?" said Michael. He waved his hand dismissively. "I don't care about the ice cream—it's the coolers themselves. These things amount to freezers, if we can find a generator. Even if we can't, they'll still make good ice boxes."

He bent down and tried to lift one end of one of the coolers. With a grunt of effort, he lifted it several inches off the floor and then set it down.

"Somewhere between one hundred and fifty and two hundred pounds, I figure. With some help, I could lift it onto something, but I'd rather not."

He turned toward the corner of the store where his daughter was rummaging around. It seemed to be the place where large tools were kept—shovels, rakes, that sort of thing.

"Hey, Shane!" he called out. "You see anything that looks like a chain hoist?"

She looked at him, and then back down. "I'm not sure what you're talking about, Dad, but there's something here that might be one. It's got chains, anyway."

Michael headed that way. Meanwhile, Melanie and Alyssa started examining the shelves in those parts of the store that hadn't been left behind by the passage of whatever force had brought them here.

"Oh, boy," said Melanie. "Snack cakes and cookies, lots of them. Also energy bars." She pointed at one still intact refrigerated wall unit. "That's got some mostly processed meat, packaged sandwiches and frozen vegetables, but other than that...Every variety of potato chips or corn chips, packaged pastries, canned meat, canned vegetables..." She stuck out her tongue. "Yuck. One bag of potato chips is nice. Day after day after day? Not so much."

"Look on the bright side," said Alyssa. "A lot of this stuff has a shelf life measured in centuries. Honey never goes bad. They say the same about Twinkies but I think that's probably an old wives' tale."

Michael returned with a complicated gadget in his hands. "With this manual chain hoist, we should be able to handle anything. It's not all that big, but we're not trying to hoist engine blocks. Now what we need to find is some sort of support to hang it from. A children's swing would be perfect."

"I'll look!" said Shane. She ran outside. About a minute later she was back, shaking her head. "No go, Dad."

They wound up using two stepladders and an expanding ladder as the cross brace. That held the hoist while they pushed and tugged the refrigerator units far enough under it to lift them up enough to slide what Michael somewhat grandiosely called a "travois" under them. The "travois" was nothing more than a section of the store's outer wall that had been sliced off by the passage of the mysterious force that had so thoroughly wrecked the place.

Michael then lowered the tanker trailer's landing gear to disengage it from the tractor's fifth wheel. He saw no reason to try to cross unpaved wilderness hauling the heavy vehicle. The tractor weighed a little over ten tons all on its own.

That done, he used the tie-down ratchet straps and ropes from Dawes' pickup toolbox to attach the travois to the back of the tractor. Once again, they had to use the rather flimsy stepladder arrangement to hoist the store wall up high enough to make the contraption a travois instead of just a flat sled.

"You realize that if OSHA gets wind of any of this, the fines'll bankrupt us," said Melanie.

"What's O-Sha?" asked Miriam.

"It's the federal agency that regulates workplace procedures to make sure they're safe," said Alyssa.

"Spoken like a true professor," scoffed Michael. "OSHA is the horde of guv'ment busybodies that do their best to make the daily lives of hardworking men and women miserable with their pettifogging rules."

It was obvious even to Miriam that he was joking.

Alyssa smiled. "I take it you're owner-operators, not fleet drivers. If you had corporate managers setting the safety rules, you'd have a kinder attitude toward government regulators."

"Well, sure," said Michael. With a grunt, he finished setting the travois up in place. "Guv'ment regulators are just annoying imps and goblins. Corporate managers answer directly to Lucifer himself."

He stepped back and examined their handiwork. "Okay, now we've got to set up some kind of walls on either side of the travois so everything doesn't fall off. This is likely to be a bumpy ride."

They used larger items like generators—they found two, both intact—propane storage tanks and five-gallon water bottles tied in place with ropes for the purpose. Then, tossed anything they thought might be useful into the space thus created, after which they loaded up the bed of the pickup.

By the time they were done—which meant they had run out of space, not loaded everything they wanted—it was late afternoon.

Melanie glanced at the sun, whose orb was just beginning to touch the horizon. "You're not planning to drive at night, I hope."

"Hell, no," said Michael. "We'll start early tomorrow morning. We'll need to make a second trip anyway, once we find a place for a permanent campsite. We didn't get everything we wanted, not by a long shot."

He squinted at the setting sun. "Is it just me who's disoriented, or is the sun setting at the wrong time? If I remember where this store was positioned, we should still be in midafternoon."

"I'm pretty sure you're right," said Alyssa. "Come nightfall, we can look at the stars, see where Polaris is sitting in the sky to find north."

"Who's Polaris?" asked Shane.

"It's the North Star, honey," answered her mother. "It sits right where the north pole is located. You follow a line set by the two stars at the end of the Big Dipper's cup until you spot the star at the end of the Little Dipper's handle. That's Polaris."

That night, after the last vestiges of the sunset had faded away, they went back outside to study the night sky. It was extraordinarily dark; much more so than any of them had ever encountered in their past. The moon wasn't up yet, and there was no light source except starlight.

Alyssa looked at the night sky, then pulled out her phone. She checked the compass function. North, magnetic north, wasn't pointing at the North Star. Not quite. "Something is a little off here," she muttered.

"What?" asked Michael.

"I'm guessing," said Alyssa, "but I think Polaris is in the wrong place. Not much, but the wrong place. Either that or my compass in the cell phone is off.

"It's above the horizon, but not quite in line with where the magnetometer built into my cell phone says it should be."

"Are you sure that you're looking at Polaris?" Michael asked.

Alyssa gave him a look, which he couldn't see in a night this dark. "Yes, I'm sure." She showed him the star map on her phone.

"What does that mean?" asked Shane.

Alyssa pointed to a spot in the sky. "You see the Big Dipper and the end of the Little Dipper. Well, that star is Polaris, the North Star, but if we are where we were on the surface of the earth, it ought to be just a bit off of where it is. That could mean that we're in another part of the world, but the grass, the animals we've seen, and the terrain features all suggest that we're pretty close to the same place on Earth that we were before this happened."

"That, in itself, is a bit strange," Michael said. "From the beginning, I've been assuming that we got caught in one of the temporal displacements that Peffers and O'Connell were trying to measure. I've been wondering if their measuring device somehow attracted the...what was it they called the things... temporal bolide."

"What are you talking about?" Alyssa asked.

"Shortly before this happened, a couple of scientist types asked us to carry a data-collecting device on the back of the Peterbilt's cab. It was pretty obvious that they were looking to figure out what was going on with the West Virginia incident and the prison and the cruise ship."

Alyssa nodded, which no one could see, then said, "Yes, I know about the temporal swaps. At least, we've all been assuming they were swaps. They could have been displacements. Land from the past arrives in our time, and land from our time goes into the future. The argument for that would be that if they went into the past, we should see something in the archaeological record."

"I think they must be swaps then in spite of the archaeological record," Melanie said, looking around. "Or else there would be a lot more light pollution. I rule out nuclear war or holocaust because if we'd gone far enough into the future for that to be it, the stars would be more different than they are."

Alyssa had been thinking about what the Anderles had said. "Did you put the box on your truck?"

"Yes," Melanie said. "Oh, my god. Do you think that could be what caused it?"

At that point, what Michael Anderle wanted to do was go to the back of the Peterbilt and take a sledge hammer to that "harmless box of sensors." Or better yet, to take the sledgehammer to Peffers and O'Connell, which was impossible as well as useless. He didn't attack the box, because he realized that if there was ever going to be any chance of them getting any help, it was probably going to be from that box. Assuming that they really had experienced what happened to Grantville, West Virginia, from the inside. Something that he was still far from convinced of. It was just the least insane theory he had for what had happened. "Okay. Assuming that we were caught in an event like what happened to Grantville, and further assuming that it was a swap, why isn't there any archaeological evidence of Grantville arriving in seventeenth-century Germany?"

"The many-worlds hypothesis," Alyssa said without hesitation. "The arrival of Grantville in that other history sent their timeline off in another direction."

"Which would mean that our arrival here could send us off into another timeline," Michael said.

"Not could. Has," Alyssa said. "Assuming that Grantville went into the past and didn't show up in our history, then anything, even a pebble arriving in the past, sets up a new timeline, even if it never does anything you can measure."

Everyone was silent after that. They still didn't know, not for sure. But it was the best theory they had.

"So, how far back?" Melanie asked.

"I have no idea," Alyssa said. "But if I take a few more observations, measure the movement of Polaris overnight, and the distance between Barnard's Star and its near neighbors, I might be able to get a rough estimate. Also the positions of the moon, Venus, Mars, Jupiter and Saturn make a sort of complicated clock. Over the next few nights, I'll try to get a look at the planets. Jupiter has a year that's twelve years long, and Saturn twenty-nine. Once we get a rough idea, the locations of the planets should let us narrow it down."

Alyssa did look at Barnard's Star and compare what she saw in the night sky to what the app on her cell phone said she should be seeing. In fact, she fiddled with her phone and let it take a five-minute exposure picture of the night sky where Barnard's Star was located, then compared that picture with what she should be seeing. Barnard's Star wasn't where it was in the twenty-first century. Her best guess was that they were between five hundred and two thousand years in the past.

The distance between Mars, Jupiter and Saturn narrowed that, and by working for most of the night, she figured that they were either right around a thousand years in the past, or seventeen hundred years in the past, or just possibly four hundred years in the past.

The next morning, she explained, finishing with, "I'm not at all certain, but my best guess is sometime around the year 1005 of the Common Era, give or take a year."

There was silence for a while. Then Shane said, plaintively, "A *thousand* years? We've traveled that far back in time?"

"Well, we have to have traveled back at least a few centuries," said Alyssa. She pointed up at the sky again. It was daylight.

"Without the light pollution the star field was clearer and brighter than you could find it almost anywhere on the planet Earth when we lived there. That let me get images that were better than I expected. I'm pretty sure of my numbers."

"In other words, whatever civilization is out there can't have reached the industrial revolution," said Michael. "So no lights at night beyond fires of one kind or another. And whatever cities might exist, most of them can't be all that big."

"Could we be even farther back in time than one or two thousand years?" asked Shane.

"I don't think so," said Alyssa. "A lot of the constellations have gotten a little distorted, but most of them are still recognizable, and Barnard's Star simply hasn't moved enough.

"My best guess is the year 1005. That's pretty good news for us, actually."

"Why?" asked Shane.

"There was a time when enormous mammals roamed North America. The Pleistocene megafauna, they're called: wooly mammoths, giant sloths, cave bears, saber-toothed tigers, dire wolves, there were a lot of them. But they all went extinct by ten thousand years ago. So the only thing we'll be facing in the way of wildlife will be pretty much the same animals we had in our time. More of them, of course. But if we need to defend ourselves, our guns will be able to handle the job. We'll be dealing with mountain lions, not saber-toothed tigers. Grey and red wolves, not dire wolves."

"But are we still in North America?" asked Melanie.

"Yeah, I'm pretty sure we are," said her husband. "The fact that we can recognize so many constellations means we're definitely still on Earth." He reached out his hand and swept it across the landscape. "This terrain looks just like what we were driving through and if that isn't Midwest/Great Plains prairie grasses and flowers, I'd be very surprised."

"There sure are a lot of them," said Shane. "Hey... wait a minute! Aren't there too many flowers? We're in August. Well, we were, anyway."

Her mother chuckled. "Honey, if we can be shifted back in time a thousand years, I figure whatever force did it wasn't too fussy about which season it dropped us into. Judging from the number and variety of flowers we've seen, I bet we're now in springtime. Probably sometime in late April or May."

"Now that would *really* be good luck," said Michael. "We'll have half a year to get ready for winter instead of two months.

"Out of idle curiosity, Professor Jefferson, is there any subject you *don't* know a lot about?"

Melanie and Shane laughed.

"Sure!" Alyssa said smiling. "I don't know diddly-squat about cars, for instance. My husband teases me—teased me—about it."

She was silent for a moment. Then she said, "Jerry liked to say that the only car part I knew the name for was Triple A."

Another little laugh was shared by the group, even her two young children.

"We'd better get some breakfast," said Michael. "We've got a lot to do today. Except you, Alyssa. You were up half the night taking star sightings. Get some rest."

Alyssa Jefferson got into the upper bunk in the cabin of the Peterbilt, but she couldn't sleep. She stared up at the ceiling of the Peterbilt's cab. The ceiling she could see wasn't metal, but some sort of fabric. It was a soft gray color, like most of the cab's interior.

Alyssa found it soothing. The ceiling was low, but not so much as to make her claustrophobic. Taken as a whole, the cab was quite spacious, in fact. She and her children had enough room on the upper bunk to sleep comfortably. It was on the cozy side, granted, but didn't feel cramped.

Actually, the cab's main effect on her—and a powerful one—was to make her feel safe. Sleeping in the Peterbilt felt a lot like sleeping in a small but very strong fortress. They were high off the ground. No one, man or beast, could reach the doors without climbing up a few feet. The Anderles had carefully locked the doors.

The biggest bear in the world couldn't break into the truck. In fact, she doubted even a Tyrannosaurus rex could have managed that—assuming the thought would have occurred to the monster, which it wouldn't have. The Peterbilt—just the tractor alone—weighed quite a bit more than the biggest Tyrannosaurus—more than ten tons compared to seven or eight. And there was simply no comparison in terms of speed and power.

A bigger danger, of course, would be other humans. But if Alyssa was right, and she was quite confident her estimates were not far off the mark, they were now living about a thousand years in the past. If she remembered her somewhat haphazard reading on the subject correctly, the native populations in North America practiced agriculture but still relied heavily on hunting. That was because the only domesticated animals were dogs.

Their tools and weapons were mostly made of stone, wood and bone. The only metal widely used was copper, and that was almost entirely used for decoration. Tin deposits were very rare in North America, so bronze wasn't used, and the only people who worked with iron were in the Pacific Northwest and they didn't do any mining. They worked with iron retrieved from ship-wrecked Japanese and Chinese vessels. These were usually ships that drifted ashore on currents, not ones that foundered on North America itself. Alyssa had been surprised to discover that this cross-Pacific contact almost certainly predated Columbus' voyage.

But for all practical purposes, the people she and her companions would encounter were still in the late Stone Age when it came to weapons and tools. The likelihood that any of them could figure out how to open a modern lock was effectively nil. True, they could try to break into the cab of the truck and would probably manage that fairly soon—at which point they would encounter Michael Anderle's Glock 23 .40 caliber pistol. And if the thirteen rounds in the Glock's magazine weren't enough, he'd also brought George Dawes' Desert Eagle into the cab of the truck. There had been no extra ammunition in his pickup, but the .357 Magnum magazine had contained a full nine rounds.

So. Neolithic aggressors versus more than twenty rounds from modern pistols. And by the time Michael was out of ammunition, Melanie would have had time to bring into play either of the rifles they had hanging on a rack in the back of the cab. Alyssa could do that herself, for that matter. If she rose up a bit and stretched out her hand, she could reach both of the weapons from her position on the upper bunk.

She felt safe. Very safe, in fact. And that turned out to be a mixed blessing, because the relaxation that produced enabled her mind to focus on the one thing she dreaded thinking about most. Jerry was gone—and almost certainly gone forever. She'd lost her husband and her young children had lost their father. Alyssa was a scientist. She had a solid grounding in physics as well as chemistry. The recent temporal displacements had been the talk of the scientific community since the first one had happened back in the year 2000. No one ever came back. By now it was well known that, assuming anyone survived, they were stuck in whatever time they ended up in.

The tears finally started coming then. There seemed to be no end to them.

CHAPTER 3

THE CREEK

General Store
April 12, 1005 CE

The next morning, right after sunrise, they drove the tractor and the pickup westward. Michael picked that direction for no better reason than he had a hunch they were still east of the Mississippi River. If so, the closer they got to the huge waterway, the more likely they were to run into tributaries that would provide them with the running water they needed.

They drove very slowly, of course—never more than five miles an hour and often slower than that. The prairie they were crossing was generally flat and unobstructed, but "generally" is an expansive word. On more than one occasion they had to take detours to get around various obstacles.

Michael was worried that his improvised travois would come apart from the rigors of the day's drive. But it proved to be surprisingly sturdy. It helped a lot, of course, that as slowly as they were going the contraption was never subjected to sharp and violent bumps.

And they either got lucky or Michael's guess was accurate. The pickup was in the lead, as it had been from the beginning, and Shane was riding in the bed perched atop the wide toolbox. That gave her a very good view of the terrain they were crossing.

A bit less than two hours after they began the drive, she pointed to the left and shouted, "There's a tree line! I see a tree line!"

Slowly and carefully, her mother steered the pickup toward the line of trees in the distance. Alyssa, sitting in the cab alongside her, held Melanie's rifle in her hands so it would be readily available if needed. The plan was that Melanie would be the shooter unless whatever danger appeared came very suddenly. Then Alyssa would take her chances. She hadn't been on a firing range in at least five years.

It didn't take more than twenty minutes to reach the tree line. Michael and the tractor arrived five minutes later. By then, the people in the pickup had all climbed out and were inspecting what they'd found.

Sure enough, it was a creek—and just the sort of creek they'd hoped to find. It varied in width between ten and fifteen feet, was fairly shallow—between one and two feet deep in most places, although there was a pool thirty yards upriver where the creek widened to thirty feet and the depth reached five or six feet. Best of all, the water was quite fast-moving, which was likely to result in a healthier water source than would be provided by a sluggish stream. The water was very clear.

After Michael got out of the tractor and inspected the area, he proposed that they set up their camp a short distance upriver from the pool. They could use the pool for laundry and bathing during most of the year, and set up sanitary facilities forty or fifty yards downriver from the pool. They weren't sure yet that they would stay here, but it was a good prospect and close enough to the country store for them to make the trip fairly regularly. For now, it was a good campsite, and it might even make a good permanent campsite.

From that vantage point, they were on a crest in the terrain that sloped downward at a shallow angle. In the distance, perhaps half a mile away, they could see a river flowing slowly to the southwest. It was much wider and deeper than the creek they'd parked next to, but nowhere near the size of a river like the Mississippi. They could only see the stretch of the river nearest to them, because another rise in the landscape—you couldn't really call it a hill—blocked their view further to the north.

"At a guess," said Melanie, "I think that's probably the Kaskaskia River—or the version of it in the here and now, anyway."

"I'm not familiar enough with the geography here to have an opinion," said Alyssa, "but an alluvial river on a flat plain will move all over given a few centuries. So let's go with Kaskaskia."

Michael followed the line of the river to the southwest. "If you're right, it'll flow into the Mississippi down there somewhere." He turned around and pointed north. "And, assuming Alyssa's right about the time we're in, Cahokia is up there. Which means we're right in the middle of the Mound Builders territory."

"How far away is Cahokia?" asked Melanie.

He shrugged. "Its ruins are just across the Mississippi from Saint Louis, so anywhere from thirty to fifty miles would be my estimate. But I could be way off."

They began unloading the pickup and the travois. They made no attempt to organize anything—just unload it as fast as possible so they could make another round trip to the wrecked country store before sundown.

"Should anybody stay here to guard the stuff?" asked Melanie.

"From what?" said Michael. "We've got all the food that might draw animals in airtight containers or coolers of one kind or another. So the only real risk I can see is that some people might come across the camp before we get back. But we haven't seen any sign of human inhabitants in the area since we arrived."

"S'okay with me," said Alyssa. "I think we should all stick together anyway, at least until we've got a better sense for what's around here."

It didn't take them more than half an hour to unload everything. They were able to drive a bit faster on the way back to the store, partly because the travois was no longer loaded down but mostly because they knew the way now. They could avoid the worst obstacles without having to stumble across them.

When they arrived at the store, it was still short of noon. At least, according to their watches it was. Whether those watches were still synchronized with the time of day according to the nonexistent Royal Observatory in Greenwich, England, was anybody's guess. But they seemed to be pretty closely in harmony, judging from the sun's position in the sky.

Michael took a shovel out of the bed of the pickup and headed toward the stand of grass where he'd pitched the remains of George Dawes the day before. "Before I do anything else, I'm going to dig a grave for poor Mr. Dawes. I've been feeling guilty about it since yesterday. The rest of you can start looking through what's still in the store to see what you think we should take with us."

But he was back in less than a minute. "Honey, get your rifle out of the pickup." He headed toward the cab of the Peterbilt. "And I'll holster up the Glock."

"What's wrong?" she asked. But she didn't wait for a reply before heading for the pickup. Melanie had known her husband for years. The man was not an alarmist. If something had him worried, there was a good reason for it.

"Dawes' body is gone," he said. "Not a trace of it left beyond a little blood."

"That's actually good news, I think," said Alyssa. "A bear or a pack of wolves would have eaten the corpse where they found it. It's the big cats who have the habit of hauling a carcass away for later eating. Well, leopards do, anyway. I'm not sure about other cats. But there were never tigers in North America and the American lion went extinct thousands of years ago. So what we'd be dealing with is a cougar."

"And they don't hunt in packs and they aren't all that big anyway," said Michael. "I think you're probably right, Alyssa."

Melanie made a face. "Not that big," she said, mimicking Michael's baritone voice. "Hon, I've *seen* a mountain lion in the wild. Damn thing ran across the road right in front of me when I was driving. You want my opinion, it looked plenty big enough to make a snack out of me."

Alyssa laughed. "I bet it did! They're a hell of a lot bigger than a house cat, that's for sure. But they're still much smaller than a lion or a tiger, Melanie. Even the males rarely weigh more than two hundred pounds."

"So what?" demanded Melanie. "I weigh one hundred and forty-five pounds—and I got no fangs or claws." She hefted her Winchester Model 70. "I'm keeping this right next to me. A 150-grain bullet with a muzzle velocity of twenty-seven hundred feet per second is a great equalizer."

Michael climbed down from the cab with his Glock in a holster. "I'm not making fun of you, dear. I'm carrying this around until we're out of here. But I don't really think we've got much to worry about. Now, let's get started."

"We need something to make walls on the travois," said

Melanie. "There's not much left in the way of big items, though. You got any ideas?"

"There's one big item," said Michael. He nodded toward the store's restroom, which had survived the passage of the Ring of Fire. "I want to take that toilet back with us."

"That's going to be awfully heavy," said Alyssa doubtfully. "Are you sure we really need it?"

"You ever used an outhouse?"

Alyssa sniffed. "Whatever sharecroppers were in my family tree were a long way back. I grew up in Hyde Park, literally a stone's throw from the University of Chicago. So, no. The only outhouses in my vicinity would have been in museums, maybe."

Melanie chuckled. "Now you're in for it. Michael's favorite bit of trivia when it comes to the joys of outdoor camping involves the denizens of outhouses."

Michael grinned. "Spiders love outhouses—especially black widows. So there you are, sitting on moist warm wood, which the critters adore. Up they come…"

"Yuck!" Alyssa threw up her hands. "I retract everything I said! By all means, let's salvage the toilet."

Michael headed for the restroom. "I'll take off the door, too. We need to salvage as much lumber as we can take back with us. That'll also provide us with the walls we need for the travois."

Using a couple of crowbars they found in the tool section of the store, Alyssa and Melanie started prying off whatever boards looked to be still usable. There turned out to be quite a few, more than they would have expected. The Ring of Fire's peculiarly sharp edge—if that was the right term for it—cut wood cleanly rather than smashing it into pieces.

Meanwhile, Shane and Alyssa's two children roamed about, looking for anything of use they'd overlooked the day before. There was quite a bit, although that was mostly because there was a lot of space on the travois and in the pickup bed—and the operating philosophy was, *if in doubt, take it, because you never know what might turn out to be handy.*

One item the children unanimously agreed could be dispensed with was several bags full of Styrofoam cups. "We already got enough cups and glasses," said Shane.

But Alyssa overruled them. "No, we should bring them with us."

Michael had finished with loading the toilet into the pickup and had come back into the store. "I don't really see the point, Alyssa," he said. "The kids are right—we've already got enough stuff to drink out of to last us for years."

"You said yourself just yesterday that we have no idea what we're going to be facing in the way of possible human enemies, didn't you?" she replied.

"Well, yeah, but—"

Alyssa pointed at the bags full of Styrofoam cups. "We've got lots of diesel in that tanker of yours, right?"

"Yeah. Thousands of gallons."

Alyssa nodded. "With diesel and Styrofoam, I can make napalm. Gasoline will work too, but diesel's better." She pointed to a dozen or so big pickle jars that were still on one of the intact shelves. "And we should take whatever glass or ceramic containers we can find to hold the napalm, whether or not we want the contents. We'll need to figure out a way to make catapults so we can fire them a good distance. Oh, and we should grab however many sponges and rags we can find for fuses."

Michael and Melanie stared at her, then looked at each other.

"Beware of chemists in dark alleys," said Michael.

They got back to the camp with just enough daylight left to unload the travois; after which, Michael removed the travois from the tractor.

"I'll leave at sunrise tomorrow to get the tanker. You can unload the pickup while I'm gone," he said. "But leave the toilet for me until I get back. It's a heavy bastard."

Camp Peterbilt
April 12, 1005 CE

When Michael got back with the tanker in tow, it was early in the afternoon. The first thing he noticed was that Melanie and Alyssa were both standing in the bed of the pickup peering at something in the distance. Melanie was holding her rifle by the barrel, propped up against the bed of the pickup. He could see the back of Shane's head inside the cab of the pickup and assumed the other two children were with her.

He pulled up next to them and lowered the window on the driver's side of the tractor. "What's up?"

Alyssa pointed toward the rise that blocked their view of the river to the north. "We've got company."

Michael reached into the glove compartment of the tractor and drew out a pair of ten-by-forty-two binoculars in a case. He extracted the field glasses and started scanning through the windshield. The sun was high enough in the sky not to be producing a glare in the windshield, so his view was not significantly obstructed.

It took him only a few seconds to spot what his wife and Alyssa were referring to. Several people—men only, he thought, although he wasn't sure—were crouched down on the rise that impeded the view of the river to the north. Two of them that he could see held bows, although only one had an arrow nocked.

He wasn't sure exactly how many people were on the rise, because they were all obviously trying to hide. He was sure there were at least five people over there, and there might be two or three more hidden behind some heavy brush.

He considered climbing into the back of the cab and bringing down his own rifle, but decided to hold off for the moment. The closest people watching them from the rise were at least two hundred and fifty yards away. That was within the maximum range for target practice with a bow that had enough draw weight, but no one he knew ever tried to hunt at that range. Most experienced hunters didn't try to shoot at prey farther than sixty yards away—and he was quite sure that whoever these people were, they were all very experienced hunters. Much more experienced than any bow hunter in the twenty-first century who hunted for sport. These people hunted to keep themselves and their families alive.

The point being, he'd have plenty of time to get his rifle if it turned out he needed it. Melanie's .308 caliber rifle had a scope on it and she was a very good shot with very steady nerves. As good as Michael was, in his opinion, and he could bring down targets with his rifle at this range fairly easily. If the people over there decided to attack, Melanie would put them in a world of hurt all on her own.

He was hoping it wouldn't come to that. He and his wife and Alyssa had spent a fair amount of time discussing how they would handle contact with the indigenous folk if—which was far more likely to be *when*—they encountered them. They were all in full, even fervent, agreement that their operating philosophy if at all possible should be guided by the slogan *give peace a chance*.

Which wasn't the same thing as *don't study war no more*—as Alyssa had demonstrated with her cold-blooded willingness to develop weapons using napalm. She had two young children to keep alive, no matter what.

He decided he'd seen enough and slung the eyeglasses over his neck. Then he did go into the back of the cab and take down his rifle. After making sure it was fully loaded, he shoved two boxes of ammunition into a shoulder satchel—one box for his gun, and one for his wife's—and climbed down from the cab of the tractor and into the bed of the pickup.

"Here," he said to Alyssa, handing her the binoculars. He set the satchel with the ammunition down on the floor of the pickup's bed—taking advantage of the motion to peer through the rear window to see how the three children were doing.

They were all avidly watching everything on the rise opposite them. Shane was sitting at the wheel, with the keys in the ignition and herself obviously ready and willing to charge the foe. She was a pretty good driver for a twelve-year-old, although her experience was only on gravel roads and a few infrequently traveled county roads. Michael had never let her drive the Peterbilt, but that was just because she was still too small to be able to handle all the controls involved. Once she'd grown enough, he would teach her.

In big parking lots to begin with, of course. For the time being, her grandparents were always willing to let her practice with their car. Well, her grandmother was a bit dubious, but her grandfather had no qualms about it. He'd learned to drive motor vehicles on a farm when he was younger than she was, and he'd taught Michael at the same tender age.

But what Michael found most amusing was the attitude of Alyssa's two children. Both of them were standing on the passenger seat and propping their weight in front of them on the dashboard. It was crystal clear from their stances that neither one of them was infused with the spirit of *give peace a chance*.

No, no. In the case of the four-and-a-half-year-old boy and the six-year-old girl, the spirit was along the lines of *Go ahead, suckers! Try something!*

When Michael rose back up, he smiled at Alyssa and said, "I don't think your kids are devotees of Mahatma Gandhi."

She gave him an exasperated look. "And you were, at their

age? Gimme a break. Little kids are all a bunch of Goths and Vandals. It takes a while to civilize them. More or less."

About half an hour later, the people on the rise began leaving. They were clearly skilled outdoorsmen, because most of them vanished without their departure being noticed until later, when the Americans realized there was no one still watching them from the rise. Didn't seem to be, anyway.

"D'you think they'll be back tonight?" asked Alyssa.

"Yes," said Melanie. "And they'll come a lot closer. The moon still isn't showing more than a slight crescent, so it'll be dark."

"Do we have any flashlights?" asked Alyssa.

Michael grinned. "We've got something one hell of a lot better than flashlights."

"Well, yeah, the truck headlights. But we can't really illuminate anything with them except whatever is straight ahead."

Melanie was looking a bit startled. "Are you thinking of Eddie's spotlights? I'd forgotten all about them. Do you think they still work?"

"Easy to find out, but I don't see why they wouldn't. They've just been sitting in the back of that compartment for . . . what's it been? Four years?"

"At least."

Michael hopped out of the bed of the pickup and headed toward the Peterbilt. Melanie now had a wry smile on her face. "It just goes to show you never know when something oddball might prove handy," she said to Alyssa. "We had a friend named Eddie Kettering—another trucker—who retired a few years ago. He had a pair of spotlights he insisted on giving to us. 'To make sure you don't get taken by surprise by anybody,' he said."

She shook her head. "He was always a bit paranoid. Anyway, we accepted them, just to avoid hurting his feelings." She pointed to Michael, who was at the side of the truck rummaging around in an exterior compartment. He emerged holding up a pair of spotlights, both of which had long extension cords attached to them.

"How do you attach them?" asked Alyssa.

"They have suction mounts. I'm not sure how well they'd hold up if you tried driving a long stretch with them, but we'll be stationary so they should work fine. You want a hand, hon?" she asked Michael when he reached the cab of the Peterbilt.

"Yeah. Each of you stand on either side of the truck so I can hand down the extension cords to you."

It didn't take very long to set up the spotlights. Michael attached the suction mounts to the roof of the cab, one on either side, and they ran the extension cords through slightly opened cab windows. Once those were plugged into outlets inside the cab, Michael climbed up into the driver's seat and handed one of the two remote controls to Melanie, who was sitting in the passenger seat. Alyssa moved a few yards to the front of the truck to report on how well the gadgets worked.

Extremely well, as it turned out, once they changed the batteries on the remotes. Both spotlights were still completely functional, even after years of sitting idle. The remote controls allowed anyone in the cab to direct the beams through very wide angles, vertically as well as horizontally.

"I can't tell how bright they'll be at night," Alyssa said, returning to the truck. She pointed toward the sun, which was still high in the sky, which had almost no clouds in it. "The sun pretty well washes out the beams."

"At night, they should be plenty bright," said Michael. "We'll find out in a few hours."

"You really think they'll come back?"

"They'd be crazy not to. It'll be almost pitch dark so they can get much closer to us than they could in the daytime. And I'll bet dollars to donuts we won't be able to hear them moving out there. We're talking James Fenimore Cooper woodsmanship."

Alyssa smiled. "Actually, Cooper always had skulkers in the woods stepping on twigs and making noise," she said. "Mark Twain made fun of him for it. But I get your point." She looked over to the rise where the visitors had appeared earlier.

"Do you think they'll attack us, Michael?"

He shrugged. "They might, but I doubt it. Not, at least, until they have a much better sense of what they're facing. Try to imagine what this tractor and trailer look like to people still in the Stone Age. Especially ones who don't have draft animals and probably don't even use wheels except for maybe toys."

Alyssa looked at the decor painted on the Peterbilt. "So that's why you plastered this garish fire-breathing dragon all over your tractor? To scare off indigenous warriors in the event of a time travel escapade."

Michael grinned. "Think ahead, I always say."

Melanie sniffed. "I tried to talk him out of it." By now, Shane and Alyssa's two kids had gathered around the tractor. "But my daughter stabbed me in the back and sided with her father."

"Hey, I think it's cool!" protested Shane.

Melanie sniffed again. "It's just like you said, Alyssa. Buncha Goths and Vandals."

The strangers were all women and children, but their gear and, especially, the strange house had the young men of the tribe more than a bit nervous. Also, the hunting party had visited this place only a week ago and there was no one here. How had they gotten all this stuff here in so short a time, especially if they were alone?

It was all just too strange. So they were approaching the women in the strange shiny house cautiously. Then, coming around a clump of trees, came a monster. It was like some giant lizard made of fire. Or like a carving. But it moved. It was as big as a house, and it moved.

Suddenly the strange little house that the women had been in got a whole lot stranger. It was like the giant lizard demon, but smaller. Could it move too?

The big demon moved up next to the smaller one without once lifting one of its feet. And one of its ears opened and a giant climbed out, then went back in, got some things and came out again.

They didn't know what it was, but considering it had been sitting in the head of a demon, it was probably magic. For that matter, so was the giant.

To the hunters of Jabir, the village a bit over a mile away on the other side of a hill, the word "demon" didn't mean what it would mean to a twenty-first-century Christian. The word they used could mean demon, angel, god, spirit, or basically anything supernatural and powerful. They didn't make a distinction between good demon, i.e. god or angel, and bad demon, i.e. devil or imp. They were all chancy to deal with.

What was clear here was that whatever these people had or whatever had these people, it, and presumably they, had great power and were chancy to deal with.

So they continued to watch for a while, then they backed away. It was clear that this was work for the shamans.

Jabir
April 12, 1005 CE

It didn't take the hunting party long to get back to Jabir after they got behind the hillock. Jabir was a village of the Kadlo clan of the River People, and it was home. Achanu, the leader of this hunting party, told the tribal elders about the strange moving houses and the people who lived in them.

Priyak flatly disbelieved them. He was the senior shaman of Jabir, an old man dedicated to the priesthood in Hocha and generally disrespectful of the chiefs and the women's council. Gada, the younger shaman, was less dismissive, but far from convinced. For that matter, Achanu's uncle Hamadi, the senior chief, wasn't convinced either.

"I don't blame you, uncle. I wouldn't believe it either if I hadn't seen it with my own eyes. All I can say is come and see."

Hamadi did just that. It took him only an hour. He never got close and didn't stay long, just long enough to confirm that his nephew and the others hadn't been smoking mushrooms.

Even before he sent the hunters back to get a good look, Hamadi sent a message to Roshan in Hocha, telling the clan chief what he'd seen.

CHAPTER 4

SACRIFICE

Camp Peterbilt
April 12, 1005 CE

"Okay, the sun's down," said Melanie, peering through the windshield of the Peterbilt.

Michael checked his wristwatch. "7:56 P.M."

"Same as I've got," said Alyssa. "Given the time of sunrise, I'd say that puts us sometime in late April, maybe early May. Either way, we haven't reached the summer solstice yet."

"Yay!" said Shane. "I don't have to go back to school for at least three months."

Alyssa smiled. "I hate to be the bearer of bad tidings, girl, but from here on out you're on home schooling time, which means summer vacation ends whenever your parents say it does."

"That's not fair! These things should be guided by fixed rules—like a constitution—not by the whims of tyrants."

"When did your mother and I graduate to tyrant status?" asked Michael. "Last I heard—which was maybe an hour ago—we were still a paltry mom and dad. But you can cheer up, kid. For a while yet, your education's going to lean heavily in practical directions."

"Like what?"

"Like helping Alyssa make napalm bombs. Like helping me

figure out how to make some kind of catapult. Like helping your mother design and build traps for rabbits and wild turkeys."

Shane's eyes got very round. "Oh, that's *cool*. So you're back to mom-and-dad status."

"If I can change the subject," said Alyssa, "when do you think anyone's going to show up? For that matter, are we sure that they will?"

"Hell, who knows?" said Michael. "Not before ten o'clock, I wouldn't think. The twilight won't fade for another half hour or so, and they'll probably wait until then before starting to move. I'm not sure how far they have to travel to get here, since we still don't know where they live. But they'll be moving quietly, which as dark as it'll be, means slowly. As to whether they'll try a sneak, they already did. They snuck up during the daylight, and then slunk away without saying hi. That indicates less than honorable intent, to my way of thinking. So, yes, I'm pretty confident that they will try to slip up closer in the night, unless they have some sort of taboo about night operations."

"So when do we turn on the lights?"

"Let's figure on doing a quick look-see with the spotlights at ten-thirty, and then every half hour after that."

Melanie looked back at Alyssa, who was perched on the lower bunk. She was holding Michael's rifle; seated to her right, Shane was holding Melanie's. Each of them had a box of ammunition also. No one wanted to have to resort to the guns. But . . . no one knew what they were facing, either.

Alyssa shrugged. "Michael's plan seems as good as any."

All the lights were out in the cab, and it was getting darker as twilight faded. Michael glanced at his wristwatch again. "Damn, I didn't think of this. My watch is an old-fashioned one where the hands go round and round. I can't see it in the dark."

Melanie frowned. "So's mine."

Alyssa clucked her tongue. "You do know we entered the twenty-first century more than three decades ago? Relax. My watch is digital. I'll call out the time."

"Ten-thirty," said Alyssa. She spoke softly, almost in a whisper, even though no one on the ground outside the cab could possibly hear her unless she shouted.

Michael and Melanie both switched on their spotlights and,

using the remotes, began scanning the area in front of the truck.

They didn't have to spend more than a few seconds doing that. Four men—no, five—were caught in the glare. They were crouched down at the edge of the small clearing that the truck was parked in. They'd probably been there for some time, since they were no longer trying very hard to stay out of sight in the foliage.

To say they had startled expressions on their faces was putting it mildly. All of them except one had their bows ready, with nocked arrows, but not one of them even began to draw back the string. They just stared into the lights, as if paralyzed. Michael was reminded of times he'd visited his grandparents on their farm and his grandfather had taken him and his brother out at night to hunt rabbits and other crop-eating pests. His grandpa would drive slowly down the farm roads in the fields while one of the boys scanned the rows of crops with a spotlight. Any rabbit caught in the light would just freeze, whereupon the brother who had the gun duty would shoot the critter with a .22 semiautomatic. If you needed to take more than one shot to kill a motionless rabbit, you'd hear about it afterward. Grandpa Anderle had sarcasm down pat.

Michael already had the engine idling. Now he turned on the truck headlights—which were much brighter than the spotlights—revved the engine and pulled on the lanyard above the driver's window that operated the air horn. That was an eighteen-wheeler's horn, which was really LOUD. Between the lights suddenly coming on, the engine revving and the horn going off, their hope was that any skulkers would think the enormous monster in the dark had suddenly come awake.

And it was really, really pissed off.

It worked. All the men—there turned out to be seven of them—vanished almost instantly. Four of them fumbled and dropped their arrows. Two of them lost the grip on their bows as well. One had the presence of mind to recover it. The other just ran off.

They were all wearing what looked like peaked caps, not the stereotypical feathered headwear of Hollywood movies nor the turbans that were the characteristic headgear of southern Indian males of later centuries. In the dark, it was hard to make out the rest of their clothing, except that they all seemed to be wearing leggings, probably made of deer hide.

Within a few seconds, they were gone.

"Think they'll come back?" asked Melanie.

"Not tonight," said Alyssa, choking down a laugh that was partly amusement but mostly just relief.

"One of us will have to stay awake and on guard for the rest of the night," said Michael. "I'll take the first watch, from now until one o'clock, unless either of you wants it. The second watch can go from one to four in the morning and the third from four until seven."

He shook his head. "But I'll be really surprised if they come back. Not tonight, anyway. They're going to need at least a day to settle their nerves and try to figure out another plan. Clearly, sneaking up on the sleeping demon ain't gonna work."

"I can stand watch!" said Shane.

"Me too!" chimed in Miriam. Norman didn't say anything. He seemed to be unusually thoughtful for a child not yet five years old.

"You can stand watch with me, if you want to," said Michael. "But not on your own, Shane."

She muttered something that sounded like *tyrant*. But maybe it was *errant*. The younger children didn't put up a protest when their mother explained in very clear and simple English that they weren't doing anything for the rest of the night except getting some sleep.

Jabir
April 13, 1005 CE

They ran most of the way back to the village. And ran into Priyak, the village shaman who had accepted the influence of the Hocha priests.

Gada was less happy with the city, but it was undeniable that the priesthood of Hocha could tell when things were going to happen, when the sun would rise and where the stars would be, and they knew of drugs and medicines that healed the sick and sickened the well. He didn't like them, and he didn't like the gradual increase in the number of sacrifices, but he didn't know how to counter them.

So he kept his mouth shut as the humiliated warriors were bullied by Priyak into allowing the sacrifice of two Kadlo girls to the monsters that had appeared on Jabir land.

Gada did have a word with a couple of Kadlo trackers, suggesting that they follow the tracks of the huge monster and its child back to where they came from.

Camp Peterbilt
April 15, 1005 CE

So far as any of the Americans could tell, no one from the native population of the area showed up the next day or the night that followed. Of course, they might have missed one or two observers, given the natives' skill at moving unnoticed through wilderness. But it was unlikely they'd failed to spot a large party.

The following morning, though, an hour after sunrise, two figures could be seen coming up the shallow slope that led to the small clearing where the Peterbilt was parked. Using the binoculars, Melanie spotted three other people who remained on the rise near the river.

The people approaching them were making no effort to hide or move surreptitiously, and as they drew nearer it became clear that they were both women—and very young women at that. The hide skirts and leggings they were wearing could have been male apparel as well, but they were also bare-chested, which made their gender obvious.

"Look at that!" Shane exclaimed. "Their tits are showing!"

"Shane, don't be rude when they get here. Different folks, different customs."

"What are 'tits'?" asked Norman.

Melanie chuckled. "Alyssa, you can handle that one."

Alyssa explained the matter—quite smoothly, without stumbling; Melanie was impressed—the two young women came closer. When they were about fifty yards away, they stopped and looked back. They were now close enough that their expressions could be seen. Both of them were clearly scared and wanted nothing more than to flee back to where they came from.

Melanie wasn't surprised. If she'd been in their position, she'd have been terrified.

"They're just girls," muttered Michael. "I don't think either of them is more than sixteen or seventeen years old."

Melanie had come to the same conclusion herself. "Do you think... maybe that's a good sign. Sending teenage girls who are pretty clearly unarmed is about as nonthreatening a party to a parlay as you can imagine."

"True," said Alyssa. "But I can think of one alternative explanation, which is a lot grimmer."

Michael grunted. "Sacrifices? Feed a couple of virgins to the demon, in hopes of propitiating the monster?"

"Something like that. Not long after we moved to Carbondale, Jerry and I and the kids went to visit the museum at Cahokia. It's pretty damn impressive. But one of the things I remember is that archaeologists have uncovered several places where human sacrifice had been carried out." She pursed her lips. "And most of the victims were young women."

"Oh, swell," said Melanie. "How large-scale were these sacrifices?"

"Well, nothing on the scale of the Aztecs, or any of the other Mesoamerican cultures. There was only one big site where sacrificial killing was carried out—only one that they've found, anyway. The sacrifices at other sites were much smaller in number. And they mostly seem to have taken place in the period between 1000 and 1200 CE."

"What's CE?" asked Shane.

"It stands for 'Common Era,'" explained Alyssa. "What used to be called AD—Anno Domini."

"Does that dating mean anything?" asked Michael.

Alyssa shrugged. "Archaeological data's always hard to interpret, when you don't have a written language to go with it. But that period was the peak of Cahokian power. It declined rapidly thereafter, and by 1400 the site had been abandoned. The point being that I think it's really going to make a difference to us *which period* we're in now. After looking at the planetary clock and the position of Barnard's Star, I'm pretty sure we're in 1005 CE. So about all we can hope for is that the more massive human sacrifices haven't gotten started yet."

"They're coming forward again," said Michael. "What do you think we should do?"

"If you guys eat them I'm going to be really upset," said Shane. "Even if Dad did paint the truck to look like a dragon."

That produced a burst of laughter in the cab, which by the grin on the twelve-year-old girl's face was the result she was aiming for.

Looking out of the window, Melanie saw that the girls were less than thirty yards away now and were holding hands.

"Christ, they've got to be petrified. Well, we can put a stop to that, at least. Which one of us goes out there?"

"Probably not a good idea to send me," said Michael.

"A three-hundred-pound troll?" said Melanie. "Not a good idea, even if you are clean-shaven. No, it's got to be either me or Alyssa. Seeing a woman's more likely to relax them."

She and Alyssa eyed each other for a moment. Then Alyssa puffed out her cheeks and slowly exhaled the air. "Probably better if it was me," she said. "I'm smaller than you are." She glanced down at her hand. "The one possible drawback might be my skin color. It might seem strange to them."

Melanie held up her hand. "My ancestry's mostly Swedish. I'm about as much lighter-skinned than they are as you are darker. And I'm blonde, to boot. So I think that issue's probably a wash. On the other hand..."

Now she glanced at Alyssa's chest. "Wearing the kind of clothes we do, our gender might not be immediately apparent to people who dress the way they do. That might tilt things in my direction, since...ah..."

Alyssa chuckled. "It's more likely that you'll remind people of Jayne Mansfield than I will."

"Well..."

"There's a simple solution to that problem. Switch places with me." Once Alyssa was in the passenger's seat of the truck, she began unbuttoning her blouse. "Help me get this bra off, Melanie. The cab's a little cramped for this sort of thing."

A few seconds later, she was nude from the waist up and climbing out of the cab. "Wish me luck."

Watching her walk slowly toward the two girls, who had stopped again, Michael said, "I am really coming to like that woman. Running into her was a pure stroke of luck."

"Yup," said Melanie.

"Why is Mommy naked?" asked Miriam.

"Oh, boy," said Melanie.

"When in Rome," said Michael. "Which, in this instance, I interpret as this is a woman's job."

"You gutless bastard."

Michael made no riposte, for the good and simple reason that he agreed with his wife. He *was* a gutless bastard, being firmly of the opinion that there were some issues a man had to be a damn fool to stick his nose into, this being one of them.

By the time that little exchange was over, Alyssa was more than halfway toward the two girls. Michael brought up the binoculars and tried to find the people observing the scene from the distant rise in the landscape. That took a few seconds, because all of them—he could spot four, two men and two women—were crouched down. They weren't exactly hiding, but they were trying to make themselves inconspicuous.

One of the men seemed pretty old. He was wearing an oddly shaped piece of headwear—not so much a hat as something that looked like part of a costume. It was made of wood or bone and painted with facial features that were apparently meant to be frightening. His chest was covered with what looked like beadwork. The other man was clearly younger, but how much younger Michael couldn't tell at this distance. Like the men who'd tried to sneak up on the truck two days earlier, he was bare-chested, but he wasn't carrying a bow—although there might be one lying near him in the brush.

He then shifted the binoculars' focus to the two women, which was easier to do because they were standing together and weren't crouched down as much as the men. Again, there seemed to be a difference in age. One of the women looked no older than the two who'd come up the slope. The other looked a lot older, from what Michael could tell. She had graying hair, unlike the black hair of the younger woman. She was also not bare-chested, but was wearing some sort of sleeveless chemise. Unlike all the other clothing Michael had seen the natives wearing thus far, the chemise didn't look like it was animal skin. It looked like some sort of woven fabric. In general, all the natives looked like Native Americans: brown skin, black hair, high cheekbones, and a bit barrel-chested.

By the time he'd finished his examination of the onlookers, Alyssa had reached the two girls. For a few seconds, all of them just stood there, staring at each other. Then Alyssa pointed to herself with a forefinger and spoke. Michael assumed she was saying her name. She repeated the gesture and the one-word speech and then pointed to the girl to the left.

The two girls looked at each other, and then the one Alyssa

hadn't been pointing at tapped her chest and spoke, following which she pointed to her companion and spoke again. To Michael, it looked like introductions had been made, though he couldn't make out the words.

It was a start.

Alyssa now pointed to the Peterbilt and turned toward it, gesturing with her hand to indicate that the two girls should follow her. She walked a few steps and stopped. The girls hadn't moved. Again, Alyssa gestured that they should come with her. The wave of her hand wasn't peremptory; it was an invitation, not a command.

The girls looked at each other, then back at the people on the rise. Then turned back toward Alyssa, who was waiting patiently. The taller of the two girls—she was the one who'd responded to Alyssa's introductions—took her companion's hand and more or less tugged her in Alyssa's direction. That was enough to get the three of them moving toward the truck.

Back on the rise, Achanu rose to his feet, ignoring the agitated hissing command to stay where he was that came from the old shaman, Priyak. One of the girls who'd been forced to attend the demon by the tribe's shamans was his cousin, Oaka, which angered him. Like many of the young men of the clan, especially those like himself of chiefly lineage, Achanu was resentful of the growing influence of Hocha's priesthood.

Their village of Jabir was not under the direct authority of the great city called Hocha. Like most outlying villages, their status was ambiguous. They did not send regular tribute, but were expected to supply workers for the mound-building projects of Hocha's priests—which could sometimes prove to be a major burden.

Hocha had not called upon them to provide sacrifices. *Not yet.* But Achanu wondered how long that would be true. Sacrifices had been rare before the rise of the new priesthood—and as a rule, satisfied by the death of people who were old and sickly, and mostly volunteers. The sacrifice of girls and young women, which was the preference of the new priests, was abhorrent to many—Achanu and his uncles included. His mother also.

The shamans should have resisted the influence of the new priesthood, but all too often they sought to curry favor with them. There were some exceptions, but Priyak was more typical of the breed. They got away with it because the new priesthood of Hocha knew things that normal people couldn't know. Things like when to plant the corn to get a good harvest. It proved that they had a special relationship with the gods.

The shaman now half-shouted a command for Achanu to crouch back down, but he ignored it also. He would normally have obeyed, since Priyak had been a clan shaman for many years and Achanu had just turned seventeen. He could not even claim warrior status yet, since he had neither been in a skirmish with another clan or tribe nor brought down a bear or bison on his own.

But enough was enough. More to the point, he was sure all three of his uncles would support him if Priyak brought charges before the women's council—who were themselves, despite their usual conservatism, also growing displeased with the new priesthood.

For a moment, he considered leaving his spear behind, but decided against it. A spear of the sort he had in his hands was a short thrusting weapon with a crossbar, designed to kill or at least fend off bears and other large game. Bows and javelins were the weapons of a warrior planning to engage in combat.

Plus, unlike the enormous demon atop the slope, he was not wearing war paint. That alone should make his peaceful intentions clear.

He started down the rise, moving slowly because the footing was a little treacherous. The rocks were sometimes loose and much of the hillside was covered with brambles. They were in flower but not producing fruit yet.

Once he reached the bottom of the hill, he started up the slope toward the demon. He could see that his cousin Oaka and Jogida were looking down at him, along with the very dark-skinned woman who had come to meet them.

The most frightening thing Achanu had seen yet was that the dark woman had come *out* of the demon. He had seen her do it! One of the demon's ears, which had been lying flat against its skull, had spread wide and she had emerged from it. The ear was so huge that she had had to climb down the demon's cheek to reach the ground.

What sort of person could live inside a demon's head?

He would not let his cousin face danger alone. A man should have been sent here in the first place to parlay with a monster, not two sixteen-year-old girls.

It was obvious to Alyssa that the two girls knew the young man coming up the slope. One of them—the taller one—had shouted out what she was pretty sure was a name, presumably that of the young man.

Young man? As he got closer, she could see that he did not look to be much older than the two girls at her side. All had black hair and dark brown eyes in light brown faces. They had high cheekbones. They all looked healthy and none had much in the way of lines around mouth or eyes. She'd thought the young man was older at first because of his self-possession. The man had been walking steadily but a bit slowly up the slope, as if not to alarm anyone. And he was holding the rather ferocious-looking spear—and using it—like a walking stick, not a weapon.

She heard the door of the Peterbilt's cab open and looked back. Michael was now climbing out of the cab—and he was carrying his rifle.

Alyssa was nervous at first, but relaxed once Michael reached the ground. He came forward much like the youngster coming up the hill—a bit slowly, and holding the rifle in the carry position. The three natives would certainly not understand how a firearm worked, so the carry position would seem unthreatening.

The boy coming up the slope was now near enough that Alyssa could see the spear's blade was some kind of stone, not metal. Flint or obsidian, given its dark color. Obsidian was always dark—black, usually—whereas flint came in a number of shades. But flint was common in the Midwest, while obsidian was not. You needed fairly recent volcanic activity to produce obsidian and that was found in the western parts of North America.

But there could be trade routes, she reminded herself. Even Paleolithic cultures often engaged in long-distance trade. Neolithic ones did it routinely.

When the youngster coming up the slope saw Michael, he stopped for a few seconds, and then came on more slowly than before. Alyssa had to suppress a nervous laugh. To a man of this day and age, Michael must look like a giant! The youngster staring up at him was no more than a few inches over five feet tall and probably didn't weigh more than one hundred thirty or one hundred forty pounds. Michael was a foot taller than him and easily weighed twice as much. Some of that weight was early middle-age flab but most of it was bone and muscle—and the truck driver was very strong. Alyssa had seen the sort of weight he could move around.

And now an ogre had emerged from the demon's head! For a moment, Achanu was strongly tempted to run back down the slope. But stubborn pride kept him in place long enough for him to realize that the creature wasn't really a monster, just an incredibly large man. It helped that he had what seemed like a friendly smile on his face, and wasn't holding his peculiarly shaped club in a threatening manner. The big man had yellow hair and skin as light as the woman's was dark. And as he got closer, Achanu could see the eyes were the color of the sky.

So. Now what?

Achanu's decision to ignore the plan worked out by the shamans and the village elders and come up here on his own had been impulsive, driven by festering anger and resentment. What was done was done, but now he had to figure out what to do next.

He turned to his cousin. "What did they tell you to do when you reached the demon?"

"Not much," said Oaka. Her lips twisted into a wry, bitter smile. "I think they thought it was most likely that the demon would eat us."

She was probably right. "They didn't give you *any* instructions?"

Oaka shrugged. "If we remain alive, I am supposed to stay here while"—she nodded toward the other girl, Jogida—"she returns to the village and brings back her two younger brothers."

That was still more of the priestly attitude. *Use sacrifices of the weak.* Jogida's youngest brother was still a toddler. "And then what?"

She shrugged. "Spend the night up here, I guess. They didn't tell us much."

"That's because they don't know what to do, so they're waving you and Jogida around—and now Faris and Ubadan too—like bait for a fish. Ubadan can't even talk yet!"

Oaka looked up at the demon. "Very big fish. Maybe we're too small to interest it."

Achanu had always liked his cousin's sense of humor. Oaka was a cross-cousin, too, not a parallel cousin, so marriage between them was not prohibited. He'd thought about it from time to time. Looking up at the demon, which brought a quite vivid image of his own mortality, he decided he'd better start thinking about it more often and more seriously.

"Here's what we'll do, then," he said. He now turned to Jogida. "You may as well leave now." He glanced at the strangers who lived in the demon. They both still seemed friendly and relaxed. "I don't think they'll object or try to stop you. Don't come back today. Instead, take the time to gather food and blankets and whatever else your little brothers need. Come back tomorrow morning."

"What do I say to Priyak if *he* objects?"

"Ignore that insect. Just ignore him. He's too old and decrepit to do any harm to you."

"What if the women's council objects? Or the chiefs?"

They couldn't just be ignored, unlike a shaman who'd brought disrepute on himself by his subservience to the priests of Hocha. "Talk to my uncle Hamadi as soon as you reach the village. Tell him I am working out another plan."

His plan was really no better thought out than the one concocted by Priyak, but he saw no reason to point that out. His uncle Hamadi had confidence in him and he was influential among the chiefs. And his mother sat on the women's council.

"Go," he said. "Go now."

CHAPTER 5

CAMP PETERBILT

Camp Peterbilt
April 15, 1005 CE

While the three young natives had been talking, Alyssa listened to the language they were speaking as attentively as possible—which, of course, wasn't saying much. None of the languages spoken by the indigenous inhabitants of the Americas had any close connection to the languages of Europe, Asia or Africa.

Theirs was a mellifluous language, at least to her ears. It had more vowels and fewer consonants than English, in that respect sounding a bit like a Romance language—Italian more than French or the two Iberian tongues. But the words would be completely different, as would the grammar and syntax.

It was going to be hard for the three American adults to learn the language, but they did have one great asset: her two children and, to a lesser extent, Shane. Kids under the age of ten could learn languages with amazing speed and once they did, spoke it with a native accent. The skill began to drop off in a child's teenage years, and by the age of eighteen it wasn't any better than that of an adult. Shane was still young enough that she could probably learn the natives' language—or languages; there could well be more than one commonly spoken in the area—almost as quickly as Miriam and Norman. Just as quickly, if she had an aptitude for it.

53

It would help if they could figure out a way to have native children spending a lot of time with the people from the future. They'd pick up English just as fast as the American kids would learn their language. Having bilingual speakers on both sides of the equation would make a real difference.

That would especially be true when it came to a written language. The natives would not have one. No native language in North America had a written form until after Europeans arrived. The civilizations in Central America did, but whatever influence they might have had on native societies to their north did not extend to the development of any sort of writing.

She thought it would be easier to teach people with no written language to read English than to develop their own form of writing. All the more so if...

She turned to Michael. "What do you folks have in the way of written texts in the truck?"

He frowned. "What exactly do you mean by 'written texts'? Things written on paper? Not a whole lot. Most of what we have is on our laptop."

He looked back at the truck, scratching his jaw. "Melanie and I are Episcopalians, so we do have a written copy of the *Book of Common Prayer.*"

"Not the Bible?"

"No." He smiled and shook his head. "Melanie and I aren't big fans of the Old Testament. We didn't see any reason to haul around something neither of us would read. We do have the four gospels, though—but only in an audio edition. Other than that..."

His smile got rather sly. "We do have a video of *Jesus Christ Superstar* on our laptop."

Alyssa's mind was starting to race. She herself wasn't particularly religious and her husband Jerry was a straight-up agnostic. She'd been brought up in the African Methodist Episcopal church, but she'd drifted away from the church and stopped going to services once she started college.

Clearly, the Anderles were more devout than she was, but they didn't strike her as being inclined toward either doctrinaire reasoning or religious intolerance. And if so...

"We need to found a Christian church here. Or at least get something similar up and running."

Michael stared at her. "Huh?"

"Michael, *think.* We're going to be stranded here for the rest of our lives, in a world—and its societies—that are still Neolithic. Its religious beliefs and practices will be what for lack of a better term I'll call pagan. And no matter what claims Wiccans make about Druids, I don't know of any pagan religion that I'd want to belong to—or even be close to."

She used her chin to point to the north. "Cahokia is up that way, not more than a hundred miles from here. A culture that, whatever its strengths and graces, practices human sacrifice. I'll be the first to agree that Christianity—or Judaism, or Islam, or Buddhism, or any of the great world religions—have their faults and an historical track record that often stinks to high heaven. But they all developed a universal moral code, they all *eventually* accepted that all people are people, and so far as I know not one of them ever practiced human sacrifice."

Michael grimaced. "Not as such, no. But plenty of religions— including Christianity—had no trouble burning *other* people at the stake or chopping off their heads. You name the cruelty and they all committed them, at one time or another."

Alyssa started to say something, but he waved her down. "Look, I'm not arguing with your main point because I agree with you. So does Melanie. Because of her Swedish heritage, she studied some Scandinavian history. I remember her telling me that while there were things she admired about her ancestors she was sure glad she didn't live among them. They practiced human sacrifice too—and their victims were also mostly young women. Not to mention—"

He broke off, because the three native youngsters seemed to have finished whatever discussion they'd been having. Some of it had sounded like an argument, although not a hot-tempered one. Now, the shorter of the two girls started walking down the slope.

"We'll continue our discussion later, Alyssa," said Michael. "Right now we've got to figure out what to do about these two who seem to be planning to stick around."

"Yeah, sure. As for what they plan to do ..." She glanced at her watch. "We're still in early afternoon. Whatever else, we're going to need to feed them and figure out a place for them to sleep. Adding the two of them to the truck cab is going to get awfully crowded."

"Why don't we start by feeding them," Melanie proposed. She

pointed toward one of the ice cream coolers that they'd placed close to the tanker, where they were shaded for most of the day. The generator kept their interiors below freezing, but the shade helped.

"Ice cream?" said Michael. "What kind of lunch is that?"

"They've almost certainly never had any," said Alyssa. "It's bound to cheer them up and help them relax. We can make some actual food later. We'll need to defrost something out of the coolers anyway."

It seemed as good a plan as any. Melanie went over to one of the coolers and extracted two ice cream sandwiches. Then, after a moment's consideration, took out six more. The native youngsters would probably be suspicious if offered something unfamiliar to eat unless they saw their hosts eating it as well.

Besides, she was in the mood for ice cream. The natives weren't the only ones who'd been under tension.

She came back and passed them all out, including to Shane and the Jefferson children. Then, moving slowly so the natives could see what she was doing, unwrapped one end of the sandwich bar and started eating. Alyssa and Michael followed suit. Needless to say, the kids hadn't waited for anybody.

After a few seconds' hesitation, so did the teenagers. Melanie had to struggle a little to keep from laughing at the expressions that came to their faces after they took their first bites: surprise, astonishment and enthusiasm, in equal measure.

Once the ice cream was finished, which didn't take long at all, Melanie went back to the coolers to decide what to prepare for dinner. That would still be several hours away, but at least some of the food would have to be defrosted. She could cook frozen vegetables straight out of the bag, but not meat.

Which meat? The coolers held frozen steaks, pork chops and chicken parts. After thinking about it, she decided on chicken legs and pork chops. She had no idea what, if any, eating implements the natives used. Eating steaks or chicken breasts without using a knife and a fork would be awkward—and for all she knew, they were completely unfamiliar with using them to eat food. They might very well never have seen a fork before.

Pork chops and chicken legs could be eaten easily with just fingers. So that's what she pulled out.

They'd set up a grill whose heat was provided by a propane

tank not far from the coolers, with an upended basin that they used as a place to defrost food. She placed the frozen chops and legs on it, still in their plastic wrapping.

Meanwhile, Michael had been trying to figure out what sort of sleeping arrangement they could set up for the boy and girl. He had no idea what customs they had which regulated whether and in what manner the two of them could share sleeping quarters, and he decided he wasn't going to worry about it. They'd chosen to come of their own volition; or, if they had been pressured to do so, it had been done by their own people, not his. They could damn well take what they could get.

The starting point was obvious. The only thing they had which was mobile and large enough to form the basis for a shelter was the section of broken-off store wall that Michael had used as a travois. It had gotten pretty beaten up over the two days it had been used to haul stuff, but it was still intact and didn't have any large holes or tears in it.

The travois was lying on the ground not far away. Gesturing for the boy to come with him, Michael went over and lifted the travois up on one edge. He started to indicate that the boy should lift the other end, but he'd figured it out for himself and was already doing so.

Smart kid. Michael pointed toward a pair of birch trees near the creek which were about five feet apart. The two of them lifted the travois and carried it over there. It wasn't all that heavy but its size and shape made it a bit unwieldy. It didn't take them more than a few minutes, though, before they had the travois leaning up against the trees at roughly a sixty-degree angle. That created a space between the bottom of the travois and the tree trunks that was about four feet wide, roughly the size of a double bed.

Michael made some gestures indicating that they now had to move the travois out of the way, so they propped it against another tree about ten feet away. He then went to the pickup bed and climbed into it, opened the big toolbox and removed a hammer, following which he began rummaging for nails. Soon enough he'd found a dozen that were the length he needed.

While he did so, the boy came within eight feet of the pickup and watched, fascinated. The girl came over and joined him. They spoke a few sentences, which Michael guessed were along the lines of:

You think it's another demon? Maybe the big one's cub?

I got no idea. At least it's not wearing war paint.

Or maybe they were just guessing at what else might be in the toolbox. Not having any common language at all was frustrating.

He hopped out of the truck, placed the hammer and nails close to the birch trees, and headed toward the pile of lumber they'd brought back from the wrecked store. It wasn't much of a pile, not more than twenty boards of various widths and lengths. Michael started with the bathroom door and then added two boards which were a foot wide and long enough. That would be enough to close at least most of the space between the two trees. There would still be open spaces at either end of the quasi-A-frame dwelling he was constructing, but it would be better than nothing. At least it would cut down any breeze and even at night the temperature this time of year didn't drop below fifty degrees.

By the time he got the door and the boards nailed to the two birch trees, the boy and girl had figured out what came next and had brought the travois over to lean it back against the trees again. They made the angle somewhat wider than he had, closer to fifty degrees than sixty, which would give some more room.

He considered tying the top of the travois to the trees but decided that wasn't necessary. Unless a really strong wind came up, it wouldn't move. And the only way such a wind could develop would be if a storm was passing through—and in that event they'd have no choice but to bring the two youngsters into the truck.

Now. What to use for a mattress? And was there any way to seal off at least one of the ends of the structure?

He discovered that both problems were being addressed by the Neolithic youngsters. They had moved to the opposite bank of the creek, where the soil looked to be considerably wetter, cutting down rushes with short knives. He'd noticed that both of them had knives in sheaths attached to thin belts, but he hadn't thought much about it. The blades weren't more than three inches long, not really suitable to serve effectively as weapons. (And the boy had his quite ferocious looking spear anyway, so why bother fighting with a knife?)

Without thinking about it, he'd assumed the stone blades would be fairly dull. But watching the quick and efficient way the two natives were sawing off rushes, he realized they were razor sharp. How...?

Alyssa happened to be standing next to him and must have spotted the frown of puzzlement on his face. "Don't make the worst mistake any of us can make in our new here and now, Michael. These people have a far more limited technology than we do, but it's not because they aren't just as smart as we are. They simply haven't had time yet to expand it as much as we have."

She used her chin to point across the creek. "I haven't gotten a close look at them yet, but now that I see them in action I'm willing to bet those blades are obsidian. If so, they must have obtained them through trade since there's no source of obsidian that I can think of within hundreds of miles of here."

"Can a stone knife really be that sharp?"

"Yes, both obsidian and flint can be sharper than steel. In fact, an obsidian blade is much sharper than even the best steel blades. Some surgeons still use them today, for certain procedures. The big problem with obsidian is that it's very brittle, so it breaks much easier than any metal blade will."

Again, she pointed with her chin. "They've grown up using them, so they're very skilled and know the blades' strengths and weaknesses. That's why they can cut down so many rushes this quickly with such short knives."

Both of the young people by now had their arms full. They waded back across the creek, dumped their loads inside the newly erected lean-to, and went back for more.

"They're walking through the creek without taking their moccasins off," said Michael. "That won't damage them?"

"Not if it's deerskin leather, which I'm sure it is." Alyssa looked down at her own footwear, which was designed for streets and carpets, not wilderness. "We should look into whether we can get some moccasins ourselves. The boots you're wearing look pretty sturdy but these shoes of mine..." She made a face. "At least they're not high heels. But they're not going to last long in the Stone Age."

The boy and girl had apparently decided they'd piled enough rushes on the area inside the lean-to to make a suitable mattress. Now they moved further down the creek and started cutting down what looked to be coarser and taller grasses. Or maybe they were sedges. Neither of the Americans was up on the fine distinctions between rushes, sedges and grasses. Michael asked Alyssa how much she knew, and her response was: "About all I know is that there are more than ten thousand species of grasses."

Her tone of voice held a trace of exasperation. *Dammit, I do not know everything.* She relented after a couple of seconds and added with a smile, "You know, we're always called omnivores but people are actually the world's most prodigious grass-eaters."

"What do you mean?"

"Cattle and sheep and bison and reindeer—even goats—have nothing on us. Wheat? That's a grass. So is rice, maize, barley, oats, rye, millet, sorghum—and then there are grasses we Americans don't eat but other people do. Teff is grown and eaten in East Africa, for instance. Oh, yeah—and sugar cane is a grass, too."

The natives returned to the lean-to, each with their arms full of cut grass. They dumped these outside the lean-to, though, not in it. As the boy headed back to the creek to gather more, the girl started using the long grass to form what amounted to walls and windbreaks in areas that weren't shielded by the travois or the nailed-up boards. She did the work very quickly. Clearly this was something she had plenty of experience in doing.

In the end, other than providing the travois and some boards, the only contribution the Americans made was donating an extra blanket Melanie found in the truck and a pair of brightly colored beach towels.

"We do pass by a beach now and then with some time to spare," Michael explained, sounding a bit apologetic. Alyssa suspected that owner-operator truck drivers had a work ethic that was a tad excessive.

Late in the afternoon, Melanie had the dinner cooked: pork chops, chicken legs, rice and broccoli. She and the other two American adults were struck by the reaction of the two young natives to the meal. None of these foods was familiar to them. Apparently—so Alyssa said, anyway—there were no pigs in the New World until the Spanish brought them from Europe. The origin of chickens was murkier, since there was some evidence they'd arrived in South America in pre-Columbian times due to trade with Polynesian voyagers. But none had yet arrived in North America.

"Of course, all sorts of fowl have been hunted here for centuries—probably for millennia." Alyssa paused long enough to finish off a drumstick, which she tossed into an empty can since they hadn't decided yet how they wanted to dispose of uneaten food. Leaving such things as bird and animal bones with bits of meat still on them lying around was really not a good idea. But burying them seemed like a lot of work.

"If I remember right, at least some of the New World tribes and nations domesticated turkeys. Or kept them in captivity, at least. And some of the game birds are native to North America, I'm pretty sure."

"I know grouses and quails are," said Michael. He finished off a pork chop and disposed of the bone in the same can. "Doves, too, I think. I don't know how easy they'd be to hunt with bows, though. I was using a 12-gauge shotgun."

What the boy and girl seemed to find the strangest foods, though, were the rice and broccoli. The rice they clearly liked; the broccoli, they seemed dubious about. But they finished everything on their plates—and were fascinated with them as well.

But what fascinated them even more were the electric lights that Michael and Melanie set up while there was still enough daylight to see outdoors. The store had had plenty of light bulbs, fixtures and wiring, some on the surviving shelves and others being used in the store itself, to enable them to string lights all around the Peterbilt—and run a line into the lean-to as well, complete with a small portable lamp, so the boy and girl could have light through the night if they wanted it. Power was provided by the two generators they'd found in the store.

Once sundown came, Michael turned on all the lights. Except for the huge truck, nothing seemed to astonish, impress, flabbergast and excite the boy and the girl as much as the lights. And make them quite anxious, too, at first.

Shane settled their anxiety by leading them into the lean-to where they'd be sleeping and show them how to operate the lamp that had been hung in there. After turning it on and off a dozen times or so, the natives began exuding the confidence and savoir faire of well-traveled adventurers.

The three American adults had remained seated around the table they'd brought out of the store's wreckage. Michael turned away from looking at the lean-to from whose innards a light kept coming on and going off.

"I'm glad they seem to be enjoying themselves," he said, smiling, "but we're going to have to start preparing for when the gasoline runs out in a few months."

"Runs out?" asked his wife. She glanced at the enormous tanker trailer that was now hitched back up to the tractor. "Michael, there's at least two thousand gallons of gasoline in that thing. We could drive back and forth coast to coast in the pickup half a dozen times before we ran low on gasoline; at least we could if there were any roads."

"Closer to three thousand gallons." Michael shook his head. "The problem is that gasoline doesn't have a very long shelf life. Give it a few months and it'll start going bad. The diesel will go bad too, although it'll last about a year."

Alyssa opened her mouth, then closed it. Michael noticed and gave her a squinty-eyed look.

"I think you want to correct me on this subject," he said, "but you're twitchy about being considered a goddamn know-it-all." The smile came back. "Face it, lady. You *are* a goddamn know-it-all, but on the other hand I'm not a thin-skinned jerk. So spit it out. What's wrong with what I said?"

"Nothing's *wrong* with what you said, Michael. But your way of looking at it presupposes the world we came from. Diesel will go bad after a while and gasoline will go bad even faster, that's true. But there are simple ways to prevent it. Or, at least forestall it—but you can forestall the problem for a long time."

He gave his head an abrupt shake. "I never heard anyone say that."

"That's probably because they were practical fellows and in the modern world we came from, people ran through gasoline and diesel so quickly that few people worried about—or even thought about—what might happen to the fuels if you just let them sit around for months and years." She smiled, now. "But I'm a chemist, remember? Chemists are like the illuminati of legend."

She raised both hands and wiggled her fingers. "We *knooo-ooow* things. Secret things."

Both Michael and Melanie laughed. So did Miriam and Norman, who'd stayed at the table and were following (sort of) the adults' conversation. They didn't really understand it, but they found their mother's finger antics amusing.

"Here's what happens," Alyssa continued. "The reason diesel goes bad is because microbes grow in the diesel/water interface. All you have to do is add sulfur to the fuel to kill them. In a modern environment, there are good reasons to keep sulfur content in fuel low—which is why the government regulated it. But"—she spread her hands, indicating their current surroundings—"in the world we're in now, pollution isn't yet a big issue."

"How much sulfur?" asked Melanie. "And where would we get it?"

"I don't know how much we'll need, but it can't be much. A few thousand parts per million, would be my guess. We'll have to experiment with test batches. Getting sulfur shouldn't be too hard, since it's one of the half dozen most common elements on the Earth—tenth most common in the whole universe. The natives may well already use it for some purposes such as medicine and fumigants. Since they've got obsidian, they already have some trade with people further west who live in volcanic areas. Sulfur's easy to find in such areas. One way or another, though, I don't think getting our hands on sulfur will be a big problem. It better not be, since we'll want it to make gunpowder too."

Both the Anderles stared at her. "I keep forgetting," said Melanie. "You chemists are the world's original greedy slavering weapons-makers, aren't you?"

Alyssa flashed her grin. "Well, yes—but we also created the Nobel Prizes, one of which is a prize for peace."

"What do you need to do to keep gasoline from going bad?" asked Michael.

"That's even simpler. Just stir it around in the tanks regularly."

"Huh?" Michael repeated.

"Gasoline is a homogenized distillate of oil. That means that gasoline isn't one liquid, it's several different liquids mixed. All those liquids are present in crude oil and a fractional distillation process is used to separate them out and mix back together only the ones you want. The mix determines the octane. What happens when gasoline 'goes bad' is that those different mixed-together liquids become unmixed. This is especially a problem if the gasoline includes alcohol as part of the mix because alcohol weighs more than gasoline. It also absorbs water from the air so you end up with lower proof alcohol in the bottom of your tank where you are getting your gas from. If this happens in your car's gas tank you are pretty much screwed. But if this happens in a sealed storage tank like the one on your tanker truck, that's another matter. You still have all the liquids, you just need to re-homogenize them. And that takes swirling the fuel around with a stick. That's probably not going to restore your gas to perfect, but it's going to turn it back into usable gasoline, and you can keep it up for a long time."

She thought for a moment. "One last thing. We need to create shade for the tanker trailer. And figure out if there's any other way to keep the fuel as cool as possible."

Alyssa got a pensive look on her face. "We shouldn't have any trouble getting as much sulfur as we need and we can make charcoal. So that just leaves the third and largest component of gunpowder to find, which is saltpeter. Probably the fastest and simplest way to get saltpeter is to just find out from the people who already live here where there's a large cave used by bats. Where there's bats, you'll find guano, and lots of it."

Michael whistled tunelessly for a few seconds. "I guess we should start calling you Mommy Warbucks."

"Very funny. The much bigger problem is figuring out how to make guns to put the gunpowder *in*. Because there's no tin worth talking about on this continent, we'll have to skip over bronze and go straight to iron." She pursed her lips and ran fingers through her hair. "Given the low technology in the here and now, bog iron's probably our best bet. The natives won't know how to make iron from it until we show them, but they'll certainly know where it can be found."

"Do you know how to make iron?"

"I've never actually done it myself, but there's nothing too difficult about it theoretically." An angelic smile came to her face. "Mommy Warbucks, remember?"

"What are 'warbucks'?" asked Miriam.

Achanu and Oaka wound up leaving the lamp on throughout the night. Partly that was because they were so charmed by it, and partly because they had issues to discuss.

One issue in particular.

"Do you want to get married?" asked Achanu.

Oaka abruptly sat up. "No!" she said. "I'm too young. So are you. The women's council would never agree—and you know it."

Achanu waved his hand as if fending off an insect. "I didn't mean *now*. I meant"—he waved his hand again, this time in a gesture which indicated the uncertainties of life—"sometime in the future. Next year, maybe."

"I'd still be too young." But she was smiling now. "Maybe the year after that."

They then spent a goodly portion of the night engaged in activities which would have appalled any right-thinking Americans. The sexual mores of their people were a lot different in many ways from those of their continent's future. Theirs was a matrilineal culture, for one thing. Men had a monopoly on what Americans would call the executive branch of government, especially anything involving war. But chiefs had to be approved by the women's council, which also operated as the equivalent of a judiciary. It wasn't an "egalitarian" society in the American sense of the term, but it was very far removed from a patriarchal one.

Just for starters, as was usually true in matrilineal cultures, "bastardy" was a meaningless term and there was no fetish concerning virginity. In fact, despite their youth, neither Achanu nor Oaka were virgins, although their sexual experience was still rather limited. Girls her age were careful to avoid getting pregnant, but that was simply for practical reasons. If they did miscalculate and wind up having a child, it was not viewed as any kind of catastrophe nor did it bring down social punishment. All children were brought up communally, anyway.

The "rights" of fathers were strictly limited. The male authority figures for children were their maternal uncles and, if still alive and alert, their grandfathers. Husbands were tolerated, and some of them were even well liked by their wife's extended family. But gods help a man stupid enough to mistreat his wife, especially in any physical manner. Every one of his wife's brothers and uncles—and, if still capable of it, grandfathers—would beat him within an inch of his life. And his own family wouldn't take his side. Serve the bum right.

So, Achanu and Oaka enjoyed themselves that night. The fact that they could see what they were doing was an unforeseen benefit.

CHAPTER 6

TRICKS AND TOOLS

Country Store
April 14, 1005 CE

It was a day before the girls approached the demon, when Pefif and
Gorth got to the strange place where the demon had apparently
come into the world. Pefif and Gorth hadn't found it difficult to
track the two monsters. A blind squirrel wouldn't find it difficult
to track them. Then they got to the place where they had come
into the world, and they hadn't come in alone.

There was a wall. The wall was not very tall, no more than
a few inches and usually much less, where their world and the
grass and trees of their world just stopped, and a different world
started.

Pefif and Gorth didn't want to cross that wall, short as it
was, because who knew what might happen to them if they did.

Finally, Pefif got down on his hands and knees and put his
head past the wall, so he could look at it. It was as smooth as
a water-smoothed stone and as flat as . . .

It was flatter than anything he'd ever seen in his entire life.
But there was a place, a gap in the wall, where the monsters had
climbed out, breaking the wall with their round feet. And that
path made it clear that the wall was nothing but earth. The area
that had been changed was wide, but longer than it was wide, and

a part of a building was in it. Part of the building was missing and it was the part that would have extended out of the changed place. There were also tracks within the changed place.

They considered going into the elongated circle, but this was a matter for shamans, not hunters. They went back to Jabir and told Gada what they'd found, but by then the decision to send the girls to feed the demons had been superseded by the fact that the demon apparently didn't eat young girls, but made them comfortable and set up camping places for guests.

"Good work, you two, but for now we will leave the demon people's place to them," Gada told them.

Kadlo Mound, Hocha
April 16, 1005 CE

The runner sat on the pad and sipped water as Roshan watched. "Hamadi sent me because I had seen the demon building," the lad said. He couldn't have been more than seventeen.

"So tell me what you saw," Roshan demanded.

He did and it was frankly unbelievable. Roshan wouldn't have believed, except the lad had a token from Hamadi and Roshan trusted Hamadi. Roshan would have been happier if Hamadi had waited until they knew more before he'd sent the runner, but Roshan knew what Hamadi was thinking. If the demon thing was a threat, something that might destroy the village and kill everyone, he wanted the clan warned.

Roshan considered telling the priests. *No. If they don't know already, why haven't their stars and magics told them? And if they do know, why weren't we warned?* Increasingly, Roshan was coming to dislike and distrust the priesthood. They had a lot of power and a lot of influence, but he lived here in Hocha and saw the way they used that power to abuse anyone who showed the least resistance to them and to demand anything they happened to want.

Roshan's immediate reaction was to go to Jabir and see the thing for himself, but he couldn't. He was the clan chief of the Kadlo. His movements would be watched. But he needed someone to go look. He needed more information than this terse report and description of a building that could move like some sort of giant snail. Fazel. He was the senior shaman of the Kadlo, and didn't trust the priest kings of Hocha any more than Roshan did. No. That wouldn't work. The priests would be watching him even more closely than they watched Roshan. Rogasi. It would have to be his nephew Rogasi. He was a good lad and thoughtful, and Roshan wanted to get him away from the influence of the priesthood anyway.

Roshan called in his nephew and made the arrangements. Hamadi's messenger and Rogasi would leave in the morning.

Camp Peterbilt
April 16, 1005 CE

Jogida returned the next morning, carrying her fifteen-month-old brother Ubadan in a baby pouch on her chest and towing her five-year-old brother Faris by the hand. Ubadan was asleep. Faris was awake, alert, and intensely curious about everything.

They didn't come alone, though. Three adult males came with them. Two appeared to be in their thirties and one was a decade or so older. There were also two women. One seemed to be the same age as the two younger men, and the other wasn't what you'd call "elderly" but was on the border of the term. That was a guess on Michael's part. He wasn't great at guessing ages, but she had a little gray in her hair and lines around her mouth and eyes. Yet she wasn't an old crone.

Oaka and, especially, Achanu were delighted to see them. One of the younger men was his uncle Hamadi and the other was Tomar, also one of the clan's chiefs. The older man was Gada, the one (and only) shaman in the village of Jabir whom Achanu liked and approved of.

The younger of the two women was his mother, Etaka. The older woman, Kasni, was the head of the women's council.

Achanu knew exactly what this signified. Jabir's chiefs and the women's council had finally had enough of the growing power of Hocha priests. They were now taking their own path. Whether they could persuade the rest of the clan to do the same remained to be seen, but he thought they had a good chance of doing so. Jabir was the second largest of the clan's villages, and the chiefs of the largest village, Kallabi—the women's council even more so, from what his uncle Hamadi had told him—were riven with disputes. For the moment, at least, Kallabi did not speak with one voice.

The demon and its human attendants, of course, was the factor that had swung opinion around—and since it now dwelt very close to Jabir, his was the village that had been most quickly and powerfully affected.

Exciting times!

Michael had exactly the same assessment as Achanu, although he didn't know any of the specific political and social factors involved. But all he had to do was observe the self-assured and self-confident bearing of the newcomers to know that decisions were going to be made and carried out by the people who could do so.

The first thing that happened was that introductions were made all around—and this time initiated by the natives, not the outsiders.

The second thing that happened was that one of the two younger men gestured for the Americans to follow him. His name was Hamadi and Achanu seemed to have an attachment to him. He led them to the lean-to and spread his hands to indicate that this was the immediate issue he wanted to deal with. That done, he moved slowly up the creek, stopping about every twenty feet or so to indicate that he wanted to erect a similar structure in those spots. How similar was unclear, of course. Obviously, he couldn't duplicate the lean-to.

Four such structures brought them to the pool. Leaving a space—presumably to provide easy access to the pool—Hamadi then made clear he wanted to erect two more structures moving away from the creek at a ninety-degree angle. The end result would be six structures of some kind forming an L shape around the Peterbilt. The structures would be close to the truck, but not crowding it.

Hamadi then collected the women and children and, using simple but clear sign language, made clear that these would be the people inhabiting whatever structures were constructed. Achanu was included in the mix, as was the older man Hamadi. Hamadi then made gestures indicating that neither he nor the other man his age would be part of it.

"That all seems clear enough," said Melanie. "They want to settle a bunch of women and children, up through teenagers—including at least one boy—and at least one old man. Well, oldish man." She paused for a moment, to recall his name. *Gada, that was it.* "Gada looks to me like he's somewhere in his fifties."

Her husband had his hands planted on his hips and spent a bit of time looking up and down the creek, gauging how big such an addition to their area would be. Their "turf," as he thought of it.

"I'll want to see an example of the kind of building he wants to put up here," Michael said. "I assume we're talking about homes of some kind. If nothing else, I want a better idea of how many people we're talking about. Fifty's one thing; five hundred, another. But if I'm reading his mind right, so to speak..."

"I like what I think he's proposing," said Alyssa. "Basically, we—and our three kids—will be immersed in a society mostly made up of women and children. That'll be a perfect environment for us to get to know them—and their language—and vice versa. But he's making clear that there won't be very many men of fighting age in the mix."

"It still wouldn't be hard for them to send warriors up here at night and overrun us," said Melanie. Her tone was matter-of-fact. "I doubt there's much danger of that, myself, but we can't ignore the possibility."

"Ignore it, no," said Michael. "We'll have to make sure we maintain a watch from the truck at all times, and never leave it unoccupied. But I don't believe there's much danger, either. What I think is that this young chief of theirs is a very smart cookie and it looks like he's related to the boy, by the way. What he and his people can learn from us will put them in a much stronger position."

He looked at both Melanie and Alyssa. "Are you both okay with this? If so, I'll go take a look at whatever village or town they've got around here. There's got to be one. I'd guess it's on the other side of that rise"—he nodded toward the nearby little hill—"that blocks our view of the northern stretch of the Kaskaskia."

"We should only send one of us, though," said Melanie. "And I don't think it should be you, Michael."

"Neither do I," said Alyssa. She glanced down at her still uncovered chest. "I'm the youngest—not to mention the smallest—of us, and I'm the one wearing a costume that's the closest to theirs. To put it another way, I'm the least threatening adult whereas Michael"—her glance now went to him—"is the opposite. I'd rather he stay back here in reserve, since he's potentially a lot more threatening than I am."

There was silence for a few seconds. Then Michael said, "Okay, makes sense. You want to take my Glock with you?"

Alyssa shook her head. "I don't see the point. If it's an ambush and they swarm me, I'm screwed anyway. I'm an academic, not John Wesley Hardin. By the time I fumbled the pistol out of the holster, I'd be cut to ribbons."

Michael chuckled. "True enough." In a baritone that even managed to carry a tune, he softly sang: "*John Wesley Hardin was a friend to the poor.*"

"Much as I love Bob Dylan," said Alyssa, "he got that all wrong. John Wesley Hardin was a murderous psychopath. But I admit I wouldn't mind having him coming along with me. Just in case."

She started walking toward Hamadi. "May as well do it now."

Alyssa's skill with impromptu sign language wasn't up to par with Hamadi's, but it wasn't bad. It didn't take him more than a minute to figure out what she wanted. He waved Achanu and Oaka over and had them come along, presumably to reassure her with people she already knew, more or less. The two older women, Etaka and Kasni, also joined them.

She got back in the middle of the afternoon, after five hours—long enough for Michael and Melanie to start getting a little worried.

"Sorry it took so long," said Alyssa, sounding not sorry at all. "I wound up spending more than two hours sequestered with Kasni and Etaka and six other women having a sign language equivalent of an introductory get-together."

"A hen party, huh?"

Both Alyssa and Melanie bestowed a look upon Michael that was not complimentary.

"Sorry," said Melanie. "Hubby's usually better trained than this, but now and then the underlying male chauvinist subconscious comes to the surface."

Alyssa wasn't actually offended, since Michael's tone of voice made clear he'd been joking. A stupid joke, granted.

"Actually, no," she said. "It became clear soon enough that that group of women carried a lot of weight in the natives' society. I'm not positive yet—sign language only takes you so far—but I think their culture is matrilineal. Oh, and they call themselves 'Kadlo,' by the way. Or 'the Kadlo,' maybe."

"Is that good or bad?" asked Melanie. "Sounds good to me, but I may be missing something."

"No, it's good. Patriarchy is a real pain in the ass, especially in primitive societies."

Michael was frowning a little. "You mean women are in charge?"

Alyssa shook her head. "I said matri-*lineal*, not matri-*archal*. Matriarchy is pretty much a myth, anyway." She sniffed. "You won't find women running the show by bullying everyone the way men so often do."

"You tell him, girl!" said Melanie.

"A matrilineal society is a lot more egalitarian," Alyssa continued. "I have a friend—had a friend—at SIU who was an anthropology professor. She was part Cherokee, which is relevant because the Cherokees—I think all the southern tribes, if I remember right: Choctaw, Creek, Chickasaw and Seminoles also—were matrilineal. She could get downright enthusiastic on the subject."

She looked around to see if there was somewhere to sit. Happily, in her absence someone had set up the folding chairs they'd found in what was left of the store. She'd been on her feet since daybreak and plunked herself down.

"It's quite likely, you know, that the Cahokians—the Mississippian culture, I should say, since that's what anthropologists and archaeologists insist we should call it—were the ancestors of at least some of the native tribes. The Choctaw and Chickasaw, anyway. Maybe not the Cherokees, since their language is Iroquoian, which means at some point they migrated down from the north.

"Never mind. You've got to forgive academics for our obsessive fussing over details. The point I'm trying to get at is that if the later tribes, about which we know a lot, are any sort of guide to the Kadlo, then men will be in charge but under some pretty strict limits. The women will have a council of some kind and they not only have to approve someone's elevation to chieftainship, but they'll act as judges when disputes arise. *Plus*"—here she gave Michael something of a scowl—"they don't have to put up with too much crap from their husbands. Women keep their own property in a matrilineal society and can always give their husbands the heave-ho if need be."

"Yikes," said Michael. But he was smiling. By now, Alyssa had gotten to know the Anderle couple well enough to know that while their marriage wasn't perfect—no one's ever was—it was pretty damn good.

"If I can change the subject," said Melanie, "what sort of structures—buildings, whatever—do they want to put up here?"

"What they want to do—I'm almost sure I'm right about this—is put up half a dozen of the same kind of houses that they live in. Oh, yeah—I forgot to mention this. Michael was right." She turned her head and pointed toward the rise. "Their village isn't too far on the other side of that hill. Not more than a mile, I'd say. They're right on the river."

"What sort of houses are they?" asked Michael.

Alyssa grimaced a little. "Nothing I'd want to live in. Basically, their homes are big thatched huts. They're pretty sturdy, I'll say that for them. There was one under construction which I had a good look at. They sink the posts that form the walls into trenches that are at least two feet deep, and then seal them and weatherproof them with wattle and daub."

"What's 'wattle and daub'?" asked Shane.

"Wattle are strips of flexible wood or thick reeds that form a lattice they weave into the posts. Daub is a mixture of clay or mud and straw that they seal it all up with. It's a primitive construction method that goes back thousands of years, but it works. Those places wouldn't stand up to a tornado, but I'm pretty sure they could handle anything short of that."

"Even the roofs?" Melanie sounded skeptical. "I don't know as I'd want to sleep under nothing much more than piled up grass or straw. What keeps water from seeping through in a heavy rain?"

"First, they know what they're doing and usually weave different materials together. Second, the thatching is very thick. What happens is that only the outer layers absorb water. That wet layer then acts as an insulating material." She shrugged. "Thatching's also been used for millennia. The big problems I'd have living in one of those buildings are that there are no windows and I'm pretty sure they'd get smoky in the winter from heating fires. And, of course, dry grass catches fire pretty darned easily."

"Or every day from cooking." Melanie still sounded skeptical.

"They mostly cook outdoors, even in winter. At least, I think they do. There are plenty of outdoor cooking areas." She gave Melanie a smile that had a definitely sly look to it. "Finally, don't forget the key thing."

"Which is?"

"Neolithic people are the opposite of wimps."

Michael laughed. "I won't argue that, for sure! Still..." He reached out and patted the upholstered wall of the cab. "I'm not trading in the truck, even if it is a bit crowded. Speaking of which, how many people live in one of their huts?"

"More than you might think, given that they aren't really very spacious. Anywhere from half a dozen to a dozen, would be my estimate."

Michael made a face. "Damn. I take back what I said about our cab being crowded."

Alyssa shrugged. "It's another way to stay warm in winter. The odor probably gets pretty heavy, though, especially in January and February."

There was silence for a few seconds. Then Melanie said: "So what do we tell Hamadi? Or sign language him, I guess I should say. Do we agree to let a bunch of them move in next door to us?"

Michael scratched his jaw. "How do we say 'no'? I mean, if they insist, what are we going to do? Shoot a bunch of them? Look, he's being polite about it—seems to be, anyway—and I don't really think he means us any harm. Besides, we need them. We're three adults and three kids, no group this small can survive for long on its own. So I say, yes."

"Me, too," said Alyssa.

"Okay, then." Melanie looked to their daughter, and then up at the two Jefferson kids, who were perched on the top bunk and had been following the discussion with keen interest. "What do you kids think?"

"It'd be nice having more kids around," was Miriam's immediate reply. "Adults can get kinda boring."

Jabir
April 15, 1005 CE

After the dark-skinned woman left, the women's council discussed her and the other strangers.

Etaka leaned forward. "We never should have let Priyak use the girls that way."

Kasni lifted a hand and said, "Don't complain. It worked out well." Etaka gave her a dirty look and she continued. "It did,

Etaka, and if you stop to think for a moment, you'll realize it. Priyak was trying to prove that the gods were displeased with your family."

"And you let him," Etaka said, still angry.

"With the way you'd been mouthing off to the priesthood and complaining about the labor tax, we had little choice. When the demon arrived, *someone* was going to have to be sent to talk to the gods. Since they arrived at our village, that meant it was one of ours that was going to be sent. And if it wasn't your daughter, it would have been one of ours."

Jogida's father had been killed two years ago and her mother had died of an infection six months earlier, and the family hadn't been particularly important even before the deaths. She and her brothers were basically living on the village's charity. So she'd had no one to speak for her when it had come time to choose a sacrifice.

Oaka, on the other hand, was from a prominent family. So Priyak's selection of her was a warning that just because your family was important didn't mean you were safe from the gods.

"Did you see her clothing?" Jogida demanded partly to change the subject. They hadn't learned very much from Alyssa Jefferson. She was a healthy young woman, but soft. They could tell that from the way she moved. Also smart and curious. She'd been quick to examine everything from the new house to the mortar and pestle. Wealthy, they could tell from the clothing as if arriving in demons didn't prove that well enough.

"Yes, I saw it," Kasni agreed, happy with the change of subject. The people had thread and woven cloth, but it was expensive and time-consuming to make. And none of it was as good as the cloth that the dark-skinned woman who called herself Alyssa wore. "It was all woven. Even the top of her shoes were white woven fabric. And she climbed down into the Kechu hut."

"Should we even continue that," Jogida asked, "if we are going to send the Kechu to stay near the demon people?"

"Hamadi is clever," Kasni said. "He wants to send as many of the young girls to stay with the demon people as we can. He hopes that will keep them out of the eyes of the priests of Hocha."

"Priyak is reporting everything we do to the priests in Hocha," Etaka said.

"Then," Kasni said, "if the priests want them for sacrifice, they will have to apply to the demon for them."

"And you think they will say no?" Jogida asked.

"I think they won't ask! Priyak is terrified of the demon people. You can see it in everything he says. And I suspect the priests of the city are going to be just as frightened. Besides, it's the Hocha priests who insist we must send young girls to the gods."

That was perhaps the biggest problem the women's council had with the Hocha priesthood. All the priests were male, and most of the sacrifices were female, and it was known among the women that young girls could avoid being chosen by being "friendly" to the priests. But the doctrine of the priesthood was that the gods brought the rains and controlled the crops, expected to be paid for that service, and preferred young women.

The priests did know when the rains were going to come. It was the new priesthood who had brought corn to the region. That the priesthood had an in with the gods was clear.

But now these new people who came riding in demons, not in canoes, had welcomed their young girls and not eaten them.

"Fine. Hamadi is clever, but that's not what I want to talk about," Jogida said. "Her clothing, her devices. She knew things and knew how to make things."

"Another reason to send young women to them. We want to know if they are the ones that make the things that they have. Or are those things made by demons?" Kasni said.

Jabir
April 16, 1005 CE

Alyssa was back in Jabir. This time she'd brought the children. It was, in fact, sort of a shopping trip. not that any money was changing hands. These people were apparently still in the barter and gift-giving system. Through gestures and the few words they'd acquired so far, Alyssa had been invited to Jabir to gather gifts from the families of Jabir to help them get set up in their camp.

Gada looked over at the older shaman. Priyak was incensed by the demon woman's presence in the village. Jabir was a fairly wealthy village, but that didn't mean everyone in the village was well off. And, recently, among the poorer families there had been a couple of cases of a known, but still fairly uncommon, illness.

"I think we should take the demon woman to see Shuna and Kaliba." Shuna was poor. Her husband was not a good hunter or a good worker. She had her hut and her share of the fields, but not much else, and her family disliked her husband, so were unwilling to give her aid which she would just give to him. She had a daughter, Kaliba, who was showing the first signs of the illness. She had the rash and the sensitivity to sunlight, but her hair was just starting to thin.

"Let the demon woman see our sick?" Priyak demanded, outraged, then considered. "Why not? Maybe she'll catch it and die."

That was, Gada acknowledged, a point. And Gada still wasn't sure of these demon people. If the demon woman did catch it from the child, that would tell them something about the power and weakness of the demon people. But Gada's impression of the demon people in general was that they were as kind as they were powerful, so he hoped that this Alyssa, who seemed to be the wise woman of the group, might know something to help.

"Alyssa." One of the shamans waved at her. She wasn't sure of his name. Not the really old one, the middle-aged one. He gestured to her to come with him. They entered a small hut near the edge of the village, and the shaman showed her to a pallet where a little girl was seated. The girl was about five and naked to the waist. She had what looked to Alyssa like a rash around her neck, though it was hard to tell in the darkness of the hut. Alyssa picked up the girl, and took her to the door of the hut, and the girl covered her eyes. *Pellagra*, Alyssa thought immediately. *Niacin deficiency.*

"Well, I don't have niacin pills. What foods contain niacin?" She stopped dead in her tracks. Corn contained niacin. But pellagra was common in Spain after the introduction of corn because they didn't know how to treat it to make the niacin available. Nixtamalization it was called, because the Aztecs used it and didn't suffer from pellagra. Why didn't these people know about it? You treat the corn with lye diluted in boiling water. It made the corn taste better, made it easier to grind, and made the niacin more available for digestion. It also got rid of a bunch of carcinogens that occurred naturally in corn. *Wait!* She stopped herself. Yes, she could do nixtamalization, but it would take time and corn wasn't the best source of niacin anyway.

Meat. This kid needed to eat meat every day for a while, until her symptoms abated and until Alyssa could get nixtamalization going on a scale that would be useful.

She took the little girl back into the hut, then grabbed the shaman by his hand, and took him back to the area in Jabir where the villagers traded or gifted each other. There was dried turkey and squirrel meat.

She picked up some squirrel jerky, hoping that the drying process hadn't removed the niacin. Holding it in one hand, she pointed to it with the other. "Feed this to the girl."

The shaman, Gada, that was his name, looked blank. Still holding the squirrel jerky, she dragged him back to the hut. Dragging him inside, she pointed to the girl and the jerky, then made eating motions. "Every day until she gets better."

Gada wasn't slow or stupid, not in the least, and he knew the illness. Further, he knew that it struck most often in families who were down on their luck and eating mostly corn and beans with not much meat in their diet. That wasn't universal. Some of the more wealthy people had the same symptoms, but as he thought about it he realized that many of them preferred the sweet corn to the more savory flavors of meats. Nor was it universal the other way. There were poor families that ate mostly corn and beans that didn't have the illness, and he had no explanation for that. But that didn't matter. Meat was the cure for the illness. That was what mattered, assuming that she was right. He nodded his agreement. He would see to it that the little girl got meat stew every day, and he would learn if it worked.

Camp Peterbilt
April 17, 1005 CE

Michael watched the men at work and shook his head. Just for safety's sake, they were keeping someone in the Peterbilt at all times while the men and women of the village apparently called Jabir were digging holes in the ground to do something. Michael wasn't sure what. They were doing it with wood and stone tools, mostly wood. And it was going to take forever at this rate.

They had brought most of the tools from the country store, not to mention the seed rack for garden seeds. What they hadn't brought from the store was the five sacks of seed corn that had been stacked on the front porch and cut in half by the whatever it was. They should have brought those. Over the last couple of

days, they had been hosted by the villagers and seen the fields
where they were planting corn and it was mostly planted by now.

Michael watched the men and women digging out holes to
become the foundation for what he supposed would be houses
and came to a decision. He called Achanu over. "Bring five"—
Michael held up a hand with fingers spread—"and come here."
He accompanied his words with gestures. Achanu said something
in their language and went off to collect some friends, while
Michael went to speak to his wife.

He climbed up into the Peterbilt and said, "I'm going to take
some of the natives and go to the country store."

"What for?"

"Seeds. Remember that stack of seed sacks on the front
porch of the country store that we didn't bother with? I think
we should have."

"I thought they were done with planting?"

"They are, but only just," Michael said. "I figure there's still
time if we use the pickup to help clear a new field or two."

The young men of Jabir were nervous about climbing into
the bed of the pickup truck, but they did it. There were shouts
of dismay when Michael started the truck, and more when it
started to move. But they settled down quickly enough once
they were moving.

Until they got to the few hundred yards or so of blacktop that
was all that had come back with them. At which point, Michael
put on the gas. Not a lot, but they got up to thirty-five before
he started braking. Then he pulled into the parking lot of the
country store, and led the young men to the sliced sacks of seed
corn. The birds and squirrels had been at it, but there was still
a lot of the seed corn left. Using show and tell, he got them to
load the corn sacks and loose corn into the back of the pickup
and they were assiduous in collecting up every seed. The walls,
most of them, and several of the windows were still there, even
still unbroken, and it occurred to Michael that a window in the
huts they were making might make them a lot more livable.

He climbed up into the back of the pickup and pulled out a
hammer, and went to work on a wall next to a window. He got
the two-by-four stud loose and started on the paneling below

the window. It was plywood with artificial wood paneling on the outside and painted sheetrock on the inside. He was collecting the nails while the locals were collecting the seeds. Achanu came over to watch, and asked about the nails. Michael could tell that much. Unfortunately, he couldn't tell *what* Achanu was asking about the nails. Michael showed him a bent nail and then used the hammer to unbend it a bit, and something about that impressed the heck out of Achanu.

Meanwhile, one of the young men Achanu had brought with him had cut himself picking up a broken piece of glass. He'd dropped it and it had broken into smaller pieces, which seemed to upset the kid more than the cut. They got him bandaged up, then headed back to Camp Peterbilt.

CHAPTER 7

WEALTH AND MONEY

Jabir
April 17, 1005 CE

That evening Achanu showed his uncle and the women's council a handful of the corn collected and explained, "Michael took me and five others to the place where they came into the world, and collected up this. He pointed at our fields and indicated he wanted to plant this corn if it wasn't too late."

"It's not," Etaka said. "We have planted later than this in other years. It doesn't hurt the harvest much."

"Which is why the priests are upset with you," Hamadi said. "You are supposed to leave such knowledge to the priesthood and not interfere."

"Then don't tell them. The demon people want to plant their corn. There is no reason not to help them."

Over the next few days the people of Jabir started preparing a field for the demon people seeds. Meanwhile Alyssa wanted to nixtamalize corn, which needed lye.

Camp Peterbilt
April 18, 1005 CE

Alyssa gathered up the sack from the general store and headed out. They were all busy, but Alyssa wasn't going to wait. She needed to persuade the local shaman, Gada, and that older one, Priyak, that they needed to nixtamalize their corn to prevent pellagra. She had no clue how she was going to explain it to them, but the first step was to get lye. And for that, she needed wood ashes and a pot. She left the kids in the care of Shane and headed off to Jabir to collect as much campfire ash as she could get and as large an earthenware pot as she could, so that she could make lye.

"Where are you going?" Melanie Anderle asked.

"I have to make lye," Alyssa told her.

"I'd like soap too, but is it that much of a priority?" Melanie asked.

"Not that I would object to soap, but no. This is to nixtamalize corn."

"Nixtamalize?"

"It's a way of treating corn that the Aztecs, heck, most of the South and Central American cultures had before the Spanish arrived..." Alyssa explained about niacin and pellagra and the little girl, ending with, "I have to figure out some way of convincing the locals to nixtamalize their corn or there are going to be a lot of sick kids as corn becomes a bigger part of their diet."

"And you need lye for this?"

Alyssa nodded. "Calcium oxide or calcium hydroxide will work, but we have more wood ash available than seashells, so yes, lye."

"Back in the pioneer days, what you did to get lye was to make a V-shaped box with a hole in the bottom of the V. You put ashes in the bottom of the box then poured water through the ash, catching the lye in a metal pan. You don't want to use earthenware because the lye is caustic and will definitely score the glaze on the earthenware pot," Melanie said.

Alyssa looked a question at her.

"I think that comes from one of the Little House stories, the books, not the TV show," Melanie explained.

"Okay," Alyssa agreed. "Do we have metal pots?"

"There were some at the general store."

Again Alyssa nodded, then went off to Jabir to collect wood ash from the fire pits that were located outside the huts of the villagers.

Gada joined her as she collected the ash from the stone-surrounded campfires that were located in several places in the village of Jabir. Not every house had a fireplace next to it, but there were several which were shared by two or three huts. They had roofs, but no walls, so people could cook even when it rained.

Alyssa was thinking. First, that these people really needed bricks for brick fireplaces and chimneys, and second, that money wasn't the root of all evil.

These people didn't have money, at least not full money, but they did have poverty and class. The little girl with pellagra was also generally undernourished, and there were clear distinctions in wealth even within the village. Poverty, class and want didn't require money. But if this society was to survive, it darn well did *need* money.

Gada followed the demon woman around the village and as soon as she started collecting ash, he set several of the people of Jabir to collecting more of the ashes from the fire pits around the village. He knew from her gestures that it had something to do with Kaliba's illness, and Kaliba wasn't the only person in Jabir who was starting to have the symptoms. She was just the worst so far, and that meant that even if the cure was meat, people were going to keep getting sick with it because meat was hard to come by, especially for the poorer families.

If there was some other magic that the demon people had that would stave off the illness, he wanted to know about it.

Three hours later, carrying sacks and baskets full of wood ash, they walked back to the demons' camp to find that under the other demon woman's instruction, the giant had constructed a strange wooden pot with a hole in the bottom. The ash was placed in the wooden pot, and hot water was poured over the ash. It drained through the ash and into one of the strange not-copper containers that they'd found at the magic place where the demon people had come into the world.

The liquid that poured out the bottom of the wooden pot smelled bad. He stuck a finger in it, and it was slippery. The demon woman immediately grabbed his hand and pulled him over to a water container and washed his hand with water.

Gada felt foolish, realizing that the demon woman was protecting him. He knew better than to stick his fingers in another's magic, but he wanted to know how this worked.

He had to know. He'd known people to die of the rash that Kaliba suffered.

Then she put corn in a pot, added water and a little of the slippery liquid. Then, using gestures, she indicated that they would boil it for a time, long enough for the sun to move so far. He guessed about an hour, maybe two. Then it would be allowed to steep in hot water for a full day.

And suddenly he understood. It was a stroke out of the blue. Like the gods slapping him on the head. There was a process that was sometimes used. It made the corn easier to grind and it changed the flavor, made it taste better, Gada thought. That was what she was doing here. Not exactly the way they did it back in Jabir and in the other villages and clans who farmed the river basin. That was to simply boil the corn in a pot with some wood ash in the pot as well.

The reason it had fallen out of favor was that it required extra wood and the wood was getting harder to find as the trees were used up from the land right around the villages. And now that he thought about it, he realized that when the corn was more commonly treated that way, there had been less of the rash.

Camp Peterbilt
April 20, 1005 CE

"It's going to take a lot of experience and experimentation before we start producing good-quality parchment," said Alyssa, "but I'm pretty confident that even the first crude versions of it will make an adequate surface to write on."

Melanie's mouth was tight with distaste. "Sounds yucky, though. I mean, scraping off blood and flesh and fat. Not to mention a lot of work. You're sure we can't make paper?"

Alyssa shook her head. "Not any time soon, no. It's another case of we need the tools first to make the tools to make the tools. In this case, the tool we need most is a screen. To make paper, you make a mush out of fibers, plant or animal fibers, and spread them on a screen to let the water out. The screens are made of fine steel wires very close together, but not quite as close as the strings in a fabric shirt. We can't make the wires yet. Not in the quantity we need, anyway."

"What about that stuff the Egyptians used?" asked Michael. "I can't remember the name but it was something close to 'paper.'"

"You're talking about papyrus. The problem there is that so far as I know the plant they made it from doesn't exist in North America in this time. Even if it did, you'd have to import it from places like Florida and Louisiana. No, folks, I think it's either parchment or clay tablets like the ancient Sumerians used. And those are bulky and awkward."

There was silence for perhaps half a minute, as Michael and Melanie pondered the problem. Then Melanie got a crooked smile on her face and said: "Look on the bright side. We've now got teenagers, boys and girls both, who think that working on anything the weird people who live in the dragon want them to work on is an exciting adventure." She was referring to the dragon paint job on the Peterbilt.

Michael's expression was skeptical. "Even if it means hours scraping a stretched deer hide with an obsidian knife?"

"How is that any worse than a lot of the labor these people do?" said Alyssa. "How long do women spend grinding maize using a mortar and pestle? Or making thread with those little twisting things that they hang down and spin?"

"Let's raise it with Etaka and see what she thinks," said Melanie.

Achanu's mother had become, along with Hamadi, their main liaison when it came to practical projects the Americans wanted to propose. She didn't speak more than a word or two of English, but she was very good at making herself clear through gestures and examples. It helped that she had her son and Oaka to help her through the rough patches. Those were the two teenagers who were at least starting to get a feel for how the new language worked—and about the only ones other than small children able and willing to help Americans improve their Kadlok.

Field near Jabir
April 22, 1005 CE

Men and women, boys and girls, were all in the field of grass and brush, chopping and pulling up the brush and chopping holes in the grass, apparently preparing the field for the seeds. They had apologized about the field. It was a "tired field," they explained, one that had been planted for three years and by now was offering yields that were not so good. The locals were preparing the field, but they weren't plowing the field. They were hoeing the field using stone hoes. The labor was intense.

Alyssa had an idea. They had quite a few two-by-fours and a lot of nails. She took one of the two-by-fours about eight feet long, and hammered eight-inch nails through it, one every foot or so. Then she attached two I-bolts to it, one on either end, and tied ropes to the bolts, then to the back of the pickup. Then she had Melanie drive the pickup out to the field that was being prepared for planting. She dumped her creation out of the back of the pickup, then placed it with the nails sticking down into the earth, and had Melanie put the pickup in gear, at which point the two-by-four came right out of the ground. Next, she tried standing on it. That made no difference, except she fell on her butt.

She discussed it with Melanie and they went back to camp and attached another two-by-four to the first, making a T. They tried it again. It worked, sort of, if someone stood on the bar of the T, which wasn't easy to do. More experiments, and they could use it to rip out most of the bushes.

Then Shane suggested replacing the nails with sharpened bits from the body of the Civic. That took a bit of work, but by the eighth of May they had a plow that had eight cutting heads about a foot apart, and then they cleared the field for planting in a day.

At that point, the villagers of Jabir pointed out that there was, near the field they'd just cleared, another field. It was one that didn't flood and it was covered in a mat of thick prairie grass, which in turn was supported by roots that held the land together and made hoeing it into a usable field way more work than it was worth. At the villagers' direction, Melanie and Shane plowed that field too.

It wasn't the back forty that a tractor would have done in an afternoon. It was about ten acres of land. But the truck had a hundred and forty horses under its hood. And the plowed field was one that the village of Jabir had never before been able to use.

Camp Peterbilt
May 5, 1005 CE

Alyssa grabbed a hammer from the tool kit in the Peterbilt and went over to the stack of walls and started to pound on bent nails. The stuff from the country store had been brought but the bringing had done some damage—nails being pulled loose and bent as the walls were pulled apart to be piled into the bed of the truck. So now Alyssa was sitting on the ground, taking nails that had been pulled out of two-by-fours and using a hammer to pound them straight, then putting the straightened nails in a basket provided by the women of Jabir.

Meanwhile, the pickup, still acting as a tractor, was plowing up the ground where the new houses of Camp Peterbilt were to be built.

Alyssa, Melanie, and Michael were learning a lot. The natives dug out the earth to a depth of two feet, give or take. Not just the posts. The whole floor space. Then they stuck posts even deeper into the earth, another six inches or so. They added the wattle and then added the daub over that. And once they had the walls in, they took some of that earth from inside and raised a mound about six inches high around the outside of the building, presumably to keep the rain from draining into the house. A "door," usually a leather flap, was attached. Then they put on a roof of rushes.

All that was standard, the way these people did it most of the time. But there were some additions this time: pieces of glass were placed in wood frames which were woven into the wattle, and the daub was carefully applied to leave the windows clear. And some of the two-by-fours from the country store were added to make window frames for windows that would have leather flaps that could be closed on cold days and opened in warm weather.

The pickup plow was used for building the houses, to loosen the earth so that the men and women of Jabir could simply shift the loose earth to the baskets for removal, rather than actually digging up the hard ground. It was still a lot of work, but these people were used to work. They were always working. Even sitting around, they were peeling tubers or working hides or shaping clay for vessels.

Which was part of the reason that Alyssa was sitting on the ground, pounding bent nails flat. With everyone working, she felt guilty just sitting around.

But it was only part of the reason. The nails were galvanized steel and valuable.

After the trip to the arrival point, the floodgates were open and the people of Jabir, in cooperation with the demon folk, traveled the just over eleven miles to the arrival point and brought back everything, down to but not including the concrete slab the country store was built on. But the roof, from shingles to beams, was carefully removed and transported to Camp Peterbilt.

Now that they were building the houses, and starting to get to know each other, the villagers were offering them payment for the stuff from the country store and for the work done by the Peterbilt and the pickup.

It came as a surprise to Michael, Melanie, and Alyssa that the locals had money of a sort. The archaeologists seemed to think that it was a barter system. That wasn't completely accurate. They had found themselves in a culture that was making the transition from a barter to a monied economy. They had pennies in the form of dried beans. They used a base-twenty counting system; a cob of corn was worth twenty of the dried beans and they had stone ax heads that were worth four thousand beans, and other tools and tokens that were worth other specific amounts. The problem with the money was the same as the problem with using cigarettes as money in prison. Cigarettes got smoked, and beans and corn got eaten. Even ax heads got used and broken. For archaeologists, the problem was that unless there happened to be natives to tell you about it or a written record, there was no way to tell that an ax head was money. Or, for that matter, beans. So there was "no archaeological evidence that the Mississippian culture had money."

But they did, and they were insisting on paying the demon people for everything they provided. It was, in fact, a matter of pride for them to pay their own way. There was still enough of the gifting economy in the mix so that the giver gained status and the accepter lost status. And while they liked the demon people, the people of Jabir had no desire at all to be their supplicants.

Alyssa dropped a nail in the basket, picked up another bent one, and started straightening it. They needed a better money, but Alyssa didn't know jack about how to create money. She knew that there was crypto currency and all sorts of stuff, but when it came right down to it, about all she knew about money was how to balance a checkbook, or keep track of how much she spent using her debit card.

Well, there's another thing I don't know about for Michael's list. After her comment about not knowing about cars, Michael had started keeping a list of things she didn't know about. It had grown fairly long by now, but things fell off the list as she learned about them.

Shane came over. "Alyssa, how do you make a spinning wheel?"

"I don't know," Alyssa admitted. "It pretty much has to do what the locals are doing with their...what do they call those things again?"

"*Fasriw,*" Shane said. It was a word in the local language for the device. Alyssa didn't know the name for it in English. She thought it might be *spindle* but wasn't sure. "And that's why I'm here. I've been trying to use the *fasriw,* but my thread sucks and it's a lot of work. We need something better."

So for now Alyssa left the nails to be straightened later, and went off with Shane to watch Jogida make thread using pounded hemp fiber and a *fasriw* and try to figure out what she was doing with it, so that she could come up with a tool to do the same thing faster and easier.

It turned out that the *fasriw* spun the fibers into a thread, then the thread was wrapped around the stick and you couldn't do both at once. You spun, then wound, then spun, then wound, and it took skill and practice to keep the width of the yarn consistent.

From that, Alyssa guessed the function of a spinning wheel, but had no clue of how one might be made. This wasn't chemistry, it was mechanical engineering. Not her field at all.

"Here's what you do. Go tell your dad that you have found something else I don't know anything about and it's his job to tell you how to make a spinning wheel."

Shane grinned and said, "Dad said you'd say that. He doesn't know how either. He wants to know if you can draw a spinning wheel."

"I'll try." Alyssa could draw. She was no Rembrandt, but she'd taken art classes in college and knew how to sketch.

By now they were writing on parchment.

Kadlo Mound, Hocha
May 12, 1005 CE

Rogasi's black hair was cut off short using scissors from the country store. It was neatly done, but Roshan wished it hadn't been. It was too noticeable, too different. Most young men wore their hair at shoulder length, cut with stone tools, so this shorter haircut was noticeable even under his peaked cap.

Rogasi opened a pouch and pulled out several sheets of cured hide that was scraped thin. On the scraped hide were pictures of the demon houses which didn't look much like snails after all. Their bottoms weren't flat, but had wheels. There were also images of other things that they found at the place where the strangers had come into the world.

Then, quite enthusiastically, Rogasi started to explain about windows and glass and plows and steel pots, which were like clay pots but much harder to break than pots made out of copper. "But it's not copper, uncle. It's different. And their wise woman...she seems to know everything. She has skin that's very dark, almost black, and her hair is strange and very curly."

Roshan listened to it all and started to worry because the priests of Hocha weren't going to let this stand. It was a threat to their power. He wasn't sure what they'd do, but they would do something. He sent Rogasi back to Jabir with a warning for Hamadi.

Jabir
June 25, 1005 CE

Carefully, Tudis whittled the hub. Making a round hub flat on both ends wasn't easy with stone tools. It could be done, but that wasn't how he was doing it. He had bought a steel knife from the demon people. It was a "box cutter" that had been in the back of the "pickup truck," in one of the "toolboxes," and it had cost a deer. He carved another sliver off the piece of wood, making one side a little flatter.

Four hours later, he had the part the demon people called a hub. It had two rods sticking out and eight holes around the outer edge.

He'd made the rim over the last three days. It was a straight piece of wood that he'd bent into a circle by soaking and steaming and careful shaping. It also had holes. Now, using thick sinew from an elk, he strung the rim onto the hub, tightening the cords until the wheel was balanced. His wheel was three feet tall when he was done. And then he started working on the wheelbarrow.

It was a lot of work, but the "pickup" couldn't be everywhere, and the corn crop was looking especially good this year. Being able to use a large wheelbarrow to collect the corn would save *a lot* of time when the crops were ready for harvest.

Finished with this project, he gathered up the wood shavings to use as starters for future fires. Then he went to the new stove to collect his dinner.

The demon people didn't think of it as a stove. It was made of bricks, about three feet tall, with a hole in one end where you could stick in a shovel to pull out ash, and it had places to hold earthenware pots and plates over the fire. Dinner was corn and bean stew flavored with squash, berries, and venison cooked tender.

The bowl he was eating from had been thrown on a potter's wheel and it used a glaze that the wizard Alyssa had come up with.

Camp Peterbilt
June 30, 1005 CE

Alyssa sifted the powdered shells into the clay. It would act as a modifying agent, keeping the clay from cracking during drying and firing. "Sorry, Shane. I know the process and you're right about the Pilgrims doing it, but I can't make glass yet."

"Why not?" asked a clearly frustrated Shane.

Alyssa looked over at the girl. "Heat! Heat is the key to all of it, making bog iron into steel, making really good pottery, making glass, everything hinges on really hot fires. Over three thousand degrees Fahrenheit for steel, about the same for glass, and between twenty-two hundred and twenty-eight hundred degrees for stoneware. What our hosts have are pit kilns which max out at around two thousand. Even just working bog iron takes temperatures in the same range as stoneware, around twenty-two hundred degrees. To get that sort of heat, you need a blast furnace. That means a bellows and something other than a person to power it. We have to have bellows and we have to have bricks, or at least earthenware pipes to control the flow of air into the fire in a way that will produce a lot of heat, while, at the same time, controlling the types of gasses that the material we're melting are exposed to.

"That goes for all of it, iron, steel, stoneware, glass, all of it."

INTERLUDE

Leo Dingley looked up at the white-painted walls of the underground lab. He rubbed his eyes as he tried to ignore the headache that was more from the complexity of the data on the screen than the lights. They were banks of LEDs anyway, not fluorescents. There was a quiet hum from the AC unit and Leo needed a break. He got up, went and got a bottle of water from the mini fridge, then went to look over Margo's shoulder.

"What's got you so engrossed, Margo?" asked Leo. He leaned over her shoulder, gazing at the complex geometry being displayed on the monitor screen she was sitting before. There was no computer in sight, just the monitor. The computer it was connected to was two levels below them in the huge laboratory that had once been a deep mine and was far larger than any PC.

What was showing on the monitor was a fractal pattern of great complexity, ninety-nine percent and more of which was unmoving. It hadn't always been unmoving. A few days after the event, a lot of it, maybe as much as ten percent, had been moving. And in the moments just after it, a fair percent had been moving and then seemed to disappear. But by two weeks after the event, that ninety-nine percent had stabilized and had remained unmoving since. Most of it was right where it had been from the beginning, but a big chunk was still some distance away.

"These...doohickeys, I call them, for lack of a better term." Her forefinger indicated six luminous squiggles whose shapes were constantly in flux. "I can't for the life of me figure out what they are. The other stuff has mostly stopped moving."

Leo scanned the rest of the screen. "You're looking at a representation of the time track made by the truck, right?"

She nodded. "Yes. The truck, the other truck, the store, or at least the part of it that got sent into the past. That part's clear enough."

He squinted. "You call that 'clear enough'? To me it looks like a bowl of spaghetti, except everything has an angular shape."

She chuckled. "Better you stick to your own field of expertise. Yes, believe it or not, this is pretty clear. Pretty damn clear, in fact. By now, after all the time we've spent crunching the numbers—"

A voice came from behind them. "For which—ahem, I despise false modesty—I had to develop the math. Took a while."

Margo waited until the interruption was over. "Hello, Malcolm. Nice to see you again. *As I was saying*, we can now pinpoint the time and place of arrival of the truck to within three kilometers and within nine months—well, closer to eight and a half months. Trying to narrow the time any further would take far more effort than it's worth, if we could do it at all."

Leo straightened. "You can locate the space and time of transit *that* closely? I had no idea you'd made so much progress. The accuracy with which we were able to track the course of Alexander Correctional Institution's strane wasn't nearly that precise."

The term "strane" was an acronym that had developed over the years since the scientific project had been launched following the disappearance of the West Virginia town of Grantville more than three decades earlier. It stood for Spacetime Transportation Event. Bolides caused stranes sometimes, but, from the readings, not always.

Margo shrugged. "The instruments we had then were a lot more primitive—"

"Please!" complained Leo. "I prefer 'less refined,' if you don't mind."

Margo's lip curled. "That's like calling an outhouse 'less refined' than a fancy ladies room at an upscale hotel in New York. But, *as I was saying*, we didn't have instrumentation as sophisticated as what we have now. And what's more important is that the instrument package wasn't directly attached to the object that underwent the strane."

Again, she pointed at the screen. "The data that enables us to create this image is coming to us directly from the truck that took the monitor unit for the thousand-year-long ride they both went on."

"Don't let her kid you," Leo said. "A lot of our data is based on carbon dating of the stuff we found after the strane passed. That gave us a range, and I could then use math and nuclear signature to refine the data."

"And that's coming in real time?" Richard asked. "I mean, one-to-one correspondent time?"

Now they were venturing into Leo's field of expertise. "Yes," he said firmly. "However mutable space-time may be and however many timelines may exist, one thing we're sure of by now is that a unit of time in every one of the multiple universes is identical. A second in Universe One is exactly the same as a second in Universe Umpty-Quadrillion."

He now pointed at the screen. "Everything you're seeing there is happening in real time, just as we experience it." His lips quirked into a sardonic smile. "Insofar as you can interpret what you're seeing, anyway. Good luck with that. If you can figure out how half a dozen luminous shape-shifting blobs fit into what looks—to me, anyway—like a fractal nightmare, have at it."

Malcolm O'Connell pursed his lips. "I wonder..."

He looked around and pointed at a monitor on a nearby desk. "Is that hooked up to Freddie?"

Leo got a pained look on his face. "I really wish people would stop referring to a computer that cost sixty million dollars as 'Freddie.'"

Margo ignored him. "Yes, it's functional."

Malcolm headed toward it. "I may—just possibly—have an answer to Leo's question. If I'm right, it won't take long."

A few minutes later, Malcolm straightened up from working at the computer. "Come over here, you two. I have something very interesting to show you."

Margo got up from her chair. She and Leo went over to Malcolm's computer.

"The first thing I established," said O'Connell, "was that while the shapes of the six objects—blobs, to use Leo's term—do change constantly, their luminosity stays exactly the same. Never varies in the slightest. So let me show you how they rank in those terms. I'm rounding off slightly just to keep the display easy to follow, but even if you use precise figures there isn't enough difference to worry about. I'm indicating each blob by a letter."

The following list appeared on the screen:

A. 100
B.   50
C.   40
D.   30
E.   15
F.   13

"Okay," he said. "Translating those figures into units of mass, using exactly the same ratios, here's what you get. I'm expressing this in kilograms."

A. 134
B.   67
C.   54
D.   43
E.   23
F.   21

"And now..." A note of triumph came into his voice. "Look at this."

A. 134   134   Michael Anderle
B.   67   67   Melanie Anderle
C.   54   54   Alyssa Jefferson
D.   43   40   Shane Anderle
E.   23   20   Miriam Jefferson
F.   21   17   Norman Jefferson

"The figures in the second column are the last recorded weights of these six people before they were swept up in the strane."

They had gotten everything they could about all the people who'd been caught in the strane. Even the old guy who'd been cut in half. That had included government records and an investigator asking questions.

"The figures for the three adults match perfectly. The figures for the three children vary slightly. The luminosities shown on Margo's screen are larger than what was on record, but that's exactly what you'd expect. They're children. They get bigger over time—and the increase is in line with the amount of time that's passed between the last record while they were still in our timeline and what's showing now."

Margo's eyes were wide. "But ... could we just be looking at a coincidence?"

Leo's head had started shaking even before she finished the sentence.

"No. Not a chance. That's ..."

He looked down at O'Connell. "You're the mathematician among us, Malcolm. What are the odds that six completely unrelated objects would show this close a matchup under these circumstances?"

"I'd have to have Freddie crunch the numbers to give you anything close to precise statistics. But as a mathematician, all I have to do is look at these numbers to tell you that the odds we're looking at a correspondence, not a coincidence, are astronomically huge."

Leo nodded. "That's what I thought. And the only way I can interpret the fact that these luminous objects are moving constantly on the screen—which they do, Margo, yes?"

"Yes. They move more or less but they never stop moving entirely."

"Then those six people still have to be alive. And since they are all in about the same place relative to the point the strane arrived, Alyssa Jefferson and her two kids must have hooked up with the Anderles after all six of them survived the strane."

"You realize what that means, if it's true," said Margo.

Malcolm nodded. "It means that—probably, we can't be sure—at least most of the people who've been caught up in all the stranes we know about have to be alive as well." In a whisper, he added: "Jesus, Joseph and Mary. Whatever else they were, at least the stranes weren't a slaughter."

Leo waggled his hand back and forth. "Well ... probably. But we can't be sure without"—he nodded at the screen—"this kind of evidence. What if Grantville, the cruise ship, or Alexander Correctional got dropped in the ocean? Or somewhere off the

planet entirely? On Venus—or on the sun itself? Or just somewhere in empty space?"

"You're such a bundle of joy, Leo," groused Margo.

"Just saying."

"Except we know that a chunk of seventeenth-century Germany arrived in West Virginia in 2000. That a chunk of the
Cretaceous landed in Alexander Correctional's location and a bit
of Formosa Island landed in the Caribbean when the *Queen of
the Sea* disappeared. So it's unlikely that they landed in space or
the middle of Venus. There seems to be something tying them
to the surface of the planet."

"Maybe." Leo shrugged. "Or maybe the baddies have some
way of controlling the bolides."

Malcolm shook his head. "Whatever the reason, nature or
intent, I think Margo has the right of it. And the reason I
think so is because"—he pointed at the screen—"here we have
people moving around. And they are right about the time that
the chunk of prairie they were replaced by comes from. That
means that it's a swap when a strane happens. At least, all of
them we've recorded have been. Statistically, given the immensity
of the universe compared to those portions of the Earth which
are habitable, the fact that all of the displacements have gone to
places where people could survive almost has to be intentional."

Leo scratched his jaw. "Point. So now what do we do?"

"Well, whatever else, we've got to tell Alyssa Jefferson's husband," said Margo. "And the Anderles' families."

Malcolm frowned. "Are you sure about that, Margo? I mean,
Alyssa's husband—I don't recall his name—"

"Jerry," Margo provided.

"Yes, Jerry. The poor guy has spent months going through
the grieving process. Do we really want to reopen that wound? I
mean, it's not as if anyone can *do* anything about the situation."

"At least he'd know that his wife and two kids were still
alive," said Leo.

Malcolm shrugged. "Not for him, they wouldn't be. Separated
by a thousand years in time. How is that any different from his
point of view from them having died?"

Leo and Margo exchanged a glance. Sometimes, the fact that
Malcolm O'Connell had been a lifelong bachelor showed.

"I've got a wife and two children myself, Malcolm," Leo said softly. "Trust me. There's a hell of a difference. Even if I couldn't ever see Rachel and Steve and Horace again, just knowing they were still alive would be far better than thinking they were dead. A lot."

"It doesn't matter anyway," said Margo. "We don't have any right to keep this information from Jerry Jefferson. We're not tin-pot gods and goddesses. We're telling him. As soon as possible. End of discussion."

After they finished explaining the significance of their data to Jerry Jefferson, he swiveled his chair and just stared at a wall for more than a minute. Then he wiped his face and swiveled the chair back.

"Have you shown this new evidence to the Joint Committee on Catastrophes?" he asked.

"We've sent it to them, yes," said Margo. "And we got the usual 'we will take it under advisement' verbiage.

"We're making progress, though. At least they've stopped trying to pass off the stranes as 'acts of terrorism.'"

Jefferson grunted. The sound had a sarcastic undertone. "Acts of terrorism by unknown terrorists for unknown reasons. The reason they've dropped that after all these years since Grantville is because nobody in the nation outside of drooling idiots thinks it's anything but drooling idiocy."

He rose from the chair. "But I think what you've got now is enough to blow the lid off and finally get the U.S. government to take it seriously. That's because now you can put faces on it. Three faces—Alyssa's, Miriam's and Norman's. No, four—you'll have mine too." He waved his hand. "And that of the Anderles' families. But the punch in the government's gut will come from my wife and kids—and me. Now you've got a man who *knows* his wife and children are still alive. Stranded like no one in history has ever been stranded, but alive—and he wants to get them back or go join them, whichever is possible."

Leo winced. "Probably neither, Mr. Jefferson."

Jerry gave him a level gaze. "Do you *know* that?"

"Well . . . no, we don't. But—"

"Screw the 'but.' Why aren't we trying to find out, if we don't know?"

"Well . . ."

"Be expensive as all hell, for starters," said Malcolm. "I mean, like the Apollo program that put men on the moon."

"And how much was that?"

"In today's dollars? Somewhere around two hundred and fifty billion dollars," said Margo.

"That's *all*?" demanded Jerry. "We spend three times that much on the military *every year*. The Apollo program's cost was spread over an entire decade. Which is about how long what I'm proposing would take, right?"

Leo ran fingers through his hair—at least, where there was any left. "Longer than that, Jerry, would be my guess. The Apollo program was mostly just engineering. We'd need a lot of pure scientific research before there'd be anything for engineers to do. You want my guesstimate? Fifteen to twenty years—and at the end of that time, the answer might very well be 'no, we can't do it.'"

Jerry nodded. "Makes sense. It also makes the cost less of a sticker shock. Correct me if I'm wrong, but I would think funding research wouldn't be as expensive as funding whatever it takes to do a time-travel expedition."

"Probably not, no." Malcolm smiled wryly. "Unless the research turned up a way to just duplicate H. G. Wells' time machine. Which I seriously doubt."

"Okay. I'll quit my job and we can start with you hiring me. I don't need much." Jerry's tone of voice became bleak. "Seeing as how I no longer have a family to support."

"But...hire you to do what?" Margo asked.

Jerry shook his head. "You really are babes in the woods. Or have just spent too many years in the ivory tower. I'm a manufacturing sales rep, Margo, which is just a fancy title for salesman. I'm good at it—and what you need most of all, to kickstart everything, is a good salesman."

His expression was determined; you could even call it grim. "Put me in front of the Special Committee and see if they can still get away with platitudes. A father who knows his wife and children are still alive and knows where and when they are and wants to go rescue them. Or at the very least, share their fate. That'll stir things up. You watch and see."

PART II

PART II

CHAPTER 8

THE TWO TOWNS

Jabir
June 15, 1005 CE

Shane watched the man as he set fires in the large tree trunk, thinking that this seemed a lot of work and, worse, it would probably be really heavy when he was done. The man was making a dugout canoe, like the two others already in the village. It looked like an *awful* lot of work, and Shane as well as two of the local girls were watching the work.

By now, movement between Jabir and Camp Peterbilt was common and the children of both villages played together, often watching the adults work on this or that. Shane tried to explain that she was worried about the weight, but while she was learning the local language, she wasn't all that good at it yet. So they watched as the trunk was burned, then the char was cut away and it was burned again to hollow out the log. It was hard work, and the girls got bored long before it was done. They decided to go back to Camp Peterbilt and talk to Alyssa about the canoe and how it was built. They reached that agreement through a combination of words and hand signs.

Arriving in Camp Peterbilt, the children found Alyssa sitting on one of the chairs that they had collected from the country store. It was set in front of a table that had been made from shelves that had held baked goods in the store. On the table sat Alyssa's computer. The Peterbilt was comfortable, but it was a cramped space. By now they all spent most of their time outside, assuming it wasn't raining and the bugs weren't too bad.

Running up to the table, Shane shouted, "How do you make a canoe?"

"Use your indoor voice, Shane," Alyssa corrected. Then, looking around, added, "Well, speak with a bit less volume, anyway."

"Sorry, Mrs. Jefferson," Shane said in a quieter voice. "So how do you build a canoe?"

"I don't know. I've never made a canoe," Alyssa said, then continued after a quick moment of thought, "There are several ways. There are dugouts like our friends use, there are kayaks like the Eskimos used back in our time, and I assume they use now. Those are made with a wood framework covered by skins and the skin is wrapped around the whole body of the canoe, so that only the kayaker's body sticks out. I think, but can't be sure, that Native Americans, our friends' descendants, made canoes out of tanned and treated hides over a framework of wood. Modern, twenty-first-century canoes are made from aluminum or fiberglass, neither of which are available to us. Wait a minute... I think there are also birchbark canoes or at least there used to be and..." She trailed off. "Why do you want to know?

"Tarak is making a dugout," said one of the other girls. "What about birchbark?" She was learning English or trying to and one of the words she knew was "birch." Her people used birch trees for quite a few things, so if you could make canoes out of birch that might be useful. Lots of the things the demon people knew were useful.

"What Makas said," Shane clarified. "He's chopping holes in a big log, then lighting fires in it and chopping out the ash..." She went on to explain how the dugout canoe was being made, which fit quite well with what Alyssa knew about the process. Then she finished with, "But their canoes are really heavy. And making them seems like a whole lot of work."

Alyssa considered. She knew that dugouts were among the oldest known boats. It was probable that birchbark canoes would be an improvement, and the locals used birch trees already. Unfortunately, that was about the limit of her knowledge of the construction of canoes. "Go see your mom and dad and suggest a birchbark canoe. But don't try to build a full-size one at first. Make a scale model first, a couple of feet long to test the concept and get practice."

An hour with Mom and Dad gave the girls the basic parameters for the two-foot-long, four-inch-wide-at-the-center birchbark canoe. After that, they returned to Jabir and started building their toy.

It took them two weeks and five tries before they had something that they were happy with. Then they showed it to Tarak.

Tarak looked at the model boat and at the dugout he'd just finished and wasn't sure whether to laugh or cry. What he really wanted to do was punch someone, preferably one of the demon people. He wasn't sure whether he wanted to punch them for showing the kids how to make a birchbark canoe or for not showing them how to do it before he spent over two weeks digging out the dugout.

Takiso Village
June 30, 1005 CE

Tarak rowed the dugout up to the shore of the river. Then he climbed out and with great effort pulled the heavy boat up onto the shore. Then he started to brag on the boat, telling the people of the Purdak clan how long he'd worked on it.

Takiso village was on the other side of the Talak River and the people were sharp bargainers. But there was no way that Tarak was going to try to sell the canoe to a tribe of his own clan. He sat with them and ate fish and corn stew, then let them steal his brand-new canoe for not much more than half of what it was worth. Then he went back to Jabir and built a birchbark canoe.

Camp Peterbilt
July 4, 1005 CE

Michael Anderle looked at the device with amusement and a little trepidation. It had taken a while, but they'd learned the date of the last winter solstice and actually measured the summer solstice just a couple of weeks ago. Alyssa Jefferson had calculated based on information in their computers and determined the date. It was July fourth.

Neither hot dogs nor watermelon were available, but they did have turkey sausage wrapped in corn flour, leavened with baking powder that Alyssa had come up with. They also had barbecued deer. And, of course, corn on the cob. Only the early corn. The more active harvest would be in a couple of weeks and "their" corn, the corn from the general store, wouldn't be ready until August.

The sun set, the fuse was lit and a few seconds later the flame gushed out of the clay volcano and sparks flew off the device.

The children oohed and awed.

Shane was impressed and not impressed. It wasn't a spark on the fireworks from her last Fourth of July, but for Missus Jefferson to do it in the here and now, making the flame burn in different colors, that was impressive.

Jogida's little brother Faris had to be grabbed to keep him from trying to grab the fire.

With her little brother firmly in hand, Jogida came over to Shane and asked, "What *adwhsik* is for?"

Adwhsik was a new word or at least one that Shane didn't remember off the top of her head, but from Jogida's finger-pointing and the burning clay mountain that Missus Jefferson had made she guessed it meant strange fire or . . . no. She knew the word for fire and it was nothing like *adwhsik*. Maybe ceremony. Yes, that was probably it.

"It's the birthday of the country we come from."

"What is country?"

Shane spent the rest of the evening talking with Jogida, then with Jogida, Oaka and Achanu; then with Jogida, Oaka, Achanu, Hamadi, Gada and Kasni about what a country was and how it differed from a village or a clan.

Over the next weeks and months, the women's council and the chiefs of Jabir discussed the concepts of country and nation and how they differed from village and clan or clan and grouping of clans that looked to Hocha and sometimes called themselves the Hochi and which the plains tribes called the river people or the settled people.

Kadlo Mound, Hocha
July 8, 1005 CE

Roshan smiled at his nephew. "What are the demon people talking about now?"

"Birchbark canoes and nations." Rogasi smiled back.

"I know about canoes. What is a nation?"

For the next few hours, Rogasi explained to his uncle what a nation was and even the basics of democracy. The idea of democracy wasn't completely strange to Roshan. Decisions were often made in villages by consensus, where the minority went along with the majority without actually agreeing. The idea that it could be used indirectly and in larger groups? That was new.

Overall, he was more interested in the drawing of the birchbark canoe and Rogasi's description of how it was made.

Camp Peterbilt
July 8, 1005 CE

Michael attached the leather flap to the wooden tube. This was his third attempt to create a bellows. He'd learned a lot in the first two. But it turned out there was a *whole lot* to learn. The bellows, based on their combined memories of western movies and tv shows, turned out to be a lot more complicated than they expected.

The only reason the women of the village maintained an interest in the process was what the locals had used before. The locals had used pit firing, and pit firing has many drawbacks. It uses a heck of a lot of fuel and it doesn't get the pots quite hot enough. It's also a heck of a lot of work, even aside from all the work of gathering up the fuel. There's a lot of work in just manning the fires. Then there was the mess it made. The pottery wasn't vitrified by hot air. It was actually *in* the fire, so it came out of the pit covered in ash and had to be scrubbed. While the fire was burning, you were working in heat and smoke. And then there was this huge pit full of ash and soot to clean up.

The one-way valve needed to be bigger. At least, some of the one-way valves needed to be bigger. In the first couple of versions, they'd spent a whole lot of labor sucking air into the leather sacks.

"We should use wood," Jogida said. "For the one-way valve we should use wood, not leather."

"It won't make a good seal," Oaka complained.

"So we put leather on the wood," Jogida insisted.

It was a good idea, Michael agreed. The wood would let them make a larger flap, which would let in more air more easily. They had bricks made in a fire pit using oil-soaked wood, so they had their kiln, and even that was making better pottery faster. But it still wasn't getting quite hot enough, according to Alyssa. Certainly not hot enough to turn bog iron into wrought iron.

Back to the drawing board, and next time they would use a piece of wood for stiffness.

A few hundred feet away, an older woman sat at a table with a rotating wheel built into it. She dumped a chunk of clay onto the wheel and started spinning it with her foot. This was doable because the potter's wheel was actually two wheels, one on the top with the clay on it and the other connected to it by a rod. She turned the lower wheel with her foot, which turned the upper wheel. It was all held in place by a framework and there was grease on the rod so that it would spin easily.

Then, using her hand, she started shaping the clay into a bowl. It took her about five minutes to shape the medium-sized bowl, a job that would have taken the better part of two hours before the demon people had brought the potter's wheel to them.

Bowl finished, she used a copper wire to cut it off the table and carefully set it on a shelf to dry. Then she grabbed another clump of clay and started the process again.

Another woman was seated a couple of feet away from her, using her feet to pedal a pedal-powered lathe. It wasn't complex, just a round chunk of wood with pedals on it, attached by cord to another round piece of wood that was, in turn, attached to one end of the lathe. Push the pedals, the end of the lathe spun, spinning a piece of wood. And using a piece of the demon people's steel sharpened to a cutting edge, she cut the wood in an intricate pattern. It wasn't anything that she couldn't have done by hand with stone tools. Flint was actually sharper. But this was a lot easier, and a lot easier to control. This piece would be the leg of a chair.

All over Jabir and Camp Peterbilt, these changes were making life better and easier for the people of Jabir. Come harvest time, they would help even more.

Jabir fields
August 10, 1005 CE

The wheelbarrows were out in force, moving among the rows of corn, collecting ears as they matured. It was handwork, cutting the corn with stone knives. No John Deere reapers here. But the locals were absolutely thrilled with how well it was going and how fast.

Melanie was watching the locals and her fellow time travelers. By now all of them were mostly used to the long hours of work that were so common in this time. These people didn't work and play. They went from heavy labor to light work, then back to heavy labor. Light work was often accompanied by discussion and gossip, but folks kept their hands busy even then. It was only when watching *Jesus Christ Superstar* and attending religious services that they weren't chatting. That, and hunting.

Using a camp knife, Melanie cut another corncob from a stalk and went on. Even with the new tools, harvest was an "all hands on deck" time. She put the corncob in the wheelbarrow and went on to the next stalk.

Three hours later, they gathered in Jabir for a feast, and it was a good feast, though Melanie really and truly missed butter and all the other milk products. The ice cream had made some of the locals sick because a high percentage of the locals had never developed the lactose tolerance of western Europeans. No milk products meant no reason to change the gene.

No butter, no cheese on the table, and Melanie missed it. Surprisingly, she missed it more than she missed processed sugar. Though perhaps not quite as much as she missed salt. These people had some salt, but the Gulf Coast was a long way away and while they did trade that far, it made such things expensive and used with moderation.

Not that there weren't spices. The natives did trade up and down the Mississippi, which they called the Talak. The river that the natives called the Talak was the Missouri River down to its confluence with the Mississippi, then the Mississippi. Spices were small and easy to carry, so there were spices from a fair chunk of the continent mixed into the stews and slathered onto the barbecued meats and vegetables.

Camp Peterbilt
August 20, 1005 CE

The harvest was in, even the sweet corn from the country store, which had larger cobs and produced a corn with sweeter kernels than the locals' corn did. Also, just about every kernel of corn had sprouted, which was a whole lot better than the local corn managed. Those three things meant that the sweet corn was a prized commodity. Which, oddly enough, meant that there was going to be less of it to eat, at least for now. Just about all of it was being set aside to be planted next spring.

Kadlo Mound, Hocha
August 24, 1005 CE

Roshan sat in the main living area of the family house, eating a corn stew that was made with food from Jabir. The corn was sweet and there were other plants, tomatoes and squash. It was squash, but a different sort than they had.

It was an interesting meal and Rogasi had explained that it was a special gift from Hamadi, to show Roshan what the demon people had been growing from the seeds in the general store. "That's what the demon people call the building that was in the place where they entered the world."

Rogasi was wearing a cord around his neck, and on the cord was an emblem. It was two sticks, a longer vertical one with a shorter one crossing it horizontally about two-thirds up from the bottom.

When he asked about it, Rogasi explained with enthusiasm about the TV and the movie *Jesus Christ Superstar*, even singing some of the songs. Rogasi had a smooth tenor voice and he sang well. He also sang in the demon people speech, then translated each line.

The meal and the discussion were interesting and, to an extent, compelling. The style of the songs were different than

Roshan was used to, but not too different. Not so different that they lost their magic.

The next morning, after Rogasi was on his way back to Jabir, Roshan told an acquaintance from the village of Pasire about the food and even a bit about the beliefs of the demon people, at least the part about the cross god arranging things so that no one ever needed to be sacrificed again.

Eldladi was a chief of the Gruda clan, and Roshan was trying to get his support against the rumor that the high priest of Hocha was going to demand a larger sacrifice this year.

Eldladi wasn't convinced by Roshan, mostly because he didn't like Roshan. What he was persuaded of was that Camp Peterbilt would be an excellent place to raid for quite a lot of wealth, and for young women. If the priesthood were going to ask for more sacrifices this year, he wanted those young women to come from the Kadlo, not the Gruda. It would also please the high priest, who had been trying to persuade him to attack the strangers because the priests of Hocha saw the big dragon demon as a challenge to their authority.

Camp Peterbilt
September 3, 1005 CE

Over the spring and summer, the Peterbilt, and especially the pickup, had helped the village of Jabir carry earth and dig ditches and canals to get the water to the crops of maize, squash and beans, which were the mainstays of the local diet. The Kadlo, and other clans associated with Hocha, did hunt and fished rather more than they hunted, but the majority of their food was crops grown in the earth without the aid of horses or oxen. They gardened, instead of farming.

But for the village of Jabir, the pickup truck pulling a plow changed that. The villagers were restricted to the soft ground on the alluvial plain of the Talak River and its tributaries, because the stone hoes they used didn't work well on the heavy soil of the grasslands. Also, all the Pilgrim stories notwithstanding, these Native Americans didn't do a lot of fertilizing. It was use a field until the crop diminished, then switch to another for a couple of years to let the first field recover. But with the plows pulled behind the Peterbilt, the fields not in the floodplain could be plowed and planted. That was where the seed corn from the general store had ended up.

Alyssa's composting pits had provided fertilizer for the fields of Jabir. The effect was that more maize, squash and beans were sown and what was sown grew better and produced more. It all made for the largest and lushest crop that Jabir had had in living memory. Totally aside from the extra field that had been planted with twenty-first-century sweet corn, which had shorter stalks and larger ears, not to mention quite a bit more sugar in each kernel of corn.

Melanie climbed into the cab of the Peterbilt on the driver's side, because Alyssa was comfortably sprawled on the passenger seat and Michael and Shane were perched side by side on the lower bunk. In times past, she would have locked the door behind her but they no longer bothered with that, even at night. That wasn't simply because the settlement that had grown up around the truck was absent from crime; it was also because at any time of day or night two young men maintained an unobtrusive guard over the Peterbilt. That was true whether it was occupied or not.

The Americans weren't sure, but they thought that was being done at the command of Hamadi. Achanu's uncle was the one chief who resided in the new settlement. The others visited from time to time, but they kept their residence in the village of Jabir.

"They're still at it," said Melanie, gesturing with her head toward the window. "I mean, Jesus, how many times can you watch *Jesus Christ Superstar*?" On her way into the cab of the truck, Melanie had walked past the shaded area next to the tanker where their TV was set up on a chair. At any given time, half a dozen to a dozen people would be gathered sitting on the ground and watching the musical. Not far away, a somewhat smaller group was listening to the gospels.

"I know one girl who's watched it forty-nine times so far. She says they really like being able to run the subtitles at the same time."

"Did she tell you in English or in Kadlok?" asked Alyssa.

"English." Shane shook her head. "It's like pulling teeth to get them to talk Kadlok to me—and I try. The only ones who will do so more or less readily are Achanu and Oaka."

"The kids our age mostly talk Kadlok to us," said Norman. "I'm getting pretty good at it," he added proudly. Then, a bit grudgingly: "So's Miriam."

His older sister sniffed. "I speak it better'n you. It's 'cause you're too quick to slide back into English."

Michael was frowning; in puzzlement, not disapproval. "What do you think accounts for the difference? I've noticed it myself. Every Kadlo I try practicing their language with almost always makes me switch to English, except the little kids. It makes things easier, sure, but sooner or later we've got to learn their language. There are only six of us, and probably sixty thousand of them when you include Hocha, the big city north of here."

"I think that's on Hamadi's orders," said Alyssa. "And I think Kasni backs him up. Which means probably the whole women's council, too. From what I've been able to see so far, the chiefs will squabble with each other fairly frequently, but not the women on the council. They stay disciplined, always speak with one voice." She sniffed also. "Don't let their egos run the show like some other gender I can think of."

Michael chuckled. "I've always known women were natural conspirators. But to get back to the question, why do you think Hamadi is being so strict about it?"

"I think there are two reasons," answered Alyssa. "First, Hamadi is smart—very smart. Having his people learn English opens up a lot of resources and possibilities for them, while teaching us Kadlok doesn't, beyond personal convenience."

"How does that work? I mean, there are only six of us and a lot of them. It would seem that having us learn their language would be easier."

"Easier, yes. But less useful," Alyssa said. "Learning a new language is learning a new way of thinking. I think Hamadi has decided that our way of thinking will buy them more than just having us explain how some tool works in Kadlok."

"That, and the fact that English amounts to a secret language as long as they speak it and the other tribes don't," said Michael. "And their language isn't written down yet. He's been especially keen on having them learn to read and write, once he figured out what literacy was."

"Which took him maybe five minutes," said Melanie. "And I think it didn't take much more time than that for Kasni and

Achanu's mother Etaka to grasp what he was explaining to them later. What's the other reason you think he's doing it, Alyssa?"

Her brow furrowed and her eyes narrowed. "Well, this is conjecture, but from what I've been able to piece together—mostly from the women, not Hamadi himself—there's a lot of tension between the people here in Jabir and the Kadlo who live in Hocha. More precisely, between the chiefs and the priests who seem to have a lot of influence in Hocha. I'm not sure, but I get the feeling that a lot of the chiefs in Hocha aren't very happy with the priests, either."

"I've gotten that same impression," said Michael, nodding. "In my case, from talks I've had with that friendly young shaman whose name I can't pronounce."

"Aegluniket," said Melanie. "It's a tongue twister, all right."

Michael spread his hands. "I won't swear to it, mind you. Agel-whazid and I talk a weird pidgin polyglot that mashes Kadlo and English together and probably mangles both."

"I can't figure the shamans out at all," said his wife. "That old one, Priyak, seems hostile to us."

"As near as I can tell," said Alyssa, "the relationship of the shamans to each other—and the lay population—is more analogous to Jewish rabbis than Christian priests. Outside of maybe Israel, rabbis don't have a hierarchy or a central authority. The influence they have is mostly whatever esteem and respect they have with the people around them. So, some shamans are allied with Hocha priests—Priyak's clearly one of them—whereas others stay independent of them or are allied with the chiefs."

"Who aren't themselves necessarily unified, am I right?" That came from Michael.

"Certainly not to the extent the women's council seems to be," said Melanie. There came another sniff. "I refer you back to my comments—okay, wisecracks—about gender differences. That said, I get the impression that most of the chiefs lean the way Hamadi does, including at least some of the ones in the big city, which I'm pretty sure is what archaeologists called Cahokia."

"Does that city have a name?" asked Michael.

"They call it Hocha, but I'm not sure if that's its name or if it's just their word for city," said Alyssa. "Or maybe 'the big city.'"

Alyssa shrugged. "Or it may just be that it doesn't have a name because it grew up as a conglomerate of small towns." She smiled. "Except for some of the people who live in Manhattan, I don't think I've ever heard someone from New York say they came from there. It's always 'I'm from Brooklyn' or 'I'm from the Bronx.' But to come back to my point, I think the chiefs—most of them, anyway—don't like the growing power of the priesthood. Whether that's for what you might call ideology or just a power struggle, I don't know."

"Could be both," said Michael.

"Yes, it could. Probably is, in fact. That's the way politics usually works."

"Interesting times we live in," said Melanie. "Which is a Chinese curse, if I recall correctly."

"What concerns me is the fact that all the priests are men," Alyssa said. "Remember when I pointed out that this was a matrilineal culture?"

She got nods all around.

"Well, there should be women shamans, or wise women, if you prefer. But there don't seem to be. There are the women's councils, but all the 'magic' seems to be the province of the shamans or the priests."

"Is there a difference between the shamans and the priests?" asked Shane.

"There seems to be," Alyssa said. "They use different words for the priests in the city and the village shamans."

CHAPTER 9

RAID

The Peterbilt
September 7, 1005 CE

Alyssa wasn't sure what woke her up. At first, she had a muzzy sense that it was something happening in a weird dream she was having—which, as was usually true, she stopped remembering as soon as consciousness started returning. But then she bolted upright.

That was a scream she'd heard! Someone was screaming.

From the sounds coming from the bunk below her, she knew someone was already getting up. Probably Michael, who was a light sleeper, unlike herself and Melanie.

Less than two seconds later, one of Michael's big hands was on her arm shaking her awake. "Something's wrong!" he said urgently. "I need you to hand me the rifles—and a box of ammunition for each of them. *Get moving, Alyssa.*"

Already sitting up, all she had to do was reach out to the gun racks and grab one of the rifles. That was Michael's .30-06, which was always on the bottom rack. Once she handed that one to him, she reached for Melanie's .308 and started fumbling for the ammunition boxes.

"Turn on the lights," she hissed. "I can't tell which box is which."

The lights came on before she finished the second sentence. That must be Shane turning them on. She was a light sleeper like her father, and she was the one closest to the light switch. From the muffled sounds she was making, Melanie was still coming awake.

There was another scream from outside. Like the first scream, it sounded like a woman's voice. There were words being screamed, though, it wasn't just a terrified noise. Alyssa had no idea what they meant. Her knowledge of Kadlok was still very rudimentary.

Then she heard a man shouting. She recognized Hamadi's voice, although she didn't understand what he was saying either. But there was no mistaking the urgency and anger involved.

"I think we're being attacked by somebody," Michael said. By now he was in the passenger seat in the front of the cab, opening the glove compartment and taking out the Glock. He turned and handed the pistol to Alyssa.

"Stay here and guard the kids," he said. They'd already discussed and agreed upon what they'd do in such an event. He and Melanie would exit the truck with their rifles while Alyssa stayed behind with the pistol. The problem they faced was that while Alyssa had shot a rifle on a firing range, she hadn't done so in a long time and had never hunted at all. She was well coordinated and could undoubtedly have become a good shot with some practice—but they didn't have enough ammunition for her to do that. So, she'd be the one to stay behind in the truck.

Before climbing out of the cab, Michael took the Desert Eagle out of the glove compartment. He'd jury-rigged a holster for it, which was nothing much fancier than a belt loop, since there hadn't been a holster with the pistol in Mr. Dawes' pickup.

After Michael exited the cab, Melanie followed him. They both used the passenger door since it was quicker to climb out of than the one on the driver's side. Plus, the area they'd be in was less visible from the trail leading up from the river than the one on the other side of the truck.

Once they were gone, Alyssa moved forward and occupied the driver's seat. She had a good view from there and, at short distances, could stay in touch with the Anderles using their cell phones. The Peterbilt was Bluetooth and Wi-Fi capable, tying all their phones into a local network.

There wasn't much light, since the sun was just coming up.

Still, using the binoculars, she could start to piece together what was happening.

The first thing that was obvious was that they were, indeed, under attack. She could see at least two dozen men coming up the slope. All of them held either bows or javelins, and had some sort of clubs attached to belts at their waists. And in case there was any doubt at all of their intentions, they all had war paint on their faces and most of them had painted their torsos as well. Their chests were protected by armor—it looked like bleached animal bones laced together—but the design of their war paint was still quite visible, especially on their bare arms. Black and red were the predominant colors, with either one or the other used as a solid band painted around the eyes, giving the impression that they were wearing masks.

And they were yelling. War cries, presumably.

Glancing to the side out of the window, Alyssa could see that Hamadi had rallied seven or eight men, which was about all the adult or teenage males who lived in the settlement next to the truck. The Kadlo had deliberately kept the population mostly women and children to allay whatever fears the Americans might have.

That had been considerate of them, but Alyssa now wished they hadn't done it. Hamadi and the men with him were no better armed than their assailants, and there were a lot fewer of them. On their own, they didn't have much of a chance.

She heard the first unmistakable flat crack of one of the American rifles.

So far as she could tell, that shot missed whoever the intended target had been. But there was another loud *crack!* that followed almost immediately, and a third *crack!* not more than a second later. Two of the men coming up the slope collapsed. One of them lay still; the other started sliding down the incline, dead or unconscious. Michael and Melanie were firing rounds designed for hunting, with no consideration given to the laws of war regulating the types of ammunition permitted. Alyssa didn't want to think of the horrible wounds that had just been inflicted upon those two men.

The attackers coming up the hill fired a volley of arrows—at Hamadi and his little group. If they'd seen Michael and Melanie off to the left by at least twenty yards, they hadn't realized that they'd been the origin of whatever had struck down their two comrades.

All of the arrows except one failed to hit their targets because

Hamadi had his men sheltering next to trees or on the back side of huts. The only injury inflicted was a shallow gash on the shoulder of...

Achanu, she realized. What was a boy that young doing on a battlefield? Other than thinking himself immortal, like so many teenagers did.

There came another double cracking sound. Two more assailants folded instantly. Alyssa had never seen a real gunfight so she'd been expecting to see bodies sent flying by the high-power bullets, as they usually were in movies. But instead they were just cut down like grass by a scythe. Most of them fell forward, not backward.

By the time the attackers were able to notch new arrows, another volley was fired by Michael and Melanie. One more fell to the ground. The second shot hadn't apparently hit anyone.

That was followed by a ragged volley of arrows fired by Hamadi and his men. Two of the attackers were struck, although only one of the wounds looked to be serious. That one penetrated a man's chest just below the collarbone. He sagged, and then dropped to his knees, although he still kept a grip on his bow.

The injuries caused by the other two arrows seemed fairly minor, at least to Alyssa's inexperienced eyes. Neither man dropped his bow and one of them even managed to nock an arrow and fire it at Hamadi's men.

At Achanu, specifically. The boy had been so startled by his first arrow wound that he still hadn't taken adequate shelter. Luckily, this second arrow fired at him missed—but not by more than a few inches.

Hamadi yelled something at him. Again, Alyssa's rudimentary knowledge of Kadlo didn't enable her to understand what he said, but the gist of it was clear enough from the context. *Get behind shelter, you idiot!*

A chorus of war cries brought Alyssa's attention back to the band of assailants. She saw that many of them had now seized their war clubs and were charging toward...

Michael and Melanie had to be their targets, although Alyssa couldn't see them. Both fired again. One man dropped instantly, the other stumbled and clutched his left leg, from which blood was gushing. *An artery*, Alyssa wondered, though she didn't know of any major artery on the thigh just above the knee. The femoral artery was higher up—or at least she thought it was. But her knowledge of anatomy was hardly that of an expert.

Despite the new casualties, the assailants kept coming. There were fewer of them, now—the Anderles' gunfire had been wither-ing at that close range.

Michael came into view coming forward of the truck.

What the hell is he doing?

Then she saw that he had the Desert Eagle held in his hands. Both hands, using a double grip.

His assailants weren't more than ten yards away now!

Suddenly remembering the air horn, she reached up and yanked the lanyard down—and kept it down for several seconds.

It then occurred to her, a bit late, that she might have thrown off Michael's aim. She probably had, in fact—she could see him hunch his shoulders. But however startled he might be, Michael was very familiar with the Peterbilt's air horn, which his Neolithic opponents were not at all. If he was a little startled, they were stunned into immobility.

The Desert Eagle steadied and Michael started firing. He obviously wasn't concerned with saving his ammunition, either. *Boom—boom—boom—boom—*

At that range, none of his shots missed. All but one hit center mass, and the one that didn't shattered a man's shoulder. He might survive, he might not—but either way he was out of the action.

Then Melanie came into view also, her face distorted in a grimace of rage and fear. She brought her rifle to her shoulder and fired. Another man went down. Alyssa could *see* the foun-tain of blood spraying out of his back where the bullet exited his body. He'd die almost instantly.

And then Hamadi and two veteran warriors arrived, with their own clubs in hand, and it was all over. The surviving attackers turned and ran back down the slope. Hamadi struck down one of them, who moved too slowly, with a blow to his head that probably caved in the back of his skull.

By then, the rest were out of range of any clubs—but not of Melanie's rifle. She was so furious she shot one of them in the back.

"Hey, leave off, hon!" shouted Michael. "It's all over and we need to save what's left of our ammunition."

Alyssa tried to count back from memory. Michael would have

fired... six rounds from his rifle, she thought. Melanie about the same, or maybe one more. And Michael had used up about half the clip in the Desert Eagle.

Not too bad, all things considered. It had been a completely one-sided battle.

Which wasn't quite over yet, she realized. The attacker who'd been struck by an arrow in his chest was still where he'd been, and still on his knees. His head was drooping forward and he seemed barely conscious.

Hamadi came up to him and raised his club. Alyssa hissed softly, assuming he was about to kill this man also with a blow to the head.

But, no. He did strike him—struck him very hard—but the blow was to his right shoulder. That knocked him over and probably knocked him unconscious, but it wouldn't have killed him.

She was a little surprised by that display of mercy. Then, seeing the pitiless way Hamadi was gazing down at the man, realized that she was probably misreading his intentions. He'd want the man to talk once he regained consciousness—and Alyssa doubted very much that Hamadi was going to read him his Miranda rights.

Michael and Melanie were now back at the cab door. Michael opened it and handed his rifle up to Shane, who'd moved from the lower bunk to the passenger seat at some point during the fracas.

"Be careful, Shane," he said. "The barrel might still be hot. Hold it by the stock."

She took the rifle and brought it up, slapping the barrel with her hand as she did so. "Yeah, it's pretty toasty. What do you want me to do with it?"

"For the moment, just lay it down on the floor behind you." He raised Melanie's rifle, now. "Do the same with this one, when you're ready. And then"—gingerly, he held up the Desert Eagle—"just put this back in the glove compartment."

While she was handling that, Michael turned back to his wife. "How are you doing, hon?"

She leaned against him, with her head on his shoulder and her arms around him. Her face, always pale, was now almost as white as a sheet. She shivered a little. "I don't know. Right now, I just feel numb. But I think there's something chattering in the back of my brain. I doubt if I'll get much sleep tonight."

"Probably not. I barely slept at all, the first time I was in a firefight in Afghanistan. And the second time wasn't much better. Combat's stressful under any conditions, but it's a lot worse—especially when it's all over—when you know for sure you killed someone."

She looked up at him. "You never talk about that. Did you... I mean..."

"Kill anyone? Yeah. Two men that I know of, for sure. It was a pure bitch. The worst of it was that one of them was a kid. Couldn't have been more than eighteen years old." He shivered himself, very briefly. "And I wasn't much older than he was at the time."

He started to add something, but Hamadi came around the front of the truck. He still had his war club in his hand, but he wasn't being threatening.

Quite the opposite, Alyssa thought. He was looking at the Anderle couple as if he were seeing... well, not ghosts. But it had probably crashed home on him that people who lived inside a huge demon and seemed to control it had to be demonic themselves. They'd done most of the killing in the brief battle—which had been more like a massacre.

Alyssa tried to estimate how long that clash had lasted. It had seemed like a long time, but looking back she realized that from the first shot being fired to Melanie shooting one of the fleeing men, not more than...

Jesus H. Christ. Two minutes? Not even that, maybe. And in that short period of time Michael and Melanie had killed... how many of the assailants? She couldn't remember exactly. Eight, ten or more, and another they'd badly wounded.

She looked forward through the windshield, trying to find that wounded man. She spotted him almost at once. He was lying prone, his left shoulder soaked with blood. But the blood wasn't gushing so it couldn't have hit an artery and—

And... nothing. His skull was also coated with blood, which had also stopped flowing. She realized that Hamadi—maybe someone else—had finished him off with a club strike. Probably because with that terrible a shoulder wound he wasn't going to be able to talk very soon, so the Neolithic version of triage had been applied.

Now she was shivering, and wasn't sure if she could stop.

Hamadi said something to Michael which Alyssa didn't understand. From the blank expression on his face, it was clear that Michael didn't comprehend the words either.

"He wants to know if either of you were hurt, Dad," said Shane.

Michael shook his head. One thing they'd managed to establish was that head gestures meant the same thing to people of both cultures. A nod was positive and a lateral shake was negative.

Hamadi gazed at Michael for another few seconds, his face impassive. Then he flipped his war club around to seize it by the knob at the business end. The weapon seemed to have been carved from some sort of hardwood, probably a branch.

He extended the club to Michael, handle first. After a moment's hesitation, Michael grasped it and held it up. It was nicely balanced, which surprised him a little. Once again he had the lesson that Alyssa emphasized so often driven home to him. The technology of the natives might be limited, but it was not crude. Within whatever range they'd come to understand something, they were very adept at it. Their minds were just as capable as those of people from the twenty-first century, they just didn't have as great a knowledge of the universe and how it worked.

Yet.

Acting on impulse, he repeated Hamadi's action—flipped the club around so that he was holding it by the knob, and held the handle out for Hamadi to take it back.

The native chief grunted faintly, took the club and smiled. Michael knew he'd instinctively done the right thing. What had been a friendly living arrangement was now something more solid and durable. Call it an understanding, even an alliance.

"I think we're in for a lot of dickering, in the weeks ahead," said Alyssa.

Melanie smiled. "Ya think?"

Michael nodded. "And I figure we'll start with proposing an actual sewer system. Things are starting to get a little stinky around here. That one toilet we set up downstream was okay for half a dozen people but it's not up to handling... How many people are living here now? About fifty?"

"About that," said Alyssa. She eyed Hamadi thoughtfully for a moment. "And I'll be very surprised if it doesn't start expanding rapidly."

Melanie frowned. "Hey, wait a damn minute! Michael and I

have listened to a lot of time travel stories. H. G. Wells' *The Time Machine*, Ray Bradbury's *A Sound of Thunder*, Robert Heinlein's *The Door Into Summer*, L. Sprague de Camp's *Lest Darkness Fall*—the list goes on and on."

"Don't forget the granddaddy of them all, Mark Twain's *A Connecticut Yankee in King Arthur's Court*," tossed in Michael.

"And I don't remember where a single one of those stories," Melanie continued, "*not one*, even mentioned toilets, much less dwelling on the gross details."

Alyssa chuckled. "Melanie, what part of the word 'fiction' are you having the most trouble with?"

"Very funny. Dammit, it's not *fair*."

Jabir
September 8, 1005 CE

To Hamadi, the raid wasn't just a surprise. It was a shock. And there was no way such a raid would have happened without the concurrence of the Hocha priesthood. Raids didn't attack villages. They attacked hunting parties, and it was rare that many men were involved. It was usually fewer than five. But not this time. They'd killed—well, mostly the demon people had killed—eighteen and the rest had run off, so at least twenty-four had attacked, and perhaps as many as thirty. That was a large enough raid to start a clan war.

And if this had been the days before the new priesthood, that's exactly what would be happening. The Kadlo would be gathering its forces to attack the Gruda in response. A part of Hamadi wanted to be doing just that. But the other chiefs wouldn't go along, not with Hocha sitting there on its mounds with its city guard ready to punish any clan that attacked another without its consent.

On the other hand, the raiders had all come from one village, the village of Pasire on the west side of the Talak River. Scouts were out even now, tracing them back to the Agla River, where they must have landed their canoes. There would be some empty canoes heading back down the Agla to the Talak. It was a safe bet that the raiders would tow them back; a dugout was an expensive piece of equipment.

And if Hocha had sanctioned this raid, there was no reason to think that it wouldn't sanction more. Not that the Pasire would be taking part. Not after losing eighteen warriors. And it would take some time. But how much?

Hamadi consulted with the other elders of the village and came up with a plan. They would turn the camp of the demon people into a fort. That, after all, was at least half the purpose of the mounds in Hocha. They talked it out and set Gada to work on the design of a fort. He'd learned more of the demon people's ways than the rest of them had.

Kadlo Mound, Hocha
September 14, 1005 CE

Roshan waved Lomhar in. Lomhar was a senior chief from another Kadlo village. "Did you hear the news about the attack on Camp Peterbilt?"

"Yes." Lomhar grinned a rather feral grin until he saw Roshan's expression. "What is it?"

"The Gruda are very upset and Ho-Chag Kotep is furious." Ho-Chag Kotep was the high priest of Hocha, in effect the Priest King of Hocha and indirectly of all the river people.

"They attacked us!" Lomhar was clearly incensed even though he wasn't from Jabir.

"I know, Lomhar," Roshan said. "I'm from Jabir and Hamadi is my cousin. The fact that they were attacking just makes it worse, as they see it. The Gruda raided one of our villages. To do that, they had to have at least the tacit consent, but more probably the active pushing of Ho-Chag Kotep. The reason was to take us down a notch and to prove that the demon people's magic isn't all that strong after all."

Roshan rubbed his face then continued. "Instead, Pasire lost a lot of warriors and they can't even complain to the priest of Hocha that we broke the peace because they were the ones attacking."

"Oh," Lomhar said. "They want revenge."

Roshan nodded. "And they can't get it directly. Lomhar, I have a source in the priesthood. They are going to choose your daughter for the sacrifice." He watched as the blood drained from Lomhar's face. They were colleagues, not really friends, but he hated to see the man's face look like that. Hated it so much that he suggested the unthinkable. "Take her away, Lomhar. Get her out of Hocha, away from the priests."

Now Lomhar looked at Roshan in shock. Refusing to provide the sacrifice demanded could cause the destruction of a clan, and the girl would end up sacrificed anyway. "If I take her to Kallabi, they will just send a canoe."

"Don't take her to Kallabi or any of our villages. Not even Jabir. Take her to Camp Peterbilt. From what I am told, they are building a fort there because of the attack."

CHAPTER 10

FORT PETERBILT

The Peterbilt
September 18, 1005 CE

Hamadi and several of his men had built a scale model of what they had in mind. What they wanted to do was greatly expand the perimeter of the settlement, enclosed by a palisade, the end result of which would be a huge increase in the area it covered. That would be enough to absorb the entire population of Jabir and leave room for a few hundred more people. That was if you packed everyone in, though. As always, communication was difficult because of the language barrier, but several of the young men—especially Achanu—had become adept enough to do a fair translation. The lingua franca that was starting to emerge, at least for the ones who were best at it, was moving from a pidgin to a mostly English-based creole. The end result was a cumbersome form of communication, but it was far better than the pure sign language they'd started with.

The first thing that became clear to Michael, to his relief, was that the way Hamadi saw the transformed settlement around the Peterbilt was analogous to a medieval keep. Most of the people would continue to live and work in Jabir except in the event of an enemy attack, at which point they could retreat into the settlement which was designed for defense.

The new settlement would now occupy both banks of the creek and would expand upstream to incorporate the pool. Even if the creek flow was cut off or diverted, the pool was big enough to provide drinking water for several months, even in midwinter.

The palisade wouldn't simply be a wall of logs erected by sinking them into the soil. It was designed to be a wooden version of a medieval curtain wall. At periodic intervals, bastions would provide fighting platforms for the defenders. Michael could see one big problem with the design, though. There was no provision made for incorporating the Peterbilt into the defense. The only entrance and exit to the settlement would be through a narrow gate located not far from the creek. There would be no way to bring the truck into action except by ramming the palisade and knocking it down, or laboriously removing a part of the wall to use as a bridge.

That problem, however, Michael ascribed to simple ignorance on the part of the natives. They had never yet seen the Peterbilt in any but its slowest gears, moving at barely more than a walk. That was because while they had used the Peterbilt to help build the road between the camp and the village, they had more often used the pickup truck. The Peterbilt was saved for pulling big rocks out of the ground and that sort of thing. They knew it was strong, but they had no idea how fast it could move if it was provided with a reasonably level and unobstructed surface. Leaving aside a very small number of top sprinters, the average human male—even ones in good condition—typically ran between eight and twelve miles per hour. Even going fifteen miles an hour, the truck would outpace them, and with a prepared surface—it didn't have to be a paved road, just a wide enough pathway with the big rocks, logs and stumps removed—the Peterbilt could easily move at twice that speed. Any enemy would be faced with a ten-ton monster capable of moving as fast as a grizzly bear or a pack of wolves.

That problem would be easy to solve. It would require quite a bit of labor to do it properly, true, but nothing beyond the resources of several hundred people. Especially when you added in the use of a pickup truck pulling locally made devices to break up and move the dirt, and the Peterbilt to move heavy stuff.

He rose to his feet and gestured for Hamadi and Achanu to accompany him. The chief would have to agree to Michael's proposal and he needed Achanu to translate for him. Semi-translate, at least. Of the six Americans who had come through the Ring of Fire, Michael's language-learning skill was the worst. His daughter Shane, who was very good at it, liked to tease him on the subject.

Hamadi and Achanu returned to the hut which served the chief as his headquarters about an hour later. Michael was no longer with him.

"You can come out now," he said. Three people emerged from a well-disguised side room. It was cramped in there, since the room was only three feet wide, but unless someone knew what to look for—or did a careful comparison of measurements of the hut's exterior to its interior—they'd never realize the hut contained more than a single, central room.

Two of the people were men in late middle age. The third was a young girl, just on the edge of her teenage years.

With the addition of three more people, the hut's central room became a little crowded, since it was already occupied by Hamadi, Achanu, their wife and mother Etaka, Kasni from the women's council, and the young shaman Aegluniket.

"What did he want?" asked one of the men. His name was Lomhar and he was one of the major chiefs of the Kadlo. He'd come here from Hocha and had arrived this morning, just before daybreak. That arrival time had been deliberate. Neither he nor the two people who'd come with him could afford to be seen. The priests had an extensive network of spies. There were bound to be some in Jabir, at least one of whom was likely by now to have gotten himself or herself into the new settlement.

"He wants us to create a new gate through which the demon can pass, and then smooth out a pathway that will allow it to reach Jabir and the river."

"So in case a battle happens, he would set loose the demon?"

Hamadi nodded. "Yes. He said as much."

Lomhar made a face. "Now that I've seen the monster"—he'd been able to get a look from the open doorway to the hut, which faced it—"I'm not sure that's a good idea. Can he really control the demon, once he sets it loose?"

The other man in late middle age shook his head. "That is not a demon, Great Chief. Now that I've finally been able to see it"—he nodded toward Aegluniket—"and question him, I realized that it is not anything like a demon."

Everyone in the room except the young shaman looked surprised by that announcement, but no one thought to scoff at it. This man was Fazel, accepted by most Kadlo as their wisest shaman.

"What is it, then?" asked Kasni.

Fazel was dressed in the traditional garb of a shaman. That was not too dissimilar from the clothing worn by all adult male Kadlo, but it included an elaborately wound turban on his head and a kilt-like leather apron to which various implements were attached. Except for a small obsidian-bladed knife, the implements were all... peculiar.

Perhaps the most peculiar was an intricately carved wooden staff whose shaft appeared to be a coiled snake but which ended in the head of a bear. Tufts of some sort of animal fur formed a sort of collar below the bear head.

A modern archaeologist would have recognized it as a type of caduceus, although not one which had ever appeared in ancient times in the eastern hemisphere. The Kadlo themselves called it a *burlin*.

Fazel detached the *burlin* from his apron and held it up high enough so all could see. "This is what it is."

"A *burlin*?" asked Lomhar. His tone was simply one of surprise, though, with not a trace of derision. A shaman took great time and care designing, carving and shaping his burlin. It was his culture's analog to a wizard's wand, and only a fool took such a thing lightly.

Fazel nodded. "Far greater and more powerful than mine—or a *burlin* made by any shaman of our world. But that should not surprise us."

He turned toward Achanu. "You have spoken the most to the Amrikanz, yes?"

Achanu hesitated. "Well, except for my cousin Oaka. She has the best command of Inglizh of any of us."

Fazel looked to Hamadi. "Can she be trusted?"

Before the chief could answer, both Kasni and Etaka answered simultaneously: "Yes."

Etaka added a somewhat peeved, "Of course she can. She is my niece. Well, my mate's niece, but her mother is like a sister to me."

Fazel glanced at Lomhar. The great chief nodded, but added: "She will have to remain with us in this hut until we leave, though."

"Go get Oaka," commanded the shaman. His younger counterpart Aegluniket rose and left the hut.

After he left, Lomhar asked Fazel what he meant by likening the demon to his *burlin*.

"A demon is a *creature*—call it a monster, if you wish—that has a life of its own and a mind and will of its own. I've listened carefully to every account of the behavior of"—he nodded toward the door—"that giant out there and one thing that became as clear as lake water to me is that no one has ever seen it do anything except when one of the Amrikanz was inside it. That is the behavior of a *creation*, not a creature. The Amrikanz *made* that thing for their own purposes, just as I"—again, he held up his *burlin*—"made this for my own purposes."

He shrugged. "And why should that be surprising?" He looked at Achanu. "You told me the Amrikanz themselves deny that they have any magical origin or powers. They say that what seems to be such powers are simply the result of the knowledge they have because they come from the far future. A thousand years in the future, they said, am I right?"

The teenage boy nodded. "Yes, that's what they told me. I didn't believe them, though. That just seems ... impossible."

The shaman looked around the hut, catching everyone with his gaze. "From now on, *believe them*. Have they ever lied to you?"

Now everyone in the hut looked at each other.

"Not so far as I know," said Hamadi.

"Do you have any reason to distrust them?"

Again, that collective mutual gaze.

"No," said Kasni firmly.

"Then don't," said Fazel. "That would not just be wrong, it would be *stupid*. These people can be an enormous help to us, if we behave properly toward them." With his chin, he pointed toward the door. "Anyone who can make a *burlin* like that one is *powerful*."

He looked at Hamadi. "So to answer your original question, I think the only horror involved in setting the giant loose is one that will fall upon our enemies. Not us."

Hamadi took a deep breath. Then, smiled very crookedly. "And a horror it is likely to be. They were terrifying in the battle.

Between us of Jabir"—he twirled his finger, indicating the entire settlement—"we killed one of the warriors who came at us and wounded three others, only one of them seriously. The other two escaped. The Amrikanz—one man and one woman, that's all—slaughtered sixteen of them. None were wounded except one, whom Pavak finished off, but he would have died from the wound anyway."

"They did it with those weird-looking clubs of theirs," said Achanu. He barked a laugh. "And we thought they were just ceremonial staffs!"

Fazel smiled. "Some people make the mistake of thinking that of my *burlin* also. Those killing clubs of theirs are *burlins*. Next time you see them, ask them how the clubs work. If I'm right about them, they will simply give you a truthful answer."

Aegluniket and Oaka returned then. The girl was obviously nervous at being in the presence of the two men from Hocha.

As to the girl, Oaka gave her no more than a glance.

"We are told that you can speak with the Amrikanz better than anyone in Jabir," said Lomhar. "We wish to ask you some questions."

"That's all," said Fazel. He smiled at her. "You don't need to be worried."

Oaka nodded. Lomhar gestured at Fazel, inviting him to be the one to question the girl.

"Do the Amrikanz have a name for their . . . giant? The one they live in."

"They call it Pidrebild. Or sometimes the Pidrebild."

"Have you ever been inside it?"

Oaka shook her head.

"Have you seen the inside of Pidrebild."

"Some of him."

"Why do you call it 'him'?"

Oaka looked at him as if he were a bit addled. "A thing that fierce is not likely to be a woman."

"Why do you think the Pidrebild is fierce? From what I've been told, it has never done very much except scare some of you who were spying on it—and then, only using very bright fires and loud noises."

Oaka got a stubborn look on her face. "I've heard the way

the Amrikanz talk about him sometimes. *They* think he's fierce. Or can be, anyway."

Fazel nodded. "That, I don't doubt at all. What did Pidrebild look like on its—his—inside?"

Now, Oaka's expression became uncertain. "It's very hard to describe. The way I think the palace of the Paramount Priest must look in Hocha." Her hands made vague gestures. "Very... splendid."

Lomhar got a sour expression on his face. Clearly, his opinion of the Paramount Priest of Hocha was not... splendid.

Fazel nodded. "Now tell me of their creed. The god they worship. The god of the cross."

Oaka seemed on surer ground now. "They are not priests themselves. They make that very clear. And they say they only have with them some parts of their beliefs. What they call 'books,' often. From what I can tell, their faith—that's the word they often use—is based on their god who sacrificed himself to save his people."

"Save them from what?"

"They call it 'damnation.' It means punishment—punishment that never ends—for doing evil."

"What do they consider evil?"

"Murder. Adultery. Lying. Theft. Worshiping false gods. Disrespecting your ancestors. Those seem to be the evils they are most concerned with."

"What do they think of human sacrifice?"

"They consider it what they call an 'abomination.' A very great evil that is unforgivable."

Silence came to the hut for a few seconds. Then a sort of sigh moved through the room as if they'd all been holding their breath.

Lomhar now spoke. "So the god of the cross sacrificed himself for the benefit of his people. And the gods of Hocha priests demand that people must be sacrificed—children, sometimes, one of whom was my own daughter—to feed their bloodlust."

By the time he finished speaking, his face was like a stone mask.

"Not a difficult choice to make, is it?" said Fazel.

"No, it is not," Lomhar agreed, then went on: "Except for the crops and other disasters that the priests insist are only prevented by the sacrifices."

"Alyssa says that we just need fertilizer and crop rotation to keep the crops healthy," Oaka said. She'd watched *Jesus Christ Superstar* quite a lot and she knew that the Pharisees had wanted to have Jesus sacrificed, but they'd already given up the practice so they needed Pilate to order it. She wasn't sure how much she believed of the religion of the cross, but after a summer spent in close association with the Peterbilt people, she was sure that she didn't believe in the gods of Hocha anymore. She'd been to the place where the god had brought the Peterbilt to this world, and that was more than the gods of Hocha had ever done.

CHAPTER 11

REFUGEE

The Peterbilt
September 19, 1005 CE

Lomhar and Fazel left the next morning, well before daybreak. As with their arrival in Jabir, they wanted their departure to go unnoticed by anyone except the people they'd met with.

The young girl did not go with them, however. She was a problem left behind that promptly got dropped onto the Americans. Before daybreak, someone rapped on the driver's side door of the Peterbilt. It turned out to be Kasni and it soon became clear that none of the three American adults had a good enough facility with the emergent creole language to follow everything she was saying.

So, Shane was assigned to translate.

"They want to know if we're willing to keep that young girl with us. Here in the Peterbilt, I mean. She's one of the nieces of one of the top chiefs in Hocha and the priests have singled her out as a soon-to-be sacrificial lamb."

Alyssa nodded. "Makes sense. My guess had been that the priesthood was using the threat of sacrificing members of high-ranked families as a way to keep them in line."

"They're *that* blatant about it?" demanded Michael.

"It's been done all through history, Michael—and, yes, it's usually blatant because the people doing it wield the whip."

Alyssa's expression became stony. "Do you know what the biggest risk factor was for a black man getting lynched during the Jim Crow era? I'll give you a hint: it had nothing to do with white women, although that was often the public excuse presented."

Michael and Melanie shook their heads. "No. What was it?" asked Melanie.

"Being a successful businessman and pissing off your white competitors. I was told by a colleague of mine at SIU—she was a professor of European history, especially the seventeenth century—that the same pattern characterized the witch hunts that were so prominent and frequent in that era. Accusing someone of being a witch and getting them executed was a way to settle scores with political or commercial rivals."

She was sitting in the passenger seat of the truck and swiveled so she could point an accusing finger to the north. "I'm willing to bet that's what's happening in Hocha. The priests use the threat of sacrifice—which they carry out, too—as a way of intimidating the chiefs."

Michael scratched his jaw. "Well, that certainly would go a long way to explain why some of these chiefs have been so friendly to us. 'Hey, look at the great big demon and its people we found.'"

"It also explains why they're so keenly interested in Christianity," said Alyssa, swiveling back. "I'm also willing to bet—okay, smaller stakes, a lot of this is pure speculation—that the natives' religion before the advent of the priests was pretty formless. Animism and pantheism, for the most part, interpreted by shamans who often disagreed with each other. Then the priesthood gets rolling, with a much more sophisticated and coherent pantheon of deities, and people start gravitating toward them. It's hard for those who are skeptical to resist, because they don't have a coherent alternative. Then—"

She chuckled, but there wasn't much humor in the sound. "*Voila.* It turns out the Peterbilt people have a *much* more impressive religion to offer, which includes motion pictures on a TV screen, singing, this amazing way of freezing words and ideas into fixed written forms—and to top it all off, a really simple but impressive symbol for all of it."

"That's right," said Shane. "They usually call Jesus the god of the cross or just the cross god. Some of them are starting to get tattooed with crosses, too."

"All right—but we've got to make a decision. Do we take the girl into the truck? And why do they want that, anyway?"

Shane provided the answer. "Kasni says the priests have spies everywhere and they're bound to have some in Jabir—they can even name one of them, that nasty old shaman Priyak. By now, she says, at least one or two have to have gotten a place for themselves in this settlement. They have to keep Zara—that's the girl's name—hidden until they're ready to challenge the priests openly. Kasni didn't give a time period for that, but—"

"We're talking months, at a minimum," said Michael.

His daughter nodded. "That's what I think, too. Anyway, Kasni says the one place they can be sure no one will spot Zara is if"—here, Shane grinned cheerily—"she's inside the belly of the demon."

Melanie grimaced. "It's already pretty crowded in here."

"There's an easy solution to that," said Alyssa, "which I've been thinking about anyway. We make a deal with Kasni. Zara gets to hide in the truck if she's willing to provide me and my kids with a big enough area in that triple-sized hut they'd built for her."

Michael and Melanie stared at her. "Are you...sure about that, Alyssa?" asked Melanie. "I mean, I'm willing to bet the bunk you share with your kids is a lot more comfortable than anything Kasni can provide you with. The natives sleep on what amounts to grass and reed pallets."

She made a face. "Probably got bugs in them."

Alyssa's chuckle, this time, had quite a bit of humor in it. "Actually, they do a pretty good job of keeping their quarters clean and pest-free. But let's face it, come winter we're all going to have it rough." She glanced into the cab. "Yeah, you'll be able to keep the truck warm—but you got neither a toilet nor a shower in here, and no way to cook food. Right now, that's not a big problem. Come the winter solstice, we're all going to be freezing our butts off."

"I'm trying not to think about it, thank you very much," grumbled Michael.

"Look, let's face facts. A few months from now—no more than a year—we're going to be caught up in what amounts to a civil war." Alyssa's expression got stern. "We have *got* to improve our language skills, especially we three adults—and we have to do it as quickly as possible. Having me and my two children immersed in Kadlo culture is the best and fastest way I can think of to do that."

There was silence for a little while. Then Michael shrugged and said, "I can't argue with that." He glanced out the driver's side window. Kasni was still out there, waiting patiently. To his daughter, he said, "So go cut the deal, kiddo."

After Shane left the truck Melanie turned to Alyssa and said, "Has it struck you that what we founded and are now following is not the Christian religion that you and I grew up in?"

Alyssa laughed. "Yes, that and more. *Jesus Christ Superstar* is hardly a blanket endorsement of Christianity. It was written in the nineteen sixties and raises a number of questions about the *truth* of Christianity. Heck, Judas is its second lead. It paints Christ as a man torn by indecision."

"But also a man that sacrificed himself so the rest of us wouldn't need to," Michael said.

"Sure, but if you start with *Jesus Christ Superstar* you're going to end up with a lot of doubters in the congregation," Alyssa insisted. "I've been getting secondhand questions like was Judas damned for all time and was he doing what Christ or God wanted him to. Both of which are right out of songs in the movie."

"I grant that," Melanie agreed, "but one clear message is 'if you turn someone over to the Pharisees to be sacrificed, you're going to end up hanging yourself.' And that's a message that clearly resonates with these folks."

Michael nodded.

Shane knocked on the window and told them about the deal she'd made.

It tied in with the new town that they were now working on, the medieval keep. Alyssa and the kids would move into Kasni's hut but only temporarily. They were going to build a new hut with a fireplace and a stone chimney, which would be for Alyssa and the kids.

"They get to learn what a fireplace and a chimney are, and I figure we can use some of the metal from the sliced car to make a top for the fireplace so that the heat will stay in the house while the smoke goes out."

Over the next few days, the design of the Jefferson house was formalized. It would include a bedroom, a main room and a lab for Alyssa. But it was going to take a while to finish, and in the meantime the full-immersion language and culture lessons could commence.

The Peterbilt
September 22, 1005 CE

Melanie Anderle was driving the Ram truck. Michael was in back with half a dozen of the villagers from Jabir on a contraption. "This is taking backseat driving to new heights," Melanie complained over her phone, only half joking. Her phone was tied into the truck by Bluetooth and Michael's was in his pocket and hooked into the Peterbilt's Wi-Fi hub, and Michael was telling her in detail how fast to go and when and where to turn. That was because the six villagers from Jabir were manhandling a device that they already had or at least had used. Hocha collected taxes or tribute in the form of labor from outlying towns, including Jabir. That labor was used to make the mounds and streets of Hocha. A lot of it was done with men carrying baskets of earth from one place to another, but some was done with large groups of men pulling not quite plows that cut up the ground so that it might be moved more easily.

With the Ram truck to pull the device, it had been modified in the village not to just cut up the ground but to load it into a sliding scoop contraption. It wasn't a fresno scraper but it performed something close to the same function of moving a great deal of earth in a comparatively short time. Compared to a bulldozer, it was slow and wasteful. Compared to a bunch of guys with baskets, it was incredibly fast. And that didn't even include the fact that the truck didn't get tired. The drivers did and so far today Alyssa, Michael, Melanie and even Shane had taken at least one turn. Melanie was on her second turn. But a great deal of earth had been moved enough to make the road under construction between Fort Peterbilt and Jabir wider and more solid, solid enough to take the full weight of the Peterbilt.

Over the fall, using the pickup truck and the Peterbilt as tractors pulling plows made from what was left of the Honda and copper that the people already worked, they cut a new town out of the earth. Ditches were emptied and mounds were built. Plots were dug out so that the houses' floors were three feet below ground level so that they would leak less heat. Rocks and clay were made into chimneys to keep the heat in while guiding the smoke away. Trees were pulled up by their roots using the pickup or the Peterbilt, then split with copper wedges. Wattle-and-daub walls were built and the glass from the country store was used to make windows for several homes. What would have taken two hundred people to do by hand was done by twenty, using the truck for pulling and hauling. The weak point was the gate that was big enough to let the Peterbilt out and the stretch of flat ground right in front of it where there was no trench to delay an attacker. But even that was less a weak point than a trap.

But building the town wasn't all they were doing. Language lessons and religious education were ongoing both in Fort Peterbilt and the village of Jabir.

The children played together and learned each other's languages, shared games and toys.

And full immersion worked. By late fall Alyssa understood the local language quite well. She didn't speak it nearly as well, but she understood. She was also teaching the locals English, but not just English. She was teaching them chemistry and the germ theory of medicine. And Alyssa wasn't the only one. Shane had her slate computer. Mostly it had games, but it also had PDF copies of her books from her last year of school. The sixth grade didn't go deep into any fields, but it gave a decent overview of English, math, general science and geography. Geography included, for instance, a map of North America that was much more accurate than anything that the locals had. Shane found herself teaching what she'd learned in the sixth grade to teenagers and grown-ups.

Fort Peterbilt
November 5, 1005 CE

As it turned out, Alyssa was wrong about how long it was going to take the locals to produce the wire screens necessary for paper making. They had examples of metal screens in the engines of the cars and Alyssa's Honda was scrap anyway. The locals already had copper, though not brass or bronze. They were already making copper wire, if slowly and by hand. But combining the knowledge the Peterbilt people brought with what they already knew, they made a pedal-powered wire puller on their own, and started making screens.

The motivation for this wasn't to make paper. No, it was a complaint Shane had made about the lack of screens to keep out flies. The locals weren't any fonder of flies than the Peterbilt people, and a way of keeping them out of the house really appealed.

Besides, they had the money to buy the copper. Their plates and bowls were selling well all up and down the Talak River.

Of course, once they had the screens, making finer screens to make paper became an option.

The Peterbilt
November 11, 1005 CE

"What's this word?" Zara asked and Shane rolled her eyes. She couldn't help it. For over a month now Shane had been Zara's teacher, companion, and the only person who spoke a language she could understand.

When Zara had questions, she had only one person to ask. And Zara always had questions. Shane looked. The word was "outcomes" and it was in Shane's sixth grade math book, so she tried to explain what an outcome was and how it differed from a result like the result of two plus two. The most irritating thing about Zara was how fast she learned. Zara had grown up with no written language. Everything she'd learned in her life, she'd learned by memorizing it. She memorized the alphabet in about an hour and her numbers in about five minutes.

Not that the people of Hocha didn't have numbers, but math and, especially, dates were the province of the priesthood in Hocha. It was part of the secret knowledge of the priests that, according to the priests, let them tell the farmers when to prepare the ground, sow the seeds, water the crops, and harvest the crops all at the right time of year.

This is vital information for farmers. It wasn't that the farmers didn't notice when the days got longer or that the stars in the sky were in different places at different times of the night and the year. But the precision that the standing pillars in Hocha provided was important as a proof of divine knowledge.

Now, though, full information on how to determine the date easily and consistently was in Shane's sixth grade textbooks.

The Peterbilt people's calendars were, in their way, more of a revelation to the locals than the cell phones that held them. There are 365.2422 days in a year. One leap year every four years would keep things consistent for the next hundred years.

Zara thought that the decimal point was sheer genius.

"There can only be one result, two plus two is always going to be four. But there can be different outcomes. If you spin a wheel it might stop on one or two or three." She pointed to the page of the book which showed a spinning arrow on a wheel divided into thirds.

"Outcomes," Zara said, "outcomes, outcomes, outcomes."

Then she went back to struggling through the math book, and two minutes later she was asking Shane what another word meant.

Gada's house, Fort Peterbilt
November 12, 1005 CE

Today Shane's slate computer was in Gada's house as she showed him the earth science textbook. And there on a page was a picture of the near side of the moon and right next to it a picture of the far side.

Gada looked at the picture, then simply stared. Shane didn't get it. Shane was just at that point where she was young enough to learn Kadlok but old enough to actually know something about the tech knowledge of her world, so she spent a lot of time explaining things to grown-ups.

On the whole, she wished she was back in the Peterbilt explaining things to Zara. She could tell by Gada's expression that it was important to him, but she didn't get it. It was just a photo of the far side of the moon, taken by a satellite she guessed, or maybe one of the Apollo missions. And it couldn't be the slate computer. He was used to that, by now.

Finally Gada managed to look away from the image of the far side of the moon and look at Shane. He realized that she didn't understand why he should care. And he had no idea how to explain it. Not a big thing in itself, it was the back side of the moon after all, but profound in the way it impressed the shaman.

He also learned math that he'd never imagined and the shape of North America. He learned the shape of all the continents, but it was North America that interested him most. He learned that every action has an equal and opposite reaction. He learned so much so quickly that he thought his mind might explode.

It wasn't all one way. The Peterbilt people learned which animals were common to the area, which were dangerous, which were good to eat. They learned which plants had medicinal value, which were poisonous and which were good to eat, how to dry and smoke meats and fruits, where the clays for making pots were located. In exchange, the Peterbilt people introduced the potter's wheel, turning a job that had taken hours into one that took minutes.

A discussion of the way the Honda Civic's body had been made led one of the villagers to invent stamps for shaping small clay items. And every innovation made the priests in Hocha seem weaker and less knowing in comparison.

Zara was seen. Not immediately, but no one can spend all their time in a Peterbilt. It wasn't that Zara didn't want to. She was quite reasonably terrified of the priests of Hocha. And the Peterbilt was fascinating, but not as fascinating as Shane with her schoolbooks and games on her slate computer.

In spite of all that, you can't spend all your time in a small room with no place to go to the bathroom. It was only a few weeks after she moved in that she was spotted. It took another month before word filtered back to Hocha and even then the priesthood did nothing.

The first attack on the Peterbilt people had been a disaster and by the time Zara's location was learned, the demon was surrounded by a ditch and a wall. A ditch and a wall that the people of the village of Jabir shouldn't have been able to build. So the priesthood waited, indecisive but growing angrier by the day.

Alyssa discussed it with Michael and Melanie after treating wounds of the hunters of Jabir. "Neolithic societies, according to my archaeologist friends, were very violent and were characterized by endemic warfare. My friends say, based on excavated skeletons, that as many as thirty percent of the males either died of violence or suffered major and possibly mortal wounds." She grimaced. "And from the things we've seen, they were right.

"But if the societies were very violent, the individual battles were not—largely because they weren't battles to begin with. They were raids, like the attack that caused the building of Fort Peterbilt, but even smaller, with usually no more than ten men fighting on either side. The twenty or so guys that attacked us were an army. By local standards anyway.

"Remember, the fighting was mostly held at a distance. The weapons principally used were javelins and bows and arrows. Usually no more than two or three men died in such fights, and it was not unusual for there to be no fatalities at all.

"That means that the body count when they attacked us probably sent shockwaves through the whole society. I think it's going to be very hard for the priests of Hocha to assemble large bodies of warriors, and will take a lot of time.

"Assuming they can manage it at all."

Gada's house, Fort Peterbilt
December 25, 1005 CE

Gada opened the door to his house and looked out at a snow-covered field. Fort Peterbilt was looking awfully festive as Christmas morning rolled around. There was a Christmas tree near the Peterbilt. It had brightly colored strings tied to the limbs and little sacks filled with nuts and sweet treats. It made Gada smile.

Shane, Miriam, and Norman had told the locals all about Christmas and Santa Claus. Gada had questioned the parents about the celebration. The thing was, none of the Peterbilt people had been of the "don't celebrate Christmas because it's a pagan holiday" sort.

"It's mostly an excuse to have a nice feast and give presents to the children," Alyssa explained.

"And each other," Michael added, with a grin at his wife. "Good food and good fellowship."

As it happened, the priests of Hocha also had a celebration held on the shortest day of the year, but that celebration involved the sacrifice of young women in order to persuade the gods to change their minds and bring back summer.

Yes, Gada thought. *This is much better than what they will be doing in Hocha in a few days. First, it doesn't involve killing teenage girls.*

In a little while Santa Claus would be welcomed into Fort Peterbilt and the jolly old elf was bringing all sorts of presents to good little girls and boys.

He smiled again at the snow-crowned Christmas tree and went back inside to get into his Santa outfit.

Over the next four hours, Gada went around the homes in Fort Peterbilt and delivered presents and treats to every house. And every house was decorated, including Christmas trees and Christmas feasts. All in celebration of Jesus deciding to be born into a human body to end forever the practice of human sacrifice.

He reached the Peterbilt and noted the rumble as its engines idled, keeping the interior warm and powering the lights and other stuff. The first Christmas since the arrival of the Peterbilt people was a white Christmas.

The most popular present was a carved and painted Peterbilt truck with wheels that actually spun. And, of course, a pickup truck. But there were also scarves and shirts, because knitting—or maybe it was crocheting—had been developed by the folk of Jabir.

He gave Melanie the scarves.

Melanie smiled and shook her head. All she'd been able to tell the locals was that there were little hooks on long sticks and women could use them to make cloth of a sort. That had been enough, as it turned out. The locals had brought her several examples of hooks and she'd approved the ones that looked most like what she'd remembered. Then the women had gone off with thread and experimented. Melanie wasn't at all sure what they'd come up with was either knitting or crocheting, but it seemed to work.

Melanie got half a dozen knit scarves. They used a hemp thread that the locals had had before the Peterbilt people had arrived.

Then they all went back to Gada's house, where there was a Christmas feast laid out, turkey and yams, but also venison and fish, and every sort of treat the locals could come up with.

CHAPTER 12

NOT ENOUGH KNOWLEDGE

Jefferson house, Fort Peterbilt
February 26, 1006 CE

Alyssa looked out the window to see snow falling on the ground. The window was the rear window from her Honda Civic, seated unopenable in one wattle-and-daub wall of her house. It was cold in the house, but not that cold. The hood—part of the hood—of the Civic was now a stove top, oven and fireplace with a chimney of clay and stone that allowed the fire to heat the house, at least the front room of the house, without smoking up the interior. The same process was now being used in Jabir and the village of Kallabi, though much of Kallabi's priesthood disapproved.

The people who had fireplaces with flues and dampers were happy they had them, feeling that they were a great innovation in winter. Also for cooking in rainy weather.

Nature called and Alyssa went to use the chamber pot. It was clay turned on a potter's wheel and glazed in a purple so dark it was almost black. It also had a lid. It wasn't that they couldn't make the pipes for a proper toilet, it was just that they couldn't make the plumbing for a lot of toilets. Not with everything else they had to do. So most of the houses in Fort Peterbilt used chamber pots that were emptied into a large wheeled barrel that was then taken out to a pit about a hundred yards outside the walls and far from the river to minimize runoff.

151

Having finished her business, Alyssa went to the fireplace and added some sticks to the fire. Then she poured hot water into a pot and added ground corn and dried berries, and some dried wild turkey meat. This formed a porridge that was the standard breakfast in Fort Peterbilt. The kids would be up soon.

Four hours later, Alyssa was working in her laboratory when there was a disturbance at the gate. More curious than concerned, Alyssa left the house and looked at the gate.

The gate was two heavy wooden doors held in place by hand-made steel hinges. It was kept open during the day, but closed and barred at night. The steel hinges had been forged from a part of the frame of her Honda Civic.

Steel could be deformed well below its melting point. Besides, over the winter, Michael had built a bellows for a smithy to provide forced air to make the fire hotter, allowing them to shape iron and to melt copper, which the locals already had. And apparently had had for centuries. Copies of the bellows Michael built were now being used to make stoneware and they were working on making glass.

But right now, the delegation in fancy robes and headgear, including a face mask, were pushing their way toward the Peterbilt. Along with them was Priyak.

There were also some warriors, also dressed a bit differently than the folks from Jabir. Alyssa was pretty sure they were the priesthood from Hocha. The ones her kids and the native kids had taken to calling the Pharisees.

Michael was climbing down from the truck and he had the Glock in its holster on his belt. Shane was running hell-for-leather toward the Peterbilt from the outdoor communal kitchen.

Shane got to the Peterbilt before Michael met the delegation and Melanie was on her way when Alyssa saw Zara in the cab of the Peterbilt, unlocking the door to let Shane in.

Alyssa looked back at the delegation, who'd apparently seen Zara through the Peterbilt's windows.

They stopped and started having an argument among themselves. Priyak was more familiar with window glass. Several of the houses in Fort Peterbilt had at least some glass inset into their walls. There'd been a lot in the remains of the store, and even a small piece let some light in and let someone look out.

But the Peterbilt, with its front windshield and its side windows, was *impressive*. Especially to someone who'd never seen glass before they arrived in Fort Peterbilt.

They were still arguing when Michael reached them, followed shortly by Gada, Achanu and Hamadi.

Then the priests started talking. Alyssa could understand them, barely. There was apparently a difference in accent between the people who lived in Hocha and the people who lived in the villages.

"You will bring us the girl, Zara!" said the guy in the face mask. "The gods demand it."

Achanu said, "They want you to give them Zara. They say the gods demand it."

"My god doesn't," Michael said. He didn't speak loudly, but he did speak firmly and he spoke in Kadlok.

Fazel arrived in time to hear that, and nodded.

"The gods will destroy you if you deny them," the priest in the mask said. "It's happened before."

Alyssa knew that the Kadlo had legends of earlier peoples who were destroyed because they refused to provide proper sacrifice to the gods. Crops failing, people starving, cannibalism, all because the tribe had failed to provide proper sacrifice to the gods. So the threat wasn't an idle one.

That was, she realized, one of the great differences between the modern religions and the ancient ones that existed earlier. Those earlier faiths had almost universally offered retribution for failing to show the gods proper respect in this world, not in the next. Fail to make sacrifices, and next year's crop will fail, and you and your family will starve. Nothing, or at least very little, along the lines of reward or punishment in the hereafter. What Joe Hill called "Pie in the sky by and by."

"The crops will fail if the land is overused," Alyssa said. "It has nothing to do with the sacrifices you make. It's a matter of chemistry and biology." Some of that was said in Kadlo, but some words were in English. There weren't words for the concepts in Kadlo. No terms for sciences or nonspecific learning. It wasn't that they didn't use chemistry and biology. They did and in some cases quite effectively, but there was no field of study of the bodies of knowledge. There were coppersmiths, potters, flint knappers, farmers, fishermen, hunters, and so on, but no chemists or biologists. Not outside of Fort Peterbilt and the village of Jabir, anyway.

"You don't know anything, woman," Facemask said.

"They know what the far side of the moon looks like," said Gada. "Which means they know more than you do."

By now there were quite a few people gathered around. The village of Jabir had a population of around seven hundred people and perhaps two hundred of them had moved to Fort Peterbilt over the fall and winter. Partly to learn from the Peterbilt people, but partly for things like the chimneys and the window glass. That migration was mostly the crafters of Jabir, potters, coppersmiths, flint knappers and the like. What Benjamin Franklin had called the middle people. They'd come for the pottery, wheels, and the bellows for the forges, and so on.

And now they stood around and watched as the Peterbilt people stood their ground and refused to yield to the priests of Hocha. Jesus may have let the Pharisees take him, but the people of Fort Peterbilt wouldn't be Peter to deny Jesus three times before the cock crowed, or Judas selling him out for thirty pieces of silver.

"Give her to us!" bellowed Facemask.

"No!" said Michael, not shouting, but not whispering either.

The delegation from Hocha looked around and realized that there was virtually no one on their side.

Then, with their tails firmly, if figuratively, between their legs, they left.

"There is going to be trouble over this," Gada said.

"You think—" Michael started, but Gada shook his head and said, "No. You did the right thing, but they won't let it stand. If Fort Peterbilt is a place safe from them, they are weakened badly. They *can't* let it stand. And I suspect that they are even more terrified of Alyssa than of you. For, if it's fertilizer and crop rotation that prevent famine, then who needs the gods and who needs *them*?"

"What will they do?" Alyssa asked.

"That's the thing that bothers me. I don't know what they can do."

"What about a straight-up attack like the one last spring, but bigger?" asked Shane, who at thirteen was a bloody-minded girl.

"That might be their only option," Gada agreed, "or at least it might seem that way to them."

"In that case, we need to get ready," Michael said.

"Catapults and claymores," said Alyssa. "We have a good stock of black powder." Over the last year since their arrival, Alyssa had made hundreds of pounds of black powder. Most of that had been used in construction. Fill a large crockery pot full of black powder, bury it in a hole, then use a copper wire to send it a spark, and you have a much bigger hole. Or you've removed a tree trunk, or a large rock.

And as she thought about it, the same thing could be done with the same pot and chunks of rock to make a poor man's claymore. They didn't have much of her Honda Civic left. Every bit of the steel in that car was in use, either in its original form, like the two wheels of which each were part of a one-wheeled cart now, or the passenger seats that were now in the Jefferson house. Or like what was left of the engine block. It was hammered into plows, and the blade for a wooden bulldozer attachment for the pickup truck.

Meanwhile, since the priesthood in Hocha knew about her, Zara was released from the Peterbilt. By now, with nothing to do but read Shane's sixth grade textbooks and practice English, she was well versed in a sixth grader's knowledge of math, geography, general science, and English.

She, with relief, moved out of the Peterbilt and into the Jefferson house with Alyssa and her children.

For the next several months, the Pharisees of Hocha took no action.

The spring crops were planted, more goods were made, iron and steel was made from bog iron, pots and ornaments were made from clay and fired in a brick kiln. Wood was carved using steel blades and, in general, the village of Jabir and Fort Peterbilt got richer.

Forge, Fort Peterbilt
March 27, 1006 CE

Bajak pulled the bloom of iron from the forge using the tongs, then used the hammer to whack it, collecting a burn on his arm as a bit of hot flux flew off the iron bloom. It stung, but he didn't lose his hold on the bloom of iron.

Bajak wasn't nearly as tall as Michael Anderle, but for his people, he was a big man. He stood five feet nine inches tall and weighed close to two hundred pounds, mostly muscle. He was thirty-five years old and a poor hunter, but an excellent flint knapper and carver.

Now he was trying to add the skill of blacksmithing to his repertoire. He hammered the bloom several more times until the red glow had faded, then put it back in the forge. The Peterbilt people were doing what they could, but increasingly, Bajak was coming to the conclusion that they themselves didn't understand what they were trying to teach the people.

Even the Peterbilt people didn't know enough. As he thought about it, Bajak realized that he rather liked it like that. They had given him the start. He would figure out the rest.

The bloom was glowing red again. He pulled it out and went back to hammering.

Three hours later, Bajak had a chunk of iron. He put it back in the fire and once it was red hot again, he started hammering it into a sheet, but not a thin sheet. It would be roughly half an inch thick when he was done. But it would be four inches long and six wide and he'd be able to attach it to a log and have his own anvil.

Jefferson house, Fort Peterbilt
March 27, 1006 CE

Alyssa sat in her house in the light of a lamp with paper and pen. The paper was locally made, as was the ink. The pen was a sharpened turkey feather. And Alyssa was trying to remember the processes for creating or refining vitamin C. It wasn't all that urgent. Corn provides some vitamin C, but cornmeal provides none. For that matter, the same process that made niacin available for preventing pellagra also removed the vitamin C, causing scurvy, assuming that you didn't get the vitamin C somewhere else like fruits or vegetables.

She sighed and got back to work. In spite of Michael's claims that she was a "know-it-all," she didn't know nearly enough.

Fort Peterbilt
July 4, 1006 CE

Alyssa lit the fuse and the string of firecrackers went off with a *crack, crack, crack, crack!* This was the second Fourth of July in this time. The locals had had a bit over a year to learn what it was about. The United States of America. As it happened, Shane's sixth grade textbook was on world history, not American history. So no one had a copy of the United States Constitution. On the other hand, the Anderles were reasonably well read and Alyssa Jefferson was a darn know-it-all. Between them, they'd cobbled together a fairly decent approximation of what was in it.

Three branches of government: legislature, executive and courts. Executive and Legislature elected by the citizens. The locals found elections an interesting concept and not altogether foreign to what they did.

Protection of individual rights. That one had raised some eyebrows. They were a tribal people and the village, the clan, came first.

Everyone is equal before the law. Again, some raised eyebrows. Different people in the clan held different status. The notion that that wasn't fair had come as a bit of a shock.

You have the right to speak your mind and to follow your own beliefs. Sure. Within reason. But some of the stuff that people believe is pretty stupid.

Really? Even the stupid and offensive stuff? You can't be serious.

You can't be forced to give evidence against yourself? But how do you prove someone did something if they won't admit it?

The right to keep and bear arms? But considering most arms in the here and now were clubs or bows and arrows, that wasn't all that much of an issue. After all, you could make your own and most people did.

Though, considering the Peterbilt people's weapons, the locals could see how it might become one over time.

Slowly, the notion of a nation made up of states was starting to take hold.

Shane's sixth grade textbook did discuss city states which were close enough to the villages like Jabir for a comparison.

Jabir decided to experiment with elections to the women's council.

Jefferson house, Fort Peterbilt
July 17, 1006 CE

Melanie almost didn't make it outside before she threw up. And, for a moment, Michael was concerned about something in the food. But then he remembered. He'd been through this before with Shane.

Michael had been just back from the Stan and still in the army when Melanie had started puking last time. Seven months later, Shane had arrived. Things had been tough for a while after that, with Michael just out of the army, having to take any job he could to make rent. He'd learned to drive a big rig in the army, so he had the skills to find good-paying work, but not work that would let him help with the baby. All those memories came rushing back as Melanie was puking her guts out next to the Peterbilt. It hadn't been an easy time. But they'd had modern medicine and healthcare. In the here and now, making a baby was a lot more dangerous.

Michael started to worry.

A couple of hours later as they discussed the issue with Alyssa, they got even more worried. Alyssa was a chemist and a chemistry professor with a good but not infinite knowledge of chemistry. She could make dietary recommendations, but the first one was useless. "If we had domestic animals, I would recommend milk and cheese. But we don't." She scratched her head. "Eggs, probably turkey eggs, since we don't have chickens. Also cruciferous vegetables, but we don't have those either. Spinach is native to Asia. These people have to get calcium somewhere.

"Some of that's growing in the gardens," Shane said. "We have tomatoes and there was cabbage and brussels sprouts in the seed rack at the general store. And they already have berries."

"Good point. Beans, maybe. Yes, probably beans and fish. There are a host of other vitamins and minerals that we are going to need to work on. We need to talk to the local women, and then I'm going to have to do some chemistry."

PART III

PART III

CHAPTER 13

ATTACK

Kadlo Mound, Hocha
August 10, 1006 CE

Months had passed and the fall sacrifice was only a month and a half away. Lomhar was under increasing pressure to bring his daughter back from Jabir.

"They say that because you hid your daughter away, showing disrespect to the gods, the rest of the sacrifice will have to be doubled." Jakun's face was red as he leaned over the table to hiss in Lomhar's face.

"Then send your children home to your village," Lomhar said.

There were eighteen villages among the Kadlo. But the Kacla had twenty-two, the Purdak twenty-five, the Gruda twenty-one, and the Lomak seventeen. Altogether, it was one hundred and three villages that looked to Hocha to one extent or another. The villages averaged out to something like six hundred people per village. That was sixty-one thousand people and there were fifteen thousand people in Hocha itself.

But the clans weren't all enamored of the rule by the priests in Hocha. What had held them in line was the fear that if the priests were defied, the gods would take revenge and the crops would fail.

Neolithic farmers were *never* far from starvation, so the promises of someone who could, or claimed to be able to prevent crop failure, were powerful. That was true no matter where or when you lived, if you lived close to the edge.

But Jesus didn't demand sacrifices to make the crops come in. Instead, he had sacrificed himself to save his followers, asking only that they be good to one another. And his angel, Peterbilt, had brought teachers to protect the harvest without the need of sacrifices.

By now Lomhar was utterly convinced of that. Since he'd refused to give his daughter to the priests, he pretty much had to be convinced of that just to be able to live with himself. "The priests can't prevent or cause crop failures. It's beyond their power and always has been. So collect your daughters and take them out of Hocha. Take them home to your village and use compost."

"Compost" was a Kadlok word. The Kadlo, all the clans, had been using compost to some extent for hundreds of years. But it was just something some of the women did and the priests insisted that it didn't make much difference. The floods both fertilized and made the ground easier to hoe. That was part of the reason that their culture was centered around the Mississippi River system. That, and the fact that with canoes the river system made trade practical from the headwaters of the Mississippi all the way to the Gulf of Mexico. What Alyssa Jefferson had done over the summer and fall was provide a coherent explanation for how it all worked. One that didn't involve the pleasure or anger of gods. Alyssa Jefferson had used her knowledge of chemistry combined with the knowledge of Gada, the shaman, and of the women's council to come up with a better mix of leaves, fish guts, poop and other things to provide the corn, beans, squash and other crops really good food.

Then add in the fact that the Ram truck having made it possible for the village of Jabir to plant almost twice the land it had the year before meant that as this last fall's crop came in, the villagers of Jabir had more than twice the food they'd had the year before. And with the freezers, they had even more. Then there was the pickling and preserving that they'd introduced.

And visitors from Jabir were bragging about it all up and down the river.

And there was the writing. The priests and shamans had already had tools to record specific things. How you knotted a pouch to tell you which herb was in it, that sort of thing. But writing was flexible. It could record anything. And the mathematics of Shane's textbooks was spreading first from Jabir to the other villages of the Kadlo clan, then from those villages to the villages of the other clans.

All that knowledge, especially the math, was making things very tense in Hocha.

Kadlo Mound, Hocha
August 17, 1006 CE

The knock at the door of Lomhar's hut was quiet. It wouldn't have woken Lomhar where he slept. However, Lomhar's servant Akvan, the son of his cousin, slept in the front room. Akvan was friends with an under-priest of the temple. As it happened, they were very close friends and Akvan wasn't all that pleased with Lomhar's actions. Not that he didn't like Zara, but the gods' displeasure could destroy everyone. And that sort of defiance of the priesthood could bring retribution on the whole Kadlo clan.

"Ho-Chag Kotep has issued an order for Lomhar's arrest," Akvan's friend said.

"I was afraid of that," Akvan whispered back. He hated the idea of his clan leader being sacrificed, but Lomhar had brought it on himself.

His friend reached out and grabbed him by the shoulder. "You don't understand. It's for the whole family. They will take you too if you're here. You have to come away."

"But I've always been loyal to Hocha and the priesthood."

"It's gone beyond that, Akvan. The council is going to crush Jabir and destroy the demon Peterbilt. All the Peterbilt people are to go under the knife. You have to get away."

Akvan looked at his friend in shock. Then said, "All right. I'll collect my gear and go back to Kallabi."

"Good. I have to go. I wasn't supposed to warn you." No one knew about their relationship.

Akvan started to collect his things, then he stopped. Why had his friend warned him? If it would really offend the gods, was warning him any different than taking Zara off to the Peterbilt people at Fort Peterbilt?

Every day the Peterbilt people of Fort Peterbilt offered more things that brought the priesthood's power to influence the gods further into question. And everyone around him seemed willing to put aside the will of the gods for no more than what they wanted.

In all his life, he'd never really doubted the gods or the idea that they could be persuaded to leave people alone, even protect people, if they were just paid off.

And Akvan had accepted that. Accepted even that if the gods required it, he would go under the knife. The needs of the many outweighed the needs of the few.

But not, apparently, if the few included people you cared about. And as angry with his father's cousin as he'd been for these last months, he did care about Lomhar and his wife, Zanni. They had welcomed him and treated him well, much better than some of the servants in Hocha.

Hating himself as a coward and a traitor to the gods, he went to wake his father's cousin.

An hour later, Lomhar was talking to Roshan. "They are coming for my family. We have to leave."

"Yes, you do," Roshan agreed.

"You're from Jabir. You should leave too."

"No. That's part of the reason you need to leave. They're counting on me reacting when they come to take you. If you're not here, I won't be forced to defend you and defy them. Without that, they have no cause to take action against me or any of the other Kadlo chiefs. If they do, that will cause the other clans to rebel, at least some of them."

Roshan was a convert to the cross god. He even wore the cross openly. But he had not actually defied the priests in any way that would let them take action against him. "No, Lomhar. Take your wife and that nephew of yours and warn the Peterbilt people. I will stay here and watch. We need to keep watch on what the Pharisees are doing."

Talak River
August 18, 1006 CE

The Talak River tied Mississippian culture together. Goods and ideas flowed up and down it. Its fish and the wildlife that surrounded it and its tributaries fed the people of the Mississippian culture. This far upriver it was traveling at less than two miles an hour, but a canoe added about two and a half to that, so they were traveling at a solid four miles an hour down the Talak, taking turns at the paddles. Lomhar, Zanni, and Akvan managed about fifty miles before they stopped for the night. This morning, they'd all woken with sore muscles from yesterday's trip. None of them were as used to this sort of effort as they thought they were. Life in Hocha had softened them.

Two hours later they were at the mouth of the Agla river, what the Peterbilt people knew as the Kaskaskia. Then things got harder. Now they were traveling upstream and the flow that had helped them now slowed them. Where they could, they pulled the canoe close into the shore and got out and walked, pulling the canoe along behind them. It was faster and less work to walk pulling the canoe.

Still, it was well past noon when they reached Bashk Creek that Fort Peterbilt was next to, and another hour before they reached the fort. The big gates of the fort were closed, but the small one next to the creek was open.

They tied the canoe to a log and squished up to the gate.

Almost immediately runners were sent to Jabir. The runners made excellent time. By now there was a wide road of packed earth and gravel from Fort Peterbilt to Jabir. It went along the creek to the Agla River, then along the Agla to Jabir.

Fifteen minutes later, now in dry slippers, Lomhar met with Hamadi and the other clan chiefs of Jabir along with Michael Anderle. Shortly after they started talking, Michael sent for Alyssa Jefferson. She was, after all, the one who had built most of their defenses, at least the burning-and-blowing-up part of them. Michael was the main designer of the catapults, but the napalm to go in them was all Alyssa's.

"Why arrest you?" Hamadi demanded. "They must know it's going to enrage the other clan chiefs, and not just the Kadlo clan chiefs, but the chiefs of all the clans. It was a stupid move."

"They didn't want him telling us what they had planned," Michael said. "How long will it take them to raise a force?"

"It depends on the size of the force; the priest guards are over seven hundred men. But they can't send them all or there might be a revolt in Hocha. But if they leave a hundred in Hocha, that will let them send around six hundred men armed with bows and gunpowder bombs."

There had never been any way of preventing the knowledge of how to make black powder from getting out. The apothecaries of the Kadlo were familiar with all the components of black powder. They just didn't know about mixing them to make an explosive. Knowing that, Alyssa hadn't even tried. She'd shown Gada how to make it and use it, and anyone else who wanted to know and had something that sounded like a good reason. She'd been a lot more reticent about the napalm she made from fuel oil and Styrofoam.

"That's not nearly enough," Alyssa said. "And they darn well ought to know it."

"I've been thinking of that the whole way here," Lomhar said. "I think that Michael is right. The reason they decided to arrest me when they did was because they'd sent for levies from the other clans. Not for labor, but to make an army. That's also why they waited till the crops were in. Between the preservation from last year's harvest and the huge size of this year's, there is a fortune in maize and beans in the storehouses."

"So what does that mean in terms of time and the size of the army?" Alyssa asked.

"A few weeks, maybe a month."

"You're forgetting something," Hamadi said. "They know you escaped. They don't know how much of their plans you know. If all you knew was that you were to be arrested, that would be one thing. Not all that important. But what if you knew their plans in detail? What if whatever spy you have in their ranks told you everything? That would be a different matter. I think they will be afraid of what you can tell us, and they will rush things, not take time to train their forces together. Instead, move as fast as they can."

"In that case, sooner. A few days to two weeks," Lomhar said.

"We need to put out scouts, and in the meantime, we need to move all our people to Fort Peterbilt," Hamadi said.

"If we're moving everyone from Jabir to Fort Peterbilt," Alyssa said, "we also need to move the food. All the corn, the beans, the squash. Also the dried meat and fish. We may be facing a siege."

Then they ran into a translation problem. Sieges take supply trains. Starving out a town takes time and a large force, but you have to feed that large force, and feeding such a large force was difficult in the Mississippian culture. Though things like sieges had happened, they weren't common. They weren't a standard part of warfare with their own name. So Alyssa had to explain the word. The Kadlo chiefs got it, but didn't think much of it as a plan for winning a war. Especially in these circumstances. But they agreed that bringing all the food to be stored in Fort Peterbilt was a good idea. More to deny it to the attackers than because they thought they would need it.

Fort Peterbilt was pretty big. It had a ten-foot-high curtain wall, but that wall was on top of a five-foot-tall mound that was behind a five-foot-deep ditch, so to get over the wall you needed a twenty-foot ladder. Or you needed to place your ladder on top of the five-foot mound. That was not an easy thing to do.

The walls had hard points. Towers that held catapults that could throw rocks several hundred feet. And there had been enough visitors to Fort Peterbilt that it was a safe bet that they knew the layout. But they didn't know everything.

Mississippian culture was familiar with copper. They used it for tools and ornaments. They knew how to find it and refine it. Add in the Peterbilt people and their knowledge, and the Mississippians now knew how to stretch it into copper wire. And after a year of experimentation, they had insulation too. It was poor insulation, but it worked well enough. Well enough for Alyssa and several of the women of Fort Peterbilt to make and install claymore mines about halfway up the inside of the ditch outside the wall and wire all those claymores into a switch box. They didn't have metal balls. Metal was much too expensive for that. It was in the words of *Jesus Christ Superstar*: "The rocks and stones themselves" were going to sing.

It took them eight days to get everyone out of Jabir.

Then they waited.

Fort Peterbilt
August 29, 1006 CE

Zara was standing on the wall of Fort Peterbilt, crying. "It's all my fault," she blubbered as she watched the army of Hocha invest Fort Peterbilt.

Shane had had about enough of that. She knew that Zara had grown up believing in the gods of Hocha. And she knew that she was supposed to respect other people's religion, even if she wasn't all that clear on why. But this was just silly. Then suddenly, where Zara was standing struck her, and she started laughing.

Zara turned to look at her, shocked and angry.

"You're Helen of Troy!" Shane pointed.

"Who?"

So, still giggling, Shane explained about Helen of Troy, at least what she knew, which honestly wasn't much.

Then she said, "No, you're right. You can't be Helen of Troy. You're not pretty enough. If Peter or Paris, or whoever it was, was going to kidnap someone, it would have been me."

The argument got rather heated then, with Shane talking about the girl who launched a thousand canoes. Which was, in its way, pretty accurate. The force had come by way of the river in canoes. In fact, a fair chunk of the force had bypassed the fort, and gone to Jabir to burn the village to the ground.

Outside Fort Peterbilt
August 30, 1006 CE

"There was no food at all?" the commander asked.

"None. They took everything."

It was bad news. The new wealth of Jabir was part of what brought the army together. People expected to get food, textiles, copper, all sorts of things. Instead, the village had been stripped of everything of value. It also meant that his just over three thousand men were going to run out of food in about a day and a half. "Well, that decides it. We attack tomorrow before dawn."

"I'd like more time to get them to work together."

"We don't have more time."

Walls, Fort Peterbilt
August 31, 1006 CE

The watchers on the towers shouted warning, and Alyssa pulled a switch. The lights came on. They were the same set of bright LED lights that they had used to scare Achanu and his friends the first night after they got here. They swept around on a pre-programmed course.

It had a similar effect, at least at first. But after screaming commands, the army came ahead.

Hocha's army, whose official name was the Paramount Priest's Guard, didn't have enough men to attack en masse all around the fort. They concentrated the attack pretty much where it was expected, the one place where the walls didn't have a ditch in front of them, the main gate. The one that was designed to let the Peterbilt out.

Michael and Melanie still slept in the Peterbilt, though Shane was spending the night with the Jeffersons and Zara more often than not these days. So Michael's duty station was next to his bed. He was in the driver's seat, starting the engine in moments. He pulled the air horn, and Melanie opened the passenger door and ran for her duty station. The air horn woke everyone in camp. People started rushing to their assigned places.

Alyssa's station was on the tower to the left of Peterbilt's gate. It let her see what was going on, and it had her switches to signal the positions on the wall. She also had her phone so she could talk to Shane, Melanie, and Michael at need, using the Peterbilt's Wi-Fi. It was also Hamadi's station for the same reason. He was in charge of the defense of Fort Peterbilt.

At Hamadi's direction, she moved the lights around to spot the enemy formation, and about then a rain of arrows started falling. It was more of a drizzle. They were decent bows, but their range was closer to fifty yards than a hundred.

The attackers were firing at a target above them, right at the edge of their range. And the outer wall of the curtain wall covered most of the defenders' bodies. That was the good news.

The bad news was that Hocha's army was spreading out as they approached the wall. Fort Peterbilt was strong. Its weakness was in the number of people available to defend the walls. A village of seven hundred had fewer than two hundred men of combat age. A lot of the women of Jabir were also on the walls, but as a rule they weren't as good with bows and arrows as the men, and not nearly as good with the war clubs.

What they could do was appear on the walls wearing men's hats so that it looked like there were more defenders than there actually were, and if necessary, drop rocks, gunpowder bombs, and napalm-filled Molotov cocktails over the walls on the heads of the attackers.

The women were in charge of the catapults.

It still wasn't enough to make up for the fact that they were being attacked by a force that was closer to three thousand than two thousand.

The defenders couldn't be strong everywhere, so they had to force the enemy to concentrate where they wanted them. Hamadi gave the order and hating herself for it, Alyssa called Melanie and Shane.

Shane was stationed at the left-side catapult; she wasn't in charge of it. That was a member of the women's council. It had been determined that the heavy weapons didn't need to be fired by men, and they needed the men shooting arrows. Shane reported, "Hamadi wants them herded to the Peterbilt's gate."

The type of catapult that Alyssa and Michael had agreed on, in consultation with the villagers, were trebuchets. That's basically a seesaw with a short arm, with a heavy weight throwing a much lighter weight with the long arm. A big advantage of a trebuchet is it can be cocked and left cocked without being ruined. That's not true of the stress-based catapults.

The trebuchet could also be aimed with a crank. Two women cranked them around to where the commander wanted them, and then one of the women pulled the cord. A clay vessel containing twenty-five gallons of napalm and a lit fuse flew through the sky and landed on the left side of the attacking force. The ceramic container shattered and the whole area was covered in fire. So were over a dozen of the attackers.

Men covered in burning gunk are not rational. They run around madly, trying anything to put the fire out, grabbing other people in the hopes of help. They put on quite a show, and the enemy bunched up toward the Peterbilt gate.

Melanie relayed the order to Kasni, who was in charge of the right catapult and the process and results were about the same. Melanie wanted to throw up. The other women on the wall looked rather pleased.

Back at the Peterbilt gate, Hamadi was watching the battle and nodding. Things, so far, were going surprisingly well.

People were starting to die, but that had become inevitable when Hocha decided to attack. More importantly, the attackers were bunching together and the demon weapons worked best against bunched attackers.

☆   ☆   ☆

The commander across the field felt very much the same way. He too wanted his force concentrated. He too wanted them in front of that huge gate. And he too had gunpowder bombs. The villagers of Jabir and Kallabi had been using the bang powder for over six months. And the priesthood of Hocha had had spies in Fort Peterbilt since before the new fort had been constructed. By now, not just the formula for what Alyssa Jefferson called corned powder, but the entire process of its production, was well known. And the army had hand bombs filled with the stuff. Heavy fired clay pots filled with corned powder and rocks with fuses that had been tested so they had a consistent burn rate.

But he also had two large bags of the corned powder each with fuses and he needed to get those bags up against the Peterbilt gate. Once the gate was blown, it was all over but the mopping up.

The heretics were doing just what he wanted them to. He shouted his orders, and the army surged forward.

The enemy was charging now and Hamadi stood there watching them calmly. Then he turned to Alyssa. "Call Michael."

Michael got his orders and revved the Peterbilt's engine to get the attention of the people at the gate. He blew the horn, one long and two shorts, and men lifted the bar from the gate, then pulled it open, and the attackers started to pour through. The gate was wide enough for the Peterbilt with a foot on either side, and the gates had stops so that they only opened so far. Just far enough to let the Peterbilt through. Not far enough to let anyone get out of the way.

Michael stomped on the gas and the Peterbilt surged forward into the mass of men pouring in the open gate. Ten tons of steel ran into the crowd, and it was already going fifteen miles an hour when it hit. It didn't slow, but it did bump as it rolled over the broken bodies of men who'd thought that they had gotten inside Fort Peterbilt.

He kept going. As soon as he was out the gate, the warriors jumped off the road into the ditches to either side of the gate. Ten feet later, Michael made a sharp right and proceeded along the flattened plain that circled Fort Peterbilt on his way to Jabir. As he drove, men jumped into the only safe place they could find, the ditch between the road and the walls of Fort Peterbilt.

Michael kept going. He needed to get the Peterbilt out of the way for the next round.

Achanu was with the group that had opened the gate. As the Peterbilt passed, it left a wake of destruction. Masses of men crushed and broken in the space between the doors of the Peterbilt gate. Then he saw something else. Two heavy cloth bags and each of them had strings running from them, and the strings were burning.

Achanu had been with the work crews using gunpowder to remove tree stumps or break rocks. He recognized what he was looking at. He ran forward over the mangled bodies, tripping and falling on a crushed rib cage to reach the two bags. He got to them. He reached and pulled the fuse from the first one, then the other. Then he grabbed the bags and, struggling a bit because each bag weighed more than thirty pounds, he brought them inside, where they wouldn't be set off by accident.

He was covered in blood and gore from tripping on the bodies, but he barely noticed that.

The enemy commander didn't see the failure of his plans. He'd been near the front and when the gates opened he, like everyone with him, had thought it was the gods smiling on them. He was dead under the wheels of the Peterbilt.

Alyssa watched the Peterbilt as it ran over people. It didn't get all that many. These were hunters. They knew what to do when faced with a buffalo stampede. Get out of the way.

The easiest way out of the way was the ditch.

In the ditch there were hollowed-out logs and ceramic pots buried in the wall side. No one noticed. They were too happy to be out of the way of the demon Peterbilt.

"Do it!" Hamadi commanded.

Hating herself, Alyssa pulled a switch. It was an alligator switch, two copper plates that fit into four plates. When the switch closed, the circuit was completed, and electricity from one of the generators went down the wires to hair-thin copper wires so thin that they couldn't carry the current. And resistance heated those wires to the melting point of copper in an instant. Way hotter than you needed to set off black powder.

Fifteen improvised explosive devices went off. The rocks and stones that were in front of the black powder "sang."

It was not a happy song.

But it was quite effective at conversion. They converted hundreds of men into hamburger, and sent body parts as much as fifty yards downrange.

At that point, the battle was over. The enemy didn't retreat. They just ran. And they kept running until exhaustion stopped them. Then, when they got their breath back, they walked.

They walked back to their villages. Some walked back toward Hocha, but they walked away. Away from Fort Peterbilt and the people who could call such power to them.

CHAPTER 14

MOON MISSION

Plains
August 31, 1006 CE

It was midafternoon and a small group of attackers, in their haste to get away from the battle, had run in the direction of the country store, part of which had been transferred by the Ring of Fire.

They were about halfway between the country store and Fort Peterbilt when they saw a glowing ball of lightning. It was three meters across, and when it was gone there was a cylinder lying on the ground. They ran again.

Inside the cylinder, Jerry Jefferson checked the readouts, then pushed a button. The top of the cylinder opened and he sat up. He looked around and cursed. He was supposed to have arrived at the country store. He moved controls and pressed buttons in the capsule, activating sensors. His sensor pack was much better than the one that had gone back in time attached to the Peterbilt.

Twenty-four years improves understanding a lot.

So Malcolm O'Connell had been right. The guidance of the temporal bolides sucked. So picking up Alyssa and the kids and going home was not going to be possible. Not until the tech got a lot better anyway.

Twenty-four years studying the slowly diminishing traces of

the temporal bolide that had taken his wife and children had taught them a lot. The atoms from the twenty-first century were subtly different in charge from the atoms of the eleventh. That was what had let them track his wife and children and the Anderles. It had also been what let them track the Peterbilt and the pickup truck as they moved about. They didn't know the details about what was going on even yet, but they knew rather a lot.

And knowing that, they had figured out a way for Jerry to send back messages. Unfortunately, there was no way for them to send Jerry a message except to make another temporal bolide, which was unlikely. This one had cost as much as the whole Apollo program had, adjusted for inflation. But at least he could tell them what was going on. He got out of his capsule and set up the signal.

It was simple in concept and a pain in the ass to construct. And it was based on the fact that an atom from this time had a subtly different atomic signature than an atom from Jerry's time. To make the readings easier they had a heavy concentration of the sort of atom that wouldn't be concentrated in this time. In this case, depleted uranium. Then they used a machine to move it back and forth at a controlled rate. That got you ones and zeros, and you were in.

The drawback was depleted uranium is a heavy material, and they needed fairly large chunks. Moving the eight chunks of depleted uranium back and forth took a lot of power and didn't happen fast, at least not fast when compared with computer speeds. The transmitter was energy-intensive and it had a slow data-transfer rate. About as good as a modem from early in the computer age. It had the equivalent of a 474 baud rate. Sucked for most things, but plenty for basic communication.

He turned it on now, let it warm up, and sent the code for "arrived safely."

Having done that, Jerry collected his rifle and backpack, and closed and locked the capsule. Then he started to call Alyssa. Started to, then didn't. He could, assuming her cell phone still worked. Part of what the capsule carried was a small but decent cell "tower," but he had spent the last twenty-four years trying to get here and only months, maybe a year, had passed for Alyssa. No one was sure how accurate the shot was going to be and Jerry knew that it wasn't anywhere near accurate enough spatially.

But the reason he didn't call was because he wanted Alyssa to see him before she heard him. The man she left was thirty-three years old. The man she was about to meet was fifty-seven. That was clear when you looked at him, but might be less clear over the phone. It was better if she saw him first. He was a healthy fifty-seven. Medical tech had improved over the last twenty-four years.

But he was still fifty-seven.

So he put on his backpack and started walking to where the Peterbilt and, more importantly, Alyssa and the kids had mostly been since shortly after they arrived in this time.

It took him four hours to walk, and he was in good shape, having trained for this for the last five years, ever since the science had led to engineering.

The lone man in a helmet and armor that walked up to the scene of the battle that evening was a shock to the natives, but at the same time, he wasn't. He was alike in many ways to the Peterbilt people they already knew.

Immediately, Alyssa, Melanie and Michael were called.

The man was wearing camouflage armor and a combat helmet with a faceplate visor that had a heads-up display built in. As soon as he saw them, he took off the helmet.

It was Jerry, Alyssa saw.

Jerry. But a Jerry changed. Older. There was gray peppering her thirty-three-year-old husband's black hair, and lines around his eyes and mouth.

"Sorry it took so long. But we had to figure out how to do it."

"How long did it take?" Melanie Anderle asked.

"Twenty-four years, two months, and three days since the temporal bolide sent you folks here."

"Are you here to bring us home?" Melanie asked. Alyssa was still just looking at him. Then she ran forward, grabbed him, hugged him, and kissed him. She was crying and so was he. It took a while before Melanie got her question answered.

"I'm afraid not," Jerry told them later, after he'd been reintroduced to his kids. They weren't as comfortable with Daddy coming back as Alyssa. And that wasn't because of how much he'd changed, at least not mostly. It was simply that a year is a long time for a girl who's just turned seven, and even longer for a boy who is five and a half.

"Why not?" Michael asked. "Melanie is pregnant. We need to get her to modern obstetrics."

"I'm sorry. I didn't know that, none of us did. But the reason we can't go back, any of us, is aim. Our aim sucks, and according to Malcolm O'Connell, it's not going to get better until there is a theoretical breakthrough. The whole thing about sending men or robots to a specific place on the moon or Mars is misleading. You can refine your targeting en route when you're doing that. This is like shooting a pistol or throwing a spear. Once you shoot it's over, you can't correct it. If they tried to send a bolide to get us, replacing us with, say, machines, it would probably miss and you know what happens to anything that happens to be in the way of the bolide wall. I don't want to risk having you guys cut in half."

"What about a bigger bolide?" Shane asked.

"Energy increases by the eleventh power of the mass transferred. Best estimate is that the one that moved the cruise ship required as much energy as our sun puts out in about twenty years.

"There is good news. I brought chicken eggs and a bunch of vegetable seeds. As soon as we move my capsule here, we can unload those and start sending them data on what's happening in this time.

"In fact, I had to promise to do that faithfully in order to get the government to pay for the project."

"Good for you. But I didn't make any promises," Michael said. He was still angry that he wasn't going to be able to get Melanie back to modern obstetrics. "And Hamadi here certainly didn't." Michael wasn't happy to learn that they were stuck here for life, not after that brief moment of hope that they could go home.

"No, but I didn't come empty-handed. Like I said I brought equipment, eggs and seeds, and, more importantly, I brought knowledge."

"What sort of knowledge?" Alyssa asked, still keeping one of Jerry's arms in a viselike grip.

"First, let me clear up a few questions. Okay, love?" Jerry asked. "The first thing that the temporal bolides taught us is that the multi-world theory is basically accurate. The second thing it taught us is that the part of that theory that says those worlds can't interact is total crap. That much was pretty much obvious from the fact that they never found the remains of Grantville in modern Germany. Well, that and the fact that our world didn't disappear. The various probability universes can interact, and anytime they do, which is pretty much constantly, a new universe is created.

"But having that sort of interaction on anything more than a subatomic scale takes a massive amount of energy."

"That's all very interesting," Melanie said, "and I would like to hear much more about it sometime over a cold brew. But, right now, what did you bring? What sort of knowledge? Anything on obstetrics, perhaps, or prenatal foods?"

Jerry grinned. "Sure. Both those and more. It's really a question of what knowledge I didn't bring. That may be overstating things a bit, but using a lot of compression and a triple redundancy, we have about ten petabytes of data. That's the equivalent of about half the stuff in the Library of Congress. It's not the Library of Congress. For one thing, the Library of Congress has a lot of redundancy, pictures and phrases that appear in hundreds of books. The system I brought stores the picture or phrase in one place and then just references it. Well, in three places, we used triple redundancy for everything.

"But we have effective instructions about how to make most everything ever made. And about medical care, including obstetrics and surgery. That doesn't make me into a surgeon, or mean that we can make everything we might want now. But we will be able to, once we build the tools to build the tools. I did bring some of those tools. Perhaps the most important is a micro 3D printer. It's slow, but it works. And there is the information to teach someone to be a doctor, even expert systems to help identify diseases and injuries, and come up with treatments. So though I can't get you back to Johns Hopkins, I brought some of Johns Hopkins with me."

"In that case, Mr. Jefferson, let's go get your capsule."

Michael used the Peterbilt to go fetch the capsule and bring it to the fort. Once it was in place and hooked up to one of the generators, Jerry pulled out a dozen more "cell phones," and pointed out that there were the chips for a thousand more once they could build bodies for them. The "cell phones" Jerry brought out weren't the cell phones of the twenty-thirties. They were glasses. Wraparound glasses that produced a heads-up display that provided the wearer with what amounted to a wearable personal computer with cell phone functions as well.

The bodies that would house the molecular chips didn't have to be standard cell phone bodies. They could be built into just about any device or put in stations elsewhere as long as they could wire the chips into them. And part of the information Jerry brought with him was how-to videos on how to build the housings and devices to hook up to the chips. The glasses fit into helmets, and turned the helmet into an interactive learning center.

And in the capsule was a projector to project movies, both entertaining and informative, onto any flat white surface, so that the classes full of people could be taught all at once. This was all in English for the simple reason that no one in the future knew the local language.

But the medical information that Jerry brought included pictures and videos of how to do a great deal, and that was vital because Melanie wasn't the only pregnant woman in Fort Peterbilt and certainly wasn't the only person in need of treatment.

Over the next weeks, months, and years, Jerry Jefferson's capsule would train doctors, engineers, scientists, and much more. But that would take years of work and the training of experts and building of tools.

Fort Peterbilt
September 1, 1006 CE

Jerry Jefferson opened the capsule as he'd practiced hundreds of times during training. Now, as then, he had an audience. "I'll never be a scientist," Jerry said. "That was obvious when I married supernerd here." He waved to indicate Alyssa. "But after years of training, I'm a competent technician, at least with this gear."

Alyssa snorted in derision.

"It's true," Jerry said. "I admit even the nerds at NTSA admitted that electrons hate me." He pronounced it Natsa.

"Natsa?" Michael asked.

"National Temporal and Space Administration. The name change came out of the research for this project. Just like the moonshot back in the twentieth, it had spinoffs. Including a *much* cheaper way to climb out of a gravity well." He plugged a cable in and checked the charge. "Anyway, as I was saying, even the nerds at NTSA were finally forced to admit that I would never be a scientist."

"I could have told them that," Alyssa said.

"But they did manage, by dint of extensive training over the course of years, to turn me into a competent technician, at least in regard to this gear.

"Alyssa's right, though," he continued. "I knew I'd never be as smart as my wife before I asked Nerdgirl to marry me. I was always a good salesman and I can tell a good story in a bar or in front of a congressional committee, but even after decades of trying, the scientists back in the twenty-first century weren't able to make me into a scientist. Which almost got me dumped from the project in spite of my personal connection." He looked and smiled at his wife.

"But like I said, I can tell a good story even before a congressional committee. Once the brain cases knew they were stuck with me, they turned their efforts to teaching me what I could learn. I *am* a skilled tech, at least with this gear, and, more importantly, I'm a fully trained librarian. At least in regard to this library. But that's less important to you right now than this."

He pulled out another panel and took out a collection of seeds in sealed plastic containers, all carefully marked. He pulled one. "This is winter wheat. Short stalked and robust." He handed the container to Alyssa and continued. "I'll pull up the particulars of how and when to plant it later. I also brought watermelon, cantaloupe, apple trees of several varieties, walnuts, all sorts of things, at least twenty seeds for each of over two hundred sorts of plant. And for some, like the winter wheat, hundreds of seeds. Some will have to wait for spring, but a few you'll be able to plant now or at least soon. What is the date?"

As it happened, the locals had had means of determining the time of year based on what twenty-first-century archaeologists called woodhenges placed in Hocha, what twenty-first-century archaeologists called Cahokia. Using those over the last year and a half had reset the clocks on their phones to match their best estimate of the date according to the position of the sun at sunrise.

It was the first of September by their clocks, and given when they calculated the shortest and longest day of the year, by the one in the capsule as well.

The next thing he pulled out of the capsule was a small box with a lens in the front. "Do you have a flat wall, preferably painted white?"

They did. The houses in Fort Peterbilt were painted in a variety of colors but several of them were white. It took him about an hour, but he set up the projector on a table pointed at the wall and started it playing educational films from the digital library in the capsule. Then, while so many of the natives were watching movies, Jerry climbed back in his capsule, put on his glasses phone so as to provide him with a heads-up screen, and started typing on a virtual keyboard. Whatever Michael said about him not being a party to any deals with the people from the twenty-first century, Jerry had made those deals and meant to keep faith with them.

The capsule was three meters long and two wide and tall, and better than half of it had arrived underground. They had learned through tests and models that sending an object back in time replaced it with an equal amount of mass from that time. That was why the ground level was a little lower in the circle around the country store. The mass of the Peterbilt, the pickup, and the building all put together amounted to about two and a half inches of extra soil back in the twenty-first century. And that meant that you couldn't drop something onto a plane a thousand years ago. Air has a lot less mass than earth and both mass and total volume within the transfer locus must match.

You had to drop it into that plane with enough mass coming as going. And the capsule was heavy. There was a lot of dense circuitry built into the thing, and to get the government to pay for the project had required that there be some way for him to let them know that he'd gotten here and what he'd found.

Report: 2
Jerry Jefferson
Fort Peterbilt
September 2, 1006 CE

Tell George not to blame me. The name was chosen by the natives. And so was the idea of building a fort, so I am assured by the natives. A case of cultural appropriation by the natives, not cultural imperialism by the time travelers.

The natives consider the Missouri and the Mississippi below the convergence to be one river that they call the Talak River. Talak is a mother goddess and the name, as I understand it, simply means mother of rivers. The Mississippi above the convergence is called the Falast River, the Kaskaskia is called the Agla, and Fort Peterbilt is located on the small river, read creek, Bashk.

As it happens, my family and the Anderles arrived in the middle of a slow takeover shift from a matrilineal culture to a patriarchal one. The city of Hocha, what we knew as Cahokia, has god kings, or to be a bit more accurate, is moving in the god king direction. To do that, they have been systematically weakening the power of local chiefs and the tribal women's councils.

Jerry stopped and considered. He was, so far, only getting one side, the version of events from the point of view of the Kadlo clan, and mostly only those members of the Kadlo who lived in the village of Jabir. It was likely that the priesthood of Hocha, which just about everyone here called the Pharisees, would tell a different story.

On the other hand, it wasn't like the people of Jabir had climbed on the Peterbilt and attacked Hocha. And the way the natives were telling it, the reason that they chose Christianity was that it didn't involve strangling young women to take messages to the gods or to accompany a god king to the afterlife.

So, in spite of what his archaeologist and Native American friends might think, Jerry figured the side he was getting was pretty accurate. Still, there was a lot more for him to fill in that didn't have the bias of reports on a war that were all from one side of the conflict. He decided to spend the rest of this report on local names, geography and the status of the stuff he'd brought.

Jerry went back to typing.

The eggs have hatched and my children have claimed them and are taking care of them under the supervision of a local young woman named Jogida. The seeds have been distributed and the projector set up. The frozen sperm samples are locked away in the freezer and will have to wait till we have cows, goats, pigs and horses to implant them in. A mission to Europe is years, perhaps decades, away and even a trip to Greenland to meet Leif Ericson and buy cattle, goats, sheep, pigs and possibly horses is a couple of years off. So for now, at least, it's steam.

There was a big argument going on, back in the twenty-first century, about whether it was better to introduce work animals like cattle and horses or engines. And like a lot of the arguments over the project, politics and perception tended to trump science. In this case the hard scientific fact was there were no horses, cattle, goats or whatever to carry the frozen sperm or fertilized eggs. But politics had put the little freezer in the capsule anyway. It was lined in aerogels and would stay frozen for weeks even without power. With power, the frozen sperm and eggs could be kept indefinitely before implanting. In order to get the horse sperm and eggs, they had leaned heavily on the supposed Vineland colony as a place to get animals for gestation. Many of the Native American tribes wanted horses because in the twenty-first it was part of their heritage and tradition. The politics and alliances had gotten pretty convoluted. Jerry went back to his report.

> *I have been recording the local language with the help of my children and I will leave it to the scholars to determine where the tribal languages of the river people fit into the linguistic history of North America. For myself I am starting to wonder if Doctor Rodriguez's "insane notions" might have a bit more validity than we thought. Several of the words sound a little Nahuanic to me.*

Doctor Rodriguez had the notion that when Cahokia fell the priest kings and their followers had retreated down the Mississippi to the Gulf Coast then been pushed farther south to Mexico to form the Aztecs. No one else had thought much of the idea, but Jerry, after hearing a bit of the local language, especially the names of the gods of Hocha, was starting to wonder. Not that it mattered in the here and now or the there and then, but it was interesting. He attached the audio files to the message and decided that was enough for now.

He pushed the button to start transmitting the report.

Deep in the capsule, a set of very heavy depleted uranium balls started moving back and forth from one side of the capsule to the other, then back in a choreographed dance. It was slow, very slow, but the computer had compressed the data and the people in the twenty-first century had the code book to decompress it. Still, his little report and the recorded words along with pictures of him, his wife and kids and the Anderles, as well as a few snaps of the natives, would take most of the night to send.

PART IV

CHAPTER 15

HOCHA

Kadlo Mound, Hocha
September 5, 1006 CE

The news from the battle reached Fazel thirdhand. The attack was a disaster. Men had left Fort Peterbilt running for their lives, and from the stories, hundreds of them had died there.

There was no coherent account, and since none of the Kadlo had taken part in the attack, none had come to the Kadlo Mound to tell what had happened. What they got was rumor and wild tales.

There was a local corn-based beer. It was low in alcohol content, but enough of it could get you drunk. And after the failed attack on Fort Peterbilt, the returning young men—they weren't an army anymore—had drunk all of it in Hocha. They had also smoked marijuana and taken mushrooms. That last had backfired. There were several very bad trips and a few deaths.

But slowly, over the fourth and fifth of September, a picture had emerged. It was cloudy and incomplete, but what it came down to was that in the field of warfare, it was cross god two, old gods none. Both attacks on Fort Peterbilt had been unmitigated disasters.

And the crops from Jabir and the added fields using the corn from the country store had all produced well. The country store corn best of all.

The cross god was winning.

Roshan was insistent. For months, he'd been wearing the cross openly here in Hocha. "It's time, Fazel. We should put up the cross."

"I don't think the Pharisees on the temple mound would let that stand, my friend."

"What are they going to do about it?" Roshan demanded. "Their army has been shattered at Fort Peterbilt, and to get at us, they have to come down from the temple mound and come up our mound."

Each mound in Hocha had a curtain wall of wooden stakes around the top. It wasn't always a high wall, but between going uphill to reach it and the wall itself, the defenders of a mound were mostly safe from any sort of attack another mound could launch. At least, if they didn't have overwhelming force. Fazel knew that, even though he wasn't a warrior. Roshan had explained it often enough over the years.

Fazel had a bad feeling, but the truth was he didn't know much of warfare. He'd been focused on other things his whole life. He was a shaman. He knew herbs and healing. He was an initiate of the mysteries, could call the spirits of animals and rivers, and with the Peterbilt people, he could calculate the number of days until the longest day of the year or the shortest. He could tell when to plant and when to reap, so that the crops were mature and harvested before the fall rains ruined them. He was skilled in many things, but war wasn't one of them. It never had been.

On the other hand, Roshan was skilled at war. He'd been a war leader for thirty years, been on hundreds of raids, and was still alive. There was no one among the Kadlo who knew more.

So, finally, Fazel nodded. Unwillingly, but he consented, and the cross went up on the top of their mound to be followed within hours by crosses on other mounds, the greater mounds of the clans and the lesser village mounds. In fact, they went up on a majority of the mounds.

Roshan was pleased. Fazel was nervous.

"Why don't you go visit Fort Peterbilt?" Roshan suggested, and Fazel left on the sixth.

Temple mound, Hocha
September 5, 1006 CE

The Priest King wasn't having a good day. In another history, his great-grandson, who would be called a God King, would be buried with many strangled young women to accompany him into the afterlife and serve him for all eternity.

But, according to the Peterbilt people, in less than a thousand years, he and his people, all of Hocha, would be forgotten and scholars would dig up their bones and argue over what they meant.

His name was Ho-Chag Kotep. He was the high priest and, in his view, Paramount Priest of all of the peoples represented in Hocha. A year and a half ago, evil demons had invaded his world and threatened his people. He'd been slow to recognize the danger. Why would such a threat appear in some little village out in the back of nowhere? Jabir wasn't actually on the edge of Hocha territory, but it was a place of no importance.

At first, he'd ignored it, then used Pasire Village to try to slap it like a mosquito. But it wasn't a mosquito. Eighteen Pasire warriors had died in the attack and two more had died from infected wounds later. The Gruda clan had been furious and it had taken him months to convince them that the losses were the fault of the demon Peterbilt and the cross devil it served.

But he learned. He'd placed spies in Fort Peterbilt and learned not just that they were holding one of the sacrifices that were owed to the corn god, but also of their secrets the bang powder and the trebuchet. They had also learned of the cleaning of wounds, of improved querns for grinding corn, all manner of devices by which the Peterbilt people were trying to lure the clans into abandoning the true gods.

A trebuchet isn't complicated, after all. Fairly simple, when you think of it. And like a bow, the person on the highest ground has the advantage. And the temple mound was the highest in Hocha. He couldn't reach Fort Peterbilt, but he could reach the Kadlo Mound. It was only a mound over.

It was while he was working all this out that the first of the crosses went up. Then more, and finally dozens, mostly from village mounds, but also clan mounds.

Well.... Now he knew where to aim the trebuchets.

Kadlo Mound, Hocha
September 8, 1006 CE

Roshan was glad that Fazel was on his way to Fort Peterbilt. He was a good man, but he worried too much. It wasn't just the height or the walls. The Kadlo had the best bang powder as well. It was made in Fort Peterbilt and they had steel arrowheads and knives. The knowledge of how to build a bellows had started in Fort Peterbilt, but now every Kadlo village had its own blacksmith turning bog iron into wrought iron and steel, even cast steel. After some discussion, and with Alyssa Jefferson's full agreement, they had decided to avoid the Peterbilt people silliness of calling iron with even more carbon in it cast iron. It was cast steel. He liked that about the Peterbilt people. They admitted it when they were silly.

He was eating his breakfast when one of his aides brought him word that a delegation from the Pharisees was below the gate. He got up and went to see what was going on. The clan mound was sixty feet high and the flat top was forty feet across. surrounded by a curtain wall. There were steps up to a gate and the delegation was on those steps. It was headed by Kaplack, a particularly officious and odious little man, whose goal in life seemed to be putting people, especially women, in the subservient role that the gods wanted them in.

The gods had a hierarchy that was to be reflected by the humans with the priests at the top, the warriors below them, then the crafters and the field workers at the bottom. And a half step down from each group were that group's women, whose proper role was not to decide, but to support. The thing was, the man was an effective public speaker who could persuade a congregation to his view. And he was in oration mode now.

"You have abandoned the true gods for this false god, Jesus, a weak and puling thing that let itself be tortured and killed like a woman. And the true gods, who control the coming of spring and fight winter back into its hole, are offended. If it were only you and your clan who your false god endangered, I would not care! *You* aren't worth my trouble.

"But it isn't only you and your clan who abandon your duty to the gods. You and the devices of the Peterbilt people tempt others to abandon their duty to the gods and to *life* itself, and if enough of you do so, then being abandoned by us, the gods will in turn abandon us and winter will not be forced back by spring and the cold time will return. And that we cannot allow, so I now give you one last chance to return in humility to the service of the gods lest you be destroyed utterly."

Roshan had had enough of this crap. Besides, Kaplack had drawn a crowd. And, worse, people in the compound were starting to listen to him. "Well, thank Jesus that it's the *last* chance!" he shouted down at Kaplack. "Maybe now you'll *shut up!*"

Kaplack just stared for a moment. Normally, his sermons weren't interrupted. They were choreographed things with the audience not responding except at specific times with rote responses. Having someone answer back must have come as something of a shock. But it was only for a moment, then he shouted, "So be it."

He lifted both arms straight up then brought them down to his sides. Then he turned and moved quickly down the steps.

Roshan was busy trying to figure out what that gesture meant, and a trebuchet, while not silent, also isn't anywhere near as loud as a cannon or a rifle. The weight drops, the arm rises, and the projectile is flung. The first Roshan knew of the attack was when a clay jar smashed into the top of the clan mound. That first one didn't hit the top of the mound, but the side nearest the temple mound. Their aim was a little off. It shattered, spraying a liquid all over the side of the mound, but didn't do more than that.

It took them three more shots to get the range and on the second of those, Roshan learned what the liquid was. The Peterbilt people, among many other things, had introduced distillation. They, mostly Alyssa Jefferson, had also refined the fermentation of mashes into alcoholic liquids. And like most of what the Peterbilt people introduced, it spread first to Jabir, then to the rest of the Kadlo clan, then to the rest of the clans. Distilled alcohol as a disinfectant, as a drink, and as a fuel for lamps had spread more quickly than most things. Especially the drinking part.

Roshan didn't know what was in the clay pots, but he suspected some blending of alcohol and lard, or maybe some sort of seed oil.

Roshan hadn't seen the battle at Fort Peterbilt, but he was increasingly coming to believe that whatever one person could think of, someone else could copy or come up with another way of doing. All these thoughts were running through his mind as he tried to rally his increasingly panicked forces. They only had about fifty men in the compound, and as many women. Plenty to fight off an army climbing up the mound in the face of their arrows, but of no use at all against pots of fire thrown from the temple mound.

The clan mound was surrounded. There were temple warriors all around the mound, staying out of bow range, but there, blocking any retreat. Then one of the jars hit the clan house and it started to burn.

Soon there was smoke and fire everywhere, and if Roshan had been able to, he would have surrendered. But there was no surrender now. Even if they did, they would all be killed. Desperate, and with very little hope, he organized the surviving men and women into a forlorn hope of a charge down the mound. If they could break through the temple warriors, they might retreat to another mound. Or, failing that, get out of Hocha to Fort Peterbilt or another village of the Kadlo.

They were fifty by the time they reached the streets surrounding the mound. Twenty by the time they broke through. Then ten. Then five. And finally, three women with stone knives and nothing else, when the mob took them down. Roshan didn't see it. He'd been killed by the third arrow to hit him before they reached the bottom of the mound.

Fort Peterbilt
September 9, 1006 CE

Fazel arrived on the evening of the ninth from Hocha, looked at the whitewashed wall of Jefferson house and the movie that was playing there and just stared, mouth opened, for several minutes.

It was the first hour of a lesson on how to make a steam engine. The overview before they got into the detailed lessons on how to build the tools to build the tools.

Then a few minutes later when Hamadi touched him on the shoulder, he came to himself and Hamadi led him to the Jefferson house, where he was introduced to Jerry Jefferson.

"How did you get here?" Fazel asked. His accent was not good. Fazel was an accomplished linguist, but he'd spent little time in Jabir or Fort Peterbilt. As the senior shaman of the Kadlo, he spent most of his time in Hocha.

"That's a long story, and perhaps one that can wait till later, when we speak each other's language better," Jerry suggested. "I am more interested in what's been happening in Hocha?" Jerry didn't speak Kadlok at all, so his answer had to be translated by Shane.

Giving up his attempt at speaking English for now, Fazel told his story in Kadlok, trusting the children to translate. "When the first of the army filtered back to Hocha, several tribes who had been slowly converting to worship of the cross god decided it was time to abandon secrecy. We didn't know about Jerry, or the new knowledge he brought. And I am starting to think we moved too soon."

"Because of Jerry?" Alyssa asked.

"No. In spite of Jerry. It worked well for the first two days. We held most of the mounds, though the Pharisees owned the largest and the Gruda clan the second largest. They and the Lomak clan were not told. We didn't trust them and we were right not to. We put up crosses, as did the Kacla and the Purdak. But the Purdak took theirs down the day I left. Meanwhile, the Pharisees have declared that if we refuse sacrifice, not only our crops, but the crops of the loyal clans, will fail. And they are insisting that even if only the crops of the loyal clans fail, it will be our fault for offending the gods.

"There were raids between mounds as I left, and they weren't going our way."

"How can anyone believe that?" Alyssa asked.

Jerry snorted. "I'm a salesman, hon. I know how people get convinced. The most effective way is to convince them to convince themselves. And to do that, you give them someone to blame. That way, no matter the evidence, they will still find a way to blame it on the other guys."

Fazel wanted to know what a salesman was, and after it was explained, he agreed with Jerry. As a pastor and a former Pharisee himself, he knew the techniques as well as Jerry did.

Fazel pointed in the direction of Hocha. "We can hold our part of the city for a while, but we may not hold it for more than a few months, and if there is a crop failure anywhere, the Pharisees of Hocha will declare that it was our fault for stealing the gods' magic for our crops."

"We need to expand Fort Peterbilt," Michael said. "Now I wish we'd gone south to the convergence of the Talak and the Agla rivers."

"Why?" Melanie asked.

"Because we need access to the Talak River for transport. I love the Peterbilt, but it really needs roads, and until we build a nation that can build those roads, our transport is going to be on rivers like the Mississippi and Missouri and their main tributaries. We need some way of getting around Hocha."

"There is a reason the city was placed there," Fazel confirmed. "It controls the trade from the great northern oceans."

At Jerry's blank look, Alyssa clarified. "He's talking about the Great Lakes. Salt matters less than size in their names for bodies of water."

The Talak and its tributaries formed a slow-moving trade network that went from the Gulf of Mexico to the Great Lakes, and to the far northwest. The Pharisees of Hocha didn't control that trade, but they did have a stopper right in the middle of it and could make it much more difficult for anyone who wanted to trade past them.

"It sounds like we need steamboats," Jerry said.

"Except the creek is only a couple of feet deep in a lot of places," Michael said. "Which is why I wish we were farther south, closer to the Talak."

"So why did you guys decide to start your revolution now?" Jerry asked.

"We were acting first out of a resentment of the Pharisees," Fazel said. "That resentment was only held in check by fear. That fear was not the straightforward fear that the Pharisees would punish us for disobedience, whether by sacrificing our daughters or by having us executed as heretics. The fear of death, either our children's or ours, was the *least* of it. The real core of our fear was the fear that the priests' *secret knowledge* did, in fact, come from the gods and therefore represented proof that the gods were on their side and would punish any who opposed them. That an attack on the priesthood, even if successful, would be followed by retribution by the gods. To put it simply, while the chiefs would be willing to fight the Pharisees, they weren't willing to fight the *gods*.

"Almost from the moment of the Peterbilt's arrival and without trying to, you Peterbilt people have been eroding that fear. Letting us see that the gods weren't necessarily on the side of the Pharisees. But it takes time and proof, then more proof for that belief to fade."

"And sometimes all the time and proof in the world isn't enough," Jerry muttered. Jerry was an atheist; he figured it was unlikely any god existed and the next best thing to impossible that it cared about prayers at all. However, he was enough of a salesman to keep his mouth shut about that.

"First by demonstrating that much of the secret knowledge of the priests was readily available to the Peterbilt people," Fazel continued without appearing to notice Jerry's comment, "and second by introducing a new god that the Peterbilt people followed, a god who didn't require human sacrifice, but instead had come to Earth and made himself human so that all the human sacrifice could be done by him, not the humans."

"Why do they call the Peterbilt a demon?" Jerry asked.

"They don't," Shane said. "The word that Mom and Dad keep insisting is 'demon' actually translates as readily to 'angel' as to 'demon.' It just means a supernatural being that answers to a higher supernatural being. What it should be translated as is the 'Angel named Peterbilt.' Even though they know that it's a thing, not an angel, by now."

"We are not going to be called the angel people," Michael said. "It's sacrilegious, not to mention incredibly arrogant."

Fazel laughed, then continued to speak to Jerry with Shane translating. "I have heard the argument before, and I tend to agree with Shane's translation. Though I understand and respect Michael's humility.

"Anyway, in secret at first, the chiefs abandoned their belief in the old gods and replaced them with our versions of Christianity. It is a version that honors and sanctifies questioning, since it is based on *Jesus Christ Superstar* as much as the recorded gospels. We use ceremonies from the Book of Common Prayer, but we have modified them somewhat under the influence of the rock opera.

"When the Pharisees lost the battle of Fort Peterbilt, it was the final nail in the belief of power and infallibility of the Pharisees. Moreover, it was proof that the cross god of the Peterbilt people would protect them even against the old gods. And if the cross god would protect the Peterbilt people and the villagers of Jabir, then the cross god would protect us from the Pharisees of Hocha. Or so we thought. But fewer of the people of Hocha agreed with us than we were expecting.

"Each clan has its own version of the cross god. Or perhaps its own interpretation, but you have spoken of the freedom of religion mentioned in your constitution and we have taken that to heart, though it weakens us in our conflict with the Pharisees."

CHAPTER 16

CAPITALISM

Fort Peterbilt
September 20, 1006 CE

News of the events in Hocha after Fazel left took a while to get back to them. The crosses had come down after the destruction, after the *murder* of everyone in the Kadlo Mound. Using that and the threat of the trebuchet had forced the retreat of the rest. The Pharisees of the old gods now owned Hocha, but some of the other clans had retreated, abandoning the city and their clan mounds. In effect, the old gods owned the city of Hocha and some of the clans, but Jesus Christ was accepted in more than half the clans, at least outside the city.

The Kacla were trying to be neutral, allowing the worship of both the old gods and Jesus and maintaining a presence in Hocha. The Purdak, after seeing the destruction of the Kadlo Mound, had retreated from Hocha and gone to their own villages. The clan chiefs of the Purdak, and especially their women's council, had been terrified and enraged by the murder of all of the Kadlo in the city. The Gruda were sticking with the old gods, but while they were happy with the murder of the Kadlo in the city, they were unwilling to undertake military operations against Fort Peterbilt, or other Kadlo villages.

The Lomak clan had broken over the matter. Several of their

villages broke with their clan chiefs and applied for membership in the Kadlo.

It was a Lomak village chieftain who'd brought the word of the final—so far—resolution.

"My village needs your help if we are to defend against the Pharisees," Kalmak said. His village of Lisyuk, like most of the Lomak villages, was on the south side of the Talak River above Hocha, that part of the Talak that the Peterbilt people knew as the Missouri River.

After discussing things inside, they went out and used the projection screen that Jerry Jefferson had brought with him to project what he knew of the course of the Talak. The village Lisyuk was around two hundred miles along the Talak from Fort Peterbilt. Sofaf was closer, at their best guess, about one hundred fifty miles upriver, about where the town of Washington, Missouri, was in the future they came from. That would mean traveling past Hocha, but that really wasn't much of a problem. The Talak River was more than a mile across there. Both villages wanted the Peterbilt to help with the plowing, or if they couldn't get the Peterbilt, a steam tractor.

"If you can get it to our side of the river you should be able to go over land between the villages," Kalmak continued.

"The Pharisees might send out boats to intercept you," Kalmak warned.

Even using the trebuchets, Hocha couldn't reach them. But they could send out canoes and Hocha had big canoes. It was how they controlled the trade up and down the river. As Hocha's power was based on their knowledge of "the mysteries," much of their economic power was based on control of the river trade.

"We need a better money," Jerry muttered.

"What was that last?" asked Jogida. She was one of the better speakers of English, but there were a lot of words.

"*Disshot*," Miriam said. The children had picked up the words more readily than the adults, but often without the subtlety of meaning. *Disshot* did indeed mean money or trade goods, but it always included the notion that the trade goods were goods, as well as stuff to be exchanged for other stuff.

Jerry looked at his wife. "Is *disshot* money, as distinct from trade goods?"

"Daddy!" Miriam, at seven, didn't appreciate her daddy—who

had gone away and gotten old, then came back—questioning her.

"Miriam," Alyssa said, and gave her a look. Miriam subsided grumpily and Alyssa continued. "I'm not sure that there is a word that means money as distinct from trade goods."

At that point, everything devolved into a language lesson. That still happened a lot, even more now than six months in. Because now they were getting into places where there was no concept in the local language for a concept that English expressed. Or there was no word in English for a local concept. In this case, while the locals were no longer a strictly barter- and gift-based economy, they weren't yet a monied economy. They were in a middle ground that didn't know how to get the rest of the way to capitalism.

Capitalism, in its broadest sense. An economy where people use money to buy and sell stuff, not the much tighter definitions of the twentieth and twenty-first centuries, where it had taken on so much political weight that the economics could no longer support the definition. Back in the twenty-first century, Jerry Jefferson had been on the conservative side of "middle of the road." In the here and now, he was just looking for a way to make the economy work better so that people wouldn't spend as much time killing each other over an old coat or a few sacks of corn.

Over the next few days Jerry learned that money is a hard thing to explain to people who haven't grown up with it.

Fort Peterbilt
October 1, 1006 CE

Alyssa Jefferson was sitting in her house wearing her new phone in a headset made partly in the mid twenty-first century and partly right here. Moore's law had not failed while Jerry had been lobbying congress to send him to this time. The computers and memory that he'd brought back in the capsule were massively more powerful than the same weight of computers would have been when she, her children and the Anderles were dropped here.

Her new phone/computer, which was only a bit heavier than a pair of glasses, fit on her face and displayed a virtual screen about three feet distant. It also used a virtual keyboard. But Alyssa was using the keyboard on her old laptop because she couldn't get used to the virtual keyboard. That was going to change because Farsak, a wood carver from Jabir, was carving her a keyboard. It wouldn't actually do anything but the sensors in the new phone would track her finger movements as she typed on it so it would act as a keyboard.

Meanwhile, Alyssa was taking a course in practical chemistry for the eleventh century taught by one of her undergrads. She was now a middle-aged woman who had been an irritating teenager a year and a half earlier in Alyssa's personal timeline. She needed the course, both because knowledge of chemistry had improved over the more than a quarter of a century while they were figuring out how to send Jerry back to her, but also because she needed to know what chemical compounds she would be likely to find in which plants. And she desperately needed that, to save children suffering from asthma, and allergies from rickets, and any number of infections and infectious diseases.

The Pharisees, among their other charming qualities, didn't approve of "wise women." But Jabir had several; they were on the women's council and they worked with the local shamans who were now calling themselves pastors. Alyssa was now one of those women. Etaka was another. A big part of the reason that Etaka had become so incensed with the Pharisees of Hocha was that Priyak had refused to let her consult with him on medical cases after an instruction from the Pharisees.

Two children had died because he wouldn't listen to her.

At least after the second attack, Priyak had left to go to Hocha. From what Alyssa had heard, he'd gotten to the city just in time to be on the Kadlo Mound when the Pharisees had used trebuchets to kill everyone.

She called up another file and listened to a lesson on how to extract and purify digitalis from foxglove, one of the seed packs that Jerry brought. They wouldn't have any until next spring, but the same techniques could be used to extract other things from other plants.

Michael Anderle was bent over the engine of the Peterbilt. He was also wearing a pair of the glasses phones, and he was also watching a display. It was keyed to the engine of his Peterbilt and it was designed to help him use locally found replacements for seals and filters and other things, so that he could keep the engine and electrical systems on the big truck operational just as long as possible.

Jerry Jefferson had brought them a lot of toys.

Melanie Anderle was with the villagers of Jabir. She was wearing the glasses too, but they were pushed up on her forehead as they all worked on harvesting beans. She wasn't harvesting. She was driving the pickup, which at the moment was filled with baskets to collect the beans. The pickup's tires had all needed patching at least once in the year and a half since they'd been dropped here, and repairing tires in the eleventh century wasn't like making a call to AAA. So Melanie was being cautious.

Shane wasn't in the village. She was on a deer hunt with the young men of the village of Jabir. She'd been invited along after she showed them the crossbow that her dad had given her for her birthday. The metallurgy of this century still wasn't up to guns, but the woodworking was plenty up to an eighty-pound-pull crossbow. And even if she had to use both hands to cock it, she could shoot it accurately at up to one hundred fifty yards.

They reached a stand of trees and Shane got down on her belly and used a branch to support the front of the crossbow, then took careful aim and squeezed the trigger.

The bolt took the deer in the chest. It leapt into the air and started running, but it didn't go far. The rest of the small herd of bucks scattered.

They reached the dying buck, and Achanu slit its throat with a flint knife and spread its blood on each of Shane's cheeks.

It was uncommon, but acceptable, for girls to hunt among the Kadlo.

Miriam Jefferson was in school and found that she liked it. She was wearing the computer glasses that her daddy had brought with him and following along as the programmed learning text taught her math.

While just turned six, Norman played with blocks with letters carved into them. Mom had gotten them made for him by a wood carver in Jabir. He was wearing the glasses too, and the augmented reality was showing him force vectors as he set the blocks as off-center as possible without them falling.

Fort Peterbilt
October 15, 1006 CE

The crops were mostly in and the locals were shifting to their winter routine, but, both in Fort Peterbilt and Jabir, it was going to be a good winter. A winter with plenty of food and a winter with chimneys. By now just about every hut in both places had brick chimneys rising from brick fireplaces and most of them had iron tops on the fireplaces so that even as the smoke went out much of the heat stayed in. And they could even cook over, or in, the fireplace.

Jabir had bricklayers. It was a new profession and one that took great pride in itself.

Oaka was seated at a potter's wheel making clay pots. She had several tools and sacks of clay as she made each pot to a precise size. The openings in the top needed to fit the lids right so that there wouldn't be much leakage, because these would also act as Dutch ovens. You want them to be covered in hot coals but not have the coal dust get into the food, so she used a premeasured piece of wood to trim the top of each pot to the same size. Standardization meant that if a piece or a lid broke, another lid would fit.

She finished the dish, moved it to a shelf to dry and started on another, then stopped. The evening was getting chill, so she put some wood in the fireplace and started a small fire. Then she filled a pot with water and set it on the metal top of the fireplace to heat. She would have warm water to wash her hands after she was done and would sleep in a warm house tonight. And most every night all winter long.

Across the room, Jogida was working at a spinning wheel. They'd been trying for a year and a half to make it work and it wasn't until Mr. Jefferson arrived that they learned what they were missing. After that, it became easy. Jogida made excellent-quality hemp thread. Using it and the crochet hooks, she was making fine crocheted clothing for herself and her little brothers, and to sell.

Jogida had lived for the better part of a year on the charity of the village, and she never wanted to be in that position again.

Her little brother, Faris, had become great friends with Norman

Jefferson, and the two often played together. Faris spoke English very well at five and a half, though his understanding was that of a five-year-old. Three-year-old Ubadan followed them around when he could. He spoke both languages interchangeably, not even seeming to know that they were two languages.

"I want popcorn," Faris demanded in English.

"May I have popcorn," Jogida corrected.

Faris started to cloud up, then seeing the look on his big sister's face, said, "May I have popcorn, please?"

"All right," Jogida agreed, and got out the lidded iron skillet. It was made from bog iron and was worth as much as a half dozen ceramic pots. Achanu had killed a deer and traded it to Michael Anderle for the frying pan, then given it to Oaka, but they all shared.

Fort Peterbilt
November 15, 1006 CE

Jerry Jefferson listened to the discussion after the latest showing of *Jesus Christ Superstar* as Alyssa translated. The latest showing was projected by the Capsule Theater. The new brick building that housed the capsule had a smooth whitewashed wall on one end. The wall was fourteen feet tall and twenty wide and the roof and walls of the Capsule Theater kept the light out so that the projector didn't need to work quite so hard to fill the whitewashed wall with images. In other words, it was a decent, if small, movie theater with the capsule providing both image and sound.

While *Jesus Christ Superstar* was still very popular and watched several times a week by people who came from many villages to see it, the locals were less enthralled by the Old Testament and found much of the doctrine that brought by Jerry Jefferson in the capsule to be not at all in keeping with *their* faith. There was just the hint of a sect based on Judas forming that focused on lines like "No talk of God then, we called you a man" and came to the conclusion that Jesus wasn't God but just a man who'd started out with the right idea, but had gone crazy with the power. They'd latched onto the Jefferson Bible as proof that the wise of the Peterbilt people rejected the divinity of Jesus. And Judas' complaints about spending and Jesus' comments about

"There will be poor always, pathetically struggling, look at the good things you've got" as proof that Jesus was abandoning his dedication to the poor and being corrupted by his power.

"It's fascinating," Jerry muttered quietly, "watching them create their own faith out of that rock opera."

"What interests me is the fact that even now that they have access to the rest of the Bible and the Apocrypha of Christianity, not to mention Buddhism and Islam and the rest, they are sticking with *Superstar* as their guiding document. Even more than the gospels."

Jerry nodded and looked at the clock. It was time for the next educational show. "Folks, we have a show on money, what it is and how it works, coming up. If you're not involved in that, can you let the people who are in?"

The audience for this showing of *Superstar* were mostly shamans from other villages. Some left and some stayed.

They and the new viewers took their seats and watched an educational cartoon about money and how it worked. There was only a little speech in the cartoon because the people creating it knew perfectly well that the people watching it wouldn't share a language in common with them. Mostly it tracked money as it moved through the economy, making trade easier and more efficient.

In the lead-up to the transfer after the scientists realized that they would actually be able to do it, a major political wrangle about what to send back with Jerry developed. Some groups wanted to excise whole chunks of history, like communism "because it had been discredited," or "slavery" because it showed Americans in a bad light, or "the treatment of Native Americans," for the same reason. At that point, black people, including Jerry, and Native Americans got their backs up and insisted that if they were going to show history, they had to show it warts and all. And others pointed out that even "failed" economic theories like communism had contributed to the understanding of the field. Then the communists insisted that communism hadn't failed, but instead had been hijacked by fascists like Stalin.

For a while, what to put in the capsule with Jerry had become a political football.

However, with the advances in data storage and computing power, the final conclusion was to send everything. At that point, universities and Native American tribes, politicians and movie studios had started producing their own videos to present what *they* thought the natives of the eleventh century would need.

This cartoon was one of those productions, designed to provide an introduction to what money was and how it worked. It was produced by the economics department of the University of Chicago in cooperation with a movie studio.

It was one of a dozen on money that were created just for the capsule and it happened to be the one that Jerry liked the best.

After the cartoon, which lasted about half an hour, finished, Jerry set up the next video, one on water filtration using charcoal. Then he, Alyssa and the members of the women's council left the theater. They went to Alyssa's house to discuss how and whether to create money. After a set of discussions, they'd determined that the creation of money should be left in the hands of the women's councils.

Kasni, head of the women's council of Jabir and an increasingly important voice in the women's council of the Kadlo, wanted to know, "Why do we need money? We have the hoes and the beans and the corn."

That was true. Corn, beans, and stone hoe heads were all used as mediums of exchange in Hocha society.

"Because," Alyssa said, "all of those are things you use and every time you eat a bean, you decrease the money supply."

It took a while, but they were convinced. Then they got down to the how. Alyssa said, "I can make a glaze for ceramic coins that will be a bright green. It's a color that will be hard to reproduce if you don't know how it's made, and we can keep that a secret.

"And with a stamp, we can make coins with images stamped into them. We can even stamp them on both sides if we leave the bottom flat."

That took some explaining, but it turned out the coins wouldn't be circular. Instead, they would be a half circle with a flat bottom to stand on while they were fired.

All that was fine. Then they had to decide how many of the coins they were going to make.

Fort Peterbilt
December 15, 1006 CE

The first of the coins were ready. They each had a raised image of the Peterbilt on one side and a denomination on the other. The women's council of Jabir had decided that they would be introduced first as gifts from Jabir to other Kadlo villages. The tradition of Santa Claus was taking hold in the towns and villages that were abandoning Hocha. And not just Santa giving gifts to children or friends giving gifts to each other, but also villages exchanging larger gifts.

By now, both the Peterbilt and the pickup were known, and it turned out that one of the major restrictions on the expansion of agriculture was the thick soil away from the rivers. It was tied together with thick fibrous roots and impractical to plow by human labor alone. And there were no oxen to pull plows. If you wanted to plow that land, you needed to use the pickup or the Peterbilt.

Kasni had realized the importance of money and wanted it in the hands of the women's council of Jabir. She was giving coins that had images of the Peterbilt on them to other villages to try to tie them to Jabir's money. It was a gamble, and very dependent on the Peterbilt people accepting the coins of Jabir in exchange for using their truck to plow fields.

CHAPTER 17

GOVERNMENT

Kallabi, village of the Kadlo
March 15, 1007 CE

Atacha, head of the women's council of Kallabi, spilled the coins back and forth in her hands. They were a gift from the women's council of Jabir and she wasn't quite convinced that they were anything but pretty baubles.

"Will you stop playing with those things?" demanded Lacoa, her sister, and another member of the women's council. They had sent canoes down the Talak to gather salt and amber to give to the people of Jabir for Christmas, and in return, gotten the coins. They had been hoping for the steel knives that they made in Jabir, but instead they got trinkets.

"We need the Peterbilt!" Atacha insisted. "We need it to clear that field." She pointed at a hill a mile east of the village.

"That's not a field," Lacoa said. "It's prairie."

The hill grew nothing but a tough, tall grass that grazers ate. It was formed of black soil tied together by the roots. You couldn't grow corn, squash, or beans in it because you couldn't plant them, and even if you did, the weeds would strangle them. Burning the field didn't work; the grass would just grow back from the robust root system.

"They plant in fields like it in Jabir," Atacha insisted, still spilling the coins back and forth in her hands.

"Because they have the Peterbilt to cut the land," Lacoa said, then stopped. "What would we trade them for the use of the Peterbilt?"

Atacha held out the coins.

"They would never do it," Lacoa insisted. She pointed at the coins. "Those were the women of Jabir showing off their new status." Jabir had been the second village of the Kadlo, second in size and perhaps third in status. Then the angel Peterbilt had landed between Jabir's hunting lands and Kallabi's hunting lands, then made the fateful decision to travel east rather than south. If they came south, they would have encountered the village of Kallabi rather than Jabir.

The place where the general store had arrived wasn't in the territory of either village; the Kadlo, all the people associated with Hocha, farmed the alluvial plain of the Talak River and its tributaries. The high plains that didn't flood on a semi-regular basis were not farmable with the stone tools and lack of draft animals that the natives had. Those were hunting lands and not controlled by the river clans.

Atacha shrugged. She was wearing a vest knitted in Jabir of thread spun in Jabir. It was a very nice vest and Atacha liked everything about it except what she'd had to trade for it. "If they refuse, it will devalue their gifts to us and embarrass them." At this point Atacha was ready for the women's council of Jabir to be embarrassed. "We have women and whole families fleeing down the Talak to get away from the Pharisees at Hocha and showing up in our village. How are we going to feed those people next winter?"

"All right, we'll try it," Lacoa agreed. They went to see the senior chief of the village.

Hamatak was a man in his mid-forties, still fit, but his age showed in his face. "Even if they do send us the Peterbilt, where will we get the corn and beans to plant in this new field?"

"From Jabir. They have those extra fields that the Peterbilt and the pickup cleared for them." Which was true. The extra seed corn from the twenty-first century, planted in fields that had been fallow for hundreds of years, had done incredibly well compared to the standard eleventh-century corn kernels.

Hamatak reluctantly agreed, though he was much more worried about pissing off the Peterbilt people than the women's council was. Hamatak was an experienced war chief and he'd spoken to survivors of both attacks on Fort Peterbilt. He wasn't sure what the angel Peterbilt could do away from its home, but he was pretty sure it could do a lot.

They boarded canoes and rowed up the Talak to the Alga, and on up the Alga to the Bashk, and to Fort Peterbilt.

Fort Peterbilt
March 16, 1007 CE

"Push!" Etaka ordered. Etaka was a midwife even before the Peterbilt people had arrived, and she'd been watching the videos of how to deliver babies that came with the capsule, so she was about as qualified to deliver a baby as anyone on Earth.

"Okay, breathe," she ordered in English. Her English had a very strong accent, but no hesitation at all. "Just a few more pushes. At least for the first one." Over the past few weeks, Etaka had been listening to Melanie's belly and had identified two heartbeats. It would be years before they could make a sonogram machine, but a stethoscope was well within their abilities.

Two minutes later, Jerry Achanu Anderle was born. Followed fifteen minutes later by Jogida Alyssa Anderle.

The village of Jabir had two Michaels, a Shane, and an Alyssa, though called by different names. The concept of godparent was anything but foreign to the locals. They lived in a rough world and having someone to look after your kids if you died was a necessity. Naming the kids after Achanu and Jogida honored the young people, not kids anymore, but respected members of the community, and offered the locals an assurance that Michael and Melanie were members of the community.

In the case of Jogida, it was also effectively making her the children's nanny. In the eleventh century, it definitely took a village to raise a child. And though the Anderles and the Jeffersons were of really high status, they were still going to need help. Jogida had been first in line to help, since she'd brought her little brothers to live in Camp Peterbilt.

Fort Peterbilt
March 18, 1007 CE

"Certainly," Michael agreed. There had been quite a bit of discussion about the introduction of money, and they had all agreed that if the money was to be accepted by the tribes, the Peterbilt people and the rest of Fort Peterbilt would have to accept it. Besides, after a year of not traveling very far at all, almost any excuse to actually go somewhere in the Peterbilt would have been enough payment.

After Michael's agreement, it was turned over to Melanie to negotiate the price for the use of the Peterbilt and the sale of the seed corn. Then they were sent to the village of Jabir to buy the squash seeds and the beans. Also, sunflowers and other seeds, while Michael drove inland away from the trees, then along the prairie to Kallabi, where Michael, with Melanie and Shane in the pickup, plowed about two hundred acres of prairie into farmland.

The news spread, and very soon the Peterbilt and the pickup were spending all their time either plowing someone's prairie into cropland or traveling to a village. And at the same time, the value of the coins that the village of Jabir made was demonstrated and the coins started being traded between the villages for other things besides the use of the Peterbilt and the pickup.

A lot of extra land was planted that spring. A fair amount of their food corn was planted, along with beans that might well have been better used in people's bellies. No one starved that summer, but some folks got kind of hungry.

In a surprisingly short time, Jabir coins were making their way up the Talak to Hocha, where the Pharisees outlawed them. This had the effect of making them even more valuable.

Kallabi, village of the Kadlo
May 15, 1007 CE

Atacha looked out at the fields full of growing corn and was not happy. The coins of Jabir were all gone now. Gone to pay for the Peterbilt and the pickup to plow the fields. Gone to buy corn and beans, squash seed and sunflower seeds.

Then gone to buy fish nets to use on the river, and all the while the status of Jabir increased and the status of Kallabi decreased.

"What's wrong now?" Lacoa asked.

"We should be making our own money," Atacha said. "In fact, since we are the senior village of the Kadlo, we should be the ones making the money, not Jabir."

"That's an excellent idea," Lacoa said, sarcasm dripping from every word. "You make us a Peterbilt and a pickup truck, and I will see about making the coins."

Atacha looked over at her sister. She didn't throw anything. She hadn't thrown things at her sister since they'd become women, but she wanted to. Atacha knew that the Peterbilt and the pickup weren't all that was happening with the money. "Also, the Kacla wanted to trade us buffalo hides for coins and the Kacla villages are all on the west side of the Talak. They weren't going to spend those coins on having the Peterbilt plow their fields. It can't cross the river. There is something more going on."

"I know that. I talked to the demon person, Jerry Jefferson, too. But I still don't really understand how it works."

Jerry Jefferson was trying, but he hadn't had the time that the other Peterbilt people had had to learn a civilized language.

"And you know that the Kacla wanted to buy bang powder to retaliate against the Gruda for that raid that stole some of their young women and sent them to Hocha for sacrifice."

"My point is," Atacha said, "it's not just the Peterbilt that the money is good for. We need to know how to do it."

"So we're going back to Fort Peterbilt," Lacoa sighed, but her heart wasn't in it. Ultimately she agreed with her sister. They did need to know how this money stuff worked. But not just them. The women's councils of all the Kadlo villages needed to know. And the Kacla and Purdak, as well. Because, if things kept going like this, then Jabir was going to just replace Hocha, and end up ruling all the villages of all the clans. That, after all, was how Hocha had happened. A little at a time, bringing knowledge, and that knowledge giving them power, which they used to gain more power. And the Peterbilt people brought a lot more knowledge than the Pharisees of Hocha had ever dreamed of having.

Fort Peterbilt
May 25, 1007 CE

Atacha and Lacoa weren't the only members of the women's councils of other villages in Fort Peterbilt. Lots of women's councils had sent one or two of their number to Fort Peterbilt to learn about money. They also sent them to learn how to avoid becoming subject to Fort Peterbilt, the way they'd been subject to the Pharisees of Hocha before the Angel named Peterbilt had arrived. Shamans from as many villages were here to learn about medicines and tools, stars and clouds. Warriors and chiefs were there to learn tactics and strategy.

By now, Fort Peterbilt was turning into a city, with as many houses outside the walls as within. And the sheer number of people was threatening an ecological disaster simply from all the feces dropped in places it didn't belong.

Lacoa was blunt. "How do we keep you from becoming Hocha?"

Shane, who was translating, immediately insisted, "We would never do that. We would never sacrifice young women."

"That's not what I'm talking about!" Lacoa interrupted. The truth was while she'd not liked it, she'd accepted that it was necessary for the next harvest. And she was less angry about the young women who had died than she was about the Pharisees lying to her about the need. Lacoa, like any woman on any women's council, was used to making hard choices for the good of the village. "Hocha started out helping us, sharing their knowledge of when the flooding would come and when to plant so that we would have good crops, and the longer it went on, the more they commanded and the less they listened. Tell him that." She pointed at Jerry Jefferson.

Shane tried to explain, and after a few back-and-forths, Jerry got it. "You want to know how to form a government."

"What is a government?" Atacha asked.

That took some explaining, and as they went through it, Jerry learned that they already had a government. It was made of traditions more than laws, but it was a government and it worked well enough for a single village. A bit less well for a clan made up of several villages, and not well at all for a nation made up of many clans.

That was ultimately how Hocha had gained power. They knew more about making a government work than the clans did. Their system was hierarchical, based on the notion of divine right, with the high priests of the gods telling everyone what to do based on their relationship with the gods.

But *direct* democracy, absent a hi-tech communication network, simply couldn't work for groups much larger than a village. And, in Jerry's opinion, even with hi-tech communications, direct democracy still didn't work, because most people were too busy doing their jobs and living their lives to bone up on every issue that a government must handle. He tried to explain the concepts of representative democracy, also known as republics, where the people chose and had the power to recall and replace their representatives, and the women got it immediately.

That was precisely what the women's councils were; they weren't all the women in the village. They were the older women who had the support of the other women. The notion of election rather than selection through consensus was new, but as they talked it out, they all realized that the consensus was at least somewhat coerced by the majority. What they had was majority rule of a sort.

It was a sort that involved a lot of extra arguing and bullying.

Fort Peterbilt
July 4, 1007 CE

This year's celebration of July fourth was almost an excuse for the meetings of the chiefs and the women's councils. Starting in April, men and women of the villages and clans that had been vassals of Hocha and the Pharisees had been arriving in Fort Peterbilt, and Jerry had been dutifully sending reports to the twenty-first century.

The reports were about the natives' interest in the form of government known as representative democracy. One thing that the more liberal factions in the twenty-first-century political landscape had insisted on was that he avoid any sort of political or social imperialism. That political faction included some Native Americans, but a majority of Native Americans were on the other side. They wanted the United States in the tenth century, but with *their* people in charge of it. They wanted it so they would be ready when Columbus got lost on his way to China.

So Jerry's instructions were not to impose either the notion of democracy or a republic on the people of this time. But not to refuse them either, if they wanted it. It turned out that what was actually happening was not exactly what anyone had expected. The locals were very interested in the information he brought and not at all worried about the seven of them, four adults and three kids, "taking over." Instead, they were examining the stuff on government that he brought back and combining it with their own customs to make something new.

The fact that the Peterbilt people celebrated the birth of their great nation that stretched from one side of the continent to the other and more, struck the locals as a good idea, and the Fourth of July struck them as a propitious date to start things off.

Jerry set his camera computer glasses to record and transmit to the module and watched as on July fourth of the year 1007 of the Common Era, the first official meeting of the Continental Congress of the United Clans of America was called to order, and Kasni was named the first Speaker of the Great Women's Council.

Slowly, over the course of months, they argued and discussed, consulted and compromised, and came up with their own notion of representative democracy.

It was based partly on the American constitution and partly on some of the tribal governments of Native Americans from the twenty-first century, but mostly it was based on the women's councils.

The new government had a congress. The congress was called "the great women's council." And after considerable debate, it was agreed that men could be members. The women's council selected the president, called "the first chief," which was distinct from the first speaker, who was the head of the great women's council.

The first chief was not allowed to sit in the women's council and was, in effect, the head of the executive branch of government. They also selected some of the sub-chiefs, those that dealt with national matters. Meanwhile, each clan would have its clan women's council, who would select the clan chief and clan sub-chiefs. And each village within the clan would have its own women's council and its own chiefs, just like now, but a little bit more formalized.

And, at the insistence of the Peterbilt people, there would also be a Bill of Rights made up of things that neither the government nor the churches, including the new Christian churches, could compel people to do, or prevent them from doing. This included the notion that no church could compel anyone to take part in any ritual of that religion. Along with the standards about not being prevented from speaking or assembling, not being forced to give testimony against themselves, the right to keep and bear arms, or not having their stuff taken or examined without due process. It wasn't exactly the United States Bill of Rights, but it was similar.

Most of the people who signed this constitution were women, though all the Peterbilt people signed it, even the kids.

Then it was decided that Fort Peterbilt would be the capital. All that took most of the summer of 1007, and in the meantime the Pharisees of Hocha were adjusting their government too. Partly this was out of desperation. Partly because it's really hard for an authoritarian government to back down, and really easy for such a government to start believing its own propaganda. Hocha was becoming more authoritarian, but it was also reaching out to the plains tribes on either side of the Talak, seeking warriors and promising loot.

And by the fall of 1007, there was a lot of loot. Steel was in production, though not on a large scale by twenty-first-century standards, or even by seventeenth-century standards. But most of the villages in the Peterbilt alliance had a blacksmith with a brick or stone forge to make the steel from bog iron. And Jabir didn't just have a smithy. It had a foundry.

Fort Peterbilt
August 31, 1007 CE

It was Jerry's arrival day. And his daughter was pulling on his arm, insisting he wake up. "Wake up, Daddy. We're having eggs for breakfast."

One year ago today, Jerry Jefferson and a cylinder full of knowledge had arrived in this century. Along with him, he'd brought seeds and a dozen eggs in an incubator. The eggs had hatched three days later, and ten hens and two roosters had been born. Careful husbanding had produced two flocks of chickens, one that was bred for meat, and the other that was bred for eggs. For the first few months, no one ate chicken or eggs. All the eggs were fertilized and used to make more chickens, but by now there were several flocks.

Alyssa rolled over and groaned. But a little later, they were all awake and dressed and Jerry was fixing eggs and trying to figure a way to get to England for cattle, sheep, goats, anything that would provide milk so that he could have a cheese omelet or, better yet, a cheeseburger. Instead, it was scrambled eggs with ground venison patties and cornbread.

The winter wheat was all carefully stored away to be planted this winter. There was still too little of it to eat.

"We have to go to England or Spain," Jerry muttered.

"Yes. Where else are we going to get smallpox?" Alyssa agreed, sarcastically.

"Where else are we going to get milk?" Jerry countered. "Also horses and cattle, pigs, sheep for wool." Jerry knew that they wouldn't be going to Europe, at least at first. Instead, they would be going to the colony in Greenland. But that wasn't a guarantee that they wouldn't run into smallpox or some other European disease that devastated the native populace. Besides, they were going to have to go to Europe eventually. They would need other varieties of plants and animals, and eventually trade and development around the world, as well as mica from the Russian steppes and silk from China.

"We have watermelon and cantaloupe from the seeds you brought and we don't need to go to Europe and risk the diseases that the Europeans brought to this continent."

Jerry disagreed. Not that he thought Alyssa was wrong about the risk. He didn't. But, one, it wasn't going to go away and they would have a much better chance of surviving it if they controlled the initial encounter. If it was their boats that made the trip, not Spanish or Portuguese boats.

Conversation turned to other things. Absent draft animals, the need for steam engines was much greater. And not just any steam engines. They desperately needed steam tractors and steam bulldozers and, yes, steamboats to ply the Talak River. The sort of heavy dugouts that the natives had had, even the birchbark canoes they had now, weren't big enough to support serious trade. They were also a lot of work to move up or down the river.

Meanwhile, with all the uses that the diesel and gasoline in the Peterbilt was being put to, they were going to run out. Probably in no more than another year or two. They were going to need more oil. They were going to need more everything, and that meant that they needed better transport.

☆　　☆　　☆

"We need steam engines," Jerry told Michael.

"Ah, yes. Now, I understand," Michael said. "I didn't the first five hundred times you told me, but now I get it. We need steam engines. Why didn't I think of that? It's not like we've been trying to make steam engines since six months after we got here. Oh, yes, it *is* like that. *Exactly* like that. It's not that easy, Jerry, even with the technical manuals and how-to videos you brought. It's taking time."

"I know, Michael, and I'm sorry."

"No. I'm sorry. Pelok got raided by one of the plains tribes. Four killed and two young women captured, and those young women are probably going to end up strangled in Hocha to ensure a good harvest next year."

Pelok was a village of the Kacla, located on the east side of the Talak River. The plains tribes were hunter-gatherers who lived in the plains east of the Talak and hunted buffalo. Hunting buffalo with bows and arrows wasn't a sport for the faint of heart. They were some tough SOBs and not overburdened with what a person from the twenty-first century would consider morals. Stealing from people not of your tribe was not just acceptable, but the next best thing to your duty. Certainly, successfully raiding a Hocha village brought respect as well as trade goods.

In the last year or two, the river people had new stuff well worth the stealing. The plains tribes called the Hocha "the river people" because they settled next to the rivers where the flooding restored the soil. So raids as well as trading had already started increasing before the blowup in Hocha, and now with the river people divided and fighting among themselves, the plains people were attacking even more. They lacked horses, but other than that were very much the spiritual ancestors of the Comanche, in that they were a migratory warrior people who weren't overly fond of the more settled farmers, and especially didn't approve of those farmers spreading out and occupying their hunting grounds.

The cold truth is that hunter-gatherers need more land to support them than farmers, and so tend to be outnumbered. So for the past hundred years or so they'd been being slowly pushed back from the river valleys. Now, with the river people at war with each other, seemed a good opportunity to get some of their own back.

All of which Michael and Jerry knew well by now.

"Another request for aid?" Jerry asked.

"Yes. They know we can't get the Peterbilt across the Talak, but they're desperate."

"Why can't we?" Jerry stopped, then said, "I'm an idiot."

"All right," Michael agreed. "Why are you an idiot?"

"The barge plans."

"What barge plans?"

"Look, when you guys were brought here, it was by accident. You had what was in your truck and what was in that part of the country store that was transferred. With me, it was different. As the designs for the capsule were worked out and the launcher was built, everybody and their brother put in their two cents. Everyone had a design for some trick or device that you would need."

"Right, I got that."

"Stacks and stacks of them, all piled on each other. I got briefed on as close as we could come to all of them. But most of them were low-probability situations. And one of them was to use the Peterbilt as a power supply for a barge. Actually, there were about forty of them, everything from pulling the engine from the Peterbilt and putting it in a riverboat to run paddle wheels to a set of rollers built into a barge that would let your spinning wheels power a prop.

"In among those designs were designs for barges that would carry the Peterbilt. Barges that could be built using wood and stone tools. Then I got here just as the big fight with Hocha was ending, and, well, for the last year I have been spending half my time teaching modern medicine to local shamans. Half of it help-ing to design everything from a new monetary system to a new government. Half of it on new farming implements, half on new crops like the winter wheat, modern watermelons, cantaloupes, saffron, and cinnamon. That's a lot of halves. Let's just say, even though I was just advising and wasn't actually doing any of it, I've been a little busy."

"If you could find your way back to the point?" Michael asked. He understood that Jerry had been busy. They had *all* been busy. For that matter, the children of Jabir who spoke English had found themselves being teachers to their parents because the new knowledge was in English. Yet, surprisingly, he wasn't unhappy. Michael had known long before the event, back when he was driving a truck, that happiness was having a job to do and getting it done. And, since the event, he'd added the notion that being too busy to worry about whether you were happy helped as well.

"The point is I forgot all about the barges and the power supply options. There are ways to build the sort of large barge that can be used to move the Peterbilt up, down, and across the river. Most of them powered by steam engines, but some of them powered by the Peterbilt or the pickup."

They adjourned to the capsule room and put on their glasses. They sat down and Jerry used his data-retrieval skills to pull up the many options for building a barge big enough to carry the Peterbilt. There was even a barge big enough to carry the Peterbilt and its trailer.

The problem with all these plans was scale. By now, the village of Jabir had over two thousand people living there, mostly moved in from other villages of the Kadlo, but more than a few from the Gruda, who were the clan most loyal to the Pharisees of Hocha. And Fort Peterbilt had twice that many who had come from every clan. But, put them all together and that wasn't enough for a building project like this. Not if they were going to plant the crops needed to survive next year and do all the other things that a city had to do to survive.

They didn't have enough people, and they didn't have enough money. This was going to have to be a government project.

CHAPTER 18

THE BARGE

Fort Peterbilt
September 12, 1007 CE

The gavel hit the table with a loud thump. "All right, everyone settle down," Kasni said, loudly but not shouting.

The chamber was full mostly of older women. They were the representatives of their tribes and villages. There were a few young women, and even fewer men. That was less because the women were unwilling to vote for men than because the men were mostly unwilling to try for a job in something called the great women's council. The Hocha language had a single word for women's council and it was followed by the word "big." But men mostly didn't run.

"You've all heard about the proposal?" Hamadi continued.

A woman raised a hand. Bota was the representative from Pelok.

Kasni nodded and waved to Bota, who stood. "I know you are all thinking that I will be in favor of this project, but I'm not. At least, not yet. Yes, we need the Peterbilt on the west side of the Talak, but we need other things too. We need bricks. We need steel knives and axes. We need steam engines. Things that we can build now. And building this giant canoe called a barge won't get us those things."

This, Kasni thought, *isn't starting out well.*

She was right. The project almost died in the first day. For essentially the reason she wanted it. It would bring a great deal of money to Jabir, if the new government funded this project. People would have to be hired to chop down trees, to split those trees into planks, to shape and dry those planks to put them together into a hull and a framework and a deck strong enough to hold up the Peterbilt. And all those people doing all that work would, one, need to be paid, and two, would be learning valuable skills that could be put to use in other ways.

The representative of every other village and every other clan who had joined the union of clans knew it. And if they were going to be paying for it, they wanted their share.

The Pharisees of Hocha had an advantage. They weren't answerable to their home villages. For that matter, they weren't answerable to anyone, if you didn't count the gods, and by now Hamadi was convinced that the gods of the Pharisees weren't just evil. They didn't exist. They were a lie, a lie told to take power.

Still, if the Pharisees had decided they wanted a big barge, they would just order it built. Except they didn't know how. But how long would that last?

Both sides had spies.

She held up a hand. It didn't stop the arguing, so she used her gavel again. Once she had something close to quiet, she said, "The Pharisees will hear of this and they don't need a barge as big as we do, if we are going to move the Peterbilt. Smaller boats than we're planning but larger than we have, made of wood planks, powered by small steam engines, or even by men with oars, will do. If they get control of the Talak, we are all threatened. What good will our walls do if they burn our fields? We are in a race."

Main mound, Hocha
September 17, 1007 CE

"Are they going to build it?" Ho-Chag Kotep, the Priest King, asked. He was a short man and a bright one. He was also a skilled political infighter. It had taken all of that to survive after the disaster of the attack on Fort Peterbilt. It was only the fact that he'd been in charge of the assaults on the cross god worshippers in Hocha that had let him and his family maintain their high place.

"I don't know, your worship," the spy master said.

Almerak had never been to Fort Peterbilt, but he had, over the years, built a decent network of spies in that place. Almerak had sent his daughter to the gods ten years ago, long before the demon Peterbilt had come to them, bringing word of the cross god. He knew that the cross god was a lie meant to anger the true gods to destroy the people, and perhaps destroy the whole world. After having sent his daughter to the god, he *had* to believe that, and he did.

But he didn't count on belief to keep his agents honest. He made sure that he had hostages for their continued honor. "My spies say that the 'great women's council' is arguing about it. Each woman insisting that this or that part of it be placed in her village.

"More to the point, should we build a steamboat?"

"Yes! And we should put rockets on it."

The bang powder was very useful for any number of things, and the priest scholars of the temple had been experimenting with it, based on comments about fireworks that Shane had shared with other children. Hocha now had bang powder rockets that would fly great distances and then blow up. They weren't all that accurate, but they had them.

In the last three hundred years or so, the priest class of Hocha had been the only place for a young man interested in science to go. Other than that, it was warrior or farmer. They had developed a system of numbers and a very perishable form of recording information. In exchange for the knowledge, the secret knowledge, and the privileges that went with it, they simply had to do their spiritual duty, including the sacrifice of young women to make sure that the next year's harvest would be good.

The fact that all that learning was located in Hocha meant they had a cadre of people who could understand concepts like buoyancy and equal and opposite reaction on first hearing them. The fact that they'd been steeped in their faith meant that they were less likely to abandon it. All put together, it meant that Hocha was quick to pick up on the technical stuff, but loyal to their faith.

They were already making birchbark canoes and double canoes with platforms between them. They were making iron and steel and using the potter's wheel and spinning wheel and, on their own, they had developed a pedal-powered paddle wheel to propel their double canoes.

Ho-Chag Kotep was confident that they could make a steam-powered barge if they decided to. The issue was cost. A great deal of their income was based on the "donated" labor of the subject clans and villages. And with the disaster of Fort Peterbilt and the failed insurrection in Hocha itself, they were short on labor and food. The harvest hadn't been good because the sort of farming they did was very labor intensive. Also, by now the villages were reinforcing their walls, and keeping their food behind the walls.

"Very well, Almerak," Ho-Chag Kotep said. "Send in Malak on your way out." Malak was Ho-Chag Kotep's counselor of the mysteries, effectively the chief engineer for Hocha.

Malak was in favor of the idea, but wondered where they were going to get the food to feed the workers who would build boats.

"We will take it from the villages of the unbelievers and use their bodies to restore the land."

Fort Peterbilt
September 25, 1007 CE

They were in Etaka's house, Kasni and three women who had become the leaders of the delegations from Kacla, Lomak, and Purdak. The great women's council hadn't developed political parties. Instead they'd stuck to clans, each clan tending to support the villages in their clan and also to control their votes.

Etaka and her daughter Oaka brought out corn cakes and a bean stew thickened with chicken and containing spices. The women sat at table to discuss the ongoing wrangle over whether to build the great barge and what parts of it should be built in what village.

"I just got word from Gada," Kasni said. "It's confirmed the Pharisees at Hocha are going to build river barges."

"And?" asked Prutsa, the representative from Abaka, a village of the Kacla clan.

"From what Gada is hearing from his friends in Hocha, they have some new weapon, some sort of flying bomb. It uses the bang powder to make it fly."

"Do they really have it?" asked Kochi, a representative from Takiso. "Or is it another lie?" Kochi was a zealous follower of the cross god, having lost one of her daughters to the old gods. She didn't want to believe that the Pharisees could do anything but steal and kill. Before the Peterbilt's arrival, she'd been almost as fanatical in her support of the old gods.

"Gada thinks they do," Kasni said, dipping a corn cake in the stew. "He's been hearing rumors about some new bang powder weapon for months. But the point is, if we don't get to work on the great barge, we'll still be arguing when they come down the Talak on their steam barges."

"Even if we agree and start building it now," Prutsa said, tapping a corn cake on the table, "they will still be coming down the river before it's half finished. The problem with the great barge is that it's a *great* barge. It's too big, it will take too long to make. We need to be building steam engines anyway. They don't need refined oil like the Peterbilt or gasoline like the pickup. That's what Jerry Jefferson says."

"We're working on it," Etaka said as she set a pot of herbal tea on the table. "We've poured steel cylinders, but they still need to be ground to a smooth finish, so that the piston will move easily, but still hold pressure. That takes a boring machine."

"And do we have boring machines?" asked Kochi.

"Yes, but they still break down a lot," Etaka admitted. Her daughter Oaka had been one of the first of the people to go live with the Peterbilt people and was a decent speaker of English, who could read and write. So she was well versed in the various projects going on in Fort Peterbilt and Jabir. She was bringing in a set of cups glazed a bright red. They were made on the potter's wheel and were light and airy for clay vessels, not quite porcelain but moving in that direction.

"*We* made a deliberate decision to focus on building the tools to build the tools, rather than hand-making steam engines," Oaka said. "Once we start making them, we will be able to make a lot of them, very quickly."

"The Peterbilt people do everything quickly," Prutsa said, not altogether approvingly.

"Not this quickly. We aren't building steam engines because we've been putting all our effort into building a steam engine factory. Part of that is that we want to use tube boilers rather than pot boilers, because they are safer. We also need relief valves that work consistently, because when a boiler blows up, people die."

"Your Peterbilt people are too soft," said Januki, the representative from Akadas, a Lomak village. She was a persuasive speaker in the great women's council, but was often silent, preferring to listen rather than speak. She was a pragmatic convert to the cross god, not one who had particularly objected to the sacrifices, but rather one who recognized the cross god offered them more. Kasni suspected that, like Jerry Jefferson, she didn't actually believe in any god. But she attended the Sunday church meetings. "Yes, someone might die now and again, but people die all the time, for all sorts of reasons. And a working steam tractor would feed a lot of children in villages where the angel Peterbilt and the pickup cannot reach."

"That's true," Oaka admitted, "but that would just be a few steam engines. Once we get this going, we'll have dozens, maybe even hundreds. And they will be safer. No steam engine is completely safe, any more than an internal combustion engine is perfectly safe."

Januki nodded, then said, "Well, that's another reason to make smaller barges rather than the big one for the Peterbilt. Smaller barges will take the new steam engine across the river to power steam tractors on the east and south sides of the Talak."

It was a good point, and for now at least, it was the final nail in the coffin for the Peterbilt barge project.

Across Fort Peterbilt, in a wattle-and-daub building, there was a hand-built steam engine using a pot boiler. It wasn't to power a steamboat of any size. Instead it was designed to take wrought steel and pound it into sheets that might then be coiled into tube boilers to run a steam engine. It was designed to be used just long enough to build a tube boiler, which would then replace the pot boiler that provided its steam, and they were just about there.

Ugar was a large man. Not as large as the giant Michael, but he stood five feet eleven as the Peterbilt people measured things and weighed over two hundred pounds. He was bright enough, but not a quick thinker in an emergency, so not a good hunter. He'd spent most of his life in the village of Kallabi and had moved here after he saw the angel Peterbilt plow the fields in Kallabi. He didn't see all that much future in digging holes to plant corn.

Once the sheet was yellow hot, he pulled it from the forge

and ran it through the rollers. Then he repeated the process, decreasing the size on each repeat until he had a sheet less than a quarter-inch thick, then he wrapped it around a dowel to form a tube. It wasn't a very long tube, about eight inches, but once he'd completed it and welded the edges, he shaped the still hot tube into a half coil and put it aside.

Then he did it again. By now he had over fifty of the short tubes.

Another worker took the tubes and added threading, so that they would fit into a "tube block." It was a design that had been developed in the twenty-first century, and like the pot boiler it was to replace, it was an intermediary step. Something that they could build, even though they lacked the tools to make long high-carbon steel pipes. It would work, and since the "tube block" was made of much thicker steel, if a break happened, it would happen at the tubes, which were to be in a box so the accident would be contained. Just a steam leak and a no longer working engine, rather than an explosion that killed dozens.

Two days later, they had their first of the compromise tube boilers. Two days after that, they had ten of them.

In still another building in Fort Peterbilt, they were making the actual engines. They were cylinders of poured steel, and they were just now getting temperatures up high enough for crucible steel. The cylinders were poured into clay molds so that the walls wouldn't need as much finishing. It was expensive, but there were steam engines waiting for the new boilers.

Outside Fort Peterbilt
October 3, 1007 CE

The steam tractor had large wooden wheels with ridges designed to sink into the ground and grip it. It had one of the new steam engines to run it. Melanie guessed that it produced about six horsepower. Not much compared to the Peterbilt, or even the Ram, but the sucker would pull a six-bladed plow through the grassland, cutting through the heavy roots. It meant that, Peterbilt or not, the river people were no longer tied to the rivers. Not on either side of the river.

Of course, when put together, the tractor was almost as big

as the pickup, but they'd made it here. It could be disassembled and shipped across the river in several loads. It would still need some big-ass canoes, but nothing like the size of the barge.

Kasni watched it with joy. At least some joy. Yes, it was a good thing. It would help all the allied clans that had signed the constitution. But it was another reason not to build the barge for the Peterbilt. And Kasni, a politician to the soles of her moccasins, wanted that barge. She wanted it steaming down the Talak, impressing all the people down the river all the way to the great ocean that the Peterbilt people called the Gulf of Mexico. She wanted it to travel up the Talak, and humiliate the Pharisees in Hocha and persuade the villages farther up the Talak that they should abandon the Pharisees of Hocha and join the United Clans of America.

The problem with the steam tractor was that the crafters in Hocha were even now working on making their own. They were using pot boilers and their engine cylinders leaked more than the ones built in Fort Peterbilt, but they worked.

The United Clans needed that barge.

CHAPTER 19

THE RAID

Sofaf village of the Lomak
October 10, 1007 CE

Gorai, head woman of the village of Sofaf, looked on as the men and women unloaded the canoes, bringing the tractor to their village. She was happy it was finally here and happy that it would be available to use for spring plowing, as well as helping in construction around the village in the meantime. It had cost enough.

Sofaf, which had switched allegiance to the United Clans after the Lomak chiefs in Hocha had stuck with the Pharisees, was a nice place located on the south side of the upper Talak, what the Peterbilt people called the Missouri. They were still farming in essentially the old way, not having the Peterbilt. They had adopted the Peterbilt people notion of fertilizer, so they didn't have as many fallow fields as they used to. They were also carrying steel knives made by their own blacksmith and steel arrowheads, not to mention the steel hoes they used to plant. In general, all that they could have from the Peterbilt people, they did have.

Not all of the Lomak villages had switched and there was considerable rancor, but they were also related to the people in the surrounding villages, which was some protection. Their cousins weren't in any hurry to raid their village.

Now their tractor was here. Their own Peterbilt, built in this time, mostly by the hands of people from this time. It wasn't put together yet, but it was here.

She went back to work. She was learning to write, and she was learning her numbers as well. She had a phenomenal memory. She had to have it, with no other way of recording information than her memory. Now that memory was put to use in allowing her to remember which sound each letter represented and how each word was spelled. She read slowly, at about second grade level, sounding out each word and often looking them up in the book.

Books, too, were a new innovation. A printing device based on a mimeograph had been put into use within days of Jerry Jefferson's arrival. Up until then, they'd been working on a movable type printing press, but didn't have it working yet. Those lead letters were hard to make, but a good piece of hemp cloth coated in something waterproof that can be pressed out worked just fine. You couldn't print as many copies, but you could print enough.

Sofaf village of the Lomak
October 13, 1007 CE

The raiders came out of the night. They landed their canoes a mile downriver and walked up to the vicinity of the village. Once there, they pulled out their rockets and rocket troughs and went to work. When everything was in place, they started shooting.

A rocket trough is much easier to carry than a catapult. They'd brought a lot of rockets.

The first Gorai knew of it was when rockets started landing in Sofaf. Like the catapult bombs from Hocha, they didn't have explosive warheads. They had incendiary warheads. The roofs in Sofaf were thatched. They made excellent kindling. In minutes, the whole village, close to a hundred and fifty houses, was in flames. With everyone so focused on putting the fires out, no one noticed as the warriors from Hocha slipped in and started killing.

By the time the fires were out, over half the village was dead. As many from smoke inhalation and being burned alive, as from Hocha steel axes and arrows. All the food from their excellent harvest had burned in the village store houses, but the parts of the tractor were, for the most part, made of steel. The fire didn't affect them at all. The rest of the villagers of Sofaf were tied up and taken back to Hocha, where they were executed except for a few young women, who were drugged and sacrificed to the river goddess, the goddess who had taught the priests about corn.

Fort Peterbilt
October 20, 1007 CE

Kasni banged her gavel again and again. The noise wouldn't die down, and the line from *Jesus Christ Superstar* ran through her mind. *If every tongue were stilled, the noise would still continue, the rocks and stones themselves would start to sing.* But this was no joyous *hosanna*.

This was rage.

It was a rage she shared. The news of the massacre of Sofaf had just reached them yesterday. Kasni was terrified, and because she was terrified, she was furious.

Before the gods of Hocha there had been frequent raiding between their ancestors. There were still stories told of those raids. Stories that Jerry Jefferson described as similar to the stories of the ancient Greeks or, for that matter, the ancient Israelites or any other group.

Then the Pharisees had come with their stories of the gods, and especially the river goddess Talak who made the ground ready for the corn, squash, beans, and all the other bounty that fed the people. They had condemned the raids, but only punished them if the village or clan that did the raiding was out of favor with the Pharisees.

People had gotten used to it, and the raids had diminished, but not stopped.

Then the Peterbilt people came and introduced Jesus and "Put away your sword." But, at the same time, when Fort Peterbilt was raided, the raiders got nothing and many of them died. They encouraged peace, but not because they were weak.

She pounded her gavel again, and it was still having no noticeable effect.

The attack on Sofaf wasn't a raid. It was a massacre. Everyone in the new congress was terrified, and everyone in the new congress was so angry they could, as Melanie would say, "chew nails and spit tacks." The problem was that most of that fury was based on fear, and though they wouldn't admit it, the chiefs were just as frightened as the women. They knew how to fight with bow and club, stone knives and fists. Even the new steel knives and crossbows, they understood.

But rockets that could be fired from out of bow range and destroyed warehouses full of grain? That was new. Even the trebuchets that had been used in the defense of Fort Peterbilt, then in Hocha to force out the Christian clans, weren't as frightening as the rockets.

But what was even more frightening than the rockets was the fact that somehow the Pharisees got them before the Christians. It shook the faith that the Christians had in the Peterbilt people and indirectly the faith they had in the cross god.

How had the Pharisees gotten rockets first?

Congress wasn't the only place that question was being asked.

"How could they have come up with rockets on their own?" Alyssa Jefferson asked Jerry.

They were in Jefferson house. Alyssa, Jerry, Zanni, Hamadi, as well as Shane, Zara, Michael, and Melanie. Miriam was on the floor in the living area playing a board game with her little brother.

"You got me," Jerry said. He was moving his hands around in the way he did when he was using his glasses as an interface to the computer in the capsule. "There was only one question about rockets. Miriam, you asked me about rockets?"

He looked at his daughter. The computer kept a record of every time Jerry or anyone accessed its files. And Jerry, who'd spent the last years of his training for this mission learning to be a librarian, had learned that you always record who asked a question or accessed a file.

Miriam looked up from the game she was playing. "Huh?"

"You asked me about rockets. It was March."

"Dad, that was, like, six months ago! How am I supposed to know about something that long ago?" Miriam was eight now, and doing well in school. She had lots of friends, mostly the children from Jabir and Fort Peterbilt. Both of which had lots and lots of children. With the medical knowledge brought back, first with the Peterbilt people and later with Jerry, a lot fewer children had died in the last couple of years. In fact, no child had died in either village for over a year.

Jerry was back in his virtual library, looking at what other questions Miriam had asked him around the same time. "Ah, here it is. The day before, you asked about 'The Star Spangled Banner.'"

"That's it. It was in my lessons and I sang it," Miriam said. "I even translated it for the girls." Miriam had a pack of six- to ten-year-old girls that she ran with. They played with dolls and studied together. "Red was easy, but rockets, well, they didn't have a word for rockets. But I remembered 'bottle rockets' from back in the other place." Miriam had stopped referring to the twenty-first century as home before Jerry had arrived in this time. It was the other place or the old place. This was home. Fort Peterbilt was home.

"Okay," Alyssa said, "you sang them 'The Star Spangled Banner.' 'And the rockets' red glare, the bombs bursting in air' told them about bottle rockets?"

"That's right," Miriam agreed, "and hot dogs, potato salad and ice cream, and fireworks at night."

"Now I remember," Alyssa said. "You asked me about rockets too, and about how to make hot dogs. That led to the whole sausage-making thing, which led to the smokehouse, and smoked sausage." Smoked sausage was now made in Jabir and sold up and down the Talak River. It was similar to, but different from, foods the locals had.

"In other words, it was just another day with another set of questions that led to new products," Jerry agreed.

"But I told you rockets were too complicated to make in the here and now," Alyssa said.

"Then I asked Dad, and he sent me an educational cartoon about Newton and the second law of motion. So I showed it to Jika and Tenaki." Jika and Tenaki were two of the girls that Miriam played with, and they were both talkative and well liked. So from there, the cartoon on basic rocketry could have gone anywhere. "But I told 'em that it was too complicated for the here and now, just like you said," Miriam told her mother.

"I guess someone didn't believe that part," Jerry said.

"I don't care if they believed it," Alyssa Jefferson said angrily. "It's true. There's a reason that people say 'it's not rocket science' about stuff that anyone can do. Rocket science is hard, complex science that takes getting everything right."

Jerry considered her. She was right and he knew it. "'It's not brain surgery' and 'it's not rocket science' were catchphrases." Then he remembered that he'd been given lessons in brain surgery. At least in how to relieve the pressure caused by a skull fracture. That there were things you could do, even without computer-controlled laser scalpels. Then he remembered something else. An argument between an engineer and an engineering manager. "It's the eighty/twenty rule. Or maybe the ninety/ten rule.

"What? It must have been three years before the mission's go date. Two of the engineers on the project, not about the basic idea, but about the exact numbers. Rick Boatright called it the eighty/twenty rule and Dian Donovan insisted it was the ninety/ten rule."

"And what is the ninety/ten rule?" Alyssa asked.

"When you're trying to improve the efficiency of something, the first ninety percent of the improvement of efficiency costs ten percent of the budget and the last ten percent of the improvement costs ninety percent of the budget."

"Okay. I've heard the same rule in reference to the efficiency of chemical processes," Alyssa agreed. "How does it apply here?"

"Because we aren't talking about a manned mission to Mars or even to the moon. We aren't even talking about an ICBM or a V2. We're talking about a bottle rocket. A little black powder in a tube stuck to a stick."

"They didn't have sticks," Hamadi said.

"Are you sure? I mean, we're working from secondhand information."

"Yes. We have a good description." Zanni had moved to Fort Peterbilt shortly before the major attack and Zanni, who was very tied in to the culture in Hocha, had become their expert on what was going on in Hocha.

"Not that good," muttered Michael.

"Yes, I know that we should have known about the raid sooner," Zanni admitted. "But the whole project was kept very close until the attack. On their way back, they had the rockets on their backs to prove they were so light that a single man could carry one. They were about four feet long, they had fins on the back, they were about a half a foot wide and the fins were angled like on an arrow, but more. Three fins, but they twisted around the body of the rocket.

"And they were painted with a feathered snake."

"Someone's figured out the gyroscopic effect," Alyssa said.

Jerry moved his hands around. "No help. That's come up forty-three times. Everything from tops to turning a bicycle."

"And throwing pots," Zara added.

"So what you're saying is we could have had rockets when Hocha attacked Fort Peterbilt?" Hamadi demanded.

"We're just people, Hamadi!" Michael said. "We've mentioned that before. We don't know everything, not even Jerry. And I thought Alyssa was the know-it-all."

"She still is," Jerry said. "I'm just a salesman, and a half-assed librarian."

"My point is: we are going to miss things. We're going to make mistakes based on stuff we think we know that doesn't turn out to be as true as we thought it was."

"I understand, Michael," Hamadi said. "I just hope others do."

"'Here lies a toppled god,'" Melanie quoted. "'His fall was not a small one. We did but build his pedestal, a narrow and a tall one.'"

"What's that?" Jerry asked.

"It's from *Dune*, I think," Melanie admitted. "One of the Dune books, anyway. I think it refers to Maud'Dib. But it's appropriate here. We are endangered not by what we know, but by the fact that we're just human beings and the people out there"—she waved at the walls—"want us to be more than that."

"Someone is going to have to make a speech," Hamadi said. "You need to explain to the congress that you were wrong."

"I'm not sure that's a good idea," Zanni said. "Admitting error could weaken us. The Pharisees never admit to mistakes if they can avoid it."

"None of that makes any sense," Shane said. "How can anyone insist on the need to sacrifice their children to the gods anymore?"

"Because people hate to admit to being wrong," Zanni said. "And the more they have committed to that mistake, the harder it is to admit it was a mistake. After you've sacrificed a daughter to the gods so that the rains will come and the Talak will flood next spring, preparing the soil for the new crop, you don't want to admit that Talak didn't want your daughter killed or, worse, that the Talak was just a river and never a god. You hold onto that belief for dear life because if Talak wasn't a god and didn't want your daughter's life, you killed her for nothing. So you have to keep believing that Talak is a god, even if it means you sacrifice another daughter."

"That's just creepy," Alyssa said.

"I know, dear, but every salesman knows it," Jerry said. "It's why encyclopedia salesmen could make a living, and why internet providers are so happy to get you to switch to their service. Because once they get you, you decide it's a good service because you don't want to admit you got took.

"Which is why Zanni has a point about the speech that Hamadi wants. People don't like to admit they were wrong, so if you stick to your story, a lot of them are going to believe you in spite of the evidence."

"But admitting we were wrong is sticking to our story," Alyssa said. "We've never claimed to be gods. We've never even claimed to be prophets or priests. We're just people who know stuff."

"Yes, I know," Jerry said. Then he sighed. "The problem is that it's less about what you said than about what other people said about you."

"So you don't think we should admit we were wrong," Michael said, starting to sound a little angry.

"No. We *have* to admit it," Jerry said. "But you need to be aware that we are going to take a political hit. It's going to hurt us, and help the Pharisees." He shook his head. "The problem is we don't want to be seen as gods or prophets, but our enemies do. They are more willing to lie than we are. It gives them an advantage in the propaganda war. And we need some way to counteract that."

"We need the big barge for the Peterbilt," Zanni said. Then, when everyone looked at her, she explained. Zanni had spent her life in the culture of Hocha, learning how the chiefs and the Pharisees interacted and operated. "The Pharisees have Hocha as this symbol of their power. The symbol of the Peterbilt people's power is the Peterbilt. It's what everyone knows about, but it's much smaller. Not as impressive as the mounds at Hocha. Not when you just hear about it. When you see it with its windows shining clear in the sunlight, it's more impressive.

"But what's really impressive about it is that it can move. We need to demonstrate that it can move across the Talak, that it can go up the river and down it, then drive around on the ground. That it's not just a pile of mud that they got someone else to move for them."

Fort Peterbilt
October 23, 1007 CE

Shane stepped up onto the platform next to the speaker and the room got quiet. She'd been selected to give the speech for a couple of reasons. First, she was young enough that she'd learned the language without much accent. Second, she was known, since she acted as translator between the adults quite often. But also because, having turned fifteen two months ago, she was very much in the age range of the young girls that were sacrificed to the river to bring the floods and the good harvests that they foretold.

She looked around, took a deep breath, and started to speak. "We are not gods, or prophets. We aren't endowed with special knowledge that only we can know. You can, given time, learn everything we know. So can the Pharisees in Hocha. We do not hide our origins or claim that the gods speak through us. We don't even claim that Jesus Christ speaks through us. Not the movie *Jesus Christ Superstar* or the gospels are us. We just happened to have them with us when we got here. My parents are Christians. Jerry Jefferson isn't. Whether you choose to be is your choice. And that choice doesn't depend on what we know, but on what you feel..."

The speech lasted almost thirty minutes, then she opened up the floor to questions and she got them. By the time she was done, most of the people in that room had the basics of how to make a black powder rocket. And it was clear that the rockets that were made in Hocha were actually inferior compared to what Alyssa Jefferson thought of as rockets.

It worked, sort of. But only sort of. The Pharisees of Hocha still claimed that their rockets were special and magical and that the "demon people" were leading the faithful away from the true gods.

On the other hand, not that long after her speech, most villages on both sides had rockets and just about every village kept guards on their walls day and night.

Report: 127
Jerry Jefferson
Fort Peterbilt
November 15, 1007 CE

The thing everyone wanted to avoid is unavoidable. It's shaping up to be a religious war. The Pharisees at Hocha

*(I know, but that's what the followers of the cross god call
them) insist that the temporally displaced persons are evil and
attempting to seduce the people away from the true gods, and
the followers of this rather unique version of Christianity are
resentful of the human sacrifice practiced by the Pharisees of
Hocha, as well as the forced labor and the gradual reduction
of the power of the women's councils.*

     *The massacre at Sofaf has hardened positions on both
sides. The Lomak clan retaliated against a Gruda village three
nights ago. It was less one-sided, but the village of Talmak
is smoking ruins and the body count was pretty high.*

Jerry sent the file along with pictures and audio recordings
of the language of this time.

PART V

PART V

CHAPTER 20

MISSION NORTH

Dock on the Agla River
March 15, 1008 CE

Michael Anderle put the Peterbilt in its lowest, slowest reverse gear and inched backward across the heavy wooden dock.

Melanie was on the barge, watching and guiding him as he carefully brought the Peterbilt across the dock, down the ramp, and onto the barge.

The ramp was heavy wood and built into the barge.

The barge had come together surprisingly well. It was big, twenty feet wide and sixty long. After a fair amount of discussion, it was equipped with its own steam engine rather than trying to get power directly from the Peterbilt. Partly that was because of the complexities involved, but mostly it was because Michael didn't want people messing with the drivetrain of his truck.

Melanie waved and Michael adjusted and continued to back as Melanie walked backward, guiding him. The front of the barge sank a bit into the mud as the weight of the Peterbilt pushed it down, then as the Peterbilt moved back toward the middle of the barge, it balanced and the front lifted out of the mud.

It was working.

After the Peterbilt was centered and tied down using hemp straps, they spent the rest of the day loading fuel and supplies.

They loaded both diesel for the Peterbilt and charcoal for the steam engine, as well as dried meat, beans, corn, and some trade goods.

Talak River
March 16, 1008 CE

Michael touched his phone in the stand next to his seat on the Peterbilt. It rang and Jerry Jefferson answered.

"So where are you?"

"In the middle of the Talak, passing Hocha now," Michael said. "Do you have a bearing?"

"Yes, I make it three hundred forty degrees."

They'd been taking regular readings, measuring angles and distance from the river to points along its banks and using math that went back to Pythagoras to measure how far they'd gone and where they were, relative to the dock they'd left from. In the process they had made a detailed map of the Talak River from the mouth of the Alba to Hocha. Using that data and the new data that Jerry had just sent, Michael pulled up the modified mapping software on the Peterbilt and looked at his location. They were just over forty miles straight-line distance from Fort Peterbilt and they'd traveled just over sixty-four miles to get here.

"Are you going to land?" Jerry asked just as a rocket was launched from Hocha. The rocket started out straight, but it then veered off to the right and landed closer to Hocha than the Peterbilt.

"Hocha just shot a rocket at us. I suspect they will claim it's a warning shot, but it wasn't. They just don't have the accuracy to hit the broadside of a barn at this distance."

"Prudence would counsel to just ignore them and steam on upriver. The closer you get, the more accurate their rockets."

"'Never tell me the odds!'" Michael quoted Han Solo from *Star Wars*, then with a laugh he continued. "This is a show-the-flag mission, Jerry. We can't be seen to be timid."

"It's your call, Michael," Jerry said doubtfully.

Michael hung up, and then hit the horn. Two short, followed by a long.

In the pilot house of the barge, which was located just over the steam engine, Achanu turned the wheel, pointing the barge at the eastern shore of the Talak. He looked over at Akvan, who was now his executive officer. "You have been here before. Where is the ground solid enough to take the weight of the Peterbilt?"

The location of Hocha was a minor puzzle to the archaeologists in the twenty-first century, just one of many. It was just a location where there was an abundance of floodplain. Lots and lots of land that flooded on a semi-regular basis, land that was easy to plant in, but not, as a rule, all that firm. But the river people had built roads, including an elevated causeway that was wide enough to take the Peterbilt.

Akvan pointed and Achanu steered for the shore. That was apparently not the response that the Pharisees had been looking for. There were shouts, and then more rockets.

None of them came all that close, but they were starting to get closer as the barge reached the shore.

More rockets were launched as the front of the barge pushed up against the shore of the Talak and the ramp came down like a drawbridge. Then Melanie climbed aboard and Michael drove down the ramp onto the shore. He drove slowly and carefully for the first couple of minutes until they got to one of the roads. Then, once the truck was on the raised earthen road, he started to pick up speed. He slowed at a corner, then there was a long straight road that went to and through Hocha.

There were wooden gates on either side of the city. Michael looked over at Melanie and said, "Ready, hon?"

She took his right hand in her left and squeezed, then gave it back to him, took a deep breath and said, "Do it!"

The Peterbilt picked up speed as for the first time in a long time Michael brought it up to respectable speed. It still wasn't fast, not compared to doing eighty along an interstate in the twentieth century. But it was doing a respectable forty miles an hour when it hit the north gate of Hocha. It barely slowed at all as the gate shattered.

Then they drove through the city and out the closed gate on the south side. Having done that, they turned around and went back through the broken gates. Then, when they reached the center of Hocha, they stopped and blew a long blast on the air horn. And then they played the recording.

Neither Michael nor Melanie were fluent enough in the language of Hocha to make such a speech, but Fazel spoke it fluently.

He'd made the speech and it had been recorded to be played if an opportunity presented itself.

> "Talak doesn't require your daughters to bring the rains that flood her and make the ground ready for new crops. It is only the false priests who demand it as proof of their power over you. They will kill you all, and all your children, before they will give up that power.
>
> "But that power is just another lie!
>
> "They have no power at all. Some have skills, but those skills aren't unique. There is nothing they can make that you can't learn to make. Nothing they can do that you can't do or learn to do. You no longer have to sacrifice your children for the rains. The rains will come anyway, and even if they don't, we can make canals to move the water to the fields, even use the Talak's strength to lift the water to feed those canals.
>
> "You are free now. If you send your daughters to them now, it is you who do it, not Talak. Jesus the Cross God will never ask you to sacrifice a child to him."

The recording ended and Michael blew the air horn again, and drove the Peterbilt out the north gate and back to the shore of the Talak.

He drove back up onto the barge, and then out toward the back of the barge, so that the weight of the Peterbilt wasn't close to the shore, and the front of the barge lifted a little. Then the ramp was pulled up and the barge backed away from the shore.

Talak River, north of Hocha
March 16, 1008 CE

The sun was setting and the anchor was dropped into the Talak.

"I hope it works," Melanie said. They were sitting in locally made lawn chairs on the barge with a folding table between them. There was stew on the table, and they all had bowls and corn tortillas.

"It was great," Achanu insisted, holding up a tortilla.

"Still worried about the whole Caudine Forks thing?" Michael asked.

"Yes, I am, and the Third Reich, Vietnam and Afghanistan, and the fact that while the Peterbilt, especially with the extra armor that we attached to the front bumper, is really good at knocking down walls, it can't be everywhere it needs to be."

"It was the chief's council's decision," Akvan said. The chief's council of the United Clans had consulted with Jerry, and had used Jerry to consult with the library that had been sent back from the twenty-first century and come up with this plan. This was a "hearts and minds" war. It was about convincing the outlying villages that the Pharisees of Hocha didn't speak for the gods.

Which meant it was all about image.

When the forces from Hocha attacked Sofaf, it was an announcement that they could do what the Peterbilt people could do, and they were "stronger," more vicious than the Peterbilt people.

The purpose of the trip to Hocha by the Peterbilt was to say, "No, you can't, and no one has to follow you." To say to the people of Hocha "No, *they* can't, and you don't have to follow *them*."

"That was the reason for the recording," Akvan insisted. He was a good kid, a bit older than Achanu, but not the natural leader that the younger man was. He was a man who needed rules.

"I just hope it had some effect," Melanie said.

Hocha
March 16, 1008 CE

Holaka rolled the corn dough out into tortillas and put them on the copper griddle. She was sixteen years old. She was the daughter of a coppersmith and she was terrified. She used a copper spatula to flip a tortilla. She wasn't afraid she would be selected to be a sacrifice, not exactly. That possibility had always been a part of her life. As a small girl she had even played at being the sacrifice and waking up in Talak's house. No, what was eating into her guts was the fear that if she was sacrificed to Talak, she wouldn't wake in Talak's house, but would just be dead. Or, maybe, wake up in the cross god's hell because she'd worshipped false gods.

Over the last two years and more, the world had changed. The teachings of *Jesus Christ Superstar* had slipped into Hocha and brought everything into question. Her parents insisted that it was all lies and that the Superstar god wasn't real. Only Talak and the other gods were. That if the sacrifices weren't made, the river would dry up and everyone would starve. She flipped another tortilla with the copper spatula, noting in the back of her mind that the copper griddle and copper spatula were both new since the Peterbilt people arrived.

There were several new things that her father made or used in his shop that came from the Peterbilt people. And if those things were real and good, how could their god be false and bad?

As it happened, she hadn't been in the square when the demon Peterbilt stopped and declared that the sacrifices didn't do anything. That Talak was just a river, not a god, and that the priests of the temple were lying to everyone. And the priests were unable to stop it, kill it, or capture it.

In many other houses much of the same questioning was going on. Some people had seen the Peterbilt break through the gates and stop in the middle of town to berate the priests and insist that the priests were liars. The priests had insisted that the demon Peterbilt had been scared off by Talak.

The fact that they'd driven through Hocha, then turned around and driven back into Hocha, made their announcement, then left, made that a rather hard sell, but they were trying.

Fort Peterbilt
March 17, 1008 CE

Jerry waved his hands in the air. At least that's what it looked like to anyone not wearing his heads-up-display glasses. To Jerry it was different.

He was looking at an augmented reality world. He could see the world around him, but overlaid were translucent boxes that opened into files of data and readings from the computer system that controlled the various radio transmitters and receivers built into the capsule and since attached to copper-wire antennas. Some of the transmitters were directional and some were networked with other antennas located in Jabir, Kallabi, and half a dozen other villages in the United Clans.

Over the more than a quarter century that Jerry had spent working to get sent back to this time, more than just him getting older had happened. Technology had gone right on expanding and improving. The transmitters in the capsule were excellent by late twenty-first-century standards. And late twenty-first-century made early and even mid-twenty-first century suck by comparison. The control and data transmittal rates would make a radio station from the late twentieth century bow its antenna in shame. But there were still limits to how far away they could send a digital signal, and even greater limits to how far away he could receive such a signal from the relatively speaking primitive transmitter in the Peterbilt.

They weren't out of range yet, but if they didn't set up a repeater station somewhere, they were going to be out of range soon. He sent them an email to that effect.

Talak River, north of Hocha
March 17, 1008 CE

"We are now on the Missouri River. Or we would be, if we were still in the future," Melanie Anderle told her husband.

"That doesn't help us find a good spot for the repeater station Jerry wants," Michael Anderle answered grumpily. He was looking out the cab at the south bank of the Talak and seeing forest. Great for hunting, but no good at all for driving a Peterbilt through.

What they needed was someplace that wouldn't be easy for the Pharisees or their followers to reach. Because a radio station would be a target for the Pharisees even more than the steam tractor was. And the last thing that Michael wanted to do was call down another raid like the one on Sofaf.

Lisyuk, south bank of Talak River
March 17, 1008 CE

Kalmak checked the guards; they were alert but bored. Lisyuk was upriver of Sofaf, or of where Sofaf had been. They were, or had been, sister villages with a lot of trade and intermarriage between them. Now Sofaf was ashes and Kalmak had lost seven close kin and many more friends and more distant kin.

There were those in Lisyuk who blamed Kalmak for the loss of Sofaf, arguing that if he'd not pushed for the alliance with the demon people, the Pharisees wouldn't have attacked Sofaf. And Kalmak wondered the same thing. Some nights he woke up in a cold sweat after being visited by his dead relatives who condemned him for defying the gods. Or dreaming of an attack on Lisyuk that ended like that one, with his family murdered by the Pharisees.

He was still up on the wall when there was a shout from the fields and someone blew on a fire basket, a small container of coals that smoldered until it was blown on, then put out a red glow for a few moments. It was harder to carry, but easier to use than flint.

"Hello in Lisyuk!" shouted the figure holding the fire basket.

"Who are you?" shouted the guard.

"Kazal of the Shulik."

The Shulik were not among the clans of the river people. They were hunters, specifically buffalo hunters, who lived to the south and west of Sofaf for part of the year. In the spring, they moved west into the plains and hunted buffalo. Then, in the fall, they moved back east to winter in the hills. They traded buffalo products for corn, beans, squash, and other goods.

"What are you doing here in the middle of the night?" Kalmak demanded.

"We went to Sofaf to trade for corn, but Sofaf isn't there anymore. What happened?"

"Come ahead," Kalmak shouted, and three men walked forward. Kalmak went down to meet the men.

Twenty minutes later, Kalmak and the three men were seated in his house with its new chimney and its new steel plate on the top of the fire pit. There were lamps to give light. They were bowls filled with tallow, with hemp to act as a wick.

The Shulik were a hard people, but they didn't like the gods of the river people. And before the Peterbilt people came, trade with them was illegal, but it was also quite common.

Kalmak found himself telling Kazal and his companions about what had happened to the village of Sofaf. When he was finished, Kazal was not overly sympathetic.

"You never should have listened to those crazy people in the mound place."

Kalmak mostly agreed, but he didn't much like hearing it from this savage. But what could he say?

Kazal shook his head, and said, "Tell me more about the Peterbilt people?"

"Better. I'll show you." Kalmak led them to the new forge

and showed them the steel knives, axes, and arrowheads. Then he showed them the stoneware jugs and the small glass diamonds that were knit together with lead to make windows in the huts. The quality of the glass wasn't good enough to look through, but they let light through. By the time the tour was wrapping up, the sun was coming up.

Kazal stayed in Lisyuk, sending one of the men with him back to his tribe to let them know what had happened to Sofaf and to let them know that Lisyuk had food and more to trade for buffalo and other goods of the great plains.

They were still in Lisyuk when the Peterbilt arrived.

Fort Peterbilt
March 21, 1008 CE

The downriver mission was just about ready, and Jerry wasn't really happy about that. He was going to be stuck here manning the computer system while Alyssa and Shane would be the Peterbilt people going with the mission south. The kids, over their strong objections, would be staying here in what was by now a full city, at least by eleventh-century standards. There were almost ten thousand people here, about half in Fort Peterbilt and the rest spread out between Fort Peterbilt and Jabir. With the Peterbilt and the pickup to do the plowing, this spring's planting would cover twice the ground that last year's had covered. There was going to be plenty of food this fall, even for the expanded population.

The computer beeped in his ear. They were getting a message from the Peterbilt. At this distance, voice or video were not an option, and even text was taking a long time.

Jerry called up the email and read. "Reached Lisyuk. There are plains natives here. If these guys had horses, they'd be Apache."

It wasn't accurate. Jerry snorted. Michael wasn't always as politically sensitive as he might be. It was unlikely that the people he was dealing with were the ancestors of the Apache. They were mostly further south, in the area of Arizona. But that location was based on evidence from six hundred years or so from now. For all Jerry or anyone knew, these might be the ancestors of the Apache. The truth was, no one knew about the way the people of the Americas moved about in the centuries before the Europeans arrived.

"Bows and arrows. They hunt buffalo using traps and stampeding them. They also hunt other animals and they want to trade with us."

Jerry considered. Missouri was on the east end of the great plains, and a lot of it was forested hill country, more of it now than in the twenty-first century. The buffalo were on the west side of the state.

He pulled up his virtual keyboard and typed. "Are they willing to move east, or do they know a tribe that lives closer to the southern Talak? We are going to need repeater stations if we are going to set up a radio and weather network."

One of the things in the capsule was a lot of integrated circuits. Most of them could be used to produce radio repeater stations, what amounted to cell towers if they were connected to the right locally made hardware. They could also be hooked up to locally made pressure and temperature gauges, as well as wind speed and rain gauges, so that a weather station could be built using the same chips as its centerpiece.

They'd loaded him up with equipment as flexible as they could think of because they hadn't known what he was going to be landing in. Fortunately, computer chips can be exceedingly flexible and the capsule came with a ROM writer so he could program the chips with read-only memory so that they wouldn't lose their programs if they lost power.

"Program" was probably overstating it. He'd been equipped with preprogrammed black boxes that could be loaded onto the molecular chips to make the chip into a phone, a repeater station, a weather station, a genetic analysis computer, or a host of other things. Jerry didn't know how the black boxes worked, but he did know that they'd been carefully designed so that they wouldn't interfere with each other.

He could use the chips he'd brought along and a steam power generator, lead acid batteries, and some other locally made components to build a repeater station that would also be a weather station, extending the range of the main computer system. But he only had a limited stock of chips and considering what had happened to Sofaf, putting one in a village that might be raided by the Pharisees' army struck him as a bad idea. Some place distant from the rivers that were the main means of transportation for the river people struck him as a useful option.

Lisyuk, south bank of Talak River
March 21, 1008 CE

Michael looked up from the computer in the cab of the Peterbilt. He'd been trading emails with Jerry Jefferson for the last hour while consulting with Kalmak and Kazal about what the "Wild Injuns" would be willing to do.

Melanie had muttered about that as they were driving the Peterbilt up onto the shore next to Lisyuk. Achanu had heard her, and knew the term from the movies that Jerry Jefferson had brought back with him. They weren't all educational. There were old movies too. He'd told Kazal and after having the "derogatory term" explained to him, he'd taken it as his own. His people were quite proud of being untamed. A wild people, unlike the settled river people.

"What do you think, Kazal? Will your people be willing to set up a radio weather station in the hills if we show you how?"

"It would be better to have some of the river people run the station, but we will guard it and make sure they are warned. Show me that map again."

"It's not going to be that accurate. We know that the Talak has changed its course in the thousand years between now and when we come from. It's stayed in the same river valley, but the specific track has changed a lot."

"I know and it doesn't make a great deal of sense to me anyway. But I know this land and my people know this land. We know where the river people villages are. If you send a group to Takiso, we can guide them through the forest to a high hill where they can set up their repeater." He pointed at the map on the screen in the Peterbilt's cab. "It will be around there, I think." He was pointing at an area about forty miles west-southwest from Takiso.

Michael pulled up the height map and found a hill there that was fifteen hundred feet above sea level, whereas Fort Peterbilt was only a bit over four hundred feet above sea level. A repeater station located on that hilltop would give them a lot of range and being on a hilltop would probably be pretty defensible, assuming they could find a good water supply, and keep it supplied.

CHAPTER 21

HILLTOP STATION

Lisyuk, south bank of Talak River
March 24, 1008 CE

Three days later, they loaded up the Peterbilt barge with about two tons of dried buffalo meat and other products of the large animals, including quite a bit of tallow, and, perhaps most importantly, they loaded up Kazal and his mate Larka and headed back.

Larka was fascinated by the steam engine. The Peterbilt's engine was magic, hidden as it was under the hood, and most of the workings invisible even with the hood opened. But the steam engine... that she could follow. That, she could make sense of. She knew from her own experience that a little water made a lot of steam, and she knew just as well that when you blew air into a tied-off piece of buffalo gut, it expanded. She put that together and the steam engine was clear and obvious to her. She loved it. A device that would do work, that would push the barge through the water. It was glorious.

Kazal watched his wife and shook his head. "You have ruined my life, Michael. She will never want to leave your repeater station." He put on an expression of mock horror. "I may have to learn to farm."

"It's not that bad," Michael said. "I doubt that there's any place to farm on that hill anyway."

Fort Peterbilt
March 26, 1008 CE

The Peterbilt drove through the gate, and up to their tanker. Michael climbed down to start the laborious process of refilling the Peterbilt's tanks from the tanker trailer. The diesel was pumped out, then stirred, then carried over to the Peterbilt, one jerrican at a time. While in Lisyuk they used the Peterbilt to plow up several fields above the floodplain so that they would be able to plant there. It had used a fair amount of gas.

While Michael was doing that, Melanie introduced Larka and Kazal to the women's council, and discussed the prospect of the weather station and "Fort Hilltop."

"We should bring Dikak into this," Etaka said.

Melanie grimaced. Dikak was a priest from Hocha, one of the priests of Xuhpi, the sun god who was considered a cousin of Talak.

Etaka saw the grimace and said, "Before you came, Hocha was the only place for someone like Dikak."

It was true and Melanie knew it. The closest thing that the river people had had to any sort of school was the Hocha priesthoods. And that put them ahead of anyone else in North America. Dikak had worked with copper, including copper wires. He knew about irrigation and other things. He also knew a great deal that wasn't true. At the same time, he was one of a group of "intellectuals" that had defected from Hocha to Jabir and Fort Peterbilt over the last couple of years.

He was a short stocky man with ritual scars on his face from ritual bloodletting to appease the sun god, and he gave Melanie the creeps. At the same time, he was probably their best local expert on electrical generation and lead acid batteries. And much of the radio repeater and weather-measuring equipment was made by him or under his supervision.

Dikak was winding a coil of wire around a cylinder when he was called to the meeting. It was a slow and laborious process with the copper wire separated so they didn't touch. You could go from one end of the cylinder to the other, then you had to stop and paint the cylinder with two coats of resin, letting each coat dry. Then you could wind the next layer and paint that. The reason they had to do it this way was because while they had insulators, the resin was one. They didn't have flexible insulators, at least not flexible insulators that would let the wires fit as closely together as they needed to for a powerful electromagnet.

Dikak wanted rubber. They had rubber in South and Central America. It said so in the magic capsule from the future. He wanted an expedition to South America to trade for latex.

"They want you in the women's council," his assistant told him. She'd been born in Jabir and moved to Fort Peterbilt when it was still Camp Peterbilt, so she spoke English better than he did and understood almost as much about electricity as he did.

Dikak was ambivalent about the project. He agreed that such a station was needed and was even convinced that they would need his batteries and generators to power it, but he didn't want to go. He'd just gotten his hut the way he liked it after he'd moved from Hocha.

The truth was Dikak wasn't good with change. He was very smart and learned many things very quickly, but he didn't deal well with new situations.

Takiso
March 30, 1008 CE

The Peterbilt moved slowly up the slight rise next to the walled village of Takiso, following Kazal. He, by now, knew what the Peterbilt needed in the way of surface to drive over. Bushes, even small trees, the Peterbilt could push through and crush, but dips in the land were another matter. So Kazal spent yesterday scouting the route, and was now walking in front of the Peterbilt, guiding it as it drove into and through the woods, pulling a small locally made trailer full of goods. Packing those goods on people's backs could be done, and probably was going to have to be done later, but as far as the Peterbilt could take them, that was how far men didn't have to carry heavy lead acid batteries on their backs. And the station was going to take a lot of lead acid batteries to operate.

Forest southeast of Takiso
April 4, 1008 CE

Kazal climbed up on the Peterbilt's running board. "That's as far as the Peterbilt can go. The creek is dry, but the crack in the earth where it flows is too much."

"Well, we did fairly well," Michael said.

They'd traveled a roundabout route, and gotten about twenty-three miles toward the hilltop that would hold Fort Hilltop.

That only left about seven more miles and the people carting the stuff up the hill weren't going to have to go quite so far out of their way. So it was going to be about a ten-mile slog through the woods and up the hill. They'd be lucky if they made five miles a day, but with any luck they would have all the gear on the top of the hill by the seventh. Of course, then they'd need to chop down the trees to build the walls, but they had steel axes and saws. Michael helped them unload, then turned the Peterbilt around and drove back to the river.

Fort Hilltop
April 7, 1008 CE

Kazal looked around. It wasn't a fort, not yet. It was a hilltop covered in old-growth forest. But it was over a thousand feet higher than Fort Peterbilt and with the derrick they were planning, they would add another hundred above that.

Right now it was just a chunk of forest with sacks stacked everywhere, and about a hundred men guarding them. A hundred men and twenty women, including his wife. They had supplies, dried corn, dried beans, dried squash, dried strawberries, black berries, and even a fair amount of dried buffalo meat and dried fish.

What they needed was water. The St. Francois Aquifer should be here, according to the data sent back with Jerry Jefferson. The issue was going to be reaching it.

Meanwhile, Kazal needed to get away from all these people or he was going to kill someone. He gathered up his gear and a few friends, and after talking to his wife, went hunting.

Larka knew her husband. He was a good man, but he was first and foremost a hunter. Organizing camps wasn't something that she felt men were suited for. She got to work organizing the labor forming crews to use the case-hardened axes to chop down trees, and collect rocks for a fire pit. "Dikak, set up your batteries?"

Dikak looked up blearily. He wasn't used to walking so far in a day. He especially wasn't used to walking so far uphill with a thirty-pound pack of equipment on his back. After a moment, he nodded, but made no other move to comply.

Larka looked at him, shook her head, and went off to other tasks. She knew the man a little by now. Eventually, in five minutes or an hour, he would get up and get to work. Pushing him wouldn't get it done one moment sooner. It would just piss him off and frustrate her.

Fifteen minutes later, Dikak got up and started setting up the batteries and the generator. The generator was powered by a small steam engine, two small cylinders, and a flywheel, which got its steam from a tube boiler. It took him an hour to get the batteries set up and connected to the chip set that was the radio. The chipsets had connection and their radios broadcast on several frequencies. So the single pair of glasses computer that they'd sent along didn't need to be plugged in. Not this close to the main radio station.

Dikak went over to Larka. "I need the computer."

"Yes, certainly," Larka said.

She reached into her pack and pulled a wooden box wrapped in leather from it. She unwrapped the box, then opened it and removed the glasses. She handed them to him.

He opened them, and put them on. He then touched his fingertips to the upper edge of the glasses so that they would know which user was accessing them, then he called up the pairing function and paired them with the local radio station that was hooked up to the bank of lead acid batteries. CONNECTED showed up in front of his face, looking like the word was hanging in the air about two feet away. At the same time, the bone conduction ear pieces that were part of the glasses said the word "Connected."

"I'm connected."

"Well, try giving Fort Peterbilt a call," Larka told him.

"I don't have the antenna hooked up yet. Just a bit of copper wire."

"Well, they have their antenna hooked up. Give it a try."

He did, calling Jerry Jefferson. His display showed only one bar, but Jerry answered. "Hello, Dikak. What's up?"

"Just a communications check," Dikak said.

"Tell him we're encamped at the location for Fort Hilltop," Larka demanded.

"I heard," Jerry said. "Good job, people. When do you expect to do the seismic tests?"

"Not for a few days." Along with the thermometers, humidity gauges, and so on that Dikak had built under the instructions of the recordings brought by Jerry Jefferson were a set of seismometers. A seismometer is just a couple of magnets, at least one of which should be an electromagnet. When the earth vibrates, one of the magnets vibrates, and you get an electrical reading. The trick is in interpreting the vibrations, and that would be done by the big computer built into the capsule in Fort Peterbilt. "I want to get the weather station set up and operating first. After all, predicting the weather is the cornerstone of the power of the priests of Hocha."

Unlike most people, Dikak didn't call the priests of Hocha "Pharisees." He wasn't sure what he believed, except he believed in electricity.

Fort Peterbilt
April 10, 1008 CE

Jerry picked up the chicken and put it in the basket. He paid the woman with two coins, a one and a five. Meat was still much more expensive than corn or other vegetables. The man behind him made a fairly rude grunt, and Jerry looked around and lifted an eyebrow. The man said something in Kadlok, but Jerry could barely understand it.

"You mind your own business," said the woman keeping the stall. She was one of the women of Fort Peterbilt and had her own flock of chickens. This time Jerry could understand. "This is Jerry Jefferson."

"I don't trust *moi*," the man said belligerently.

"*Moi?*"

"He means money," the woman said. "He's from Abaka, a Kacla village. That's why he has the accent."

Jerry nodded understanding. Each clan had its own dialect, or perhaps language, often as different from each other as Spanish and Portuguese, and sometimes as different as Spanish and French. The stranger wasn't speaking Kadlok, but Kaclak, which was either a different language or, at the very least, a different dialect of the river people tongue.

"Why don't you trust money?" Jerry asked.

"Because he's an ignorant fool," said the woman, whose name Jerry couldn't remember.

"Because it has no value. You can't eat it or wear it or use it to hoe your garden. Not that I'm needed to hoe my garden anymore, what with the Peterbilt and the pickup plowing up the land."

"Well, you still need to plant the seeds," Jerry offered, starting to sort of understand the man's speech. Jerry was still learning Kadlok, and Kaclak was quite close.

"My wife and daughters use the seed planter. And they've planted half again the fields this year." He was an older man, so his children were probably teenagers. He was also a bit stooped from doing backbreaking labor for much of his life. He shook his head. "She told me to go find a new trade and not come back until I had one."

"That's harsh," Jerry muttered. This was a matrilineal culture and in most, but by no means all, of the villages, that meant that the women owned most of the real property, land, huts, that sort of thing. So a woman who wasn't happy with her man could throw him out, which would leave him without a great deal. It didn't happen often, but it was happening more often as the men's labor was less needed. "What would you like to learn to do?"

"I'm a farmer!" the man said belligerently. Then he sighed and admitted, "I don't know how to do much of anything else."

The woman who owned the stall cleared her throat, and the man tried to buy a chicken with a stone hoe blade—one of the things that had been used as quasi money before the Peterbilt arrived—wanting change.

"And don't try to foist off that *moi* on me. I want corn or beans."

"Well, you'll not get it here," the woman said. "And that blade isn't worth much anyway. We have steel blades now."

So not only did the older man not trust the new money, his old money was losing its value. And while that was true of the stone blades, it was perhaps even more true of the corn and beans because the extra fields meant more seeds planted and more food grown, so the value of food decreased. At least the foods that were the cornerstones of the local economy. Yes, it meant that fewer children would starve this winter, but it also meant that it took more beans to buy a leather pouch or a mortar and pestle, or any of the other products that were for sale in the Fort Peterbilt marketplace. And there were a lot of new products. Aside from the seeders and the steel hoe heads, there were spinning wheels, wood lathes, tables, chairs, fabrics, printed books, many of them picture books on everything from reading and writing to how to sterilize a wound or set a broken arm.

Jerry considered. Winter wheat was growing in nearby fields and there would be enough when it was harvested to plant several fields. The natives knew how to process corn so that it provided the proper vitamins and minerals, something that had taken a while to cross the Atlantic in that other history. What was there for this man to do? "Come with me," Jerry offered. "We'll go to the capsule and see if we can find you a new job."

Putting his stone hoe back in the leather pouch, the man followed Jerry.

"What's your name?"

"Broko."

At the capsule, Jerry put on his computer and started a search for jobs for displaced farmers. There were a lot of options, but at least half the problem was that Broko didn't want to change jobs. He wasn't the brightest man Jerry had met. He knew how to farm, which he had learned at his parents' knees, and that was pretty much all he knew. He took pride and satisfaction out of the slow and simple process of hand-planting seeds and seeing them grown into the food that would feed his family. And because of that, he had resisted every change to farming, and really all the changes brought by the Peterbilt people.

It took them some time but they came up with a pretty simple way to make a produce box out of wood shavings. The shavings, about four inches across, were folded so that each sheet formed the bottom and two sides of the box, while a smaller strip was woven through them at the rim to keep the whole thing together. It wasn't much, but it would let him make a product from local trees and perhaps get by.

Jerry wished he could do better for the man, but he stubbornly rejected just about everything Jerry suggested. The truth was, the old fellow wanted the world to go back to what it used to be.

Old fellow, hell. The guy wasn't much older than Alyssa. He sent Broko on his way shortly before Alyssa got back from the lab.

"How was your day?" Jerry asked.

"Frustrating. How was yours?"

"I'll match you frustration for frustration," Jerry said and told her Broko's tale of woe.

"Ha! I bet he talked about the good old days when they sacrificed young women to the river god to bring the harvest one too many times for his wife and daughters."

Jerry didn't know. Broko hadn't mentioned human sacrifice, but then he wouldn't, not in Fort Peterbilt. The people who lived and worked here were among the least forgiving of the practices of the Pharisees. Which position, Jerry completely agreed with. He was enough of a salesman to express his distaste in less strident terms than most of the new followers of the cross god.

"Well, we have working caps, but smokeless is causing us problems." One of the things in the library was a way of making the caps for cap and ball revolvers that didn't involve nitrated mercury but used potassium chlorate instead. Potassium chlorate was much easier and safer to make and much less likely to explode while you were making it or loading it into the copper cap.

That part was working fine, and they'd been assiduous about collecting up their brass, so if they could get a smokeless powder which wouldn't clog the guns like black powder did, they could reload the brass and keep using the guns.

Jerry's guns, the ones he'd brought, were specially made so that they could use either black or smokeless powder, and they used an electric spark to ignite the powder, so they didn't even need primers. But those two guns were like ten grand apiece and utterly beyond anything they could do in the here and now.

By now they were out of unexpended rounds for the guns that had come back in the original event, and those guns were important, more for their political effect than their military or hunting uses.

There was iron made here in Jabir, and all throughout the United Clans, but everyone was still learning to use the new metal. It was going to be a while before anyone was turning out barrels in any quantity, much less the six-cylinder chambers of a revolver.

Fort Hilltop
April 15, 1008 CE

Dikak put the computer on and touched the upper rim and found himself in the augmented reality of the computer world. The computer at Fort Peterbilt was, by the standards of the mid-twentieth century, a supercomputer. For that matter, the computers built into the glasses he was wearing and the small chip that was the core of the radio and weather station were pretty darn powerful as well. The limiting factor was the data transmittal rate between the computers here and the big one back at Fort Peterbilt.

They were finally ready to do the seismic test to see what was under the hill they were sitting on and how it lined up with the information in Jerry Jefferson's database.

According to Jerry Jefferson's geological information, there should be iron here. Iron that could be mined and which would be much better for making steel than the bog iron they were using now.

Having set up the computers and attached them to the sensors, Dikak waved to Kazal, who was back from his most recent hunting trip. Kazal now hunted with a crossbow, and regularly returned to Fort Hilltop with deer. And this last time with a bear, which he'd killed more for the protection of hunter-gatherers than for the meat and grease. Not that the grease wasn't going to be useful.

At Dikak's wave, Kazal lit the fuse which led to a buried charge that was down against the stone of the ridge. Half a minute later, the small charge went off and the sensors that Dikak had put out vibrated with the blast. Dikak had made four of them, but only three of them worked. In the fourth, the rod was stuck and couldn't move through the hand-wound electrical coil.

Fortunately, three of them were enough. They located several small deposits of magnetite, or what the computers thought were magnetite, close to the surface.

Fort Peterbilt
April 15, 1008 CE

Jerry got the results of the seismic test almost as soon as Dikak did, and while it added a bit of detail, it mostly acted as confirmation of the information in the capsule computer's geological maps. If the iron was where it was supposed to be, it was a safe bet that the oil was too. So they knew where there were oil fields that could be dug, even using the materials that they had locally. At least when combined with the pickup truck's engine to provide power.

It was time for the mission downstream.

CHAPTER 22

MISSISSIPPI OIL

Fort Peterbilt
April 18, 1008 CE

Michael Anderle looked at the now mostly empty tanker trailer and sighed. For three years they had been using the gasoline and fuel oil, not just to run the Peterbilt, pickup and generators, but to help with starting fires and heating forges and kilns to make iron, steel and stoneware of all sorts, boiling water, sterilizing instruments, distilling alcohol, nixtamalization of corn, and so on and so forth.

The fuel hadn't been wasted; it had meant the difference between life and death for hundreds of people. And even when it hadn't meant life and death, it had meant a significantly improved standard of living.

But it was running out.

And they needed more oil. Jerry's database included locations for really shallow oil wells in several places that were on or near the Mississippi River, according to geological surveys in the latter part of the twenty-first century. How well that information would line up with the course of the Talak River in the year of our lord 1008 was less certain. The oil wouldn't have moved, at least not much, but the river would have shifted its course over the thousand-plus years.

That meant wildcatting, and that meant pipes and drilling

gear. Which they still mostly didn't have. It was on the list, but kept being pushed down as other things took precedence.

Michael shook his head. That had to stop. If they didn't get oil, the Peterbilt was going to stop working. If they didn't learn to refine gasoline, the pickup and the generators were going to stop. Well, the pickup was. They'd already replaced the gasoline engine on one of the generators with a steam engine.

Melanie put a hand on his shoulder, and said, "We'll get to it."

"We have to get to it now. Or next year, folks are going to be plowing the fields by hand. More importantly, the Peterbilt has become the symbol of our new nation, and having it stop working will hurt us all."

Jerry took off his glasses computer and carefully set it in its case. "There are a number of workarounds that we can do. Pipes don't have to be made of iron or steel. Wood will work if the pipe doesn't have to go too deep."

He waved at the screen where a geologist was narrating a cartoon about how to drill a thousand foot deep well using wooden pipe and a hydraulically powered cutting head.

"Okay," Alyssa said, "you guys get to work on the oil rig, while I go down the Talak with the pickup barge, and start negotiating with the local tribes."

"I'm going too," Shane said. At her parents' look, she said, "I'm fifteen, Mom. And in this time, girls are starting to ... well, you know."

"And you know that you-know-what is going to wait at least a couple of more years. Why do you want to go?"

"More like a decade," added Michael.

Shane rolled her eyes. "I need to go because, aside from Jerry, I'm best with the glasses computers."

It was true. The glasses computers were a new and different system with their augmented reality and virtual keyboards. Like learning a new language, it was easier when you were younger. Jerry had been extensively trained in it, but in spite of, or just possibly because of Alyssa's ability with the keyboard and screen systems she'd grown up with, she still hadn't gotten used to the new system. Certainly not as quickly as the youngsters had. Michael and Melanie were better than Alyssa with the new system, but not as good as Shane. And besides, they were going to be needed upriver plowing fields and negotiating with the northern and western clans.

Talak River
April 28, 1008 CE

Keneva waved to Pulok, the engineer. Pulok pulled the lever that engaged the propeller.

Keneva was the barge captain. He was a member of the Kadlo from Kallabi. A man in his forties, he'd studied with the shaman from Kallabi, then been a trader by canoe to tribes to the south of the United Clan's territory. He'd moved to Fort Peterbilt to study about the time that Jerry Jefferson had arrived.

He was proud of the boat, but what he really wanted was a seagoing ship.

The barge backed away from the dock, and Keneva turned the wheel. The barge slowly turned, and once it was close enough to pointing downriver, he straightened the rudder and called, "Okay, Pulok. Forward engines."

Pulok pushed the lever forward, then she reached down and shoved the wooden gear to the left. Then she reengaged the chain drive and the propeller started turning the other way. The barge started to move forward down the river. Pulok was from Jabir, and had been learning about the magic of the Peterbilt people since their arrival. She knew as much about steam engines and gear systems as anyone on Earth. She checked the steam gauges, and looked at the flywheel to see how fast the engine was turning. She nodded to the fireman and he shoveled a bit more charcoal into the fire box.

Then she linked the generator to the drive, and started charging the batteries.

The barge had the steam engine and generator in the back, counterbalanced by the pickup truck near the bow. There were also removable tents in the center of the barge, where Alyssa and Shane were working to map the river.

Talak River, 323 miles downriver
April 30, 1008 CE

There were people waving at them from the shore. Two days and one night of travel had taken them to somewhere near where the border between Arkansas and Louisiana would be in that other history.

They were also shouting, but in a language that was completely unfamiliar to Alyssa or Shane.

Keneva spoke it, though. Almost spoke it. He spoke a language that was spoken fifty miles upriver from here, which was sort of like this language.

He shouted back and there was some back-and-forth. He turned to Alyssa Jefferson. "They say they have oil!" he announced. What they'd actually said was "we found the black mud that burns."

"How do they know that we want oil?" Shane asked.

"Because rumor travels the Talak faster than fish," Keneva said. "They are happy to see the great Peterbilt. They say they didn't believe that it was actually this big." He grinned. "I haven't told them yet that this is just the pickup."

"Well, tell them," Alyssa said. "If they really have oil, they are going to be seeing the Peterbilt and the tanker trailer sooner than they think."

Slowly, they maneuvered the barge to ground on the east bank of the Talak, put down the ramp, and drove the pickup onto shore. The local tribe did some farming, a bit of corn, but mostly squash and beans. They were interested, but they were a small camp, perhaps two hundred people, including women and children.

Digging a well would pull a lot of resources.

Village of the Moshik
May 2, 1008 CE

The Moshik, though they did some farming, were part of a larger hunter-gatherer tribe that abandoned the river for most of the fall to hunt. Fall was when the animals were at their fattest. After hunting season, they moved back to the river for the winter and spring. They were mostly interested in the pickup as an item of curiosity and proof of magical power. Also, their notion of what was going on up north had only a distant relationship with the truth. That wasn't new to the Peterbilt people. This was a world without the internet or even written letters. The whole world was one giant game of telephone, the game where a kid whispers something to the kid next to them and it goes around the circle until it gets back to the kid completely transformed.

The Moshikains didn't believe that the Peterbilt people came from the future. That was ridiculous. Clearly they came from a mystical land of the north and the stories have been garbled by traders. And clearly they had great magic in the north.

"It's not magic," Alyssa explained.

"It's a kind of magic you can learn if you want," Keneva translated. "The Peterbilt people share their magic. And the cross god doesn't require sacrifices."

The elders nodded, but not like they really believed it. The hunter-gatherers knew about the sacrifices and they knew that it was usually the poor or strangers that got sacrificed. They had their own harsh customs, but a large part of why they stayed downriver was because they didn't want to fight people as powerful as the northern river people. What they did know was that the dark-skinned woman of the Peterbilt people had cast a mighty spell that had ended a disease among the peoples of Hocha. Based on that, they were willing to trade for oil. They didn't want a woman with that sort of power angry with them.

"Well, what do you think of their oil well?" asked Pulok.

"It's more tar pit than oil well, but there is oil coming up," Alyssa said. "Let me finish my tests. There may not be enough volatiles for gasoline."

"Should we go back upriver?" Keneva asked. At over three hundred miles they were out of radio range, even of the station at Fort Hilltop.

"Let me finish my tests," Alyssa repeated.

Fort Peterbilt
May 2, 1008 CE

Akvan read the message. What the Peterbilt people had thought wasn't exactly true, meaning the idea that the river people had no written language. They didn't exactly, but they did have knotted leather strips. They were part of the mysteries only known to the Pharisees of Hocha, but they did have them and his special friend in Hocha had taught him the magic of the knots. So, as he looked at the beaded necklace and read the knots, he knew that his friend was warning him again. He went to see Jerry Jefferson.

His father's cousin Lomhar was back in Kallabi. Akvan was in Fort Peterbilt. And he was learning a great deal.

The world was complicated, much larger than he'd thought, and much less centered on his people than he'd ever wanted to believe.

It was true that Hocha was bigger than London was at this time, but London was a primitive backwater in Europe. The big cities were Constantinople and Baghdad. Even in the Americas, Hocha was fairly small compared to South American cities.

Jerry, as was often the case, was sitting in a chair and moving his hands about in strange and mystical gestures. Jerry had explained that they weren't mystical at all, and even showed him by letting him wear the glasses for a few moments, so he could see the magical boxes Jerry moved about to find the information he was searching for.

All he'd managed to convince Akvan of was that the Peterbilt people had two different words for magic. Magic and science.

"What's bothering you, Akvan?" Jerry asked when Akvan got his attention.

"I have a message from Jokem!"

"Jokem?"

"He's a priest of Talak in Hocha."

"Is he the one who warned you to get out?"

Akvan nodded.

"Okay. What's he saying this time?"

"That I should stay away from the Peterbilt."

"Why?"

Akvan shook his head. "He didn't say why. Just that I should not be with it the next time it leaves the fort."

"That makes sense," Jerry said. Jerry Jefferson wasn't anyone's notion of a spy. But as the librarian for the database, he'd fallen into the role of spy master. Not even that, really. He was just the guy who kept the files, and determined who got to look at them. Which meant that he got to look at them, so he was about as informed about the politics of Hocha and the United Clans as anyone.

"They were deeply embarrassed and angered by the Peterbilt's trip through Hocha." Jerry sighed. "'Never do your enemy a small hurt.' That's a quote. Several people have said it throughout history, everyone from Machiavelli to an ancient Samnite. What the Peterbilt delivered in their attempt to keep casualties down was a small hurt. They embarrassed the hell out of the Pharisees of Hocha, but didn't actually weaken them. The worst thing about it, is that it probably convinced them that no matter how strong our"—he held up his hands and made quote marks—"'magic' is, we're weak because of our unwillingness to kill the innocent. So they think that if they send people to attack us, we won't respond. Not, at least, in any way that will really hurt them."

"Are you saying they're wrong?" Akvan asked, really curious. It had always seemed to him that the Pharisees were powerful because they were willing to do whatever they had to do to be powerful. Whether it was sacrificing young women to the river goddess, cutting their own faces and genitals in bloodletting rituals, or sending out warriors to attack any village that defied them.

"I'm saying their concept is wrong." Jerry held up his hands. "Never mind. This discussion belongs in a philosophy class. What I'm saying is, if your friend's friends do this thing, you'd better warn him to get his ass out of Hocha, unless you want to be scraping up his remains.

"Thank you for the information, Akvan. I'll inform the great women's council and the chiefs."

Hamadi laid the steel ax on the table. It was new, made right here in Jabir out of bog iron. It wasn't for chopping trees. This was a war ax. Hamadi was used to stone axes and clubs. This had the weight and balance he was used to, but at the same time, it could take a beating that would shatter a stone ax to nothing. He also had a new mail shirt. It was cloth, with pockets that held iron sheets. It weighed more than the bone and leather he'd worn before, but it would stop a spear or an arrow most of the time.

Hamadi had made the transition from Stone Age to Iron Age without even glancing at the Bronze Age. He was anxiously looking forward to the Gunpowder Age. He had grenades. They were made of wood with embedded stone, but what he wanted was a revolver.

Michael placed his pistol on the table. This was a meeting of the chiefs and it was custom. New custom, but custom all the same.

"You need to keep going out," Ginak, a war chief of Kacla, said. The weapon he'd laid on the table was a spiked club, much like the one Hamadi had given to Michael, and Michael had returned, after that first raid, years ago now.

"I know. I don't like it, but you're right. We can't let the Pharisees dictate our actions."

Ginak grunted and nodded. He didn't really trust the Peterbilt people. He was very much afraid that they were too soft for this world. Good people. He didn't know how many lives nixtamalization had saved, but he knew it was more than all the women the Pharisees had sacrificed since the beginning of Hocha. At the same time, the strong took and the weak gave, and that was just the way the world worked. And the Pharisees were strong.

"More than that, Michael," Hamadi said. "I think we should reconsider making another assault on Hocha."

"We can't," Michael said. "Evil doesn't mean idiots. After the first raid, they realized that the Peterbilt needs a flattish surface to drive on. They dug out a trench around the walls and put walking bridges in front of the gates. Those bridges will hold a man, even several, but they won't hold the Peterbilt or even the pickup truck.

"If we're going to hit them, we're going to have to find another way."

Ginak grunted again. "We need one of your airplanes"—he wasn't a stupid, or even an ignorant, man. He'd seen the images of airplanes flying and the descriptions of how they worked— "to fly over their walls and drop grenades on the high priest's residence mound."

"That might actually be possible. Not a real airplane, but a hang glider or a balloon." Michael shook his head. "No, not a balloon. All the cloth in North America wouldn't be enough to make a hot air balloon big enough to carry a man and a five-hundred-pound bomb over Hocha. But a hang glider . . . that we might be able to do. We'd need a long, straight, flat piece of land somewhere within a few miles of Hocha. The longer, the better. And a really long rope. Pull the hang glider along to give it some altitude." He shrugged. "It might work. I'll talk to Jerry and see what we can come up with. I wish Alyssa was here."

Village of the Moshik
May 7, 1008 CE

Shane manipulated the data and fed it to Alyssa's laptop. The oil seep was smallish, but it was a safe bet that there was enough crude there to fill up the tanker a couple of times. They were going to need more eventually, but for now it would do. Besides, there was quite a lot of tar and there was a whole lot that Alyssa could do with tar. "It's time to go back," she told Alyssa.

They would be taking Moshikain tribesmen with them on the trip back, to see the Peterbilt and the capsule and the magic pictures. It wasn't that they doubted, but people from the future was a lot to take on faith, even if they did have the pickup to show.

Talak River
May 9, 1008 CE

"I have Fort Hilltop," Shane said.

"Well, tell them we have an oil source next to the Mississippi. We won't have to go to Spindletop, at least not yet."

"Okay." Shane used the virtual keyboard to type out a message and sent it. They had contact, but it was like one bar on a phone, enough for instant messages but not for speech or large data files.

A minute later, she got a message. "Be careful. Our sources in Hocha suggest a possible attack on barges carrying Peterbilt and pickup."

She copied it to Alyssa's laptop.

The trip upriver was going a bit smoother than the downriver trip had gone. They were using oil from the oil seep. It was thick and unrefined, but it burned and that was all the boiler needed. It also didn't produce the ash that wood or coal left in the firebox. Just soot.

They were carrying a lot of local herbs and spices, as well as local plants and meats. Trade down the Talak was going to be profitable. Perhaps not so profitable as the trade up and down the Mississippi had been in the nineteenth century. After all, there weren't nearly as many people in America in the early eleventh century as there were in the nineteenth. And those people didn't have the beginnings of the industrial revolution to supply the trade. At least, they didn't have it yet. But that was going to change.

Shane would make sure of it.

CHAPTER 23

INCREASING TENSIONS

Bajak's smithy, Jabir
May 9, 1008 CE

Bajak carefully pulled the ceramic jar from the blast furnace and emptied it into the flat tray. The steel was white hot and liquid. The tray was of fine sand, just moist enough to hold its shape.

The steel poured out and formed a sheet a half inch thick, three inches wide and six long. He waited until it was starting to harden, then quickly placed it on a mold and, using a rounded wedge, he hammered the sheet of steel into the mold until it formed a U shape, round on the bottom with two straight sides.

For two years, Bajak had been working as a blacksmith, first in Fort Peterbilt, then in Jabir. He'd learned a lot in that time, both from experience and from the videos that smiths from that future time had sent back. He'd also built tools, like the mold he was using and the long, rounded chisel he used to hammer the hot steel into shape.

Bajak was building a six-shot ball and cap revolver. He knew how it had been done by gunsmiths in the 1860s in that other history, but he liked his way better. The 1860s way had too many welds. His barrel would have just a single weld when he was done. That weld would be on the bottom of the barrel, so if it split, the explosion would be toward the ground and be less dangerous for the user.

He put the U-shaped piece back in the fire to heat again. His shop was full of gadgets that he'd made over the last two years. He had a drill press with a steel bit. He had files and awls and sandpaper. He'd bought the sandpaper, but most of what was in his shop was built by him, and that wasn't all he'd built.

He did a regular business in ax heads and arrowheads, in wood files and wood saws, even steel pots and pans. He wasn't the only blacksmith in the United Clans. He wasn't even the only one in Jabir. But he was the best.

One of the best, anyway.

And he was making this gun not for Michael Anderle, or any of the Peterbilt people. He was making this gun for himself.

Because he was frightened.

The Peterbilt people were kind and strong, at least when directly defending themselves. He knew that. He'd been in Fort Peterbilt when the army Hocha sent attacked. But then, after Hocha massacred a village, all the Peterbilt had done was drive through the town and make a speech.

Increasingly, Bajak was convinced that if the Pharisees in Hocha were to be stopped, it was going to have to be the people of the United Clans that did it, not the Peterbilt people. They didn't have the stomach for what was necessary.

Because what was necessary was to burn it out, root and branch.

Temple mound, Hocha
May 9, 1008 CE

Ho-Chag Kotep looked out at his city. His many-times great grandparents had come to this place up the river almost two hundred years ago as refugees from the lands south of the sea, what the demon people called the Gulf of Mexico.

He turned back to the table and went over to the map. He had the stories from his grandfather, who had died before the demon people arrived, and the string codes, to tell him that.

The string codes were his family's great secret. He looked at the strings and the map that came from Fort Peterbilt. Without the map, he wouldn't know where the string codes were referring to. Without the string codes, he wouldn't know where on the map his family came from.

His ancestors had brought with them the knowledge of the gods of the south and had adjusted the names to make the gods like Talak, the mother of rivers who made humans from corn. And they had taught the savages of this land how to live and respect the gods.

Ho-Chag Kotep was their heir and the high priest of Talak. He lived and worked in a palace on the top of the temple mound, what the histories of that other time would call Monks Mound. Not out of any respect for the religion of Hocha. Hocha and its gods were lost in time. It was called that because Christian monks had put a settlement there.

Gods are supposed to be eternal, not to fade away and be forgotten. The demon people, with their cross god, had destroyed his future, and he hated them for it.

"How?" he demanded of his cousin. "How do we kill them?"

"It won't do any good. Even if we kill them all, the knowledge has already spread. The writing is known. They are making paper." He pointed at the map. It had place names written out on it in the script of the demon people.

"I don't care!" Ho-Chag Kotep shouted. "The gods demand that they be countered! This cross god of theirs is a lie and an abomination. The gods demand sacrifice of *us*, if the world is to continue. They created the world, not this false god of the demon Peterbilt and its lying followers, who were sent into this world to disrupt the social order and make the peasants think that they have no duty to the gods or to Hocha.

"If this is allowed to continue, the gods will abandon our people. And, first, the rains will stop, and the mother of rivers will dry up. Then the sun god will become angry and the world will burn." Ho-Chag Kotep had to believe that. More, after the things he'd done in the service of the gods, they had to be real. *Had* to be. He would die before he would give up his belief in them, for it was that belief that justified every act he had taken in their names, which justified his position of privilege and his very self.

His cousin nodded in doubtful agreement. Ho-Chag Kotep was terrified by that doubt, and the terror added to his fury.

"You must find a way to attack the demon Peterbilt."

"There is a way."

Capsule School, Fort Peterbilt
May 15, 1008 CE

The school was now a brick building with a whitewashed wall on one side. There were chairs for over sixty people to sit and watch videos sent back in time with the capsule. And the building had locally made glass windows, though the curtains were usually closed.

Right now, the screen was displaying a discussion of using black powder in digging holes and mining. Seated in the audience was a secretly devout follower of the sun god. He was learning a great deal about the effects of a contained explosion. Among the most important parts was the knowledge that the explosion must have a great deal of earth over it, else the blast will just shoot up and do little to dig the hole.

Several hours later, using the script of the demon people, he wrote out his message to the sun god's high priest, for he'd come to realize that the blast shooting up was just what was needed for his purposes and the purposes of the sun god. Fire would serve the sun god, as was its proper role.

Village of Darta in Purdak Territory
May 15, 1008 CE

Darta was still loyal to Hocha and the priests of the gods of Hocha, but that didn't mean it was willing to do without the innovations that the Peterbilt people offered freely.

Gatadi was a woman of middle years. Her husband had been killed in a hunt three years ago, and she hadn't found another. However, her property included a clay field. Mixing the clay with ash, dung, and dried grass and forming it into bricks was the work of the entire village.

There were over a hundred people mixing the ingredients and using wooden molds to form the bricks. As soon as a mold was emptied onto the sand, it was dumped in a bucket to wash, then sanded, and more of the mixture was added. They'd been at it for weeks, and the first bricks had had plenty of time to dry.

Darta was a bit over a hundred miles north of Hocha on the Falast River. The winters were cold, but brick walls and fireplaces would make a great difference in that this winter. The money was already making a difference, even if the priests of Hocha didn't approve of it.

Another man dropped a form into the water-filled barrel. That was another thing the Peterbilt people had brought. Wood barrels. They'd already had pots and plates and many other things carved from wood, but the cutting of staves and fitting them together into a barrel was new.

Gatadi, no stranger to hard work, grabbed the wet form from the barrel and placed it on the table. The form was rectangular, about two and a half inches tall and open on both the top and the bottom. She set the form on the table, and the table acted as the bottom side of the form. She grabbed a handful of sand and used it to sand the sides of the form and the tabletop that was acting as the bottom of the form. Then she took a blob of the brick mix and shoved it into the form. She pounded it into the form using her fists, then, taking a flat stick, scraped off the excess and applied a bit of sand to the top of the brick. A boy took the form over to a stretch of flat ground. He hit the form with a wooden mallet a couple of times to encourage the brick to fall out, then brought the form back to the bucket.

Many hands make light work, but even with many hands, making tens of thousands of bricks was a lot of work. But the village had an assembly line going. Several assembly lines. It wouldn't all be done this summer. There was other work to be done. But in the next few years, Darta would become a town of brick buildings, some of which would have actual basements.

Gatadi filled another mold, wondering what was going to happen between Hocha and Fort Peterbilt. For that matter, she wondered what was going to happen right here in Darta. It seemed like half the village were secret Christians.

Village of Coasblin in Gruda Territory
May 15, 1008 CE

The blast furnace went up the wall of Coasblin. It was made of clay with brick surrounding it, and it had stone shelves that you could set ceramic pots into, where iron and iron ore could be held. There was a fire at the bottom, and the shape of the chimney sucked heat up from the hot fire, directing it and magnifying the flames into a blast of fire that heated the metal, not just to the point that it turned ductile, but beyond that, to the point that it became liquid.

On another day, it might be making stoneware, or even glass. But today they were making steel. Steel for knives and axes and arrowheads, because war was coming between Hocha and the demon people.

All across the clans of the river people, the citizens and subjects were preparing, using the knowledge brought by the Peterbilt people to make their lives better.

But also to make ready for war.

For if the priests of Hocha were right, unless the cross god was brought down and his followers destroyed, the world would end as the gods abandoned it.

Village of Plack in Kadlo Territory
May 15, 1008 CE

Bivwhok, the radio man, typed on the locally made keyboard. He was a local, not one of the Peterbilt people. He wasn't even from Jabir. But he'd spent most of 1007 in Fort Peterbilt, studying electronics under the tutelage of the library and Jerry Jefferson. There were limits to what they could do, but he had, with help, built a printer and a keyboard that worked and operated within the voltages defined by the capsule. That had been enough to get one of the computer chips assigned to his radio.

Jerry Jefferson's micro 3D printer had built a screen. It was actually two tiny little screens, and to use it Bivwhok had to lean forward, placing his head in a wooden rest so that each eye saw its own screen. Jerry's micro printer took over two weeks to make the two screens. They were very expensive and Bivwhok's wife Yola, who was a senior member of the women's council, had to promise to repay a large loan. But it meant that Bivwhok could use the computer and the radio to access the main computer in Fort Peterbilt. That knowledge had already saved the lives of two villagers, one an injury and another, a sickness.

And they had weather reports. Not great weather reports, but some weather reports. Enough so that they often got a few hours' warning before rains or high winds came.

Plack wasn't the southernmost village in the Kadlo Territory, but it was over a hundred miles south of Hocha. Probably two hundred if you were trying to march an army there. So it was safer from Hocha attacks than most places, but even here the increasing tensions were making people nervous.

Bivwhok stretched and shifted. He'd lost a foot in a hunting accident almost ten years ago, and after that he'd been unable to do much but hop with a walking stick. Things were much better now, thanks to the radio. Also, thanks to the Peterbilt people, Bivwhok now had an artificial foot. It was made of wood and metal and attached to the bottom of his right leg with a leather cup, but he could walk on it, even though he still needed a walking stick. He had purpose now, and skills. The whole village was eating better and they had more stuff and better brick chimneys and hooks to hang pots over the fire. The world was better.

At the same time, it was getting scary. Even here, there were those who were afraid that if the villagers listened to the Peterbilt people, the gods would abandon them for their arrogance and the world would end.

"Bivwhok?"

Bivwhok's head jerked up at his wife's shout and he banged his nose on the wooden frame that held the little screens.

Rubbing his nose, he stood, keeping most of his weight on his left leg. It still hurt some to put weight on his right. He grabbed his cane and left the computer room to answer Yola's summons. "What is it? I was sending your message to Fort Peterbilt."

He moved the flap and stepped out of the "radio shack," which was rather more than a shack, truth be told.

The sun was bright compared to the darkness of the radio room, and he blinked a bit.

Yola said, "We have a delegation." She waved at a group of three men.

The three men were staring at his right leg and the artificial foot that was attached to it. Bivwhok's day-to-day attire was a leather loincloth, basically the same thing he'd worn his whole life. It, unlike the clothes the Peterbilt people often wore, didn't hide his artificial foot at all. Also, while he wore a moccasin on his left foot, he saw no reason to put one on the wood and metal prosthetic that the woodcarvers of Jabir had made for him from designs brought back with Jerry Jefferson. Yes, especially for Bivwhok, things were *a lot* better since the Peterbilt people came.

"Does it feel?" asked one of the men.

The others shushed him.

"Sort of, in a strange way," Bivwhok said. "I have had phantom pains ever since the accident. Long before I got this." He used the cane to tap his right foot. "But using the virtual glasses at Fort Peterbilt, they treated that, so I still have them, but they aren't as bad. And the more I use the foot, the more it feels like I can feel it. I can't really, but it can seem like I can."

Yola's half smile was there now. This was what she was after, at least part of it. Yola was his wife, and he loved her. Also, she'd stuck with him after the accident that lost him his foot and almost killed him. But he had few illusions about his wife. She was manipulative and sneaky.

"What brings you to Plack?" Bivwhok asked.

"We saw the giant canoe," said one of the men.

Bivwhok thought he was probably the leader.

"We saw it as it went south and again as it went north. We came to find out how it works."

"I can show you that," Bivwhok said. "Not as well as they could in Fort Peterbilt, but I can show you."

And he did, over the next several hours. He showed them how it could be done and he showed them that they couldn't do it, at least not quickly. They had a few copper tools and ornaments, but no iron or steel. And though you could build a boiler out of copper, it would take a lot of copper and copper came down the river from the Great Lakes. They didn't have enough, and buying or trading for enough copper to make a boiler, much less a boiler and steam engine, would bankrupt the village.

Steel, they could make, but it would mean a whole other investment, and finding the iron ore to make the steel. Even with the knowledge which Bivwhok freely shared, as that was part of the deal with Jerry Jefferson, it would still be much cheaper for them to just trade for a boiler and steam engine built in Fort Peterbilt.

They went away, saying they would think about it. But Bivwhok was worried. His feeling was that they thought the cheapest way of all to get a steam barge would be to steal it.

The world kept getting better for him and his village, but every time it got better, it also got more tempting, and so more dangerous.

CHAPTER 24

THE MINE

Talak River, 200 miles upriver of Hocha
June 11, 1008 CE

The Peterbilt pulled off the barge onto the flat ground. This was mostly outside the territory claimed by Hocha. The people here, about one hundred and fifty-seven miles east-northeast of Hocha, did some farming, but they lived as much from buffalo as from corn. They were members of the Shulik Confederation, but were a different tribe than Kazal's. That didn't mean they were uninterested in what the barge carried. Aside from the Peterbilt, the barge carried knives, axes, arrowheads, pots and pans made of steel and copper. Jerry had brought a wide variety of seeds. Conifers from Europe, as well as modern and heirloom tomatoes, and all sorts of other stuff and the technical know-how to bring the ones that didn't do it easily to seed, and last year he'd gotten a lot of seeds.

Well, the villagers of Jabir had gotten a lot of seeds, following Jerry and the capsule's advice. Those seeds were worth their weight in gold if anyone in this part of America had had any gold to trade.

Melanie and Michael were seated around a campfire in the village, discussing plants and arrowheads, but more importantly, the tools to build the tools.

"Tell me again about this crossbow?" Jaback, the local tribal leader, said. "How do you make them?"

Hunting buffalo wasn't a safe occupation and hunting them with bows and arrows didn't make it a lot safer. Spears and atlatls packed more wallop, but you had to get closer and there wasn't always a handy cliff to stampede them over. So while buffalo hunting was necessary, it had a tendency to "waste" a lot of young hunters. Anything that would let them hunt a buffalo from out of range of the buffalo's charge appealed greatly.

Michael went through the process. In some ways, crossbows are harder to make than a standard bow, but in other ways easier. Since a crossbow has a channel to send the arrow down, the balance of the bow isn't as critical as it is in a standard bow. Since the bow is cocked and the bowstring held in place, you can have a stronger pull than you can have in a standard bow. Certainly since a crossbow bolt is shorter than the arrow fired from a bow, it's easier to make.

Put it all together, and if your goal is to be far enough away from a buffalo to be safe and still kill it, a crossbow is a better tool than a standard bow and arrow.

Even better would be an elephant gun, but though they'd started making steel over two years before, they weren't up to machining barrels thirty inches long. The only rifles in the world were the ones that had come with the time travelers. Those rifles had ammunition again, reloaded by Alyssa's chemistry, but for most people, a crossbow was as good as they were going to get.

South Talak River
June 14, 1008 CE

Michael looked at the chief and shook his head. "No. You should use the crossbows. Our guns make a lot of noise."

Michael and Melanie were out with the several tribal leaders on a buffalo hunt to demonstrate the crossbows. They were outside the danger distance. Melanie cocked the crossbow and loaded the quarrel, then carefully handed the bow to a senior hunter. It wouldn't be the first time the man had shot a crossbow. They'd spent most of yesterday shooting crossbows at buffalo skins draped over bushes, and learning how much drop they could expect from the bolts at a given range. Heavier bolts dropped faster, but gave more punch at the target.

The hunter carefully went to his belly and took aim, then

jerked the trigger. The quarrel missed to the right, which didn't matter because he underestimated the drop and it buried itself in the earth twenty feet short of the target.

The buffalo looked up, then went back to his grazing.

"Squeeze the trigger, just like yesterday," Melanie reminded the man.

Cursing, the hunter sat up and reloaded the crossbow.

Then he went back to the prone position, took a deep calming breath, adjusted his aim, and squeezed the trigger. The quarrel hit the buffalo in the top half of its chest. His head came up and he bellowed. The other buffalo looked up, but no one was close to them. The wounded buffalo moved five steps...ten... then his legs crumpled and he fell to the ground.

Buffalo have only one lung. It's a rare feature, and it means that when you poke a hole in the lung, the whole respiratory system collapses, not just one air sack. A human or a mountain lion with a hole in one lung can keep operating for several minutes.

Not so a buffalo.

The natives shot two more buffalos, then let Michael and Melanie have their turn. Each of them downed a buffalo, which, by prior agreement, would be theirs to keep. That was a great deal of buffalo meat that would be worth a lot back in Fort Peterbilt.

Melanie went back to the village to get the Peterbilt, and Michael, along with the braves, started slowly approaching the herd, which moved off, leaving their dead behind.

They started to prepare the buffalos for butchering, but Michael suggested they wait.

By now, the Peterbilt was equipped with an electric winch, so when it arrived, all five buffaloes were winched up onto the back of the Peterbilt and carried back to the village whole. That made it easier for the locals to collect things like blood and intestines.

The next morning, the Peterbilt rolled back onto the barge and headed back downriver with orders for the products of Fort Peterbilt and the rest of the United Clans.

Lisyuk
June 15, 1008 CE

They stopped at Lisyuk for the night and the women's council asked them to plow a field about a mile south of the village.

"We'd wait, but you're here, and if we can get it plowed now, we can plant winter wheat come the fall."

Melanie agreed. It wouldn't take long. They'd built a road for the Peterbilt to the field.

That night they ate with the locals, enjoying fish and corn in a thick and savory stew, finished with cantaloupe.

Lisyuk was solidly in the United Clans, and an overwhelming majority of its population shared that belief. But not everyone.

Susuk had been in training to become a priest of Talak before the Peterbilt people came. And he knew with great certainty that if the gods were abandoned, they, in turn, would abandon humanity. The rains would stop. The river would dry up, and they would all die.

The truth was that Susuk would never have been admitted to the priesthood of Hocha. They had standards, after all, and Susuk wasn't all that bright. He'd been told the way the world worked as a child, and he wasn't going to change his mind just because a demon arrived from somewhere, trying to tempt them away from the true faith with lies about how the world worked. Knowing that the demon people were trying to destroy the world, he was going to kill them. But, more importantly, he was going to destroy the demon that had brought them to this world. The priests of Hocha had shown him how.

The electrical wires were buried under the road and ten pounds of the magic powder was also buried. Fifty feet away, a small box with coils of wire and a magnet sat behind a bush. The plan had been carefully thought out by the priests of Hocha and provided to Susuk.

Of course, the Pharisees of Hocha knew what was going to happen to Susuk after the Peterbilt was destroyed, but they didn't care. They'd told Susuk that once the Peterbilt was destroyed, the spell it had cast would kill his fellows in Lisyuk too.

Susuk believed it because he *needed* to believe it.

The Peterbilt moved along the road. It was rather narrow for the big truck, so Melanie was walking backwards in front of the truck, guiding Michael. The front wheels reached the mine and Susuk rammed the plunger home.

Nothing happened.

The Peterbilt continued to roll slowly forward.

Susuk, realizing the demon Peterbilt was keeping the charge from going off, desperately pushed and pulled on the plunger.

A plunger is, at its core, a simple mechanism. It's a one-stroke generator. The magnetic core moves through the coil, inducing a current. The faster it moves, the stronger the current. Susuk's first stroke was firm, but not all that fast. His back-and-forth jerks were rather faster. On the third one, the thin wire in the black powder bomb got hot enough to ignite the powder.

A black powder bomb is also a fairly simple thing, but it's subject to simple, uncaring laws of physics. Laws that the designers of the bomb didn't actually understand. Black powder burns very fast, but it burns. As it burns, a small volume of black powder turns into a much larger volume of hot gas. This produces pressure, which will burst the container, causing flow, which has momentum. And which can be directed by things like rocks in the soil and even the placement of the spark that sets it off. This is the basis of shaped charges.

The spark was on the upper end of the charge, toward the direction of the Peterbilt's front. The explosion traveled at a downward and backward angle, compressing the earth, and then encountering a largish flat stone. Which shattered, but at the same time, redirected the flow up and forward.

This did two things. It absorbed quite a bit of the force of the bomb and, two, redirected the blast so that rather than blowing up, it blew forward and up. And, of course, out. It was an explosion, after all, and it was black powder, not a plastic explosive like C-4.

Rocks blew up, bounced off the undercarriage of the Peterbilt, went down and bounced off the ground, then a piece of rock about an inch across slammed into Melanie's left leg about two inches above the ankle.

That rock shattered Melanie's tibia and ripped open her leg. She fell to the ground, but the rest of the blast front was gone before she fell into it. The other rocks ripped holes in the left and right front tires of the Peterbilt.

Several stones and a whole lot of dirt hit the undercarriage of the Peterbilt, but that brought into play something else that the Pharisees didn't get. They didn't understand just how tough thick chunks of high carbon steel are. The undercarriage of the Peterbilt was scratched and dented, but not holed.

In moments Michael was out of the truck, medical kit in hand, and running to the aid of his wife. He saw the injury, and he was back in the 'Stan. He knew what to do.

He started with a pressure bandage to control the bleeding and realized that Melanie was going to need surgery to reconstruct the bone, or she was very likely to lose the foot. The tibia was shattered, but the fibula, the smaller leg bone was still intact. It would, hopefully, hold the foot and ankle in place until they could get her back to Fort Peterbilt, where they could operate.

Michael stopped, frozen. Jerry Jefferson had brought the new computer phones, virtual reality glasses, back from the future to them all. Neither Michael nor Melanie were particularly fond of them, but they had them.

Jerry wasn't a surgeon. No one in this time was. This sort of surgery would require augmented reality. Someone was going to have to put the glasses on, and then follow along as a record-ing or a computer-generated cartoon guided them through the motions of reconstructing the shattered tibia.

But Michael couldn't do it. He could hold himself together long enough to do first aid, but not to do reconstructive surgery on his wife. He'd lose it, and she'd lose her foot.

He looked around, and there was a crowd around him. The whole village had been following along behind to watch the plowing.

When the bomb had gone off, at first they thought it was the Peterbilt, but that hadn't lasted more than a few moments. They were, by now, familiar with the sound a black powder charge buried in the earth made when it went off.

"Help me get her back to the barge," Michael shouted. Unfor-tunately, he shouted it in English. Fortunately, at least one of the people in the crowd knew enough English to understand. The women started giving orders, and Michael picked up his wife and started back to the barge.

"The wooden case next to the passenger seat." He jerked his chin at the Peterbilt, and again some of the women started giv-ing orders. He kept going.

☆   ☆   ☆

Kalmak, the senior chief of the hunters of this village, watched the situation, confused.

The women of the women's council were trying to figure out what was going on. So were the chiefs. It was all very confusing and it wasn't supposed to be happening to the Peterbilt people. They didn't claim to be gods or messengers of the gods, but whatever they claimed, people thought of them as prophets.

Prophets weren't supposed to have things like this happen to them.

And that was what brought him up short. Jesus Christ the Superstar had had something even worse than this happen to him. He'd been taken by the Pharisees, given to the Romans, and crucified.

He'd known it was coming, maybe. He'd accepted it, maybe. Certainly he hadn't wanted his followers to interfere at the risk of their lives. Or had he?

"One of you denies me," Jesus sang in Kalmak's memory.

"One of you betrays me,

"Peter will deny me in just a few hours.

"Three times will deny me."

Kalmak wasn't going to betray them. That was for sure. He shouted for the hunters of the village. "Search! Find the one who betrayed them."

The men started to run off, but he called three back. An older man and two boys. "You three stay. Guard the angel Peterbilt. Let no one touch it." Then he rushed back to the village.

Back at the barge, they opened the carved wooden case that held the seldom used virtual reality glasses, and started to hand a pair to Michael.

"No, not me. I'm barely keeping it together. I can't do the surgery."

Kalmak arrived just in time to hear that. And more than he ever had before, he realized Michael Anderle's true courage. For Kalmak had grown up in the real world, not in a fantasy. He knew from personal experience how dangerous it was to go into something like this with your emotions clouded by love, hate, or fear. He also knew from that same personal experience just how hard it was to step aside and let someone else do it if you were too upset to do it right.

Kalmak spoke, "I will do it. I have treated wounds on hunts. But my English is not good. I will need a translator."

Michael nodded and the glasses were passed to Kalmak. Virtual reality and augmented reality were just words to Kalmak, barely more than sounds. That changed quickly.

The phone, glasses, computer, had cameras on the frame so that what Kalmak saw was sent to the station in the Peterbilt and from there to the station at Fort Hilltop, then from Fort Hilltop to Fort Peterbilt. All faster than Kalmak could blink his eyes.

Once the images got to the capsule at Fort Peterbilt, they were fed into the massive computer and run through a database of wounds, refined by Jerry Jefferson adding parameters, like "right tibia shattered two inches above the ankle."

Then the closest ten or so matches showed up, and Jerry grabbed the one that looked the most like what he was seeing from Michael's glasses.

And suddenly Kalmak could see the drawing of the fractured tibia overlaid over Melanie's shattered tibia. Jerry was speaking, but after a moment that stopped and a young woman's voice replaced Jerry's. She was speaking in Kadlok, which was close enough to Kalmak's Lomak to be understood.

She was telling him what he was going to need to do. He was going to have to look for ruptured blood vessels, veins and arteries, and use sterilized thread to tie them off, or better, sew them up if he could. Carefully, using the pictures sent to him from the capsule in Fort Peterbilt, Kalmak found himself rebuilding a leg.

Melanie was losing blood, but as they'd known for years, Michael and Melanie shared a blood type. So Kalmak found himself stopping the surgery in order to set up a transfusion from Michael to Melanie. It was amazing what you could do with sterilized intestines. Fortunately, Melanie didn't have to make the transfusion tube. They had one in the medical kit on the barge.

For the next two hours, in fits and starts, Kalmak rebuilt a human. At least, her leg. And when he was done, and her tatters of skin had been sewn back together, he washed her leg in alcohol, which caused the semiconscious woman to scream and faint. Then, Kalmak wrapped the wound.

While Kalmak had been doing that, several of the women of the women's council had also been in contact with Fort Peterbilt.

So, after Kalmak wrapped the leg in leather, the women had plaster ready to make a cast.

Susuk heard Kalmak's order, and he wanted to run. But if he ran, they would hear him and catch him. He stayed still as they started to search. Then, when one of the hunters noticed the stretch of earthen road that had been disturbed when Susuk had buried the wires and came in his direction, he panicked and started to run.

He made it maybe ten feet before he was tackled.

He fought all the time, screaming that the gods demanded their sacrifices, and if they didn't get them, the world would end.

He was recognized. His mother was on the women's council and he was a member of a respected family. In spite of that, some of the warriors wanted to kill him then and there. But cooler heads prevailed. They would question him and turn him over to the women's council.

Lisyuk
June 17, 1008 CE

Three days of recovery, and two of questioning, had let the village learn a lot. The bomb hadn't done anything completely irreparable to the Peterbilt. Aside from the several holes in both front tires, there was a hose that had been cut and two that had been pulled loose. The cut tube had been repaired, and the knocked-loose tubes had been reattached.

The tires were going to be a more difficult problem. The Peterbilt carried an industrial grade jack, but new tires were a thousand years away.

They could repair the tires, but such repairs would be difficult and time-consuming. And they were going to need latex soon.

After questioning by the women's council, including his mother, Susuk admitted everything and unintentionally identified his contact. The contact was gone. He was a merchant who'd disappeared with his canoe full of stuff the day after Susuk was captured. The radios had been used to let others know who he was and where he was thought to be, but the truth was the whole village had more important things to deal with.

"What about Judas?" Susuk's mother asked. "He took thirty pieces of silver to turn Jesus over to the Pharisees."

It was an obvious and fairly desperate ploy to save her son. At the same time, the Christianity of the river people wasn't the Christianity of Europe. For that matter, it wasn't the Christianity of twenty-first-century America either. Under the influence of the rock opera, it was a religion that almost demanded that the faith be questioned.

"Judas regretted his actions and hung himself," another of the women of the council countered, and Melanie saw that many of the women of the women's council were looking at her.

"I'm not Jesus. I'm not even an evangelical." She shook her head, and tried to think. Something that wasn't made any easier by the pain in her right leg. What she wanted to do was beat the little sucker to a pulp, or maybe shoot him dead. At the same time, it was clear from the questioning that he was more than a few bricks shy of a full load.

And almost in spite of herself, she was familiar with the religion these people had made out of *Jesus Christ Superstar* and the Four Gospels on tape that they'd brought back with them. Oddly enough, Susuk's mother's point was well taken. It was also more in line with these peoples' faith than with the one she'd had before God—or whatever—had dumped her and her family in this time.

And who was she to say their version was wrong?

"I can't speak to what God wants. All I know is I was here to plow a field and help feed some people. I didn't force my way here. I was asked to come. If you folks didn't want me here, all you had to say was goodbye. It seems to me that what he was trying to do wasn't just attacking me or the Peterbilt, but attacking your right to decide for yourselves." She looked at the young man. The warriors of his tribe hadn't been gentle with him, but his face was full of belligerence and a certainty that seemed to be based as much on desperation as anything else.

"Yes, he should be allowed to question and even reject the cross god. But should he be allowed to take away your right to choose differently?"

CHAPTER 25

RESPONSE

Fort Peterbilt
June 20, 1008 CE

The Peterbilt was still in Lisyuk and so were Michael and Melanie Anderle. Shane was in Fort Peterbilt, and she was asked what she thought about the events in Lisyuk. Shane wasn't circumspect. Those crazy people in Hocha had gotten another crazy person to try to kill her parents. If they'd been back in the world she might be going through her rebellious stage right now, but that wasn't how it was working. In the here and now, she was much too busy and had much too much scope to resent her parents much.

Mom and Dad had spent the last three years just trying to help people. And, best Shane could tell, doing a bang-up job of it. So Shane was saying things like, "I'd kill them all if I could!" She didn't really mean it, but she was fifteen and upset. She was also a Peterbilt person who spoke the local language with very little accent, and who'd helped people to learn to do a bunch of useful stuff in the past three years.

Her opinion carried weight.

291

Fort Peterbilt
June 23, 1008 CE

The council of chiefs wasn't the women's council. It was the council of war leaders from each village and each clan in the United Clans.

Lomhar looked around the council and said, "We should have acted when they killed Roshan in Hocha." He sighed. "I respect the ways of the cross god. But there comes a time when a man must pick up a club. The old gods don't respect life. They think it's theirs and owed to them."

"The old gods don't exist," Hamadi said. "If they did, they wouldn't have faded away in the thousand years between now and the time the Peterbilt comes from. Real gods don't die and fade away."

"How do you know the cross god won't fade away and be forgotten," asked a chief of the Lomak.

"I don't," Hamadi said with a shrug. "It could be that Jesus Christ is as much of a smoke dream as Xuhpi. But I know there is no Xuhpi. He's a story that the Pharisees of Hocha use to frighten us, and I'm done with being frightened of them and their lies."

It was a long meeting, and if they didn't get complete consensus, finally, the doubters agreed not to protest. And those who would be taking part released their fellow chiefs and went onto a discussion of weapons and tactics.

Lomhar looked around at the chiefs. "Hocha still has more followers than the cross god. Many more, and many of them are concentrated in Hocha. Just as those converted to the cross god come here, those who hold to the old gods retreat to Hocha when their villages come over to our side. Hocha has more people than it did before the cross god came and a lot of those people are warriors. This is not going to be an easy fight."

Lomhar looked at the map of Hocha. "We won't be able to breach their walls. Not with the trench they've dug out in front of them."

For quite a while that seemed an insurmountable obstacle, mostly because these men thought in terms of raids. Raids were almost always done as much for profit as to prove a tribe's prowess or bravery.

But this wasn't a raid. It wasn't about bravery or prowess

or even loot. It was about putting an end to Hocha and all the Pharisees in the place.

By now they knew perfectly well what had happened to Sofaf, and just about every village in the United Clans had at least a few gunpowder rockets. Put it all together and that was a lot of rockets. And the Peterbilt's tanker might be getting low on fuel oil, but it was far from out.

At the same time, this was all new to them. This wasn't the sort of war that they had learned over their lives. It wasn't exactly uglier. There is very little uglier than bashing a man's head in and having his blood splash into your face and mouth. But the scope of the thing and the indiscriminate nature of the rockets and catapult bombs was new to them. New enough not to be something they fully understood, but they had that little bit of experience that let them feel how horribly dangerous it could be.

Some hours later, Hamadi looked at the map on which they'd planned their attack, and put what they were all thinking into words. "Even if this works, a lot of people are going to die. And if it doesn't work...If they break out, they will slaughter us to the last man."

Fort Peterbilt
July 2, 1008 CE

By now, Shane was well practiced with the pickup. And while she wasn't entirely sure what the chiefs had in mind, she did respect them, and she was still very angry at the Pharisees of Hocha. So when the chiefs came to her wanting the use of the pickup's barge, she agreed. She also agreed to their use of the fuel oil.

Jerry and Alyssa Jefferson weren't thrilled, but they hadn't been consulted. While the Peterbilt people were honored and respected, the government of the United Clans was firmly in the hands of the locals.

It took all of the second of July, all that night, and most of the next day to load all the ceramic warheads with fuel oil and attach them to the rockets that had been collected from over fifty villages. And Hocha would have learned of it, but Hocha didn't have a radio and it takes time to walk that far. In fact, it takes rather longer than it does for a steam-powered barge to travel that far upriver.

Pickup barge
July 4, 1008 CE

As the barge reached Hocha around noon on the fourth of July, Shane was starting to wonder what she was getting herself into. She'd seen battles before. She'd been there when the raid had been tried before Camp Peterbilt had become Fort Peterbilt, and for the major attack when so many warriors had been turned into roadkill by the Peterbilt, and even more had been made into mincemeat when Alyssa Jefferson's mines had gone off. She'd even been on the walls, relaying messages to the women manning the catapults.

Finally, they got to the shore, and following Achanu's directions, she pulled the pickup off the barge onto the flat ground south of Hocha. The back of the pickup was filled with boxes of rockets. The boxes were made of wood and they were set into the truck bed at a carefully calculated angle.

Achanu was holding up a device made of three sticks. He was looking down one stick and judging the wall of Hocha with another, and the angle with a third. The sticks were all fitted together and Achanu was saying, "Get closer...closer....There. That's good. Now straight along the wall."

Shane directed the pickup along the wall. They were about forty yards away from it and another warrior in the truck bed lit a fuse.

A few seconds later, the first rocket flew into the sky. It arched along and before it had reached the top of its arc, the second rocket was following it. Then the third, and so on, while Achanu kept saying, "A little faster...now a little slower."

The pickup was traveling between twenty-five and thirty miles an hour, and they were firing rockets a measured distance apart. It wasn't until they'd reached the end and turned around that Shane knew what the rockets were doing.

They were smoke rockets. When they landed next to the trench and wall, they burned sulfur and fuel oil and a few other things that produced a stinky and dense smoke. So stinky and dense that no one on either side could see to aim.

Shane's first thought was that the war chiefs of the United Clans had made a mistake. Then she remembered. Hocha was a city and the temple mound was a known distance from landmarks that were clearly visible from this side of the smoke, whereas she was driving a truck and the rest of the rockets were on wheeled carts that a single man could pull along at a fair clip.

She drove back to the barge. They loaded up more rockets. Achanu made some adjustments of his stick device. He grinned at her. "It's not a sextant, not exactly. It's not nearly as flexible as a true sextant would be, but if you know the locations of two points and you're going to a known third, it will get you there. And we have excellent maps of Hocha." He pointed. "That way."

A few minutes later, he had the pickup where he wanted it and said, "Stop now." Then he turned and shouted into the back of the pickup. "We're there." The young warrior in the back of the pickup looked at his compass, rotated the box of rockets a bit, then lit the fuses. They flew up and disappeared into the smoke.

On Temple Mount, Ho-Chag Kotep watched the smoke along the walls with increasing frustration. Throwing water on the fires was just adding to the smoke. He ordered blind firing. And the rockets went out, but he couldn't tell what they were hitting. Then rockets started hitting the temple mound. And they weren't smoke rockets. They were fire rockets, great, huge Molotov cocktails, filled with fuel oil.

And the buildings of the temple started to burn. Choking from the smoke, and feeling the heat of the fires, Ho-Chag Kotep started running to collect his family and get off the artificial hilltop that separated him and his from the lower people of Hocha.

By the time he had collected his family, there were flames all around the hilltop. And the funnel effect of large fires was starting to come into play. When you have a fire, the air above it gets hot and moves up, sucking in the air around it. Like a funnel funneling water. A big fire, or a lot of fires, magnifies the effect. That's what made the fire storm at Dresden so devastating in WWII. While it was true that Hocha was much smaller than Dresden, and that the rockets launched weren't a patch on the incendiary bombs dropped on Dresden, it was also true that Hocha was a city made of wood and thatch. It was just kindling for a fire like that.

The fire sucked away the air and replaced it with dense, acrid and unbreathable smoke. Many more people died of smoke than burned to death, and perhaps that was a mercy.

A small one, anyway.

☆　　☆　　☆

Lomhar watched the fires burn. It took several hours for the fire to burn out and long before that happened no one was manning the walls anymore. As soon as the funnel effect was sucking the fire away from the wall, he started sending warriors forward. They crossed the ditch with little opposition and using rope ladders climbed the walls. Those first smoke bombs had been aimed to land just behind the walls or even on them. A few had landed outside the walls. The smoke blinded the enemy, but it also made the walls somewhere between unpleasant and deadly. So most of the Hocha warriors who were manning the walls retreated back into the city, at least a little. Then the fire bombs had started and the funnel effect pulled the smoke away from the walls.

Carefully, Lomhar sent warriors forward to occupy the gates and walls.

Akvan was in shock as he went over the wall. And it was getting worse with everything he saw. Akvan had grown up in a world of human sacrifice and constant raids and counterraids between villages and clans. Also a world where disease and malnutrition were common killers of the young and the old. Seeing men and women dead wasn't new to him.

It was the scale. This wasn't one dead man or one strangled woman. A dead child or old person was fairly common in Hocha.

But this...

There were hundreds of bodies, mostly men, caught in the smoke and fire, dead and smoldering. The smell of cooked and half-cooked human flesh was everywhere. Hundreds of houses were burning or gone.

But worst of all were the mounds. Not just the temple mound where the priest king and his family lived, but the clan mounds where the clan leaders stayed while they were in the city. The flames had flowed up the hillsides like water following a spoon, turning the hilltop residences of the clan leaders into blast furnaces.

There were people alive, even a few who still wanted to fight, though not many of those. Especially not on this side of Hocha. For the fire hadn't been even. It was concentrated on the southern end of the city. That and the temple mound which had been targeted.

So it had swept north along the city and the people, especially the poor who didn't live on the mounds, had had time to run.

And run they had.

Later analysis would show that less than a third of the population of Hocha had died. There were still a lot of people living in Hocha, true believers from villages that had gone over to the cross god. There was a whole lot of very good farmland right around Hocha. The city had produced a lot of food.

Pickup barge
July 4, 1008 CE

Back on the barge, Shane was reporting on the battle. She'd gotten used to the glasses computer and was recording a lot of the battle, at least from a distance. She didn't see the devastation, but she saw enough. Enough that she didn't want to "study war no more."

But as the reports from the day came in, she realized that that wasn't going to be an option. Partly that was because though much of the leadership of Hocha was gone, killed in the fire-bombing, not all of it was. More importantly, the followers of the pantheon on Hocha still believed. They had committed so much to their beliefs that it was truly hard for them to give up the belief. Once you watched and accepted as a priest strangled a young woman so that the rains will come and the harvest will be good, it's really hard to admit you were wrong in following those people.

It was like Jerry Jefferson said. "Most of the people in Jim Jones' colony drank the Kool-Aid willingly and fed it to their kids."

Losing a couple of battles wasn't going to change that.

Peterbilt barge, Lisyuk
July 6, 1008 CE

It had taken weeks to "repair" the front tires of the Peterbilt. "Jerry-rig" would be a more apt description. The tires still wouldn't hold air, so instead there was a wooden framework attached to the wheel and the remains of the tires were lashed to that. It wasn't right, but it let them drive the thing. They went ahead and plowed the fields that Lisyuk had asked them to plow, then carefully pulled the Peterbilt back onto the barge.

Now the barge was pulling away from the dock and they were on their way back home to Fort Peterbilt.

They knew what had happened at Hocha and Melanie was appalled by the locals. How could people she knew, friends of hers, do what had been done at Hocha?

Michael was appalled too, but not surprised. He'd been in the 'Stan and had seen what the Taliban—but not *just* the Taliban—had done. He knew that the sort of thing that happened in Hocha was frigging inevitable in war. He didn't like it any more than Melanie, but he and Shane both realized that it wasn't the last time such a thing was going to happen. He knew that the United Clans' plan was to expand to fill continental North America. Peacefully, if possible. But peacefully or not, they intended for there to be a united people to face the Europeans when they came.

Fort Peterbilt
August 20, 1008 CE

Jerry finished his report, wondering what the people back in the twenty-first century thought about what was going on here. The harvest was in and stored. Work was progressing on the many projects that were ongoing, the expansion of the fields, the development of more and better steam engines and electronics and on and on.

"Jerry," Michael demanded, "who has rubber in this time and how do we get it?"

Jerry looked up to see Michael Anderle covered in mud.

"It's fairly common from Mexico all the way to South America. The word *Olmec* translates as 'the rubber people' after all. As to 'how do we get it...'" Jerry shrugged. "We don't. To get it we will need to send a fairly large trading mission to Central America, and we're all wealthy from the innovations. Well, you guys are wealthy anyway, but not that wealthy."

Jerry was referring to the fact that when the government of the late twenty-first century had sent all the stuff back in time with him, they had made it very clear that it was to be provided to the locals freely. "We aren't sending you back to get rich." There was nothing to enforce that except Jerry's personal honor, but Jerry came equipped with a full load of the stuff, even if he was a salesman.

The great women's council had set up a fund to provide for

Jerry and the capsule, but it was basically civil servant pay. Not that people weren't starting to get rich. As industries started, more wealth was created and there actually was a surplus. People started accumulating wealth.

Alyssa, for instance, was quite wealthy already because of the chemistry and engineering. She'd done both, before and after Jerry had brought the capsule.

The Anderles, with the Peterbilt and the pickup, had spent the last three years expanding the cropland and using the profits from that to start other businesses. So they were in no danger of starvation either. They actually owned the steam barges that carried the Peterbilt and pickup across and up and down the Talak River.

But the sort of mega rich "I can build my own rocket ship" that was happening in the twenty-first century didn't exist yet and wasn't going to for another twenty years at least. Probably the next hundred. "If you want a mission to the rubber trees in Central and South America, you're going to have to get the great women's council to authorize it and provide funds and military support."

Hamadi looked over at Etaka. "What do you think?"

"It depends. What about the Pharisees?"

After the fire rockets hit Hocha, the population retreated up the Falast River in the direction of the Great Lakes. With the steel plows, the seeders and other equipment, especially the Peterbilt, the fields around Hocha could be plowed and planted next year with barely a tenth of the people that it took to do the same job without them. There was going to be a lot of food next year, and not just food. They were growing hemp for making cloth, but also cotton and linen that Jerry Jefferson had brought back in his capsule. The question was: were they going to be able to keep it or were the Pharisees of Hocha going to come back next year?

Hamadi considered. He wasn't the first chief but he was an important chief of the United Clans so he'd been in on the reports and estimations. "I think we are safe for next year, possibly the year after, and we have good relations with the clans down the Talak. Also, aside from rubber, there are potatoes. I know we have the ones Jerry Jefferson brought, but there will be

other varieties as well. And, of course, gold, which we are going
to need to trade with the Norse in Greenland."

"You've been studying."

Hamadi grinned at her. "Yes. The capsule is right here. I think
we want a catamaran to make the trip, but we should make it
near the coast, where the river is deep enough so that an actual
ship will be safe from grounding."

CLANS AND PLACES

Clans of the Hocha

Kadlo: 18 villages including Plack Jabir and Kallabi

Kacla: 22 villages including Pelok and Abaka

Purdak: 25 villages including Takiso

Gruda: 21 villages including Pasire, Coasblin and Talmak

Lomak: 17 villages, mostly south of the Missouri, including Sofaf, Lisyuk

Rivers

Talak: Mother of rivers the Missouri River and the Mississippi River below the convergence of the two

Falast: Tributary to the Talak; the Peterbilt people think it's the Mississippi above the convergence of the Missouri and the Mississippi rivers

Agla: Tributary of the Talak known to the Peterbilt people as the Kaskaskia

Bashk: Creek, tributary of the Alga

Cast of Characters

Akvan:	Lomhar's servant in Hocha
Achanu:	Man of Jabir, cross cousin of Oaka
Aegluniket:	Shaman of the Kadlo
Almerak:	Spymaster in Hocha
Alyssa Jefferson:	Chemistry PhD; mother of Miriam and Norman
Bota:	Representative from Pelok
Bajak:	Blacksmith in Fort Peterbilt
Dikak:	Priest of Hocha who defected to the Peterbilt for electronics
Etaka:	Achanu's mother, member of the women's council
Faris:	Five-year-old brother of Jogida
Farsak:	A wood carver from Jabir
Fazel:	Senior shaman of the Kadlo
Gorai:	Head woman of Sofaf
Gada:	Shaman of Jabir in his forties
Hamadi:	A chief of Jabir/Kadlo; uncle to Achanu
Kazal:	Man of the Shulik tribe
Keneva:	Male, forties; a member of the Kadlo from Kallabi

Kochi:	Representative from Takiso
Januki:	The rep from Akadas, a Lomak village
Jerry Jefferson:	Husband of Alyssa Jefferson
Jogida:	Woman of the village, impoverished
Jokem:	Special friend of Akvan member of Hocha priesthood
Kasni:	Head of the women's council
Kaplack:	Priest of the old gods; a particularly officious and odious little man
Lomhar:	Major chief of the Kadlo
Malak:	Chief engineer for Hocha
Melanie Anderle:	Trucker, wife of Michael, mother of Shane
Michael Anderle:	Trucker, husband of Melanie, father of Shane
Miriam Jefferson:	Daughter of Alyssa, almost six at start of the story
Norman Jefferson:	Son of Alyssa, four and a half at the start of the story
Oaka:	Woman of Jabir, cross cousin of Achanu
Prutsa:	The representative from Abaka the Kacla
Ho-Chag Kotep:	Priest King of Hocha
Priyak:	Shaman of Jabir
Pulok:	Female engineer from Jabir; works with Keneva
Roshan:	A clan chief of the Kadlo
Rogasi:	Nephew of Roshan
Shane Anderle:	Daughter of Michael and Melanie
Tomar:	Minor chief of the Kadlo in Jabir
Ubadan:	Fifteen-month-old brother of Jogida
Zara:	Eleven when she arrives in Fort Peterbilt
Zanni:	Zara's mother